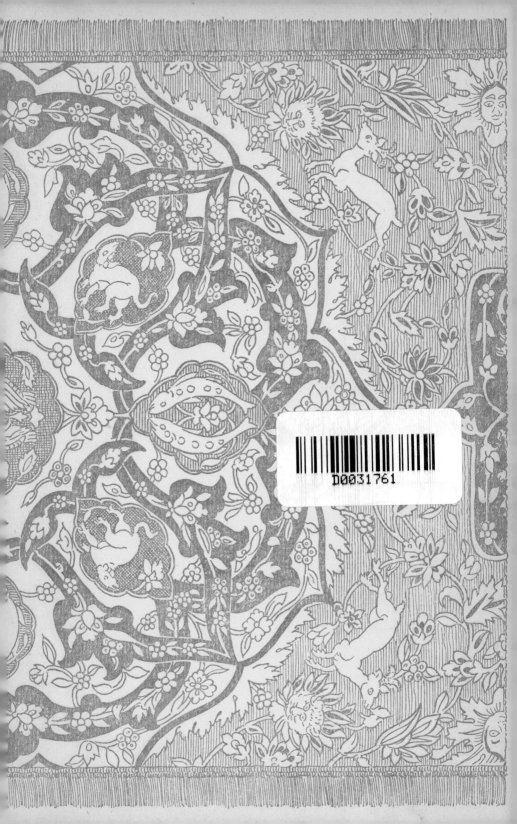

D0031761

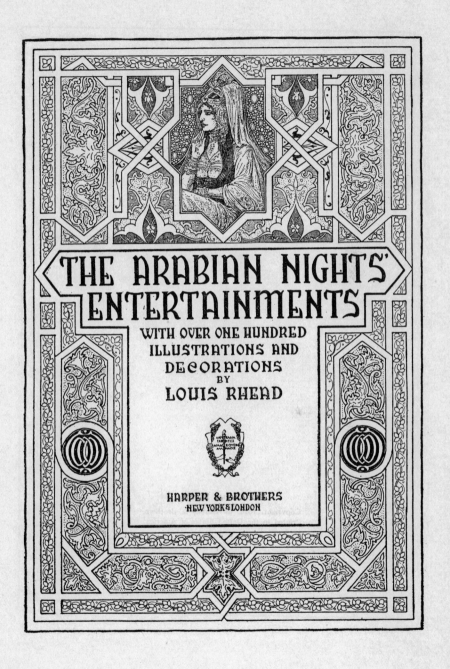

THE ARABIAN NIGHTS' ENTERTAINMENTS

WITH OVER ONE HUNDRED
ILLUSTRATIONS AND
DECORATIONS
BY
LOUIS RHEAD

HARPER & BROTHERS
NEW YORK & LONDON

CONTENTS

CONTENTS

ILLUSTRATIONS

ILLUSTRATIONS

ILLUSTRATIONS

ARABIAN NIGHTS

INTRODUCTION

THE chronicles of the ancient kings of Persia, who extended their empire into the Indies, and as far as China, tell of a powerful king of that family, who, dying, left two sons. The eldest, Shahriar, inherited the bulk of his empire; the younger, Shahzenan, who like his brother Shahriar was a virtuous prince, well beloved by his subjects, became King of Samarcande.

After they had been separated ten years, Shahriar resolved to send his vizier to his brother to invite him to his court. Setting out with a retinue answerable to his dignity, that officer made all possible haste to Samarcande. Shahzenan received the ambassador with the greatest demonstrations of joy. The vizier then gave him an account of his embassy. Shahzenan answered thus:—"Sage vizier, the sultan does me too much honor; I long as passionately to see him as he does to see me. My kingdom is in peace, and I desire no more than ten days to get myself ready to go with you; there is no necessity that you should enter the city for so short a time: I pray you to pitch your tents

ARABIAN NIGHTS

here, and I will order provisions in abundance for yourself and your company."

At the end of ten days the king took his leave of his queen, and went out of town in the evening with his retinue, pitched his royal pavilion near the vizier's tent, and discoursed with that ambassador till midnight. But willing once more to embrace the queen, whom he loved entirely, he returned alone to his palace, and went straight to her apartment.

The king entered without any noise, and pleased himself to think how he should surprise his wife, whose affection for him he never doubted. Great was his surprise when, by the lights in the royal chamber, he saw a male slave in the queen's apartment! He could scarcely believe his own eyes. "How!" said he to himself, "I am scarce gone from Samarcande and they dare thus disgrace me!" And he drew his scimitar and killed them both; and quitting the town privately, set forth on his journey.

When he drew near the capital of the Indies, the Sultan Shahriar and all the court came out to meet him: the princes, overjoyed at meeting, embraced, and entered the city together, amid the acclamations of the people; and the sultan conducted his brother to the place he had provided for him.

But the remembrance of his wife's disloyalty made such an impression upon the countenance of Shahzenan that the sultan could not but notice it. Shahriar endeavored to divert his brother every day by new schemes of pleasure and the most splendid entertainments; but all his efforts only increased the king's sorrow.

One day, Shahriar had started on a great hunting-match, about two days' journey from his capital; but Shahzenan, pleading ill health, was left behind. He shut himself up in his apartment, and sat down at a window that looked into the garden.

Suddenly a secret gate of the palace opened, and there came out of it twenty women, in the midst of whom walked the sultaness. The persons who accompanied the sultaness threw off their veils and long robes, and Shahzenan was greatly surprised when he saw that ten of them were black slaves, each of whom chose a female companion. The sultaness clapped her hands, and called: "Masoud, Masoud!" and immediately a black came running to her; and they all remained conversing familiarly together.

When Shahzenan saw this he cried: "How little reason had I to think that no one was so unfortunate as myself!" So, from that moment he forbore to repine. He ate and drank, and he continued in very good humor; and when the sultan returned, he went to meet him with a shining countenance.

Shahriar was overjoyed to see his brother so cheerful, and spoke thus: "Dear brother, ever since you came to my court I have seen you afflicted with a deep melancholy; but now you are in the highest spirits. Pray tell me why you were so melancholy, and why you are now cheerful?"

Upon this, the King of Tartary replied as follows: "You are my sultan and master; but excuse me, I beseech you, from answering your question."—"No, dear brother," said the sultan, "you must answer me; I will take no denial." Shahzenan not being able to withstand his brother's importunity, told him the story of the Queen of Samarcande's treachery: "This," said he, "was the cause of my grief; judge whether I had not reason enough to give myself up to it."

Then Shahriar said: "I cease now to wonder at your melancholy. But, bless Allah, who has comforted you; let me know what your comfort is, and conceal nothing from me." Obliged again to yield to the sultan, Shahzenan gave him the particulars of all that he had seen from his window. Then Shahriar spoke thus: "I must see this with my own eyes." "Dear brother," answered Shahzenan, "that you may without much difficulty. Appoint another hunting-match; and after our departure you and I will return alone to my apartments; the next day you will see what I saw." The sultan, approving the stratagem, immediately appointed a new hunting-match.

Next day the two princes set out, and stayed for some time at the place of encampment. They then returned in disguise,

2

and went straight to Shahzenan's apartment. They had scarce placed themselves in the window when the secret gate opened, the sultaness and her ladies entered the garden with the blacks. Again she called Masoud; and the sultan saw that his brother had spoken truth.

"O heavens!" cried he, "what an indignity!"

Then Shahriar ordered that the sultaness should be strangled; and he beheaded all her women with his own hand. After this he resolved to marry a virgin every day, and to have her killed the next morning. And thus every day a maiden was married, and every day a wife was sacrificed.

The report of this unexampled cruelty spread consternation through the city. And at length the people, who had once loaded their monarch with praise and blessing, raised one universal outcry against him.

The grand vizier, who was the unwilling agent of this horrid injustice, had two daughters, the eldest called Sheherazade, and the youngest Dinarzade. The latter was a lady of very great merit; but the elder had courage, wit, and penetration in a remarkable degree. She studied much, and never forgot anything she had once read. She had successfully applied herself to philosophy, physic, history, and the liberal arts; and made verses that surpassed those of the best poets of her time. Besides this, she was a perfect beauty; all her great qualifications were crowned by solid virtue; and the vizier passionately loved a daughter so worthy of his affection.

One day, as they were discoursing together, she said to him, "Father, I have one favor to beg of you, and most humbly pray you to grant it me." "I will not refuse it," he answered, "provided it be just and reasonable." "I have a design," resumed she, "to stop the course of that barbarity which the sultan exercises upon the families of this city." "Your design, daughter," replied the vizier, "is very commendable; but how do you intend to effect it?" "Father," said Sheherazade, "since by your means the sultan celebrates new marriage, I conjure you to procure me the honor of being his bride."

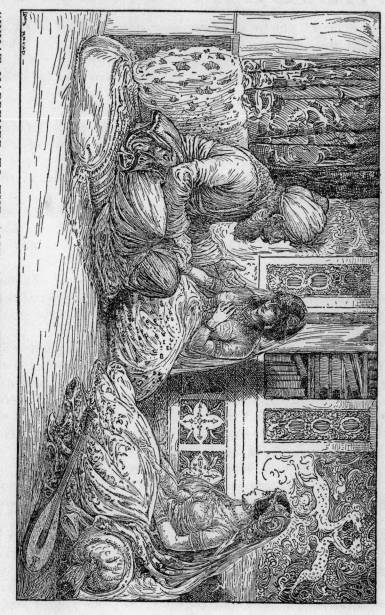

"WHAT HAPPENED TO THE ASS?" ASKED SHEHERAZADE. "I WILL TELL YOU,"
SAID THE VIZIER

ARABIAN NIGHTS

This proposal filled the vizier with horror. "O heavens," replied he, "have you lost your senses, daughter, that you make such a dangerous request to me? You know the sultan has sworn by his soul that he will never be married for two days to the same woman; and would you have me propose you to him?" "Dear father," said the daughter, "I know the risk I run; but that does not frighten me. If I perish, at least my death will be glorious; and if I succeed, I shall do my country an important piece of service." "No, no," said the vizier, "whatever you can represent to induce me to let you throw yourself into that horrible danger, do not think that I will agree to it. When the sultan shall order me to strike my dagger into your heart, alas! I must obey him; what a horrible office for a father!" "Once more, father," said Sheherazade, "grant me the favor, I beg." "Your stubbornness," replied the vizier, "will make me angry. Why will you run headlong to your ruin? I am afraid the same thing will happen to you that happened to the ass who was well off and could not keep so." "What happened to the ass?" asked Sheherazade. "I will tell you," said the vizier.

THE STORY OF THE ASS, THE OX, AND
THE LABORER

"A VERY rich merchant had the gift of understanding the languages of beasts; but with this condition, that, on pain of death, he should reveal to nobody what they said; and this hindered him from communicating to others the knowledge he thus acquired.

"He had in the same stall an ox and an ass; and one day, as he sat near them, he heard the ox say to the ass: 'Oh! how happy do I think you, when I consider the ease you enjoy and the little labor that is required of you! Your greatest business is to carry our master when he has a short journey to make; and were it not for that, you would be perfectly idle. I am treated in quite a different manner, and my condition is as miserable as yours is pleasant. It is scarce daylight when I am fastened to a plow, and the laborer, who is always behind me, beats me continually; and after having toiled from morning to night, when I am brought in, they give me nothing to eat but dry beans; and when I have satisfied my hunger with this trash I am forced to lie all night upon filthy straw; so that you see I have reason to envy your lot.'

[8]

ARABIAN NIGHTS

"The ass answered: 'They do not lie who call you a foolish beast. You kill yourself for the ease, profit, and pleasure of those who give you no thanks for so doing. But they would not treat you so if you had as much courage as strength. When they come to fasten you to your stall, why do you not strike them with your horns? They bring you only sorry beans and bad straw; eat none of these; only smell at and leave them. If you follow the advice I give you, you will quickly find a change in your condition.'

"The ox took the ass's advice in very good part, and professed himself much obliged for the good counsel.

"Next morning the laborer fastened the ox to the plow, and led him off to his usual work. The ox was very troublesome all that day; and in the evening, when the laborer brought him back to the stall, the vicious beast ran at the laborer, as if he would have pushed him with his horns. In a word, he did all that the ass advised him to do. Next day the laborer, finding the manger still full of beans, and the ox lying on the ground with his legs stretched out, and panting in a strange manner, believed the beast was sick, and, pitying him, acquainted the merchant with the fact. The merchant, perceiving that the ox had followed the mischievous advice of the ass, ordered the laborer to go and put the ass in the ox's place, and to be sure to work him hard. The laborer did so; the ass was forced to draw the plow all that day; besides, he was so soundly beaten that he could scarcely stand when he came back.

"Meanwhile the ox was very well satisfied. He ate up all that was in his stall, and rested the whole day, and did not fail to compliment the ass for his advice when he came back. The ass answered not one word, so angry was he at the treatment he had received; but he said within himself, 'By my own imprudence I have brought this misfortune upon myself; and if I cannot contrive some way to get out of it, I am certainly undone'; and as he spoke thus, his strength was so much exhausted that he fell down in his stall, half dead.

"The merchant was curious to know what had passed between the ass and the ox; therefore he went out and sat down by them, and his wife was with him. When he arrived he heard the ass say to the ox, 'Comrade, tell me, I pray you, what you intend to do to-morrow when the laborer brings you meat?' 'What shall I do!' said the ox; 'I shall continue to do as you taught me.' 'Beware of that,' replied the ass, 'it will ruin you; for as I came home this evening I heard the merchant, our master, say to the laborer, "Since the ox does not eat, and is not able to work, I will have him killed to-morrow; therefore, do not fail to send for the butcher." This is what I had to tell you,' said the ass. 'The concern I have for your safety, and my friendship for you, obliged me to let you know it, and to give you new advice. As soon as they bring you your bran and straw, rise up and eat heartily. Our master will by this think you are cured, and, no doubt, will recall his orders for killing you; whereas, if you do otherwise, you are certainly gone.'

"This discourse had the effect which the ass designed. The merchant, who had listened very attentively, burst into such a fit of laughter that his wife was surprised at it, and said, 'Pray, husband, tell me what you laugh at so heartily, that I may laugh with you.' 'Wife,' said he, 'I only laugh at what our ass just now said to our ox. The matter is a secret, which I am not allowed to reveal. If I tell it you it will cost me my life.' 'If you do not tell me what the ox and the ass said to each other,' cried his wife, 'I swear by heaven that you and I shall never live together again.'

"Having spoken thus, she went into the house in great anger, and, sitting down in a corner, she cried there all night. Her husband, finding next morning that she continued in the same humor, told her that she was a very foolish woman to afflict herself in that manner. 'I shall never cease weeping,' said she, 'till you have satisfied my curiosity.' 'But I tell you,' replied he, 'that it will cost me my life if I yield to your indiscretion.' 'Let what will happen,' said she, 'I insist upon knowing this matter.' 'I perceive,' said the merchant, 'that it is impossible to bring you to reason; and since I foresee that you will procure

SHEHERAZADE RELATING HER FIRST STORY TO THE
SULTAN

ARABIAN NIGHTS

your own death by your obstinacy, I will call in your children, and they may see you before you die.' Accordingly, he called for them, and sent for her father and mother, and other relations. When they heard the reason of their being called for they did all they could to convince her that she was in the wrong; but she told them that she would rather die than yield that point to her husband. The merchant was like a man out of his senses, and almost ready to risk his own life to save that of his wife, whom he loved dearly.

"Now this merchant had fifty hens and a cock, with a dog, that gave good heed to all that passed; and while the merchant was considering what he should do he saw his dog run toward the cock, who was crowing lustily, and heard him speak thus: 'You, cock, I am sure, will not be allowed to live long; are you not ashamed to be so merry to-day?' 'And why,' said the cock, 'should I not be merry to-day as well as on other days?' 'If you do not know,' replied the dog, 'then I'll tell you that this day our master is in great affliction; his wife would have him reveal a secret which is of such a nature that its discovery will cost him his life.'

"The cock answered the dog thus: 'What, has our master so little sense? He has but one wife, and cannot govern her! and though I have fifty, I make them all do what I please. Let him make use of his reason; he will speedily find a way to rid himself of his trouble.' 'How?' asked the dog; 'what would you have him do?' 'Let him go into the room where his wife is,' replied the cock, 'lock the door, and take a good stick and beat her well; and I will answer for it that will bring her to her senses and make her forbear asking him any more to reveal what he ought not to tell her.' The merchant had no sooner heard what the cock said than he took up a good stick, went to his wife, whom he found still crying, and, shutting the door, belabored her so soundly that she cried out, 'It is enough, husband, it is enough; let me alone, and I will never ask the question more.'

"Daughter," added the grand vizier, "you deserve to be treated as the merchant treated his wife."

[13]

"Father," replied Sheherazade, "I beg you will not take it ill that I persist in my opinion. I am in no way moved by the story of that woman." In short, the father, overcome by the resolution of his daughter, yielded to her importunity; and, though he was very much grieved that he could not divert her from her fatal resolution, he went that minute to inform the sultan that next night he would bring him Sheherazade.

The sultan was much surprised at the sacrifice which the grand vizier proposed making. "How could you resolve," said he, "to bring me your own daughter?" "Sir," answered the vizier, "it is her own offer." "But do not deceive yourself, vizier," said the sultan; "to-morrow when I put Sheherazade into your hands, I expect you will take away her life; and if you fail, I swear that you shall die."

Sheherazade now set about preparing to appear before the sultan, but before she went she took her sister Dinarzade apart and said to her: "My dear sister, I have need of your help in a matter of very great importance. As soon as I come to the sultan I will beg him to allow you to be in the bride-chamber, that I may enjoy your company for the last time. If I obtain this favor, as I hope to do, remember to awaken me to-morrow an hour before day, and to address me in words like these, 'My sister, if you be not asleep, I pray you that, till daybreak, you will relate one of the delightful stories of which you have read so many.' Immediately I will begin to tell you one; and I hope, by this means, to deliver the city from the consternation it is in." Dinarzade answered that she would fulfil her sister's wishes.

When the hour for retiring came, the grand vizier conducted Sheherazade to the palace, and took his leave. As soon as the sultan was left alone with her, he ordered her to uncover her face, and found it so beautiful that he was charmed with her; but, perceiving her to be in tears, he asked her the reason. "Sir," answered Sheherazade, "I have a sister who loves me tenderly, and whom I love; and I could wish that she might be allowed to pass the night in this chamber, that I might see her and bid her farewell. Will you be pleased to grant me the comfort of

ARABIAN NIGHTS

giving her this last testimony of my affection?'' Shahriar having consented, Dinarzade was sent for, and came with all diligence. The sultan passed the night with Sheherazade upon an elevated couch, and Dinarzade slept on a mattress prepared for her near the foot of the bed.

An hour before day Dinarzade awoke, and failed not to speak as her sister had ordered her.

Sheherazade, instead of answering her sister, asked leave of the sultan to grant Dinarzade's request. Shahriar consented. And, desiring her sister to attend, and addressing herself to the sultan, Sheherazade began as follows:

THE STORY OF THE MERCHANT AND THE GENIE

"SIR, there was formerly a merchant who had a great estate in lands, goods, and money. He had numbers of deputies, factors, and slaves. One day, being under the necessity of going a long journey, he mounted his horse, and put a wallet behind him with some biscuits and dates, because he had to pass over a great desert, where he could procure no provisions. He arrived without accident at the end of his journey; and, having despatched his business, took horse again in order to return home.

"On the fourth day of his journey, being in want of refreshment, he alighted from his horse and, sitting down by a fountain, took some biscuits and dates out of his wallet; and, as he ate his dates, he threw the stones about on all sides. When he had done eating, being a good Mussulman, he washed his hands, his face, and his feet, and said his prayers. He was still on his knees when he saw a Genie appear, white with age, and of enormous stature. The monster advanced toward him, scimitar in hand,

[16]

HE WAS STILL ON HIS KNEES WHEN HE SAW A
GENIE APPEAR, WHITE WITH AGE, AND OF
ENORMOUS STATURE

and spoke to him in a terrible voice, thus: 'Rise up, that I may kill thee, as thou hast killed my son.' The merchant, frightened at the hideous shape of the giant, answered: 'How can I have slain thy son? I do not know him, nor have I ever seen him.' 'What!' replied the Genie, 'didst not thou take dates out of thy wallet, and after eating them didst not thou throw the stones on all sides?' 'I do not deny it,' answered the merchant. 'Then,' said the Genie, 'I tell thee thou hast killed my son; and the way was thus: When thou threwest the date stones, my son was passing by, and one of them was flung into his eye and killed him; therefore I must kill thee.' 'Ah! my lord, pardon me,' cried the merchant; 'for, if I have killed thy son, it was accidentally; therefore suffer me to live.' 'No, no,' said the Genie, 'I must kill thee, since thou hast killed my son.' The Genie then threw the merchant upon the ground, and lifted up the scimitar to cut off his head."

When Sheherazade spoke these words she perceived it was day; and, knowing that the sultan rose betimes in the morning, she held her peace. "Oh, sister," said Dinarzade, "what a wonderful story is this!" "The remainder of it," said Sheherazade, "is more surprising; and you will be of my mind if the sultan will let me live this day and permit me to continue the story to-night." Shahriar, who had listened to Sheherazade with pleasure, said to himself, "I will let her stay till to-morrow, for I can at any time put her to death, when she has made an end of her story." So, having resolved to defer her death till the following day, he arose and, having prayed, went to the council.

The grand vizier, in the mean time, was in a state of cruel suspense. Unable to sleep, he passed the night in lamenting the approaching fate of his daughter, whose executioner he was destined to be. How great was his surprise when the sultan entered the council-chamber, without giving him the horrible order he expected.

The sultan spent the day, as usual, in regulating the affairs of his kingdom, and on the approach of night retired with Sheherazade to his apartment. The next morning, before the day

3 [19]

appeared, Dinarzade did not fail to address her sister. "My dear sister," she said, "if you are not asleep, I entreat you, before the morning breaks, to continue your story." The sultan did not wait for Sheherazade to ask permission, but said, "Finish the tale of the Genie and the Merchant." Sheherazade immediately went on as follows:

"Sir, when the merchant perceived that the Genie was about to slay him, he cried, 'One word more, I entreat thee; give me time to go and take leave of my wife and children and divide my estate among them, as I have not yet made my will; and when I have set my house in order, I promise to return to this spot and submit myself to thee.' 'But if I grant thee the respite thou askest,' replied the Genie, 'I fear thou wilt not return.' 'I swear by the God of heaven and earth that I will not fail to repair hither.' 'What length of time requirest thou?' said the Genie. 'It will take me a full year to arrange everything. But I promise thee, that after twelve months have passed thou shalt find me under these trees, waiting to deliver myself into thy hands.' On this, the Genie left him, and immediately disappeared.

"The merchant, having recovered from his fright, mounted his horse and continued his journey. But if, on the one hand, he rejoiced at escaping for the moment from a great present peril, he was, on the other, much distressed when he recollected the fatal oath he had taken. On his arrival at home his wife and family received him with signs of the greatest joy; but instead of returning their embraces, he wept so bitterly that they supposed something very extraordinary had happened. His wife inquired the cause of his tears, and of his violent grief. 'Alas!' he replied, 'how should I feel cheerful when I have only a year to live?' He then related to them what had passed, and that he had given his word to return, and at the end of a year to submit to his death.

"When they heard this melancholy tale they were in despair.

"The next day the merchant began to settle his affairs, and first of all to pay his debts. He made many presents to his different friends, and large donations to the poor. He set at liberty many of his slaves of both sexes; divided his property among his children; appointed guardians for those of tender age; to his wife he returned all the fortune she brought him, and added as much more as the law would permit.

"The year soon passed away, and he was compelled to depart. He took in his wallet his grave-clothes; but when he attempted to take leave of his wife and children his grief quite overwhelmed him. They could not bear his loss, and almost resolved to accompany him, and all perish together. Compelled at length to tear himself away, he addressed them in these words: 'In leaving you, my children, I obey the command of God; imitate me, and submit with fortitude to this necessity. Remember, that to die is the inevitable destiny of man.' Having said this, he snatched himself away from them and set out. He arrived at the destined spot on the very day he had promised. He got off his horse and, seating himself by the side of the fountain, with such sorrowful sensations as may easily be imagined, waited the arrival of the Genie.

"While he was kept in this cruel suspense, there appeared an old man leading a hind, who came near him. When they had saluted each other, the old man said, 'May I ask of you, brother, what brought you to this desert place, which is so full of evil genii that there is no safety? From the appearance of these trees one might suppose this spot was inhabited; but it is, in fact, a solitude, where to tarry is dangerous.'

"The merchant satisfied the old man's curiosity, and related his adventure. The old man listened with astonishment to the account, and when it was ended he said, 'Surely nothing in the world can be more surprising; and you have kept your oath inviolate! In truth I should like to be a witness to your interview with the Genie.' Having said this, he sat down near the merchant, and while they were talking, another old man, followed by two black dogs, appeared. As soon as he was near enough, he saluted them, and inquired the reason of their stay in that place. The first old man related the adventure of the merchant, and added that this was the appointed day, and therefore he was determined to remain, to see the event.

"The second old man resolved to stay likewise; and, sitting down, joined in the conversation. He was hardly seated when a third arrived and, addressing himself to the other two, asked why the merchant, who was with them, appeared so melancholy. They related the cause, which seemed to the new-comer so wonderful that he also resolved to be witness to what passed between the Genie and the merchant.

"They quickly perceived, toward the plain, a thick vapor or smoke, like a column of dust, raised by the wind. This vapor approached them; and on its sudden disappearance, they saw the Genie, who, without noticing them, went toward the merchant, with his scimitar in his hand, and, taking him by the arm, cried, 'Get up, that I may kill thee as thou hast slain my son.' The merchant and the three old men were so horrified that they began to weep and filled the air with their lamentations.

"When the old man, who led the hind, saw the Genie lay hold of the merchant, and about to murder him without mercy, he threw himself at the monster's feet and, kissing them, said, 'Prince of the Genii, I humbly entreat you to abate your rage and do me the favor to listen to me. I wish to relate my own history, and that of the hind, which you see here! and if you find it more wonderful and surprising than the adventure of this merchant, whose life you wish to take, may I not hope that you will at least remit a third part of the punishment of this unfortunate man?' After meditating for some time, the Genie answered, 'Good; I agree to it.'"

THE HISTORY OF THE FIRST OLD MAN AND
THE HIND

 AM now going," said he, "to begin my tale, and I request your attention. The hind that you see here is my cousin; nay, more, she is my wife. When I married her she was only twelve years old; and she ought therefore to look upon me not only as her relation and husband, but even as her father.

"We lived together thirty years, without having any children; this, however, did not decrease my kindness and regard for her. Still, my desire for an heir was so great that I purchased a female slave, who bore me a son of great promise and beauty. Soon afterward my wife was seized with jealousy, and consequently took a great aversion to both mother and child; yet she so well concealed her feelings that I, alas! never had a suspicion of them till too late.

"In the mean time my son grew up, and he was about ten

ARABIAN NIGHTS

years old when I was obliged to make a journey. Before my departure I recommended both the slave and the child to my wife, whom I trusted implicitly, and begged her to take care of them during my absence, which would last not less than a year. Now was the time she endeavored to gratify her hatred. She applied herself to the study of magic; and when she was sufficiently skilled in that diabolical art to execute the horrible design she meditated, the wretch carried my son to a distant place. There, by her enchantments, she changed him into a calf; and giving the creature to my steward, told him it was a purchase of hers, and ordered him to rear it. Not satisfied even with this infamous action, she changed the slave into a cow, which she also sent to my steward.

"Immediately on my return I inquired after my child and his mother. 'Your slave is dead,' said she, 'and it is now more than two months since I have beheld your son; nor do I know what is become of him.' I was deeply affected at the death of the slave; but as my son had only disappeared, I consoled myself with the hope that he would soon be found. Eight months, however, passed, and he did not return; nor could I learn any tidings of him. The festival of the great Bairam was approaching; to celebrate it I ordered my steward to bring me the fattest cow I had for a sacrifice. He obeyed my commands; and the cow he brought me was my own slave, the unfortunate mother of my son. Having bound her, I was about to offer her up; but she lowed most sorrowfully, and tears even fell from her eyes. This seemed to me so extraordinary that I could not but feel compassion for her, and I was unable to strike the fatal blow. I therefore ordered that she should be taken away and another cow brought.

"My wife, who was present, seemed angry at my compassion, and resisted an order which defeated her malice. 'What are you about, husband?' said she. 'Why not sacrifice this cow? Your steward has not a more beautiful one, nor one more proper for the purpose.' Wishing to oblige my wife, I again approached the cow; and, struggling with the pity that held my hand, I was again going to give the mortal blow when the victim a second

ARABIAN NIGHTS

time disarmed me by her renewed tears and moanings. I then delivered the instruments into the hands of my steward. 'Take them,' I cried, 'and perform the sacrifice yourself, for the lamentations and tears of the animal have overcome me.'

"The steward was less compassionate than I; he sacrificed her. On taking off her skin we found her greatly emaciated, though she had appeared very fat. 'Take her away,' said I, to the steward, greatly mortified. 'I give her to you to do as you please with; feast upon her with any friend you choose; and if you have a very fat calf, bring it in her place.' He had not been gone long before a remarkably fine calf was brought out. Although I was ignorant that this calf was my own son, yet I felt a sensation of pity arise in my breast at the first sight of him. As soon as he perceived me, he made so great an effort to come to me that he broke his cord. He lay down at my feet, with his head on the ground, as if he endeavored to seek my compassion. He was striving in this manner to make me understand that he was my son.

"I was still more surprised and affected by this action than I had been by the tears of the cow. I felt a kind of tender pity, and a great interest for him. 'Go back,' I cried, 'and take all possible care of this calf, and in its stead bring me another directly.'

"So soon as my wife heard this she exclaimed, 'What are you about, husband? Do not, I pray you, sacrifice any calf but this.' 'Wife,' answered I, 'I will not sacrifice him; I wish to preserve him, therefore do not oppose it.' This wicked woman, however, did not agree to my wish. She hated my son too much to suffer him to remain alive, and she continued to demand his death so obstinately that I was compelled to yield. I bound the calf, and, taking the fatal knife, was going to bury it in the throat of my son, when he turned his eyes so persuasively upon me that I had no power to execute my intention. The knife fell from my hand, and I told my wife I was determined to have another calf brought. She tried every means to induce me to alter my mind. I continued firm, however, in my resolution, promising, in order

ARABIAN NIGHTS

to appease her, to sacrifice this calf at the feast of Bairam on the following year.

"The next morning my steward desired to speak with me in private. 'I am come,' said he 'to give you some information, which I trust will afford you pleasure. I have a daughter who has some little knowledge of magic, and yesterday, as I was bringing back the calf which you were unwilling to sacrifice, I observed that she smiled on seeing it, and next moment began to weep. I inquired of her the cause of two such contrary emotions. "My dear father," she answered, "that calf which you bring back is the son of our master; I smiled with joy at seeing him still alive, and wept at the recollection of his mother, who was yesterday sacrificed in the shape of a cow. These two metamorphoses have been contrived by the enchantments of our master's wife, who hated both the mother and the child." 'This,' continued the steward, 'is what my daughter said, and I come to report it to you.' Imagine, O Genie, my surprise at hearing these words. I went to the stable where the calf had been placed; he could not return my caresses, but he received them in a way which convinced me that he was really my son.

"When the daughter of the steward made her appearance, I asked her if she could restore the poor creature to his former shape. 'Yes,' replied she, 'I can.' 'Ah!' exclaimed I, 'if you can perform such a miracle, I will make you the mistress of all I possess.' She then answered with a smile, 'I can restore your son to his own form only on two conditions: firstly, that you bestow him upon me for my husband; and secondly, that I may be permitted to punish her who changed him into a calf.' 'To the first condition,' I replied, 'I agree with all my heart. I will do still more; I will give you, for your own separate use, a considerable sum of money, independent of what I destine for my son. I agree also to the stipulation concerning my wife, for a horrible crime like this is worthy of punishment. Do what you please with her; I only entreat you to spare her life.' 'I will treat her, then,' she said, 'as she has treated your son.' To this I gave my consent.

[26]

THE STEWARD INTRODUCES HIS DAUGHTER

ARABIAN NIGHTS

"The damsel then took a vessel full of water, and, pronouncing over it some words I did not understand, she thus addressed the calf: 'O calf, if thou hast been created, as thou now appearest, by the all-powerful Sovereign of the world, retain that form; but if thou art a man, and hast been changed by enchantment into a calf, reassume thy natural figure!' As she said this she threw the water over him, and he instantly regained his own form.

"'My child! my dear child!' I exclaimed; 'it is Allah who hath sent this damsel to us to destroy the horrible charm with which you were enthralled, and to avenge the evil that has been done to you and your mother. I am sure your gratitude will lead you to accept her for a wife, as I have already promised for you.' He joyfully consented; but before they were united the damsel changed my wife into this hind which you see here. I wished her to have this form in preference to any other, that we might see her without repugnance in our family.

"Since that time my son has become a widower, and is now traveling. Many years have passed since I have heard anything of him; I have therefore now set out with a view to gain some information; and as I did not like to trust my wife to the care of any one during my absence, I thought proper to carry her with me. This is the history of myself and the hind. Can anything be more wonderful?" "I agree with you," said the Genie, "and in consequence I remit to this merchant a third part of his penalty."

"As soon as the first old man had finished his history," continued Sheherazade, "the second, who led the two black dogs, said to the Genie, 'I will tell you what has happened to me, and to these two dogs, which you see here; and I am sure you will find my history still more astonishing than that which you have heard. But when I have told it, will you forgive this merchant another third of his penalty?' 'Yes,' answered the Genie, 'provided your history surpass that of the hind.'" This being settled, the second old man began as follows:

THE HISTORY OF THE OLD MAN AND THE TWO
BLACK DOGS

"GREAT Prince of the Genii, you must know that these two black dogs which you see here, and myself, are three brothers. Our father left us, when he died, one thousand sequins each. With this sum we all embarked in the same calling; namely, as merchants. Soon after we had opened our warehouse, my eldest brother, who is now one of these dogs, resolved to carry on his business in foreign countries. With this view he sold all his goods, and bought such kind of merchandise as was adapted to the different lands he proposed visiting.

"He departed, and was absent a whole year. At the end of that time a poor man, who seemed to me to be asking charity, presented himself at my warehouse. 'God help you,' said I. 'And you also,' answered he. 'Is it possible you do not know me?' On looking attentively at him, I recognized my brother. 'Ah! my brother,' I cried, embracing him; 'how should I possibly know you in the state you are in?' I made him come in directly, and inquired concerning his health and the success of his voyage. 'Do not ask me,' he replied; 'you behold in me a token of my fate. To enter into a detail of all the misfortunes that I have suffered in the last year, and which have reduced me to the state you see, would only be to renew my affliction.'

"I instantly shut up my shop, and, putting aside all my own affairs, I took him to the bath, and dressed him in the best apparel my wardrobe afforded. I examined the state of my business, and finding by my accounts that I had just doubled my capital, and that I was now worth two thousand sequins, I presented him with half my fortune. 'Let this, my brother,' I said, 'make you forget your losses.' He joyfully accepted the thousand sequins, again settled his affairs, and we lived together as we had done before.

"Some time after this my second brother, the other of these black dogs, wished also to dispose of his property. Both his elder brother and myself tried every means in our power to dissuade him from his intention, but in vain. He sold all, and with the money he bought such merchandise as he considered proper for his journey. He took his departure and joined a caravan. At the end of a year he also returned, as destitute as his brother had been. I furnished him with clothes; and as I had gained another thousand sequins, I gave them to him. He bought a shop and continued to carry on his business.

"One day both my brothers came to me and proposed that I should make a voyage with them, for the purpose of traffic. At first I opposed their scheme. 'You have traveled,' said I, 'and what have you gained? Who will insure that I shall be more fortunate than you?' They returned, however, so often to the subject that, after withstanding their solicitations for five years, I at length yielded.

"When it became necessary to prepare for the voyage, and we were consulting on the sort of merchandise to be bought, I discovered that they had consumed their capital, and that nothing remained of the thousand sequins I had given to each. I did not, however, reproach them. On the contrary, as my fortune had increased to six thousand sequins, I divided the half with them, saying: 'We must, my brothers, risk only three thousand sequins, and endeavor to conceal the rest in some secure place, so that if our voyage be not more successful than the ventures you have already made, we shall be able to console ourselves with what we have left, and resume our former profession. I will give one thousand sequins to each of you, and keep one thousand myself; and I will conceal the other three thousand in a corner of my house.' We purchased our goods, embarked in a vessel, and set sail with a favorable wind. After sailing about a month, we arrived, without any accident, at a port, where we landed and disposed of our merchandise with great advantage. I, in particular, sold mine so well that I gained ten sequins for one. We then purchased the produce of the country we were in, in order to traffic with it in our own.

"About the time when we were ready to embark for our return, I accidentally met on the seashore a woman, very handsome, but poorly dressed. She accosted me by kissing my hand; entreated me most earnestly to permit her to go with me, and besought me to take her for my wife. I pleaded many difficulties against such a plan; but at length she said so much to persuade me, urging that I ought not to regard her poverty, and assuring me I should be well satisfied with her conduct, that I was entirely overcome. I directly procured proper dresses for her; and when I had married her in due form, she embarked with me and we set sail.

"During our voyage, I found my wife possessed of so many good qualities that I loved her every day more and more. In the mean time my two brothers, who had not traded so advantageously as myself, and who were jealous of my prosperity, began to feel exceedingly envious. They even went so far as to conspire against my life; and one night, while my wife and I were asleep, they threw us into the sea.

"My wife proved to be a fairy; consequently she possessed supernatural power. You may therefore imagine she was not hurt. As for me, I should certainly have perished but for her

I SHOULD CERTAINLY HAVE PERISHED BUT FOR
HER AID

aid. I had hardly, however, fallen into the water before she took me up, and transported me to an island. As soon as it was day the fairy thus addressed me: 'You may observe, my husband, that in saving your life I have not badly rewarded the good you have done me. You must know that I am a fairy; I saw you upon the shore, when you were about to sail, and felt a great regard for you. I wished to try the goodness of your heart, and therefore I presented myself before you in the disguise you saw. You acted most generously, and I am delighted to find an opportunity of showing my gratitude. But I am angry with your brothers; nor shall I be satisfied till I have taken their lives.'

"I listened with astonishment to the words of the fairy, and thanked her, as well as I could, for the great obligation she had conferred on me. 'But, lady,' said I to her, 'I must entreat you to pardon my brothers; for although I have the greatest reason to complain of their conduct, yet I am not so cruel as to wish their ruin.' I related to her what I had done for each of them, and my story only increased her anger. 'I must instantly fly after these ungrateful wretches,' cried she, 'and bring them to a just punishment; I will destroy their vessel, and sink them to the bottom of the sea.' 'No, beautiful lady,' replied I, 'for Heaven's sake moderate your indignation, and do not execute so dreadful a design; remember they are still my brothers, and that we are bound to return good for evil.'

"I appeased the fairy by these words; and so soon as I had pronounced them she transported me in an instant from the island where we were to the top of my own house, which was terraced. She then disappeared. I descended, opened the doors, and dug up the three thousand sequins which I had hidden. I afterward repaired to my shop, opened it, and received the congratulations of the merchants in the neighborhood on my safe return. When I went home I perceived these two black dogs, which came toward me, fawning. I could not imagine what this meant; but the fairy, who soon appeared, satisfied my curiosity. 'My dear husband,' said she, 'be not surprised at seeing these two dogs in your house; they are your brothers.' My blood ran

4   [35]

cold on hearing this, and I inquired by what power they had been transformed into their present shape. 'It is I,' replied the fairy, 'who have done it; at least it is one of my sisters, to whom I gave the commission; and she has also sunk their ship. You will lose the merchandise it contained, but I shall recompense you in some way; as to your brothers, I have condemned them to remain under this form for ten years, as a punishment for their perfidy.' Then, after informing me where I might hear of her, she disappeared.

"The ten years are now completed, and I am traveling in search of her. As I was passing this way I met this merchant, and the good old man who is leading his hind, and here I tarried. This, O Prince of the Genii, is my history. Does it not appear to you most marvelous?" "Yes," replied the Genie, "I confess it is wonderful, and therefore I remit the second third of the merchant's punishment."

"When the second old man had finished his story the third began by asking the Genie, as the others had done, if he would forgive the remaining third of the merchant's crime, provided this third history surpassed the other two, in the singularity and marvelousness of its events. The Genie repeated his former promise.

"The third old man related his history to the Genie, but as it has not yet come to my knowledge, I cannot repeat it; but I know it was so much beyond the others, in the variety of wonderful adventures it contained, that the Genie was astonished. He had no sooner heard the conclusion than he said: 'I grant thee the remaining third part of the merchant's pardon; and he ought to be greatly obliged to you all for having, by telling your histories, freed him from his dangerous position; but for this aid he would not now have been in this world.' Having said this, he disappeared, to the great joy of the whole party.

"The merchant did not omit to bestow many thanks upon his liberators. They rejoiced with him at his safety, and then, bidding him adieu, each went his separate way. The merchant

ARABIAN NIGHTS

returned home to his wife and children, and spent the remainder of his days with them in peace. But, sir," added Sheherazade, "however wonderful those tales which I have related to your Majesty may be, they are not equal to that of the fisherman." "Since there is still some time, my sister, pray tell this history; the sultan, I hope, will not object to it." Shahriar consented to the proposal, and Sheherazade went on as follows:

THE HISTORY OF THE FISHERMAN

"THERE once lived, sir, a fisherman, who was old and feeble, and so poor that he could barely obtain food for himself and for the wife and three children who made up his family. He went out very early every morning to his work; and he made it an absolute rule that he would throw his nets only four times a day.

"One morning he set out before the moon had set; when he had got to the seashore he undressed himself and threw his nets. In drawing them to land, he felt them drag heavily, and began to imagine he should have an excellent haul. But, on pulling up the nets, he found that instead of fish he had only caught the carcass of an ass; and he was much vexed and afflicted at having made so bad a haul. When he had mended his nets, which the weight of the ass had torn in many places, he cast them a second time into the sea. He again found considerable resistance in drawing them up, and again he thought they were filled with fish; but great was his disappointment when he discovered only a large basket, filled with sand and mud. 'O

Fortune!' he exclaimed with a melancholy voice and in the greatest distress, 'cease to be angry with me. I came from home to seek for life, and thou threatenest me with death. I have no other trade by which I can subsist, and even with all my toil I can hardly supply the most pressing wants of my family; but I am wrong to complain of thee, that takest a pleasure in deluding the virtuous and leavest good men in obscurity, while thou favorest the wicked and exaltest those who possess no virtue to recommend them.'

"Having thus vented his complaints, he angrily threw the basket aside, and, washing his nets from mud and slime, he threw them a third time. He brought up only stones, shells, and filth. It is impossible to describe his despair, but the day now began to break, and, like a good Mussulman, he did not neglect his prayers, to which he added the following supplication: 'Thou knowest, O Lord, that I throw my nets only four times a day; three times have I thrown them into the sea, without any profit for my labor. One more cast alone remains; and I entreat Thee to render the sea favorable, as Thou formerly didst to Moses.'

"When the fisherman had finished his prayer, he threw his nets for the fourth time. Again he supposed he had caught a great quantity of fish, as they were just as heavy as before. He nevertheless found none, but discovered a vase of yellow copper, which seemed from its weight to be filled with something; and he observed that it was shut up and stoppered with lead, on which there was the impression of a seal. 'I will sell this to a founder,' said he, joyfully, 'and with the money I shall get for it I will purchase a measure of corn.'

"He examined the vase and shook it, to judge of its contents by the sound. He could hear nothing; and this, together with the impression of the seal on the lead, made him think it was filled with something valuable. To decide the question, he took his knife and cut it open without much difficulty. He turned the top downward, and was much surprised to find nothing come out. He set it down before him, and while he watched it closely there issued from it so thick a smoke that he was obliged to step back a few paces. This smoke by degrees rose almost to the clouds, and spread itself over sea and land, appearing like a thick fog. The fisherman, as may easily be imagined, was much surprised at this sight. When the smoke had all come out from the vase it again collected itself, and became a solid body, taking the shape of a genie, twice as large as any of the giants. At the appearance of this huge monster, the fisherman wished to run away; but his fear was so great he was unable to move.

"'Solomon, Solomon,' cried the Genie, 'great prophet of Allah, pardon, I beseech thee. I will never more oppose thy will, but obey all thy commands.'

"The fisherman had no sooner heard these words spoken by the Genie than he regained his courage, and said: 'Proud spirit, what is this thou sayest? Solomon, the prophet to the Most High, has been dead more than eighteen hundred years. Tell me, then, thy history, and wherefore thou hast been shut up in this vase?'

"To this speech the Genie, looking disdainfully at the fisherman, answered, 'Speak more civilly; thou art very bold to call me a proud spirit.' 'Perhaps, then,' returned the fisherman, 'it will be more civil to call thee a bird of good omen.' 'I tell thee,' said the Genie, 'speak to me more civilly, before I kill thee.' 'And for what reason, pray, wouldst thou kill me?' asked the fisherman. 'Hast thou already forgotten that I have set thee at liberty?' 'I remember it very well,' returned the Genie, 'but that shall not prevent my destroying thee; and I will only grant thee one favor.' 'And what is that?' asked the fisherman. 'It is,' replied the Genie, 'to permit thee to choose the manner of thy death.' 'But in what,' resumed the other, 'have I offended thee? Is it thus thou dost recompense me for the good service I have done thee?' 'I cannot treat thee otherwise,' said the Genie; 'and to convince thee of it, attend to my history.

"'I am one of those spirits who rebelled against the sovereignty of Allah. All the other Genii acknowledged the great Solomon, the prophet of God, and submitted to him. Sacar and myself were the only ones who disdained to humble ourselves. In revenge for my contumacy, this powerful monarch charged Assaf, the son

AT THE APPEARANCE OF THIS HUGE MONSTER, THE
FISHERMAN WISHED TO RUN AWAY

of Barakhia, his first minister, to come and seize me. This was done, and Assaf captured me, and brought me by force before the throne of the king, his master.

"'Solomon, the son of David, commanded me to quit my mode of life, acknowledge his authority, and submit to his laws. I haughtily refused to obey him, and exposed myself to his resentment rather than take the oath of fidelity and submission which he required of me. In order, therefore, to punish me, he confined me in this copper vase; and to prevent my forcing my way out he put upon the leaden cover the impression of his seal, on which the great name of Allah is engraven. Thereupon he gave the vase to one of those Genii who obeyed him, and ordered the spirit to throw me into the sea, which, to my great sorrow, was done directly.

"'During the first period of my captivity I swore that if any man delivered me before the first hundred years were passed, I would make him rich, even after his death. The time lapsed, and no one released me. During the second century I swore that if any one set me free I would discover to him all the treasures of the earth; still no help came. During the third I promised to make my deliverer a most powerful monarch, to be always at his command, and to grant him every day any three requests he chose to make. This age, like the former, passed away, and I remained in bondage. Enraged at last, to be so long a prisoner, I swore that I would without mercy kill the person who should release me, and that the only favor I would grant him should be the choice of what manner of death he preferred. Since, therefore, thou hast come here to-day, and hast delivered me, fix upon whatever death thou wilt.'

"The fisherman was much grieved at this speech. 'How unfortunate,' he exclaimed, 'am I to come here and render so great a service to such an ungrateful creature! Consider, I entreat thee, thy injustice, and revoke thine unreasonable oath. Pardon me, and Allah will, in like manner, pardon thee. If thou wilt generously suffer me to live, he will defend thee from all attempts that will be made against thy life.' 'No,' answered the Genie,

'thy death is inevitable; determine only how I shall kill thee.'
The fisherman was in great distress at finding the Genie thus resolved on his death; not so much on his own account as on that
of his three children; for he anticipated with anguish the wretched
state to which his death would reduce them. He still endeavored
to appease the Genie. 'Let us lose no time,' cried the Genie;
'thy arguments will not alter my resolution. Make haste and
tell me how thou wilt die.'

"Necessity is the spur to invention, and the fisherman thought
of a stratagem. 'Since, then,' said he, 'I cannot escape death, I
submit to the will of God; but before I choose the manner of my
death, I conjure thee, by the great name of Allah, which is graven
upon the seal of the prophet Solomon, the son of David, to answer
me truly a question I am going to put to thee.' When the Genie
found that he should be compelled to answer positively, he
trembled, and said to the fisherman, 'Ask what thou wilt and
make haste.'

"So soon as the Genie had promised to speak the truth, the
fisherman said to him, 'I wish to know whether thou really wert
in that vase; darest thou swear it by the great name of Allah?'
'Yes,' answered the Genie, 'I do swear by the great name of
Allah, that I most certainly was there.' 'In truth,' replied the
fisherman, 'I cannot believe thee. This vase cannot contain one
of thy feet; how then can it hold thy whole body?' 'I swear to
thee, notwithstanding,' replied the monster, 'that I was there
just as thou seest me. Wilt thou not believe me after the solemn
oath I have taken?' 'No, truly,' retorted the fisherman, 'I shall
not believe thee unless I see it.'

"Immediately the form of the Genie began to change into
smoke, and to extend itself as before over both the shore and the
sea; and then, collecting itself, it began to enter the vase, and
continued to do so with a slow and equal motion, till nothing
remained without. A voice immediately issued forth, saying,
'Now—thou unbelieving fisherman—art thou convinced now that
I am in the vase?' But instead of answering the Genie, the fisherman immediately took the leaden cover and clapped it on the

vase. 'Genie,' he cried, 'it is now thy turn to ask pardon, and choose what sort of death is most agreeable to thee. But no; it is better that I should throw thee again into the sea; and I will build on the very spot where thou art cast a house upon the shore, in which I will live, to warn all fishermen that shall come and throw their nets not to fish up so wicked a Genie as thou art, that takest an oath to kill him who shall set thee at liberty.'

"At this insulting speech the enraged Genie tried his utmost to get out of the vase, but in vain, for the impression of the seal of Solomon the prophet, the son of David, prevented him. Knowing then that the fisherman had the advantage over him, he began to conceal his rage. 'Take heed,' said he, in a softened tone—'take heed what thou doest, O fisherman. Whatever I said was merely in jest, and thou shouldst not take it seriously.' 'O Genie,' answered the fisherman, 'thou, who wert a moment ago the greatest of all the genii, art now the most insignificant; and suppose not that thy flattering speeches will avail thee anything. Thou shalt assuredly return to the sea. I entreated thee in the name of God not to take my life, and as thou hast rejected my prayers, I ought to reject thine likewise.'

"The Genie tried every argument to move the fisherman's pity, but in vain. 'If thou givest me my liberty again, thou shalt have reason to be satisfied with my gratitude,' said he. 'Thou art too treacherous for me; I will not trust thee,' returned the fisherman; 'I should deserve to lose my life were I so foolish as to put it in thy power a second time. For thou wouldst probably treat me as the Greek king treated Douban, the physician. I will tell thee the story':

THE HISTORY OF THE GREEK KING, AND DOUBAN,
THE PHYSICIAN

"**I**N the country of Zouman, in Persia, there lived a king whose subjects were of Greek origin. This king was sorely afflicted with a leprosy, and his physicians had unsuccessfully tried every remedy they knew when a very learned physician, called Douban, arrived at the court.

"As soon as he was informed of the king's illness, and heard that the physicians had given their master up, he dressed himself as neatly as possible and obtained an audience of the king. 'Sir,' said he, 'I know that all the physicians who have attended your Majesty have been unable to remove your leprosy; but if you will do me the honor to accept of my services, I will engage to cure you without medicines or ointments.' The king, pleased with this proposal, replied: 'If thou art really so skilful as thou pretendest, I promise to shower wealth on thee and thy posterity;

THE GAME CONTINUED UNTIL THE KING FOUND HIS HAND THOROUGHLY HEATED

and, in addition to the presents thou shalt have, thou shalt be my first favorite. But dost thou tell me in earnest that thou wilt remove my leprosy without making me swallow any potion or applying any remedy externally?' 'Yes, sir,' replied the physician, 'I flatter myself I shall succeed, with the help of God, and to-morrow I will begin my cure.'

"Douban returned to his house, and made a sort of racket or bat, with a hollow in the handle to admit the drug he meant to use; that being done, he also prepared a sort of round ball, or bowl; and the following day he presented himself before the king and, prostrating himself at the monarch's feet, kissed the ground before him.

"Douban then arose, and told the king that he must ride on horseback to the place where he was accustomed to play at bowls. The king did as he was recommended; and when he had reached the bowling-green the physician approached him, and, putting into his hand the bat, which had been prepared, said: 'O King, exercise yourself with striking yonder ball with this bat till you find yourself in a profuse perspiration. When the remedy I have inclosed in the handle of the bat is warmed by your hand, it will penetrate through your whole body; you may then leave off playing, for the drug will have taken effect; and when you return to your palace get into a warm bath and be well rubbed and washed, then go to bed, and to-morrow you will be quite cured.'

"The king took the bat and spurred his horse after the ball till he struck it. It was sent back to him by the officers who were playing with him, and he struck it again; and thus the game continued for a considerable time, till he found his hand as well as his whole body thoroughly heated, and the remedy in the bat began to operate as the physician had prophesied. The king then ceased playing, returned to the palace, bathed, and observed very punctually all the directions that had been given him.

"He soon found the good effects of the prescription, for when he arose the next morning he perceived with equal surprise and joy that his leprosy was entirely cured, and that his body was as clear as if he had never been attacked by that malady. As soon as he was dressed he went into the audience-chamber, where he mounted his throne and received the congratulations of all his courtiers, who had assembled on that day partly to gratify their curiosity, and partly to testify their joy at their master's recovery.

"Douban entered, and went to prostrate himself at the foot of the throne, with his face toward the ground. The king, when he saw him, called to him and made him sit by his side, and, pointing him out to the assembly, gave him in that public way all the praise the physician so well deserved. Nor did the king stop here, for at a grand entertainment at court on that day he placed the physician at his own table to dine with him alone.

"The Greek King," continued the fisherman, "was not satisfied with admitting the physician to his own table; toward evening, when the courtiers were about to depart, he caused him to be dressed in a long, rich robe resembling that which the courtiers usually wore in the king's presence; and, in addition, made him a present of two thousand sequins. For the next few days this prince, thinking he could never repay the obligations he owed to the skilful physician, was continually conferring on him some fresh proof of his gratitude.

"The king had a grand vizier who was avaricious, envious, and prone by nature to every species of crime. This man observed with malicious fury the presents which had been bestowed upon the physician, whose great character and merit he was determined to lessen and destroy in the mind of the king. To accomplish this purpose he went to the monarch, and said in private that he had some intelligence of the greatest moment to communicate. The king asked him what it was. 'Sir,' replied he, 'it is very dangerous for a monarch to place confidence in a man of whose fidelity he is not assured. While you overwhelm the physician Douban with your favors, and bestow all this kindness and regard upon him, you are ignorant that he is a traitor, who has introduced himself into your court in order to assassinate you.'

'What is this you dare tell me?' cried the king. 'Recollect to whom you speak, and that you advance an assertion which I shall not easily believe.' 'O King,' resumed the vizier, 'I am accurately informed of what I have the honor to represent to you; do not, therefore, continue to repose such a dangerous confidence in Douban. I repeat that the physician Douban has traveled from the farthest part of Greece, his own country, solely to carry out the horrible design I have mentioned.'

"'No, no, vizier,' interrupted the king; 'I am sure this man, whom you consider a hypocrite and a traitor, is one of the most virtuous and best of men. You know by what remedy—or, rather, by what miracle—he cured me of my leprosy; and if he had sought my life, why did he thus save it? Cease then from endeavoring to instil unjust suspicions into my mind, for instead of listening to them, I now inform you that from this very day I bestow upon him a pension of one thousand sequins a month for the rest of his life. And were I to share all my riches, and even my kingdoms, with him I could never sufficiently repay what he has done for me. I see the reason of this. His virtue excites your envy; but do not suppose that I shall suffer myself to be prejudiced against him.'

"The vizier was too desirous of the death of Douban to let the matter rest where it was. 'O King,' replied he, 'it is not envy that makes me hostile to him; it is the interest alone that I take in your Majesty's preservation. Douban is a spy, sent by your enemies to attempt your Majesty's life. He has cured you, you say—but who can tell that? He has, perhaps, only cured you in appearance, and not in truth; and who can tell whether this remedy, in the end, will not produce the most pernicious effects?'

"The Greek King was naturally rather weak, and had neither penetration enough to discover the wicked intention of his vizier nor the firmness to persist in his first opinion. 'You are right, vizier,' said he; 'he may have come for the express purpose of taking my life—an object he can easily accomplish. We must consider what is to be done in this difficulty!'

5 [51]

ARABIAN NIGHTS

"When the vizier perceived the king in the disposition he wished to produce, he said to him, 'The best and most certain means, great King, to insure your repose and put your person in safety is instantly to send for Douban, and on his appearance to cause him to be beheaded.' 'Indeed,' replied the king, 'I think I ought to prevent his designs.' Having said this, he called one of his officers and ordered him to summon the physician. The latter, quite unsuspicious of the king's design, hastened to the palace.

"'Knowest thou,' said the king, as soon as he saw him, 'why I sent for thee?' 'No, sir,' answered Douban. 'I have ordered thee to come,' replied the king, 'that I may free myself from thy snares by taking thy life.'

"It is impossible to express the astonishment of Douban when he heard himself thus addressed. 'For what reason, O King,' replied he, 'does your Majesty condemn me to death? What crime have I committed?' 'I have been informed,' said the king, 'that thou art a spy and that thou hast come to my court to take away my life; but to prevent that I will now deprive thee of thine. Strike!' added he to an officer who was present, 'and deliver me from a treacherous wretch who has introduced himself here only to assassinate me.'

"On hearing this, the physician began to think that the honors and riches which had been heaped upon him had excited some enemies against him, and that the king, through weakness, had suffered himself to be guided by these. He began to repent having cured the king; but this repentance came too late. 'Is it thus,' he cried, 'that you repay the good I have done you?' The king, however, paid no attention to his remonstrances, and a second time desired the officer to execute his orders. The physician had then recourse to prayers. 'Ah, sir,' he cried, 'if you prolong my life God will prolong yours; do not kill me, lest God should treat you in the same manner.'

"You see, then," said the fisherman to the Genie, "that what has passed between the Greek King and the physician Douban is exactly similar to what has happened between us.

ARABIAN NIGHTS

"The Greek King, however," he continued, "instead of regarding the entreaties of the physician, exclaimed, 'No, no; you must die, or you will take away my life more mysteriously even than you have cured me.' The officer then put a bandage over the prisoner's eyes, tied Douban's hands, and was going to draw his scimitar. But the courtiers who were present felt so much for the physician that they entreated the king to pardon him, assuring his Majesty that they would answer for his innocence. But the king was inflexible, and spoke so peremptorily that they dare not reply.

"On his knees, his eyes bandaged, and ready to receive the stroke that was to terminate his existence, the physician once more addressed the king in these words: 'Since your Majesty refuses to revoke the order for my death, I entreat you at least to give me leave to return home, to arrange my funeral, take a last farewell of my family, bestow some money in charity, and leave my books to those who will know how to make a good use of them. There is one among them which I wish to present to your Majesty. It is a very rare and curious work, and worthy of being kept even in your treasury with the greatest care.' 'What book can there be,' replied the king, 'so valuable as to deserve such honor?' 'Sir,' answered the physician, 'it contains powers of the most curious nature; and one of the principal effects it can produce is, that when my head shall be cut off, if your Majesty will take the trouble to open the book at the sixth leaf, and read the third line on the left-hand page, my head will answer every question you wish to ask.' The king was so desirous of seeing such a wonderful thing, that he put off the physician's death till the next day, and sent him home under a strong guard.

"The unfortunate prisoner then arranged all his affairs; and as the news got abroad that an unheard-of prodigy was to happen after his execution, all the court flocked the next day to the hall of audience, to witness the extraordinary event.

"Douban, the physician, appeared presently, and advanced to the foot of the throne with a very large volume in his hand. He then placed the book on a vase, and, unfolding the cover in

[53]

which the book was wrapped, presented it to the monarch, and thus addressed him: 'May it please your Majesty to receive this book; and directly my head shall have been struck off, order one of your officers to place the head on the vase upon the cover of the book. As soon as it is there the blood will cease to flow; then open the book, and my head shall answer all your questions. But, sir,' added Douban, 'permit me once more to implore your mercy. I protest to you I am innocent.' 'Thy prayers,' answered the king, 'are useless; and were it only to hear thy head speak after thy death, I would wish for thy execution.' So saying, he took the book from the physician, and ordered the headsman to do his duty.

"The head was so cleverly cut off that it fell into the vase; and it had hardly been on the cover an instant before the blood ceased to run. Then, to the astonishment of the king and of all the spectators, it opened its eyes, and said, 'Will your Majesty now open the book?' The king did so; and, finding that the first leaf stuck to the second, put his finger to his mouth and moistened it in order to turn over the leaves more easily. He turned them over, one by one, till he came to the sixth leaf; and, observing nothing written upon the appointed page, he said to the head, 'Physician, there is no writing.' 'Turn over a few more leaves,' replied the head. The king continued turning them over, still putting his finger frequently to his mouth, till the poison, in which each leaf had been dipped, began to produce its effect. The monarch then felt himself suddenly agitated in a most extraordinary manner; his sight failed him, and he rolled to the foot of the throne in strong convulsions.

"When the physician Douban, or rather his head, saw that the poison had begun to work, and the king had only a few moments to live, he exclaimed: 'Tyrant, behold how those princes are treated who abuse their power and sacrifice the innocent! Sooner or later Allah punishes their injustice and their cruelty.' As soon as the head had finished these words, the king expired; and at the same moment the small remnant of life that remained in the head itself flickered away."

ARABIAN NIGHTS

"Such, my lord," continued Sheherazade, "was the end of the Greek King and the physician Douban. I shall now return to the fisherman and the Genie.

"When the fisherman had finished the history of the Greek King and the physician, he applied it to the Genie, whom he still kept confined in the vase. 'If,' said he, 'the Greek King had permitted Douban to live, Allah would have bestowed the same benefit on the king: but he rejected the humble prayers of the physician, and Allah punished him. This, O Genie, is the case with thee. If I had been able to make thee relent, and could have obtained the favor I asked of thee, I should have pitied the state in which thou now art; but as thou didst persist in thy determination to kill me, in spite of the great service I did thee in setting thee at liberty, I ought, in my turn, to show no mercy. By leaving thee within this vase and casting thee into the sea, I shall deprive thee of the use of thy being till the end of time.'

"'Once more, my good friend,' replied the Genie, 'I entreat thee not to be guilty of so cruel an act. Remember that revenge is not a part of virtue; on the contrary, it is praiseworthy to return good for evil.' 'No, no,' said the fisherman, 'I will not release thee; it is better for me to cast thee to the bottom of the sea.' 'One word more, fisherman,' cried the Genie; 'I will teach thee how to become rich beyond thy imagining.'

"The hope of escaping from poverty and want at once disarmed the fisherman. 'I would listen to thee,' he cried, 'if I had the least ground to believe thee; swear to me by the great name of Allah that thou wilt faithfully observe thy promise, and I will open the vase. I do not believe that thou wilt dare to violate such an oath.' The Genie took the oath; the fisherman immediately removed the covering of the vase, and the smoke instantly poured from it. The first thing the Genie did, after he had reassumed his natural form, was to kick the vase into the sea. This action rather alarmed the fisherman.

"The fear expressed by the fisherman made the Genie laugh. 'Be of good cheer, fisherman,' answered he; 'to show I intend to

[55]

keep my word, take thy nets and follow me.' So they went out, and passed by the city and crossed the summit of a mountain from whence they descended into a vast plain, which led them to a lake situated between four small hills.

"When they arrived on the borders of the lake, the Genie said to the fisherman, 'Throw thy nets and catch fish.' The fisherman did not doubt that he should take some, for he saw a great quantity in the lake; but he was greatly surprised to notice that they were of four different colors—white, red, blue, and yellow. He threw his nets and caught four fish, one of each color. 'Carry these fish to the palace,' said the Genie, 'and offer them to the sultan, and he will give thee more money than thou hast seen in thy life. Come thou every day and fish in this lake, but be careful to throw thy nets only once each day; if you neglect my warning, some evil will befall you, therefore take care.' Having said this, he struck his foot against the ground; the earth opened and he disappeared, the ground closing over him.

"The fisherman resolved to observe the advice and instructions of the Genie in every point, and to take care never to throw his nets a second time. He went back to the town very well satisfied with his success, and presented himself with his fish at the sultan's palace.

"Your Majesty may imagine how much the sultan was surprised when he saw the four fish. He took them up, one by one, examined them very attentively, and, after admiring them a long time, he said to his first vizier, 'Take these fish and carry them to that excellent cook whom the Emperor of the Greeks sent me; I think they must be as delicious as they are beautiful.'

"The vizier took them, and delivered them himself into the hands of the cook. 'Here are four fish,' said he, 'which have been presented to the sultan; he commands you to dress them.' He then returned to the sultan, his master, who desired him to give the fisherman four hundred pieces of gold. The fisherman, who had never before beheld so large a sum of money at once, could not conceal his joy and thought the whole adventure a

ARABIAN NIGHTS

dream. He soon, however, proved it to be a reality, and applied the gold to a good purpose in relieving the wants of his family.

"We must now, my lord," continued Sheherazade, "give account of what passed in the sultan's kitchen. As soon as the cook had cleaned the fish which the vizier had brought, she put them to fry over the fire in a vessel with some oil. When she thought they were sufficiently done on one side, she turned them. She had hardly done so when the wall of the kitchen appeared to separate, and a beautiful young damsel came out of the opening. She was dressed in a satin robe, embroidered with flowers after the Egyptian manner, and adorned with ear-rings and a necklace of large pearls, and gold bracelets set with rubies; she held a rod of myrtle in her hand. To the great astonishment of the cook, she approached the pan and, striking one of the fish with her rod, she said, 'Fish, fish, art thou doing thy duty?' The fish answered not a word. She repeated the question, when the four fishes all raised themselves up and said, very distinctly, 'Yes, yes—if you reckon, we reckon; if you pay your debts, we pay ours; if you fly, we conquer and are content.' As soon as they had spoken these words the damsel overturned the vessel and went back through the wall, which immediately closed up and was as if it had never been disturbed.

"When the cook, who was greatly alarmed at all these wonders, had in some measure recovered from her fright, she went to take up the fish, which had fallen upon the hot ashes; but she found them blacker and more burnt than the coals themselves, and not at all in a fit state to be put before the sultan. At this she was greatly distressed, and began to weep and lament bitterly. 'Alas!' said she, 'what will become of me? I am sure, when I relate to the sultan what I have seen, he will not believe me.'

"While she was in this distress the grand vizier entered and asked if the fish were ready. The cook then related all that had taken place, at which the vizier was greatly astonished; but, without telling the sultan anything about the matter, he invented some excuse for the non-appearance of the fish, which satisfied his master. He then sent directly for the fisherman, on whose arrival he said, 'Bring me four more fish, like those you brought before, for an accident has happened which prevents their being served up to the sultan.' The fisherman pleaded the length of the way as an excuse for not being able to procure any more fish that day; he promised, however, to bring some the next morning.

"The fisherman, in order to be in time, set out before it was day and went to the lake. He threw his nets, and upon taking them out found four more fishes, like those he had taken the day before, each of a different color. He returned directly, and brought them to the grand vizier. The vizier took them, and carried them into the kitchen, where he shut himself up with the cook, who prepared to dress them in his presence. She put them on the fire as she had done with the others on the preceding day. When they were dressed on one side, she turned them, and immediately the wall of the kitchen opened and the same damsel appeared, with her myrtle wand in her hand. She approached the pan in which the fish were, and, striking one of them, repeated the words she had used on the preceding day; and all the fish raised their heads and made the same answer. The damsel overturned the vessel with her rod, as she had done before, and went away through the wall. The grand vizier witnessed all that passed. 'This is very surprising,' he cried, 'and too extraordinary to be kept a secret from the sultan's ears. I will myself go and inform him of this prodigy.' Accordingly he went directly, and gave an exact account of all that had passed.

"The sultan was much astonished, and became very anxious to see this wonderful sight. For this purpose he sent for the fisherman. 'Friend,' said he to him, 'canst thou not bring me four more fish of different colors?' 'If your Majesty,' answered the fisherman, 'will grant me time, I can promise to do so.' He obtained the time he wished, and went again for the third time to the lake. Not less successful than before, he caught four fishes of different colors, the first time he threw his nets. The fisherman hastened to carry them to the sultan, who ordered four hundred pieces of money to be given to the man.

ARABIAN NIGHTS

"As soon as the sultan had obtained the fish, he had them brought into his own cabinet, together with the different things that were necessary for preparing them. He shut himself up with the grand vizier, who began to cook the fish and put them on the fire in a proper vessel. As soon as they were done on one side he turned them on the other. The wall of the cabinet immediately opened; but instead of the beautiful damsel there appeared a negro, in the dress of a slave. This negro was of gigantic stature, and held a large green rod in his hand. He advanced toward the vessel, and, touching one of the fish with his rod, he cried out in a terrible tone, 'Fish, fish, art thou doing thy duty?' At these words, the fish lifted up their heads and answered, 'Yes, yes, we are; if you reckon, we reckon; if you pay your debts, we pay ours; if you fly, we conquer and are content.' The fish had scarcely said this when the negro overturned the vessel into the middle of the cabinet, and reduced the fish to cinders. Having done this, he retired through the opening in the wall, which instantly closed, and appeared as perfect as before.

"'After what I have seen,' said the sultan to his grand vizier, 'I cannot think of letting this matter rest. It is certain that these fish signify something very extraordinary, and I must discover what it is. He sent for the fisherman, and when the man arrived the sultan said to him: 'The fish thou hast brought me have caused great uneasiness. Where dost thou catch them?' 'I caught them, O Sultan,' answered he, 'in a lake, which is situated in the midst of four small hills, beyond the mountains you may see from hence.' 'Do you know that lake?' said the sultan to the vizier. 'No, my lord,' answered he, 'I have never even heard it mentioned, though I have hunted in the vicinity of the mountain, and beyond it, for nearly sixty years.' The sultan asked the fisherman about what distance the lake was from the palace. He replied that it was not more than three hours' journey. On hearing this, as there was still time to arrive there before night, the sultan ordered his whole court to accompany him, while the fisherman served as a guide.

ARABIAN NIGHTS

"They all ascended the mountain; and, on going down on the other side, they were much surprised at the appearance of a large plain which no one had ever before remarked. They at length arrived at the lake, which they found situated exactly as the fisherman had reported. Its water was so transparent that they could see that all the fish were of the same colors as those the fisherman had brought to the palace.

"The sultan halted at the side of the lake, and, after contemplating the fish with looks of great admiration, he inquired of his courtiers if it could be possible that they had never seen this lake, which was so close to the city? They all said they had never even heard it mentioned. 'Since you all agree, then,' said he, 'that you have never heard it spoken of, and since I am not less astonished than yourselves at this novelty, I am resolved not to return to my palace till I have discovered for what reason this lake is now placed here, and why there are fish of only four colors in it.' Thereupon he ordered them to encamp.

"When the day closed the sultan retired to his pavilion and began an important conversation with his vizier. 'My mind,' said he, 'is much disturbed; this lake suddenly placed here, this black who appeared to us in my cabinet, these fish, too, which we heard speak—all this so much excites my curiosity that I am determined to be satisfied. Therefore I have made up my mind to execute the design I meditate. I shall go quite alone from my camp, and order you to keep my departure a profound secret. Remain in my pavilion, and when my courtiers present themselves at the entrance to-morrow morning, send them away and say I am somewhat indisposed and wish to remain alone. You will continue to do so every day till my return.'

"The grand vizier endeavored by many arguments to dissuade the sultan from carrying out his design. But all his eloquence was exhausted to no effect; the sultan did not listen to him, but prepared to set out. He put on a dress proper for walking, and armed himself with a saber; and as soon as he found that everything in the camp was quiet, he departed quite alone.

"The sultan bent his course toward one of the small hills,

which he ascended without much difficulty; and the descent on the other side was still easier. He then pursued his way over a plain till the sun rose. He now perceived before him in the distance a large building, the sight of which filled him with joy, for he now hoped to gain some intelligence of what he wished to know. When he came near he remarked that the building was a magnificent palace built of polished black marble, and covered with fine steel, so bright that it shone like a mirror. Delighted to have so soon met with something, at least worth investigation, he stopped opposite the front of the castle and examined it with much attention; he then advanced toward the folding-doors, one of which was open. Though he might have entered, he thought it better to knock. At first he knocked gently, and waited some time; but finding that no one answered his summons, he knocked a second time, much louder than before; still no one came. At this he was much astonished, for he could not imagine that a castle so well built could be deserted. 'If there is no person there,' said the sultan to himself, 'I have nothing to fear; and if any one comes, I have arms to defend myself with.'

"At last he entered and, pausing in the vestibule, he called out, 'Is there no one here to receive a stranger who is in want of refreshment on his journey?' He repeated this call two or three times, as loudly as he could; still there was no answer. This silence increased his astonishment. He passed on to a very spacious court, and, looking on every side, he could not discover a living creature. He then passed through some large halls, in which were spread carpets of silk, while the recesses were full of sofas entirely covered with the stuffs of Mecca; the curtains hung before the doors were of the richest manufactures of India, embroidered with gold and silver. The sultan went on, and came to a most splendid saloon, in the midst of which there was a large reservoir, with a lion of massive gold at each corner. Streams of water issued from the mouths of the four lions, and formed a goodly addition to a fountain that sprang from the middle of the basin, rising almost to the top of a dome, beautifully painted in the arabesque style.

ARABIAN NIGHTS

"The castle was surrounded on three sides by a garden, radiant with all kinds of flowers, with fountains, groves, and many other beauties; but what more than all else rendered this spot enchanting was the multitude of birds which filled the air with their sweetest notes. This was their constant habitation, for nets were thrown entirely over the trees, which prevented the escape of the beautiful songsters.

"The sultan continued a long time walking from one apartment to another; and everything around him was grand and magnificent. Being somewhat fatigued, he sat down in an open cabinet which looked into the garden. Here he sat meditating upon all he had seen, when suddenly a plaintive voice, uttering the most heartrending cries, struck his ear. He listened attentively, and heard these melancholy words: 'O Fortune, thou hast not suffered me long to enjoy my happy lot, but hast rendered me the most wretched of men; cease, I entreat thee, thus to persecute me, and rather by a speedy death put an end to my sufferings!'

"The sultan, much affected by these lamentable complaints, immediately rose and went toward the spot whence they issued. He came to the entrance of a large hall. Drawing the curtain aside, he saw a young man seated upon a sort of throne, raised a little from the ground. This man was handsome to behold and was very richly dressed. A look of sorrow was impressed on his countenance. The sultan approached and saluted the stranger. The youth returned the compliment by a deep bending of his head, but did not rise. 'Certainly,' said he to the sultan, 'I ought to rise to receive you, and show you all possible respect— but a most powerful reason prevents me; you will not, I trust, take it amiss.' 'Whatever may be your motive for not rising,' said the sultan, 'I willingly receive your apologies. Attracted by your complaints, and hoping to relieve your sufferings, I come to offer you my assistance. But in the first place, I beg you to inform me what is the meaning of that lake in which there are fish of four different colors; tell me also how this castle came here, and how you came to be in it thus alone?'

ARABIAN NIGHTS

"Instead of answering these questions, the young man began to weep most bitterly. 'How inconstant is Fortune!' he cried. 'She delights in hurling down those whom she has raised up. Who can say he has ever enjoyed from her a life of calm and pure happiness?'

"The sultan, touched with compassion at the youth's condition, again requested him to relate the cause of such sorrow. 'Alas, my lord,' answered the youth, 'can I be otherwise than sorrowful?' With these words he lifted up his robe, and the sultan perceived he was a man only to his waist, and that from thence to his feet he had been changed into black marble.

"The sultan's surprise may be readily imagined when he saw the deplorable state of the young man. 'What you show me,' said he to him, 'fills me with horror, but at the same time excites my interest. I am impatient to learn your history, and I am convinced that the lake and the fish have some connection with it. I entreat you, therefore, to relate your story.' 'I will not refuse you this satisfaction,' replied the young man, 'but I must forewarn you to prepare your ears and your mind—nay, even your eyes—for something that passes all belief.'

THE HISTORY OF THE YOUNG KING OF THE BLACK ISLES

 "I MUST first inform you," began the young man, "that my father, who was named Mahmoud, was the King of this State. It is the kingdom of the Black Isles, and takes its name from four small neighboring mountains that were formerly islands; and the capital, in which my father dwelt, was situated on the spot which is now occupied by yonder lake. You will hear how these changes took place as I proceed with my history.

"The king, my father, died at the age of seventy years. Immediately upon mounting his throne I married, and the person whom I chose as the partner of my state was my cousin. I had every reason to be satisfied with the proofs of affection I received from her, and I returned her regard with equal tenderness. Our union produced unmixed happiness for five years, but at the end of that time I began to perceive that the queen no longer loved me.

ARABIAN NIGHTS

"One day after dinner, when she had gone to bathe, I felt inclined to sleep, and threw myself on a sofa; two of the queen's women, who happened to be in the room, seated themselves, one at my head, the other at my feet, to fan me. These two women, supposing me asleep, began to talk in whispers; but my eyes were only closed, and I overheard their whole conversation.

"'Is it not a pity,' said one of them to the other, 'that the queen does not love our king, who is such an amiable prince?' 'Surely it is,' replied the other, 'and I cannot conceive why she goes out every night and leaves him. Does he not perceive it?' 'How should he perceive it?' resumed the first. 'Every night she mixes in his drink the juice of a certain herb, which makes him sleep all night so profoundly that she has time to go wherever she likes; and when at break of day she returns to him, she awakes him by passing a particular scent under his nose.'

"You may judge my astonishment at this speech, and how I felt when I heard it! Nevertheless, I had sufficient command over myself to suppress my emotions; I pretended to awake, and gave no sign of having heard anything.

"Presently the queen returned from the bath; we supped together, and before we went to bed she presented me with the cup of water, which it was usual for me to take; but, instead of drinking it, I approached a window that was open, and threw it out, unperceived by her. I then returned the cup into her hands, that she might suppose I had drunk the contents. We soon retired to rest; and shortly afterward, supposing that I was asleep, she got up with very little precaution, and even said aloud, 'Sleep, and I would thou mightest never wake more.' She dressed herself quickly and left the chamber.

"So soon as the queen was gone I rose and threw on my clothes as quickly as possible, and, taking my scimitar, I followed her so closely that I heard her footsteps just before me. She passed through several doors, which opened by virtue of some magic words she pronounced; the last she opened was that of the garden, which she entered. I stopped at this door that she might not see me, while she crossed a lawn; and, following her with my eyes, I remarked that she went into a little wood which was bounded by a thick hedge. I repaired thither by another way, and, hiding myself, I perceived that she was walking with a man.

"I did not fail to listen attentively to their discourse, when I heard what follows: 'I do not,' said the queen to her companion, 'deserve your reproaches for my want of diligence; but if all the tokens of love which I have hitherto given you are not sufficient to persuade you of my sincerity, I am ready to give you still more convincing proofs; you have only to command—you know my power. I will, if you wish it, before the sun rises, change this great city and this beautiful palace into frightful ruins, which shall be inhabited only by wolves and owls. Shall I transport all the stones with which these walls are so strongly built beyond Mount Caucasus, and farther than the boundaries of the habitable world? You have only to speak, and all this place shall be transformed.'

"As the queen finished this speech she and her lover reached the end of the walk, and, turning to enter another, passed before me. I had already drawn my scimitar, and as the man walked past me I struck him on the neck, and he fell. I believed I had killed him, and retired precipitately, without discovering myself to the queen, whom I wished to spare.

"Although her lover's wound was mortal, she yet contrived by her magic art to preserve in him a kind of existence which can be called neither death nor life. When I reached my chamber I returned to bed; and, satisfied with the punishment I had inflicted on the wretch who had offended me, I fell asleep. On waking the next morning, I found the queen by my side. I cannot say whether she was in a real or a feigned sleep, but I got up without disturbing her. I afterward attended the council, and on my return, the queen, dressed in mourning, with her hair disheveled and torn, presented herself before me. 'My lord,' said she, 'I come to entreat your Majesty not to be displeased at the state in which you now see me. I have just received intelligence of three events which occasion the grief I so strongly

I BELIEVED I HAD KILLED HIM, AND RETIRED PRECIPITATELY, WITHOUT
DISCOVERING MYSELF TO THE QUEEN

feel that I can scarcely express it.' 'What are these events, madam?' I inquired. 'The death of the queen, my beloved mother,' replied she; 'that of the king, my father, who was killed in battle; and of my brother, who fell down a precipice.'

"I was not sorry that she had invented this pretext to conceal the true cause of her affliction, and I concluded that she did not suspect me of having been the murderer of her lover. 'Madam,' said I, 'I do not blame your sorrow; on the contrary, I assure you that I sympathize in the cause. I hope, nevertheless, that time and philosophy will restore to you your wonted cheerfulness.'

"She retired to her apartments and, abandoning herself to her grief, she passed a whole year there, weeping and bewailing the fate of her lover. At the expiration of that time she requested my permission to build for herself, in the center of the palace, a mausoleum in which, she said, she designed to pass the remainder of her days. I did not refuse; and she erected a magnificent palace with a dome, which may be seen from this place, and she called it the Palace of Tears.

"When it was completed, she had her lover removed and brought to this mausoleum from the place whither she had transported him on the night I wounded him. She had till that period preserved his life by giving him certain potions, which she administered herself and continued to give him daily after his removal to the Palace of Tears.

"All her enchantments, however, did not avail much, for he was not only unable to walk or stand, but had also lost the use of his speech, and gave no signs of life but by looks. Although the queen had only the consolation of seeing him, and saying to him all the tender things that her love inspired, yet she constantly paid him two long visits every day. I was well acquainted with this circumstance, but I pretended to be ignorant of it.

"Moved by curiosity, I went one day to the Palace of Tears to know how the queen passed her time there; and, concealing myself, I heard her speak these words to her lover: 'Oh, what a heavy affliction to me to see you in this state! I share with you all the agonies you endure. But, dearest Life, I am always speaking to you, and yet you return no answer. How long will this distressing silence continue? Speak but once, and I am satisfied. Alas! I cannot exist away from you, and I should prefer the pleasure of seeing you continually to the empire of the whole universe.'

"This speech, which was frequently interrupted by tears, exhausted my patience. I could no longer remain in concealment, but, approaching her, exclaimed, 'Madam, you have wept enough; it is now time to have done with a grief which dishonors us both.' 'Sir,' replied she, 'if you still retain any regard for me, I entreat you to leave me to my sorrows, which time can neither diminish nor relieve.'

"I endeavored, but in vain, to bring her to a sense of her duty; finding that all my arguments only increased her obstinacy, I at last desisted and left her. She continued to visit her lover every day, and for two years she was inconsolable.

"I went a second time to the Palace of Tears while she was there. I hid myself as before, and heard her say: 'It is now three years since you have spoken to me; nor do you return the tokens of affection and fondness which I offer you. Is it from insensibility or disdain? Hast thou, O Tomb, destroyed that excess of tenderness which he bore me? Hast thou closed forever those dear eyes which beamed with love and were all my delight? Ah, no, I cannot think it; rather let me say thou art become the depository of the rarest treasure the world ever saw.'

"I confess to you, my lord, that I was enraged at these words; and indeed this cherished lover, this adored mortal, was not the kind of man you would imagine. He was a black Indian, one of the original inhabitants of this country. I was, as I have said, so enraged that I suddenly showed myself, and, apostrophizing the tomb as my wife had done, I said: 'Why dost thou not, O Tomb, swallow up this monster, who is disgusting to human nature? Or, rather, why dost thou not consume both the lover and his mistress?'

"So soon as I had spoken these words, the queen, who was seated near the black, started up like a fury. 'Ah, wretch!' cried she to me, 'it is you who have been the cause of my grief.

ARABIAN NIGHTS

It was your barbarous hand which reduced the object of my affection to the miserable state he now is in. And have you the cruelty to come and insult my despair?' 'Yes,' exclaimed I, transported with anger; 'I have chastised the monster as he deserved, and I ought to treat thee in the same manner. I repent that I have not already done it, for thou hast too long abused my goodness.' As I said this I drew my scimitar and raised my arm to punish her. 'Moderate thy rage,' said she to me, with a disdainful smile. After a moment she pronounced some words which I did not understand, and added, 'By virtue of my enchantments, I command thee, from this moment, to become half marble and half man.' Immediately, my lord, I was changed to what you see, already dead among the living, and still living among the dead.

"As soon as this cruel enchantress had thus transformed me, and by means of her magic had conveyed me to this apartment, she destroyed my capital, which had been flourishing and well inhabited; she annihilated the palaces, public places, and markets; turned the whole region into a lake or pond, and rendered the country, as you may perceive, quite a desert. The four sorts of fish which are in the lake are four different classes of inhabitants, who professed different religions and inhabited the capital. The white were Mussulmans; the red, Persians and fire-worshipers; the blue, Christians; and the yellow, Jews. The four little hills were four islands which originally gave the kingdom its name.

"I was informed of all this by the enchantress, who herself related to me the effects of her rage. Nor was even this all. Her fury is not satiated by the destruction of my empire and the enchantment of myself, for she comes every day and gives me a hundred blows upon my shoulders with a thong made of a bull's hide, drawing blood at every stroke. As soon as she has finished this punishment she covers me with a coarse stuff made of goat's hair, and puts a robe of rich brocade over it, not for the sake of honoring me, but to mock my despair." As he said this the young King of the Black Isles could not refrain from tears.

"The sultan was much affected by the recital of this strange

[71]

story, and felt eager to revenge the unfortunate king's injuries. 'Inform me,' cried he, 'where this perfidious enchantress resides; and also where is this infamous paramour whom she has entombed before his death.' 'My lord,' answered the prince, 'he, as I have before mentioned, is at the Palace of Tears in a tomb formed like a dome; and the building has a communication with the castle, in the direction of the entrance. I cannot exactly tell you to what spot the enchantress has retired, but she visits her lover every day at sunrise, after having inflicted on me the cruel punishment I have described; and you may easily judge that I cannot defend myself from such inhumanity. She always brings with her a sort of liquor, which is the only thing that can keep him alive.'

"'No one, Prince,' replied the sultan, 'deserves greater commiseration than yourself. A more extraordinary fate never happened to any man; and they who may hereafter compose your history will be able to relate an event more surprising than anything yet recorded. One thing only is wanting to complete it, and that is your revenge; nor will I leave anything untried to accomplish this end.' The sultan, having first informed the prince of his own name and rank, and of the reason of his entering the castle, consulted with him on the best means of accomplishing a just revenge. They agreed upon the steps it was necessary to take in order to insure success, and they deferred the execution of the plan till the following day. In the mean time, as the night was far advanced, the sultan took some repose. The young prince, as usual, passed his time in continued wakefulness, for he had been unable to sleep since his enchantment.

"The sultan rose as soon as it was day, and, concealing in his chamber his robe and external dress, which might have encumbered him, he went to the Palace of Tears. He found it illuminated by a multitude of torches of white wax, and became conscious of a delicious perfume issuing from various beautiful golden vases, regularly arranged. As soon as he perceived the bed on which the wounded man was lying, he drew his saber, and destroyed without resistance the little life that remained in the wretch. He then dragged the body into the court of the castle, and threw it into a well. Having done this, he returned and lay down in the Indian's place, hiding his saber under the coverlid, and there he watched to complete the revenge he meditated. The enchantress arrived soon after. Her first business was to go into the apartment in which she had immured her husband, the King of the Black Isles. She stripped him, and began with horrible barbarity to inflict upon his shoulders the accustomed number of blows. The poor prince filled the whole building with his cries, and conjured her in the most pathetic manner to have pity on him. The cruel enchantress, however, ceased not to beat him till she had completed the hundred stripes. 'Thou hadst no compassion on my lover,' said she; 'therefore expect none from me.' As soon as she had finished her cruel work she threw over him the coarse garment made of goatskin, covering this with the robe of brocade. She next went to the Palace of Tears and, on entering, began to renew her lamentations. When she approached the couch where she thought to find her lover, she exclaimed: 'Alas! what cruelty to have thus destroyed the tranquil joy of so tender and fond a mistress as I am! Merciless Prince, thou reproachest me with being inhuman, when I make thee feel the effects of my resentment—and has not thy barbarity far exceeded my revenge? Hast thou not, traitor, in destroying almost the existence of this adorable object, equally destroyed mine? Alas!' added she, addressing herself to the sultan, whom she took for her lover, 'will you always, Light of my life, thus keep silence? Are you resolved to let me die without the consolation of hearing you again declare you love me? Utter at least one word, I conjure you.'

"Then the sultan, pretending to awake from a profound sleep, and imitating the language of the Indians, answered the queen in a solemn tone. 'There is no strength or power,' he said, 'but in Allah alone, who is all-powerful.' At these words the enchantress, who never expected to hear her lover speak, gave a violent scream for very joy. 'My dear lord,' she exclaimed, 'do you deceive me? Is what I hear true? Is it really you who speak?'

'Wretched woman,' replied the sultan, 'are you worthy of an answer?' 'What!' cried the queen, 'do you reproach me?' 'The cries, the tears, the groans of thy husband,' answered the supposed Indian, 'whom you every day torture with so much barbarity, continually disturb my rest. I should have been cured long since, and should have recovered the use of my tongue if you had disenchanted him. This, and this only, is the cause of my silence, of which you so bitterly complain.' 'Then,' said the enchantress, 'to satisfy you I am ready to do what you command. Do you wish him to be restored to his former shape?' 'Yes,' replied the Sultan, 'and hasten to set him free, that I may no longer be disturbed by his cries.'

"The queen immediately went out from the Palace of Tears, and, taking a vessel of water, she pronounced over it some words which caused it instantly to boil, as if it had been placed on a fire. She proceeded to the apartment where the young king, her husband, was. 'If the Creator of all things,' said she, throwing the water over him, 'hath formed thee as thou now art, or if he is angry with thee, be not changed; but if thou art in this state by virtue of my enchantment, take back thy natural form, and become as thou wert before.' She had hardly concluded when the prince, recovering his first shape, rose up with all possible joy and returned thanks to God. 'Go,' said the enchantress, addressing him, 'hasten from this castle, and never return, lest it should cost you your life!' The young king yielded to necessity, and left the queen without uttering a word. He concealed himself in a secure spot, where he impatiently waited the completion of the sultan's design, the commencement of which had been so successful.

"The enchantress then returned to the Palace of Tears, and on entering said to the sultan, whom she still mistook for the Indian, 'I have done, my Love, what you ordered me; nothing, therefore, now prevents your getting up and affording me the satisfaction I have so long been deprived of.' The sultan, still imitating the language of the blacks, answered in a somewhat severe tone: 'What you have yet done is not sufficient for my cure. You have destroyed only a part of the evil.' 'What do you mean by those words, my charming friend?' asked she. 'What can I mean,' he cried, 'but the city and its inhabitants and the four isles, which you have destroyed by your magic? Every day toward midnight the fish raise their heads out of the pond and cry for vengeance against us both. This is the real cause why my recovery is so long delayed. Go quickly and re-establish everything in its former state; and on your return I will give you my hand, and you shall assist me in rising.'

"The queen, exulting in the expectations these words produced, joyfully exclaimed, 'You shall soon then, my Life, recover your health, for I will instantly go and do what you have commanded.' When she arrived on the border of the pond, she took a little water in her hand and scattered it about. So soon as she had done this, and pronounced certain words over the fish and the pond, the city reappeared. The fish became men, women, and children; all arose as Mohammedans, Christians, Persians, and Jews; in short, each took his former shape. The houses and shops became filled with inhabitants, who found all things in the same situation and order in which they had been previous to the change effected by the queen's enchantment. The officers and attendants of the sultan, who had happened to encamp upon the site of the great square, were astonished at finding themselves on a sudden in the midst of a large, well-built, and populous city.

"But to return to the enchantress. As soon as she had completed this change she hastened back to the Palace of Tears to enjoy the reward of her labors. 'My dear lord,' she cried on entering, 'I have returned to participate in the pleasure of your renewed health, for I have done all you have required of me. Arise, and give me your hand.' 'Come near, then,' said the sultan, still imitating the manner of the Indian. She did so. 'Nearer still!' he cried. She obeyed. Then, raising himself up, he seized her so suddenly by the arms that she had no opportunity of perceiving how she had been deceived; and with one stroke of his saber he separated her body into two parts, which fell on each

side of him. Having done this, he left the corpse where it fell,
and went to seek the Prince of the Black Isles, who was waiting
with the greatest impatience for him. 'Rejoice, Prince,' said he,
embracing him, 'you have nothing more to fear, for your cruel
enemy exists no longer.'

"The young prince thanked the sultan in a way which proved
that his heart was truly filled with gratitude; and wished his
deliverer, as a reward for the important service he had rendered
him, a long life and the greatest prosperity. 'May you, too,
live happily and at peace in your capital!' replied the sultan.
'And should you hereafter have a wish to visit mine, which is so
near, I shall receive you with the truest pleasure, and you shall
be as highly honored as in your own.' 'Powerful monarch,' answered the prince, 'to whom I am so much indebted, do you
think you are very near your capital?' 'Certainly,' replied the
sultan; 'I presume, at least, that I am not more than four or
five hours' journey from thence.' 'It is a whole year's journey,'
said the prince, 'although I believe you might come here in the
time you mention, because my city was enchanted; but since
it has been restored all this is altered. This, however, shall
not prevent my following you, were it necessary to go to the very
ends of the earth. You are my liberator; and to show you every
mark of my gratitude as long as I live, I shall freely accompany
you and resign my kingdom without regret.'

"The sultan was extremely surprised to find that he was so
distant from his dominions, and could not comprehend how it
had happened. 'It matters not,' resumed the sultan. 'The
trouble of returning to my dominions will be sufficiently recom-
pensed by the satisfaction of having assisted you and of having
gained a son in you; for, as you will do me the honor to accompany me, I shall look upon you as my son; and, as I am childless,
I from this moment make you my heir and successor.' This
interview between the sultan and the King of the Black Isles
was terminated by the most affectionate embraces, and the
young prince at once prepared for his journey. In three weeks
he was ready to depart, greatly regretted by his court and

subjects, who received at his hands a near relation of his own as their king.

"At length the sultan and the prince set out, with a hundred camels laden with inestimable riches, which had been selected from the treasury of the young king, who was, moreover, accompanied by fifty handsome nobles, well mounted and equipped. Their journey was a pleasant one; and when the sultan, who had despatched couriers to give notice of his arrival, and explain the reason of his delay, drew near to his capital, the principal officers, whom he had left there, came to receive him, and to assure him that his long absence had not occasioned any change in his empire. The inhabitants also crowded to meet him, and welcomed him with acclamations and every demonstration of joy.

"The day after his arrival, the sultan assembled his courtiers, and gave them an ample detail of the occurrences which had delayed his return. He then declared to them his intention of adopting the King of the Black Isles, who had left a large kingdom to accompany and live with him; and, lastly, to reward the fidelity with which they served him, he bestowed presents on all according to each man's rank and station.

"With regard to the fisherman, as he had been the first cause of the deliverance of the young prince, the sultan overwhelmed him with rewards, and made him and his family happy and prosperous for the rest of their days."

"Why not the entertaining adventures of Sinbad the Sailor?" inquired Dinarzade. "We will hear them to-morrow," agreed Shahriar.

THE HISTORY OF SINDBAD THE SAILOR

"IN the reign of the Caliph Harun-al-Rashid, there lived in Bagdad a poor porter, who was named Hindbad. One day, during the most violent heat of summer, he was carrying a heavy load from one extremity of the city to the other. Much fatigued by the length of the way he had come, he arrived in a street where the pavement was sprinkled with rose-water and a grateful coolness refreshed the air. Delighted with this mild and pleasant situation, he placed his load on the ground and took his station near a large mansion. The delicious scent of aloes and frankincense which issued from the windows, the sound of a charming concert issuing from within the house, accompanied with the melody of the nightingales, and other birds peculiar to the climate of Bagdad, added to the smell of different sorts of viands, led Hindbad to suppose that some grand feast was in progress. He wished to know to whom this house belonged. To satisfy his curiosity, therefore, he approached

[78]

"COME, FOLLOW ME; MY MASTER SINDBAD WISHES
TO SPEAK WITH YOU"

ARABIAN NIGHTS

some magnificently dressed servants who were standing at the door, and inquired who was the master of that mansion. 'What,' replied the servant, 'are you an inhabitant of Bagdad, and do not know that this is the residence of Sindbad the sailor, that famous voyager, who has roamed over all the seas under the sun?' The porter, who had heard of the immense riches of Sindbad, could not help comparing the situation of this man, whose lot appeared so enviable, with his own deplorable position; and, distressed by the reflection, he raised his eyes to heaven, and exclaimed in a loud voice: 'Almighty Creator of all things, deign to consider the difference that there is between Sindbad and myself. I suffer daily a thousand ills, and have the greatest difficulty in supplying my wretched family with bad barley bread, whilst the fortunate Sindbad lavishes his riches in profusion, and enjoys every pleasure. What has he done to obtain so happy a destiny, or what crime has been mine to merit a fate so rigorous?' He was still musing on his fate when a servant came toward him from the house, and said, 'Come, follow me; my master Sindbad wishes to speak with you.'

"Hindbad was not a little surprised at the compliment thus paid him. Remembering the words he had just uttered, he began to fear that Sindbad sent for him to reprimand him, and therefore he tried to excuse himself from going. He declared that he could not leave his load in the middle of the street. But the servant assured him that it should be taken care of, and pressed him so much to go that the porter could no longer refuse.

"His conductor led him into a spacious room where a number of persons were seated round a table which was covered with all kinds of delicate viands. In the principal seat sat a grave and venerable personage whose long, white beard hung down to his breast, and behind him stood a crowd of officers and servants ready to wait on him. This person was Sindbad. Quite confused by the number of the company and the magnificence of the entertainment, the porter made his obeisance with fear and trembling. Sindbad desired him to approach, and, seating him at his right hand, helped him to the choicest dishes, and made him drink

[81]

some of the excellent wine with which the sideboard was plentifully supplied.

"Toward the end of the repast Sindbad began to speak, and, addressing Hindbad by the title 'my brother'—the common salutation amongst the Arabians when they converse familiarly—he inquired the name and profession of his guest. 'Sir,' replied the porter, 'my name is Hindbad.' 'I am happy to see you,' said Sindbad, 'but I wish to know from your own lips what it was you said just now in the street'; for Sindbad, before he went to dinner, had heard from the window every word of Hindbad's ejaculation, which was the reason of his sending for him. At this request, Hindbad, full of confusion, hung down his head, and replied, 'Sir, I must confess to you that, put out of humor by weariness and exhaustion, I uttered some indiscreet words which I entreat you to pardon.' 'Oh,' resumed Sindbad, 'do not imagine that I am so unjust as to have any resentment on that account. I feel for your situation, and pity you heartily; but I must undeceive you on one point respecting my own history, in which you seem to be in error. You appear to suppose that the riches and comforts I enjoy have been obtained without any labor or trouble. In this you are mistaken. Before attaining my present position I have endured for many years the greatest mental and bodily sufferings that you can possibly conceive. Yes, gentlemen,' continued the venerable host, addressing himself to the whole company, 'I assure you that my sufferings have been so acute that they might deprive the greatest miser of his love of riches. Perhaps you have heard only a confused account of my adventures in the seven voyages I have made on different seas; and as an opportunity now offers, I will, with your leave, relate the dangers I have encountered; and I think the story will not be uninteresting to you.'

THE FIRST VOYAGE OF SINDBAD THE SAILOR

"I SQUANDERED the greater part of my paternal inheritance in youthful dissipation; but at length I saw my folly, and became convinced that riches were not of much use when applied to such purposes as those to which I had devoted them, and I reflected that the time I spent in dissipation was of still greater value than gold, and that nothing could be more truly deplorable than poverty in old age. Feeling the truth of this reflection, I resolved to collect the small remains of my patrimony and to sell my goods by auction. In short, I determined to employ to some profit the small sum I had remaining; and no sooner was this resolution formed than I put it into execution. I repaired to Balsora, where I embarked with several merchants in a vessel which had been equipped at our united expense.

"We set sail, and steered toward the East Indies by the Persian Gulf. I was at first troubled with the sickness that attacks voyagers by sea, but I soon recovered my health. In the course of our voyage we touched at several islands, and sold

7 [83]

ARABIAN NIGHTS

or exchanged our merchandise. One day, when our vessel was in full sail, we were unexpectedly becalmed before a small island which appeared just above the water, and in its verdure resembled a beautiful meadow. The captain ordered the sails to be lowered, and gave permission to those passengers who wished it to go ashore, and of this number I formed one. But while we were enjoying ourselves the island suddenly trembled, and we felt a severe shock.

"The people who had remained in the ship perceived the earthquake in the island, and immediately called us to re-embark or we should all perish; but what we supposed to be an island was nothing but the back of a whale. The most active of the party jumped into the boat, whilst others threw themselves into the water, to swim to the ship; as for me, I was still on the island, or, more properly speaking, on the whale, when it dived below the surface, and I had only time to seize a piece of wood which had been brought to make a fire with, when the monster disappeared beneath the waves. Meantime the captain, willing to avail himself of a fair breeze which had sprung up, set sail with those who had reached his vessel, and left me to the mercy of the waves. I remained in this deplorable situation the whole of that day and the following night. On the return of morning I had neither strength nor hope left, but a breaker happily threw me on an island.

"Though extremely enfeebled by the fatigues I had undergone, I still tried to creep about in search of some herb or fruit that might satisfy my hunger. I found some, and had also the good luck to meet with a stream of excellent water. Having in a great measure regained my strength, I began to explore the island, and entered a beautiful plain where I perceived a horse grazing. I bent my steps toward it, trembling between fear and joy, for I could not ascertain whether I was advancing to safety or perdition. I remarked, as I approached, that the creature was a mare tied to a stake; her beauty attracted my attention; but whilst I was admiring her I heard from underground the voice of a man who shortly after appeared, and, coming to me, asked

"THE CAPTAIN SET SAIL AND LEFT ME TO THE
MERCY OF THE WAVES"

me who I was. I related my adventure to him; whereupon he took me by the hand and led me into a cave, where I found some other persons who were not less astonished to see me than I was to meet them there.

"I ate some food which they offered me; and upon my asking them what they did in a place which appeared so barren they replied that they were grooms to King Mihragè, who was the sovereign of that isle, and that they came hither every year, about this season, with some mares belonging to the king for the purpose of having a breed between them and a sea-horse which came on shore at that spot. They tied up the mares as I had seen because they were obliged almost immediately, by their cries, to drive back the sea-horse, which otherwise began to tear the mares in pieces. As soon as the mares were with foal they carried them back, and the colts were called sea-colts, and set apart for the king's use. They told me that the morrow was the day fixed for their departure, and if I had been one day later I must certainly have perished, because they lived so far off that it was impossible to reach their habitations without a guide.

"Whilst they were talking to me the horse rose out of the sea, as they described, and immediately attacked the mares. He would have torn them to pieces, but the grooms began to make such a noise that he let go his prey and again plunged into the ocean.

"The following day they returned with the mares to the capital of the island, whither I accompanied them. On our arrival, King Mihragè, to whom I was presented, asked me who I was and by what chance I had reached his dominions; and when I had satisfied his curiosity he expressed pity at my misfortune. At the same time he gave orders that I should be taken care of and be supplied with everything I might want.

"As I was a merchant, I associated with persons of my own profession. I sought, in particular, such as were foreigners, partly to hear some intelligence of Bagdad, and partly in the hope of meeting some one with whom I could return, for the capital of King Mihragè is situated on the seacoast, and has a beautiful port where vessels from all parts of the world daily arrive.

"As I was standing one day near the port, I saw a ship come toward the land. When the crew had cast anchor they began to unload its goods, and the merchants to whom the cargo belonged took it away to their warehouses. Happening to cast my eyes on some of the packages, I saw my name written thereon, and, having attentively examined them, I recognized them as the same which I had embarked in the ship in which I left Balsora. I also recollected the captain; but as I felt assured that he thought me dead, I went up to him and asked him to whom those parcels belonged. 'I had on board with me,' replied he, 'a merchant of Bagdad named Sindbad. One day when we were near an island, or at least what appeared to be one, he went ashore with some other passengers on this supposed island, which was nothing but an enormous whale that had fallen asleep on the surface of the water. The fish no sooner felt the heat of a fire they lighted on its back to cook their provisions than it began to move and flounce about in the sea. Most of the persons who were on it were drowned, and the unfortunate Sindbad was one of the number. These parcels belonged to him, and I have resolved to sell them, that if I meet with any of his family I may be able to pay over to them the profit I shall have made on the principal.' 'Captain,' said I then, 'I am that Sindbad whom you supposed dead, but who is still alive; and these parcels are my property and merchandise.'

"When the captain heard me speak thus he exclaimed: 'Great God! whom shall I trust? There is no longer truth in man! With my own eyes I saw Sindbad perish; the passengers I had on board were also witnesses of his death, and you have the assurance to say that you are that same Sindbad? At first sight you appeared a man of probity and honor; yet you assert an impious falsity, to possess yourself of some merchandise which does not belong to you.' 'Have patience,' replied I, 'and do me the favor to listen to what I have to say.' I then related in what manner I had been saved, and by what accident I had met with King Mihrage's grooms, who had brought me to his court.

"The captain was rather staggered at my discourse, but was

soon convinced that I was not an impostor, for some people who arrived from his ship knew me and began to congratulate me on my fortunate escape. At last he recollected me himself, and, embracing me, exclaimed: 'Heaven be praised that you have happily escaped from that great peril. Here are your goods; take them, for they are yours.' I thanked him and praised his honorable conduct.

"I selected the most precious and valuable things in my bales as presents for King Mihragè. As this prince had been informed of my misfortunes, he asked me where I had obtained such rare curiosities. I related to him the manner in which I had recovered my property, and he had the condescension to express his joy at my good fortune. He accepted my presents, and gave me others of far greater value. Hereupon I took my leave, and re-embarked in the same vessel in which I had come, having first exchanged what merchandise remained for products of the country, consisting of aloes and sandalwood, camphor, nutmegs, cloves, pepper, and ginger. We touched at several islands, and at last landed at Balsora, from whence I came here, having realized about a hundred thousand sequins. I returned to my family, and was received by them with the joy of true and sincere friendship. I purchased slaves of both sexes, and bought a magnificent house and grounds. Thus I established myself, determined to forget the hardships I had endured and to enjoy the pleasures of life."

"Thus Sindbad concluded the story of his first voyage. The company continued to feast till night approached; and when it was time to separate, Sindbad ordered a purse containing a hundred sequins to be brought to him, and gave it to the porter with these words: 'Take this, Hindbad; return to your home, and come again to-morrow to hear the continuation of my history.' The porter retired, quite confused by the honor conferred on him and the present he had received. The account he gave of his adventure to his wife and children rejoiced them greatly, and they did not fail to return thanks to Providence for the bounties bestowed by means of Sindbad.

ARABIAN NIGHTS

"Hindbad dressed himself in his best clothes on the following day and betook himself to the house of his liberal patron, who received him with smiling looks and a friendly air. As soon as the guests had all arrived the feast was served, and they sat down to eat. When the repast was over, Sindbad thus addressed his guests. 'My friends, I request you to have the kindness to listen to me while I relate the adventures of my second voyage.' The company were silent, and Sindbad began to speak as follows:

THE SECOND VOYAGE OF SINDBAD THE SAILOR

"AS I had the honor to tell you yesterday, I had resolved, after my first voyage, to pass the rest of my days in tranquillity at Bagdad. But the desire of seeing foreign countries and carrying on some traffic by sea returned. I bought merchandise and set off a second time with some merchants whose probity I could rely on. We embarked in a good vessel, and, recommending ourselves to the care of Allah, we began our voyage.

"We went from island to island, and bartered our goods very profitably. One day we landed on one which was covered with a variety of fruit trees, but so desert that we could not discover any habitation, or the trace of a human being. We walked in the meadows and along the brooks that watered them;

and whilst some of my companions were amusing themselves with gathering fruits and flowers, I took out some of the wine and provisions I had brought with me, and seated myself by a little stream under some trees which afforded a delightful shade. When I had satisfied my hunger, sleep gradually stole over my senses. I cannot say how long I slept, but when I awoke the ship was no longer in view. I was much surprised at this circumstance, and rose to look for my companions, but they were all gone; and I could only just descry the vessel in full sail at such a distance that I soon lost sight of it.

"You may imagine what were my reflections when I found myself in this dismal state. I thought I should have died with grief. I reproached myself a thousand times for my folly in not being contented with my first voyage, which ought to have satisfied my craving for adventure; but all my regrets were of no avail, and my repentance came too late. At length I resigned myself to the will of Heaven, and, not knowing what would become of me, I ascended a high tree, from whence I looked on all sides to try if I could not discover some object to inspire me with hope. Casting my eyes toward the sea, I could discern only water and sky, but perceiving on the land side a white spot I descended from the tree, and, taking up the remainder of my provisions, I walked toward the object. As I approached I perceived it to be a ball of prodigious size, and when I got near enough to touch it I found it was soft. I walked round it to see if there was an opening, but could find none; and the ball appeared so smooth that any attempt to climb it would have been fruitless. Its circumference might be about fifty paces.

"The sun was then near setting; the air grew suddenly dark, as if obscured by a thick cloud. I was surprised at this change, but how much did my amazement increase when I perceived it to be occasioned by a bird of most extraordinary size which was flying toward me. I recollected having heard sailors speak of a bird called a roc, and I concluded that the great white ball which had drawn my attention must be the egg of this bird. I was not mistaken, for shortly afterward it lighted on the white ball and placed itself as if to sit upon it. When I saw this huge fowl coming I drew near to the egg so that I had one of the claws of the bird just before me; this claw was as big as the trunk of a large tree. I tied myself to the claw with the linen of my turban, in hopes that the roc, when it took its flight the next morning, would carry me with it out of that desert island. My project succeeded, for at break of day the roc flew away, and bore me to such a height that I could no longer distinguish the earth; then it descended with such rapidity that I almost lost my senses. When the roc had alighted I quickly untied the knot that bound me to its foot, and had scarcely released myself when it darted on a serpent of immeasurable length, and, seizing the snake in its beak, flew away.

"The place in which the roc left me was a very deep valley, surrounded on all sides by mountains of such height that their summits were lost in the clouds, and so steep that there was no possibility of climbing them. This was a fresh embarrassment, for I had no reason to rejoice at my change of situation when I compared it with the island I had left.

"As I walked along this valley I remarked that it was strewn with diamonds, some of which were of astonishing size. I amused myself for some time by examining them, but soon perceived from afar some objects which destroyed my pleasure and created in me great fear. These were a great number of serpents, so long and large that the smallest of them would have swallowed an elephant with ease. During the daytime they hid themselves in caves from the roc, their mortal enemy, and only came out when it was dark. I passed the day in walking about the valley, resting myself occasionally when an opportunity offered; and when the sun set I retired into a small cave, where I thought I should be in safety. I closed the entrance, which was low and narrow, with a stone large enough to protect me from the serpents, but which yet allowed a little light to pass into the cave. I supped on part of my provisions, and could plainly hear the serpents which began to make their appearance. Their tremendous hissings caused me great fear, and, as you may suppose,

I did not pass a very quiet night. When the day appeared the serpents retired. I left my cave with trembling, and may truly say that I walked a long time on diamonds without feeling the least desire to possess them. At last I sat down, and, notwithstanding my agitation, after making another meal off my provisions, I fell asleep, for I had not once closed my eyes during all the previous night. I had scarcely begun to doze when something falling near me with a great noise awoke me. It was a large piece of fresh meat, and at the same moment I saw a number of other pieces rolling down the rocks from above.

"I had always supposed the account to be fictitious which I had heard related by seamen and others, of the Valley of Diamonds, and of the means by which merchants procured these precious gems. I now knew it to be true. The method of proceeding is this: The merchants go to the mountains which surround the valley about the time that the eagles hatch their young. They cut large pieces of meat, and throw them into the valley; and the diamonds on which the lumps of meat fall stick to them. The eagles, which are larger and stronger in that country than in any other, seize these pieces of meat to carry to their young at the top of the rocks. The merchants then run to the eagles' nests, and by various noises oblige the birds to retreat, and then take the diamonds that have stuck to the pieces of meat. I had supposed it impossible ever to leave this valley, and began to look on it as my tomb; but now I changed my opinion, and turned my thoughts to the preservation of my life. I began by collecting the largest diamonds I could find, and with these I filled my leather bag in which I had carried my provisions. I then took one of the largest pieces of meat and tied it tight round me with the linen of my turban; in this state I laid myself on the ground, tightly securing my leather bag round me.

"I had not been long in this position before the eagles began to descend, and each seized a piece of meat with which it flew away. One of the strongest darted on the piece to which I was attached, and carried me up with it to its nest. The merchants then began their cries to frighten away the eagles; and

"ONE OF THE STRONGEST DARTED ON THE PIECE
TO WHICH I WAS ATTACHED, AND CARRIED
ME UP WITH IT TO ITS NEST"

when they had obliged the birds to quit their prey one of them approached, but was much surprised and alarmed on seeing me. He soon, however, recovered from his fear and, instead of inquiring by what means I came there, began to quarrel with me for trespassing on what he called his property. 'You will speak to me with pity instead of anger,' said I, 'when you learn by what means I reached this place. Console yourself, for I have diamonds for you as well as for myself, and my diamonds are more valuable than those of all the other merchants added together. I have myself chosen some of the finest at the bottom of the valley, and have them in this bag.' Saying this, I showed him my store. I had scarcely finished speaking when the other merchants, perceiving me, flocked round me with great astonishment, and their wonder was still greater when I related my history.

"They conducted me to the place where they lived together, and on seeing my diamonds they all expressed their admiration, and declared they had never seen any to equal them in size or quality. The nest into which I had been transported belonged to one of these merchants, for each merchant has his own; I entreated him, therefore, to choose for himself from my stock as many as he pleased. He contented himself with taking only one, and that, too, was the smallest I had, and as I pressed him to take more, without fear of wronging me, he refused. 'No,' said he, 'I am very well satisfied with this, which is sufficiently valuable to spare me the trouble of making any more voyages to complete my little fortune.'

"The merchants had been for some days in that spot, and as they now appeared to be contented with the diamonds they had collected, we set off together on the following day, and traveled over high mountains which were infested by prodigious serpents; but we had the good fortune to escape them. We reached the nearest port in safety, and from thence embarked for the Isle of Roha, where I exchanged some of my diamonds for valuable merchandise. We set sail for other islands, and at last, after having touched at several ports, we reached Balsora,

ARABIAN NIGHTS

from which place I returned to Bagdad. The first thing I did was to distribute a great deal of money among the poor; and I enjoyed with credit and honor the remainder of my immense riches, which I had acquired with such labor and fatigue."

"Here Sindbad closed the relation of his second voyage. He again ordered a hundred sequins to be given to Hindbad, whom he invited to come on the morrow to hear the history of the third.

"The guests returned home, and the following day repaired at the usual hour to the house of Sindbad, where the porter, who had almost forgotten his poverty, also made his appearance. They sat down to table; and when the repast was ended, Sindbad began to tell the story of his third voyage."

THE THIRD VOYAGE OF SINDBAD THE SAILOR

"THE agreeable life I led in my prosperity soon obliterated the remembrance of the dangers I had encountered in my two voyages; but as I was in the prime of life, I grew tired of passing my days in slothful repose, and, banishing all thoughts of the perils I might have to face, I set off from Bagdad with some rich merchandise of the country, which I carried with me to Balsora. There I again embarked with other merchants. We made a long voyage, and touched at several ports, and by these means carried on a very profitable commerce.

"One day, as we were sailing in the open sea, we were overtaken by a violent tempest, which made us lose our reckoning. The storm continued for several days, and drove us near an island which the captain would gladly have avoided approaching, but we were under the necessity of casting anchor there. When

8

ARABIAN NIGHTS

the sails were furled the captain told us that this region and some of the neighboring isles were inhabited by hairy savages who would come to attack us. He further declared that although they were only dwarfs, we must not attempt to make any resistance; for as their number was inconceivable, if we should happen to kill one they would pour upon us like locusts and destroy us. This account put the whole crew in a terrible consternation, and we were too soon convinced that the captain had spoken the truth. We saw coming toward us an innumerable multitude of hideous savages, entirely covered with red hair and about two feet high. They threw themselves into the sea and swam to the ship, which they soon completely surrounded. They began to climb the sides and ropes of the vessel with so much swiftness and agility that their feet scarcely seemed to touch them, and soon came swarming upon the deck.

"You may imagine the situation we were in, not daring to defend ourselves, nor even to speak to these intruders, to endeavor to avert the impending danger. They unfurled the sails, cut the cable from the anchor, and, after dragging the ship ashore, obliged us to disembark; then they conveyed us to another island, from whence they had come. All voyagers carefully avoided this island, for the dismal reason you are going to hear; but our misfortune had led us there, and we were obliged to submit to our fate.

"We left the shore and, penetrating farther into the island, we found some fruits and herbs, which we ate to prolong our lives as much as possible, for we all expected to be sacrificed. As we walked we perceived at some distance a large building, toward which we bent our steps. It was a large and lofty palace, with folding gates of ebony which opened as we pushed them. We entered the courtyard, and saw facing us a vast apartment with a vestibule, on one side of which was a large heap of human bones, while on the opposite side appeared a number of spits for roasting. We trembled at this spectacle, and fell on the earth, where we remained a considerable time, paralyzed by fear and unable to move.

KINDLING A LARGE FIRE, HE ROASTED HIM, AND
ATE HIM FOR HIS SUPPER

ARABIAN NIGHTS

"The sun was setting; and while we were in the piteous state I have described, the door of the apartment suddenly opened with a loud noise, and there entered a black man of frightful aspect, and as tall as a large palm-tree. In the middle of his forehead gleamed a single eye, red and fiery as a burning coal; his front teeth were long and sharp, and projected from his mouth, which was as wide as that of a horse, with the under lip hanging on his breast; his ears resembled those of an elephant, and covered his shoulders, and his long and curved nails were like the talons of an immense bird. At the sight of this hideous giant we all fainted, and remained a long time like dead men.

"At last our senses returned, and we saw him seated under the vestibule, glaring at us with his piercing eye. When he had scanned us well he advanced toward us and, stretching forth his hand to seize me, took me up by the poll, and turned me round every way, as a butcher would handle the head of a sheep. After having well examined me, finding me meager, and little more than skin and bone, he released me. He took up each of my companions in their turn, and examined them in the same manner, and as the captain was the fattest of the party he held him in one hand as I should hold a sparrow, and with the other ran a spit through his body; then kindling a large fire, he roasted him, and ate him for his supper in the inner apartment, to which he retired. When he had finished his repast he returned to the vestibule, where he lay down to sleep and snored louder than thunder. He did not wake till the next morning, but we passed the night in the most agonizing suspense. When daylight returned the giant awoke and went abroad, leaving us in the palace.

"When we supposed him at some distance we began to give vent to our lamentations, for the fear of disturbing the giant had kept us silent during the night. The palace resounded with our groans. Although there were many of us, and we had but one common enemy, the idea of delivering ourselves by his death never occurred to any one of us. But however difficult of accomplishment such an enterprise might have been, we ought to have made the attempt at once.

ARABIAN NIGHTS

"We deliberated on various methods of action, but could not determine on any; and, submitting ourselves to the will of Allah, we passed the day in walking over the island and eating what plants and fruit we could meet with, as we had done the preceding day. Toward evening we sought for some shelter in which to pass the night, but, finding none, we were obliged to return to the palace.

"The giant duly returned to sup on one of our companions. After his hideous meal he fell asleep and snored till daybreak, when he arose and went out as before. Our situation appeared to be so hopeless that some of my comrades were on the point of throwing themselves into the sea rather than be sacrificed by the horrible monster; and they advised the rest to follow their example, but one of the company thus addressed them: 'We are forbidden to kill ourselves; and even were such an act permitted, would it not be more rational to endeavor to destroy the barbarous giant who has destined us to such a cruel death?'

"As I had already formed a project of that nature, I now communicated it to my fellow-sufferers, who approved of my design. 'My friends,' said I then, 'you know that there is a great deal of wood on the seashore. If you will take my advice, we can make some rafts, and when they are finished we will leave them in a proper place till we can find an opportunity to make use of them. In the mean time we can put in execution the design I propose to you to rid ourselves of the giant. If my stratagem succeeds we may wait here with patience till some vessel passes, by means of which we may quit this fatal isle; if, on the contrary, we fail, we shall have recourse to our rafts and put to sea.' My advice was approved by all, and we immediately built some rafts, each large enough to support three persons.

"We returned to the palace toward evening, and the giant arrived a short time after us. Again one of our party was sacrificed to his inhuman appetite. But we were soon revenged on him for his cruelty. After he had finished his horrible meal, he laid himself down as usual to sleep. As soon as we heard him snore, nine of the most courageous amongst us, and myself, took each a spit, and, heating the points red-hot, thrust them into his eye, and blinded him.

"The pain which the giant suffered made him groan hideously. He suddenly raised himself and threw his arms about on all sides to seize some one and sacrifice him to his rage, but, fortunately, we had time to throw ourselves on the ground in places where he could not set his feet on us. After having sought us in vain, he at last found the door and went out, bellowing with pain.

"We quitted the palace immediately after the giant, and repaired to that part of the shore where our rafts lay. We set them afloat, and waited till daybreak before embarking on them, in case we should see the giant approach with some guide to lead him to us; but we hoped that if he did not make his appearance by that time, and if his cries and groans, which now resounded through the air, ceased, we might suppose him dead; and in that case we proposed remaining in the island till we could obtain some safer mode of transport. But the sun had scarcely risen when we perceived our cruel enemy, accompanied by two giants nearly as huge as himself, who led him, and a great number of others who walked very rapidly before him.

"At this sight we immediately ran to our rafts and rowed away as fast as possible. The giants, seeing this, provided themselves with large stones, hastened to the shore, and even ventured to their waists into the sea to hurl the stones at us, which they did so adroitly that they sunk all the rafts excepting that I was upon. Thus I and two companions were the only men who escaped, the others being all drowned.

"As we rowed with all our strength, we were soon beyond reach of the stones.

"When we had gained the open sea we were tossed about at the mercy of the winds and waves, and we passed that day and night in the most cruel suspense; but on the morrow we had the good fortune to be thrown on an island, where we landed with great joy. We found some excellent fruit, which soon recruited our exhausted strength.

ARABIAN NIGHTS

"When night came on we went to sleep on the seashore, but were soon awakened by the noise made on the ground by the scales of an immense serpent, long as a palm-tree. It was so near to us that it devoured one of my companions, notwithstanding the efforts he made to extricate himself from its deadly grasp.

"My other comrade and myself immediately took to flight. 'O Allah!' I exclaimed, 'what a horrible fate will be ours! Yesterday we were rejoicing at our escape from the cruelty of a giant and the fury of the waves, and to-day we are again terrified by a peril not less dreadful.'

"As we walked along, we remarked a large, high tree, on which we proposed to pass the night, hoping we might there be in safety. We ate some fruit as we had done on the preceding day, and at the approach of night we climbed the tree. We soon heard the serpent, which came hissing to the foot of the tree; it raised itself against the trunk and, meeting my companion, who had not climbed so high as I, it swallowed him and retired.

"I remained on the tree till daybreak, when I came down, more dead than alive; indeed, I could only anticipate the same fate.

"I collected a great quantity of small wood and furze, and, tying it in faggots, put it round the tree in a large circle, and tied some across to cover my head. I inclosed myself within this circle when the evening came on, and sat down with the dismal consolation that I had done all in my power to preserve my life. The serpent returned with the intention of devouring me, but he could not succeed, being prevented by the rampart I had formed. The whole night he was watching me; at last day returned and the serpent retired, but I did not venture out of my fortress till the sun shone.

"I was so fatigued with watching, as well as with the exertion of forming my retreat, and had suffered so much from the serpent's pestilential breath, that death appeared preferable to a repetition of such horror. I ran toward the sea with the intention of putting an end to my existence; but Allah pitied my condition, and at the moment that I was going to throw

ARABIAN NIGHTS

myself into the sea I descried a vessel at a great distance. I cried out with all my strength, and unfolded and waved my turban to attract the attention of those on board. This had the desired effect; all the crew saw me, and the captain sent a boat to bring me off.

"As soon as I was on board the merchants and seamen were eager to learn by what chance I had reached that desert island; and after I had related to them all that had happened, they expressed their joy at my fortunate escape from so many perils; then, as they supposed I must be in want of something to eat, they pressed upon me the best they had; and the captain, observing that my clothes were torn, had the generosity to give me some of his.

"We remained a considerable time at sea, and touched at several islands; at length we landed on the isle of Salahat, where the merchants began to unload their goods to sell or exchange them. One day the captain called me to him, and said: 'Brother, I have in my possession some goods which belonged to a merchant who was for some time on board my ship. As this merchant is dead, I am going to have them valued that I may render an account of them to his heirs, should I ever meet them.' The bales of which he spoke were already upon deck. He showed them to me, saying: 'These are the goods; I wish you to take charge of them and traffic with them, and you shall receive for your trouble what is usually given in such cases.' I consented, and thanked him for the opportunity he afforded me of employing myself.

"The clerk of the ship registered all the bales with the names of the merchants to whom they belonged; when he asked the captain in what name he should register those destined for my charge, the captain replied, 'In the name of Sindbad the sailor.' I could not hear my own name without emotion; and, looking at the captain, I recognized in him the very same person who in my second voyage had left me on the island where I had fallen asleep by the side of a brook, and who had put to sea without waiting for me. I did not at first recollect him, so much

ARABIAN NIGHTS

was he changed in appearance since the time I last saw him. As he thought me dead, it is not to be wondered at that he did not recognize me. 'Captain,' said I to him, 'was the merchant to whom these things belonged called Sindbad?' 'Yes,' returned he, 'that was his name; he was from Bagdad, and embarked on board my vessel at Balsora. One day, when he went ashore on an island for fresh water, he was left behind I know not through what mistake. None of the crew noticed his absence till four hours after, when the wind blew so fresh against us that it was impossible to return.' 'You believe him to be dead?' said I. 'Most assuredly,' replied the captain. 'Then open your eyes,' cried I, 'and convince yourself that the same Sindbad whom you left in the desert island is now before you.'

"At these words the captain fixed his eyes on me, and after scrutinizing me very attentively, at last recollected me. 'God be praised!' cried he, embracing me; 'I am delighted that fortune has given me an opportunity of repairing my fault. Here are your goods, which I have preserved with care, and always had valued at every port I stopped at. I return them to you with the profit I have made on them.'

"From the island of Salahat we went to another, where I provided myself with cloves, cinnamon, and other spices. At length, after a long voyage, we arrived at Balsora, from whence I came to Bagdad with so much wealth that I did not know the amount of it. I gave a great deal to the poor and bought a considerable quantity of land."

"Sindbad thus finished the history of his third voyage. Again he gave Hindbad a hundred sequins, inviting him to the usual repast on the morrow, and promising he should hear the account of the fourth voyage. Hindbad and the other guests retired, and on the following day returned at the same hour. When dinner was over, Sindbad continued the relation of his adventures."

THE FOURTH VOYAGE OF SINDBAD THE SAILOR

"THE pleasures and amusements in which I indulged after my third voyage had not charms sufficiently powerful to deter me from venturing on the sea again. I gave way to my love for traffic and adventure. I settled my affairs, and furnished myself with the merchandises uited to the places I intended to visit, and traveled toward Persia, some of the provinces of which I traversed, till I at last reached a port, where I embarked. We set sail, and touched at several points of the mainland, and at some of the Oriental islands; but one day we were surprised by a sudden squall of wind; our sails were torn in a thousand pieces, and the vessel, becoming ungovernable, was driven on a sand-bank and went to pieces. A great number of the crew perished, and the cargo was swallowed up by the waves.

"With some other merchants and seamen I had the good fortune to get hold of a plank; we were all drawn by the strength of the current toward an island that lay before us. We found some fruits and fresh water, which recruited our strength, and we lay down to sleep in the spot where the waves had thrown us. The next morning, when the sun was risen, we left the shore and, advancing into the island, perceived some habitations toward which we bent our steps. When we drew near, a great number of blacks came forward and, surrounding us, made us prisoners. They seemed to divide us among themselves, and then led us away to their houses.

"Five of my comrades and myself were taken into the same place. Our captors made us sit down, and then offered us a certain herb, inviting us by signs to eat of it. My companions, without considering that the people did not eat of it themselves, only consulted their hunger and devoured it greedily. I had a sort of presentiment that this herb was given us for no good purpose, and refused even to taste it; and it was well I did so, for a short time after I perceived that my companions soon lost all sense of their position, and did not know what they said. The blacks then served us with some rice dressed with the oil of the cocoanut; and my comrades, not being sensible of what they did, ate ravenously of this mess. I likewise partook of it, but fed sparingly.

"The blacks had given us the herb first to turn our brains, and thus banish the sorrow which our miserable situation would create, and the rice was given to fatten us. As these men were anthropophagi, they designed to feast on us when we were in good condition. My poor companions fell victims to the barbarous custom of these wretches, because they had lost their senses and could not foresee their destiny. As for me, instead of fattening as the others had done, I grew thinner every day. The fear of death, which constantly haunted me, poisoned the food I took, and I fell into a state of languor which was in the end very beneficial to me, for when the blacks had devoured my comrades they were content to let me remain till I should be worth eating.

"In the mean time I was allowed a great deal of liberty and my actions were scarcely observed. This afforded me the opportunity one day of quitting the habitation of the blacks, and

ARABIAN NIGHTS

escaping. I walked for seven days, taking care to avoid those places continually which appeared inhabited, and living on cocoanuts, which afforded me both drink and food.

"On the eighth day I came to the seashore; here I saw some white people employed in gathering pepper, which grew very plentifully in that place. They came toward me as soon as they perceived me, and asked me in Arabic from whence I came.

"Delighted to hear my native language once more, I readily satisfied their curiosity.

"I remained with them until they had collected as much pepper as they chose to gather. They made me embark with them in the vessel which had conveyed them, and we soon reached another island, from whence they had come. My deliverers presented me to their king, who was a good prince. He had the patience to listen to the recital of my adventures, which astonished him; and he ordered me some new clothes, and desired I might be taken care of. This island was very populous, and abounded in all sorts of articles for commerce. The pleasantness of my new quarters began to console me for my misfortunes, and the kindness of this generous prince made me completely happy. Indeed, I appeared to be his greatest favorite.

"I remarked one thing which appeared to me very singular; every one—the king not excepted—rode on horseback without saddle, bridle, or stirrups. I one day took the liberty to ask his Majesty why such things were not used in his city; he replied that he had never heard of the things of which I spoke.

"I immediately went to a workman and gave him a model from which to make the tree of a saddle. When he had executed his task, I myself covered the saddle-tree with leather, richly embroidered in gold, and stuffed it with hair. I then applied to a locksmith, who made me a bit, and some stirrups also, according to the patterns I gave him.

"When these articles were completed I presented them to the king, and tried them on one of his horses; the prince then mounted his steed, and was so pleased with its accoutrements

ARABIAN NIGHTS

that he testified his approbation by making me considerable presents. I was then obliged to make several saddles for his ministers and the principal officers of his household, who all rewarded me with very rich and handsome gifts. I also made some for the wealthiest inhabitants of the town, by which I gained great reputation and credit.

"As I constantly attended at court, the king said to me one day: 'Sindbad, I love you; and I know that all my subjects who have any knowledge of you entertain a high regard for you. I have one request to make, which you must not deny me.' 'O King,' replied I, 'there is nothing your Majesty can command which I will not perform to prove my obedience to your orders. Your power over me is absolute.' 'I wish you to marry,' resumed the prince, 'that you may have a tender tie to attach you to my dominions and prevent your returning to your native country.' As I did not dare to refuse the king's offer, he bestowed on me in marriage a lady of his court who was noble, beautiful, rich, and accomplished. After the ceremony of the nuptials I took up my abode in the house of my wife, and lived with her for some time in perfect harmony. Nevertheless, I was discontented with my situation, and designed to make my escape at the first convenient opportunity and return to Bagdad.

"While I was thus meditating an escape, the wife of one of my neighbors, with whom I was very intimate, fell sick and died. I went to console the widower, and, finding him in the deepest affliction, I said to him, 'May God preserve you, and grant you a long life.' 'Alas!' replied he, 'I have only one hour to live.' 'Oh,' resumed I, 'do not suffer such dismal ideas to take possession of your mind; I hope that I shall enjoy your friendship for many years.' 'I wish with all my heart,' said he, 'that your life may be of long duration. As for me, the die is cast, and this day I shall be buried with my wife; such is the custom which our ancestors have established in this island, and which is still inviolably observed; the husband is interred alive with his dead wife, and the living wife with the dead husband. Nothing can save me, and every one submits to this law.'

[112]

ARABIAN NIGHTS

"Whilst he was relating to me this singularly barbarous custom, the bare idea of which filled me with terror, his relations, friends, and neighbors came to make arrangements for the funeral. They dressed the corpse of the woman in the richest attire, as on the day of her nuptials, and decorated her with all her jewels. They then placed her on an open bier, and the procession set out. The husband, dressed in mourning, went immediately after the body of his wife, and the relations followed. They bent their course toward a high mountain, and when they had reached the summit, a large stone was raised which covered a deep pit, and the body was let down into the pit in all its sumptuous apparel and ornaments. Thereupon the husband took his leave of his relations and friends, and without making any resistance suffered himself to be placed on a bier, with a jug of water and seven small loaves by his side; he was then let down into the pit as his wife had been. This mountain extended to a great distance, reaching even to the seashore, and the pit was very deep. When the ceremony was ended the stone was replaced and the company retired. I need scarcely tell you that I was particularly affected by this ceremony. I could not avoid telling the king my sentiments on this subject. 'O King,' said I, 'I cannot express my astonishment at the strange custom which exists in your dominions, of interring the living with the dead; in the whole course of my travels I never heard of so cruel a decree.' 'What can I do, Sindbad?' replied the king; 'it is a law common to all ranks, and even I submit to it. I shall be interred alive with the queen my consort, if she happens to die first.' 'Will your Majesty allow me to ask,' resumed I, 'if strangers are obliged to conform to this custom?' 'Certainly,' said the king; 'they are not exempt when they marry in the island.'

"I returned home thoughtful and sad. The fear that my wife might die before me, and that I must be interred with her, distressed me beyond measure. I soon had good reason to fear; she was taken dangerously ill and died in a few days. To be buried alive appeared to me as horrible a fate as being devoured by the anthropophagi; yet I was obliged to submit. The king, accompanied by his whole court, proposed to honor the procession with his presence; and the principal inhabitants of the city also, out of respect to me, were present at my interment.

"When all was in readiness for the ceremony, the corpse of my wife, decorated with her jewels, and dressed in her most magnificent clothes, was placed on a bier, and the procession set out. As the chief mourner in this dreadful tragedy, I followed the body of my wife, my eyes full of tears, and deploring my miserable destiny. Before we arrived at the mountain I made an appeal to the compassion of the spectators. I first addressed myself to the king, then to the courtiers who were near me, and entreated them to have pity on me. 'Consider,' said I, 'that I am a stranger, who ought not to be subject to your rigorous law, and that I have another wife and children in my own country.' I pronounced these words in a heartrending tone, but no one seemed moved; on the contrary, the spectators hastened to deposit the corpse in the pit, and soon after I was let down also on another bier, with a jug of water and seven loaves. At last, this fatal ceremony being completed, they replaced the stone over the mouth of the cave, notwithstanding my piteous lamentation.

"As I approached the bottom of the pit, I discovered by the little light that shone from above the nature of this subterranean abode. It was a vast cavern, and might be about fifty cubits deep. I soon smelt an insupportable stench, which arose from the moldering corpses that were strewed around. I even fancied I heard the last sighs of some miserable wretches who had lately fallen victims to this inhuman law. So soon as the bier stopped at the bottom of the cave I stepped from it to the ground, and, stopping my nostrils, went to a distance from the dead bodies. I threw myself on the ground, where I remained a long time, and gave way to the most violent grief. Nevertheless, I did not call on death to release me from this habitation of horror; the love of life still glowed within me, and induced me to seek to prolong my days. I felt my way to the bier on which I had been placed, and, notwithstanding the intense darkness which prevailed, I

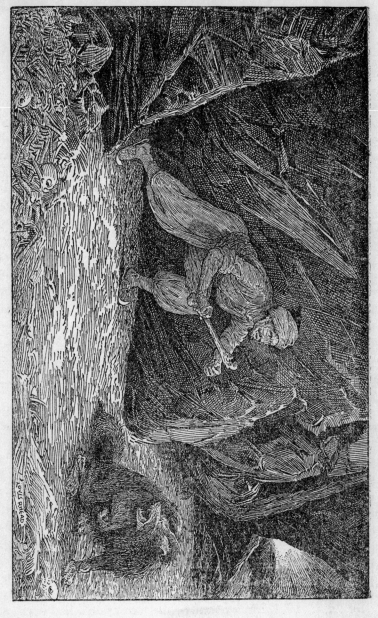

I PERCEIVED THAT THE THING WHICH I HAD HEARD PANT, AND WHICH I HAD FOLLOWED, WAS AN ANIMAL THAT LIVED IN THE SEA

9

found my bread and water, and ate and drank of it. I lived for some days on my provisions, but as soon as they were exhausted I prepared to die. I had become resigned to my fate, when suddenly I heard the stone above me raised. A corpse and a living person were let down. The deceased was a man. It is natural to have recourse to violent means to preserve life when a man is reduced to the last extremity. While the woman was descending, I approached the spot where her bier was to be placed, and when I perceived that the aperture by which she had been lowered was closed, I gave the unhappy creature two or three heavy blows on the head with a large bone. She was stunned, or, to say the truth, I killed her, committing this inhuman action to obtain the bread and water which had been allowed her. I had now provisions for some days. At the end of that time a dead woman and her living husband were let down into the pit. I killed the man as I had slain the woman; and as at that time there happened, fortunately for me, to be a great mortality in the city, I was not in want of food, always obtaining my supplies by the same cruel means.

"One day, when I had just put an end to an unfortunate woman, I heard footsteps, and a sound like breathing. I advanced in the direction from whence the sound proceeded. I heard a louder breathing at my approach, and I fancied I saw something fleeing from me. I followed the flying shadow, which occasionally stopped and then again retreated panting as I drew near. I pursued it so long, and went so far, that at last I perceived a small speck of light resembling a star. I continued to walk toward this light till I arrived at an opening in the rock large enough to allow me to pass.

"At this discovery I stopped for some time to recover from the violent emotion occasioned by my rapid chase; then passing through the crevice, I found myself on the seashore. You may imagine the excess of my joy; it was so great I could scarcely persuade myself that my imagination did not deceive me. When I became convinced that it was a reality, and that my senses did not play me false, I perceived that the thing which I had heard pant, and which I had followed, was an animal that lived in the sea, and was accustomed to go into that cave to devour the dead bodies.

"I returned to the cave to collect from the different biers all the diamonds, rubies, pearls, golden bracelets—in short, everything of value on which I could lay my hands in the dark—and I brought all my plunder to the shore. I tied it up in several packets with the cords which had served to let down the biers, of which there were many lying around. I left my goods in a convenient place till a proper opportunity should offer for conveying them away.

"At the end of two or three days I perceived a vessel just sailing out of the harbor and passing by the spot where I was. I made signals with my turban, and cried aloud with all my strength. They heard me on board, and despatched the boat to fetch me. When the sailors inquired by what misfortune I had got in that place, I replied that I had been wrecked two days since on that shore, with all my merchandise. Fortunately for me, these people did not stop to consider whether my story was probable, but, satisfied with my answer, they took me into the boat with my bales.

"When we had reached the vessel the captain never thought of doubting the tale of the wreck.

"At length I arrived happily at Bagdad, with immense riches. To show my gratitude to Heaven for the mercies shown me I spent a great deal in charity, giving money for the support of the mosques and for the relief of the poor. I then entirely gave myself up to the society of my relations and friends, and passed my time in feasting and entertainments."

"Sindbad here concluded the relation of his fourth voyage. He repeated his present of a hundred sequins to Hindbad, whom he requested, with the rest of the company, to return on the following day to dine, and hear the story of his fifth voyage. The next day, when all were assembled, they sat down to table, and at the conclusion of the repast Sindbad began the account of his fifth voyage in the following words":

THE FIFTH VOYAGE OF SINDBAD THE SAILOR

"THE pleasures I enjoyed soon made me forget the perils I had endured; yet these delights were not sufficiently attractive to prevent my forming the resolution of venturing a fifth time on the sea. I again provided myself with merchandise and sent it overland to the nearest seaport. Unwilling to trust again to a captain, and wishing to have a vessel of my own, I built and equipped one at my own expense. As soon as it was ready I loaded it and embarked; and as I had not sufficient cargo of my own to fill it, I received on board several merchants of different nations, with their goods.

"We hoisted our sails to the first fair wind, and put to sea. After sailing for a considerable time, the first place we stopped at was a desert island, where we found the egg of a roc as large as that of which I spoke on a former occasion. It contained a small roc, almost hatched, for its beak had begun to pierce through the shell. The merchants who were with me broke the egg with hatchets, cut out the young roc, piece by piece, and roasted it. I had seriously advised them not to touch the egg, but they would not attend to me.

"They had scarcely finished their meal when two immense clouds appeared in the air at a considerable distance from us. The captain knew by experience what it was, and cried out that the father and mother of the young roc were coming. He warned us to re-embark as quickly as possible, to escape the danger which threatened us. We took his advice, and set sail immediately.

"The two rocs approached, uttering the most terrible screams, which they redoubled on finding their egg broken and their young one destroyed. Designing to revenge themselves, they flew away toward the mountains from whence they came, and disappeared for some time while we used all diligence to sail away and prevent what nevertheless befell us.

"They soon returned, and we perceived that each had an enormous piece of rock in its claws. When they were exactly over the ship they stopped and, suspending themselves in the air, one of them let fall the piece of rock it held. The skill of the pilot, who suddenly turned the vessel, prevented our being crushed by its fall, but the stone fell close to us into the sea, in which it made such a chasm that we could almost see the bottom. The other bird, unfortunately for us, let its piece of rock fall so directly on the ship that it broke and split our vessel into a thousand pieces. The sailors and passengers were all crushed to death or drowned. I myself was under water for some time; but, rising again to the surface, I had the good fortune to seize a piece of the wreck. Swimming sometimes with one hand and sometimes with the other, still clutching the plank I had seized, I at length reached an island where the shore was very steep. But I contrived to clamber up the beach, and got on land.

"I seated myself on the grass to recover from my fatigue. When I had rested I rose and advanced into the island, to reconnoiter the ground. This region seemed to me like a delicious garden. Wherever I turned my eyes I saw beautiful trees, some loaded with green, others with ripe fruits, and transparent streams meandering between them. I ate of the fruits, which

ARABIAN NIGHTS

I found excellent, and quenched my thirst at the inviting brooks.

"When night came, I lay down on the grass in a convenient spot. But I did not sleep an hour at a time, and I passed the greater part of the night in lamenting my fate, and reproaching myself for the imprudence of venturing from home, where I had possessed everything that could make me comfortable. These reflections led me so far that I meditated the idea of taking my own life; but day returned with its cheerful light, and dissipated my gloomy thoughts. I rose and walked amongst the trees, though not without some degree of trepidation.

"When I had advanced a little way into the island, I perceived an old man who appeared very decrepit. He was seated on the bank of a little rivulet. I approached and saluted him; he replied only by a slight inclination of the head. I asked him what he was doing, but instead of answering he made signs to me to take him on my shoulders and cross the brook, making me understand that he wanted to gather some fruit.

"I supposed he wished me to render him this piece of service, and, taking him on my back, I waded through the stream. When I had reached the other side I stooped and desired him to alight; instead of complying, this old man, who appeared to me so decrepit, nimbly threw his legs, which I now saw were covered with a skin like a cow's, over my neck, and seated himself fast on my shoulders, at the same time squeezing my throat so violently that I expected to be strangled; this alarmed me so much that I fainted away.

"Notwithstanding my condition, the old man kept his place on my neck, and only loosened his hold sufficiently to allow me to breathe. When I had somewhat recovered, he pushed one of his feet against my stomach, and, kicking my side with the other, obliged me to get up. He then made me walk under some trees, and forced me to gather and eat the fruit we found. He never quitted his hold during the day; and when I wished to rest at night, he laid himself on the ground with me, always clinging to my neck. He never failed to awaken me in the morning, and then he made me get up and walk, kicking me all the time. Imagine how miserable it was to me to bear this burden, without the possibility of getting rid of it.

"One day I chanced to find on the ground several dried gourds which had fallen from the tree that bore them. I took a large one and, after having cleared it well, I squeezed into it the juice of several bunches of grapes, which the island produced in great abundance. When I had filled the gourd, I placed it in a particular spot, and some days after returned with the old man. On tasting the contents, I found the juice converted into excellent wine, which for a little time made me forget the ills that weighed upon me. The drink gave me new vigor, and raised my spirits so high that I began to sing and dance as I went along.

"Perceiving the effect this beverage had taken on my spirits, the old man made signs to me to let him taste it; I gave him the gourd, and the liquor pleased his taste so well that he drank it to the last drop. There was enough to inebriate him, and the fumes of the wine very soon rose into his head; he then began to sing after his own manner, and to sway to and fro on my shoulders. Finding he no longer held me tight, I threw him on the ground, where he lay motionless. I then took a large stone and crushed him to death.

"I was much rejoiced at having got rid of this old man; and I walked toward the seashore, where I met some people who belonged to a vessel which had anchored there to get fresh water. They were very much astonished at seeing me and hearing the account of my adventure. 'You had fallen,' said they, 'into the hands of the Old Man of the Sea, and you are the first of his captives whom he has not strangled. This island is famous for the number of persons he has killed. The sailors and merchants who land here never dare approach except in a strong body.'

"After giving me this information, they took me to their ship, whose captain received me with the greatest politeness when he heard what had befallen me. He set sail, and in a few days we anchored in the harbor of a large city where the houses were built of stone.

THE OLD MAN BEGAN TO SING AFTER HIS OWN
MANNER, AND TO SWAY TO AND FRO
ON MY SHOULDERS

ARABIAN NIGHTS

"One of the merchants of the ship had contracted a friendship for me. He entreated me to accompany him, and conducted me to the quarters set apart for foreign merchants. He gave me a large sack, and then introduced me to some people belonging to the city, who were also furnished with sacks. He requested them to take me with them to gather cocoa, and said to me, 'Go, follow them, and do as they do; and do not stray from them, for your life will be in danger if you leave them.' He gave me provisions for the day, and I set off with my new friends.

"We arrived at a large forest of tall, straight trees, the trunks of which were so smooth that it was impossible to climb up to the branches where the fruit grew. These were all cocoa-trees; and we proposed to knock down the fruit and fill our sacks. On entering the forest we saw a great number of monkeys of all sizes, who fled at our approach and ran up the trees with surprising agility. The merchants who were with me collected stones and threw them with great force at the monkeys, who had reached some of the highest branches. I did the same, and soon perceived that these animals were aware of our proceedings. They gathered the cocoanuts and threw them down at us with gestures which plainly showed their anger and spite. By this contrivance we obtained nuts enough to fill our sacks, a thing utterly impracticable by any other method.

"When we had collected a sufficient quantity, we returned to the city, where the merchant who had sent me to the forest gave me the value of the cocoanuts I had brought. At last I had collected such a quantity of cocoanuts that I sold them for a considerable sum.

"The vessel in which I came had sailed with the merchants, who had loaded it with the cocoanuts they had purchased. I waited for the arrival of another, which shortly after came into harbor to take in a cargo of the same description. I sent on board all the cocoanuts which belonged to me, and when the ship was ready to sail I took leave of the merchant to whom I was under so much obligation.

ARABIAN NIGHTS

"We set sail, and steered toward the island of Comari. In this island I exchanged all my cocoanuts for aloe-wood; and I then, like the other merchants, engaged on my own account in a pearl fishery, in which I employed many divers. I had soon collected by these means a great number of very large and perfect gems, with which I joyfully put to sea, and arrived safely at Balsora, from whence I returned to Bagdad. Here I sold for a large sum the aloes and pearls which I had brought with me. I bestowed a tenth part of my profit in charity, as I had done on my return from every former voyage, and endeavored by all kinds of relaxation to recover from my fatigues."

"When he had concluded his narrative, Sindbad gave a hundred sequins to Hindbad, who retired with all the other guests. The same party returned to the rich Sindbad's house the next day, and after their host had regaled them in a ssumptuous a manner as on the preceding days he began the account of his sixth voyage."

THE SIXTH VOYAGE OF SINDBAD THE SAILOR

"I FEEL convinced, my friends, that you all wonder how I could be tempted again to expose myself to the caprice of fortune, after I had undergone so many perils in my other voyages. I am astonished myself when I think of it. It was fate alone that impelled me, at the expiration of a year, to venture a sixth time on the changeful sea.

"Instead of taking the route of the Persian Gulf, I passed through some of the provinces of Persia and the Indies, and arrived at a seaport, where I embarked in a good ship with a captain who was determined to make a long voyage. Long indeed it proved, but at the same time unfortunate, for the captain and pilot lost their way and did not know how to steer. They at length found out where we were; but we had no reason to rejoice at the discovery, for the captain astonished us all by suddenly quitting his post, and uttering the most lamentable cries. He threw his turban on the deck, tore his beard, and beat his head, like a man distraught. We asked the reason of this violent grief, and he replied: 'I am obliged to announce to you that we are in the greatest peril. A rapid current is hurrying the ship along, and we shall all perish in less than a quarter of an hour. Pray Allah to deliver us from this dreadful danger, for nothing can save us unless he takes pity on us.' He then gave orders for setting the sails; but the ropes broke in the attempt, and the ship became entirely unmanageable, and was dashed by the current against a rock, where it split and went to pieces. Nevertheless, we had time to disembark our provisions, as well as the most valuable part of the cargo.

"When we were assembled on the shore the captain said: 'God's will be done. Here we may dig our graves, and bid each other an eternal farewell; for we are in a place so desolate that no one who ever was cast on this shore returned to his own home.' This speech increased our distress.

"The mountain at the foot of which we were formed one side of a large and long island. The coast was covered with the remains of vessels which had been wrecked on it; and the scattered heaps of bones which lay strewn about in every direction convinced us of the dreadful fact that many lives had been lost in this spot. Almost incredible quantities of merchandise of every sort were heaped up on the shore.

"In every other region it is common for a number of small rivers to discharge themselves into the sea; but here a large river of fresh water takes its course from the sea, and runs along the coast through a dark cave, the entrance to which is extremely high and wide. The most remarkable feature in this place is that the mountain is composed of rubies, crystals, and other precious stones. Here, too, a kind of pitch, or bitumen, distils from the rock into the sea, and the fishes which eat it return it in the form of ambergris, which the waves leave on the shore.

"To complete the description of this place, I have only to mention that it is impossible for a ship to avoid being dragged thither, if it comes within a certain distance. If a sea-breeze blows, the wind assists the current, and there is no remedy;

ARABIAN NIGHTS

and if the wind comes from land, the high mountain impedes its effect, and causes a calm, which allows the current full force, and then it whirls the ship against the coast and dashes it to pieces as it shattered ours. In addition to this, the mountain is so steep that it is impossible to reach the summit, or indeed to escape by any means.

"We remained on the shore, quite heartbroken, expecting to die. We had divided our provisions equally, so that each person lived a longer or a shorter time, according to the manner in which he husbanded his portion.

"Those who died first were interred by the others. I had the dismal office of burying my last companion; for, besides managing my share of provisions with more care than the rest had shown in the consumption of theirs, I had also a store which I kept concealed from my comrades. Nevertheless, when I buried the last of them I had so little food left that I imagined I must soon follow him.

"But Allah still had pity on me, and inspired me with the thought of going to the river which lost itself in the recesses of the cave. I examined the stream with great attention; and it occurred to me that, as the river ran underground, it must in its course come out to daylight again. I therefore conjectured that if I constructed a raft, and placed myself on it, the current of the water might perhaps bring me to some inhabited country. If I perished, it was but altering the manner of my death; but if, on the contrary, I got safely out of this fatal place, I should not only escape the cruel death by which my companions perished, but might also meet with some fresh opportunity of enriching myself.

"These reflections made me work at my raft with fresh vigor. I made it of thick pieces of wood and great cables, of which there was abundance on the coast; I tied them closely together, and formed a strong framework. When it was completed, I placed on it a cargo of rubies, emeralds, ambergris, crystal, and also some gold and silver stuffs. When I had stowed all these things so as to balance the raft, I embarked on my vessel, guiding it with two little oars which I had provided; and, driving along with the current, I resigned myself to the will of God.

"As soon as I was under the vault of the cavern I lost the light of day; the current carried me on, but I was unable to discern its course. I rowed for some days in this obscurity without ever perceiving the least ray of light. During this time I consumed no more of my provisions than was absolutely necessary to sustain nature; but, frugal as I was, they came to an end. I then fell into a sweet sleep. I cannot tell whether I slept long, but when I awoke I was surprised to find myself in an open country near a bank of the river to which my raft was fastened, and in the midst of a large concourse of blacks. I rose and saluted them; they spoke to me, but I could not understand them.

"At this moment I felt so transported with joy that I could scarcely believe myself awake. Being at length convinced that my deliverance was not a dream, I pronounced aloud these Arabic words: 'Invoke the Almighty, and he will come to thy assistance. Close thine eyes, and while thou sleepest Allah will change thy fortune from evil to good.'

"One of the blacks, who understood Arabic, hearing me speak thus, advanced toward me, and spoke as follows: 'Brother, be not surprised at seeing us; we live in this country, and we came hither to-day to this river, which flows from the neighboring mountain, to water our fields by cutting canals to admit the water. We observed that the current bore something along, and we immediately ran to the bank to see what it was, and perceived this raft; one of us instantly swam to it and guided it to shore. We fastened it as you see, and were waiting for you to wake. We entreat you to relate to us your history, which must be very extraordinary. Tell us from whence you came.' I requested him first to give me some food, and promised to satisfy their curiosity when I had eaten.

"They produced several kinds of meat, and when I had satisfied my hunger I related to them all that had happened to me. They appeared to listen to my story with great admiration.

I THEN FELL INTO A SWEET SLEEP

ARABIAN NIGHTS

As soon as I had finished my history their interpreter told me that I had astonished them with my relation, and I must go myself to the king to recount my adventures, for they were of too extraordinary a nature to be repeated by any one but by the person himself to whom they had happened. I replied that I was ready to do anything they wished. The blacks then sent for a horse, which arrived shortly after; they placed me on it, and while some walked by my side to show me the way, certain stalwart fellows hauled the raft out of the water and followed me, carrying it on their shoulders, with the bales of rubies.

"We went together to the city in Serendid, for this was the name of the island, and the blacks presented me to their king. I approached the throne on which he was seated, and saluted him in the manner adopted toward sovereigns in India, namely, by prostrating myself at his feet and kissing the earth. The king made me rise, and, receiving me with an affable air, he seated me by his side. He first asked me my name; I replied that I was called Sindbad, surnamed the Sailor, from having made several voyages; and ended that I was a c tizen of Bagdad. 'How, then,' said the monarch, 'came you into my dominions, and from whence have you arrived?'

"I concealed nothing from the king, but related to him all you have heard me tell; he was so pleased with it that he ordered the history of my adventures to be written in letters of gold, that it might be preserved among the archives of his kingdom. The raft was then produced, and the bales were opened in his presence. He admired the aloe-wood and ambergris, but above all the rubies and emeralds, as he had none in his treasury equal to them in value.

"Perceiving that he examined my valuables with pleasure, I prostrated myself before him and took the liberty of saying, 'O King, not only am I your servant, but the cargo of my raft also is at your disposal, if your Majesty will do me the honor of accepting it.' The king smiled, and replied that he did not desire to possess anything which belonged to me; that, instead of diminishing my riches, he should add to them; and that when I left

[133]

his dominions I should carry with me proofs of his liberality. I could only reply to this by praying for his prosperity and by praising his generosity.

"He ordered one of his officers to attend me, and placed some of his own servants at my disposal. The officers faithfully fulfilled the charge with which they were intrusted, and conveyed all the bales to the place appointed for my lodging. I went every day at certain hours to pay my court to the king, and employed the rest of my time in seeing the city.

"The island of Serendid is situated exactly under the equinoctial line, so that the days and nights are of equal length. The principal town is situated at the extremity of a beautiful valley, formed by a mountain which is in the middle of the island, and which is by far the highest in the world; it is discernible at sea at a distance of three days' sail. I made a devotional journey up the mountain, to the spot where Adam was placed on his banishment from Paradise; and I had the curiosity to ascend the summit.

"When I came back to the city I entreated the king to grant me permission to return to my native country, and he acceded to my request in the most obliging and honorable manner. He commanded me to receive a rich present from his treasury; and when I went to take my leave, he placed in my hands another gift, still more considerable than the first, and at the same time gave me a letter for the Commander of the Believers, our sovereign lord, saying: 'I request you to deliver for me this letter and this present to the Caliph Harun-al-Rashid, and to assure him of my friendship.' I took the present and the letter with the greatest respect, and promised his Majesty that I would most punctually execute the orders with which he was pleased to honor me. Before I embarked the king sent for the captain and the merchants with whom I was to sail, and charged them to pay me all possible attention.

"The letter of the King of Serendid was written on the skin of a certain animal highly prized in that country on account of its rareness. It is of a yellowish color. The letter itself was

ARABIAN NIGHTS

in characters of azure, and it contained the following words in the Indian language:

> "'THE KING OF THE INDIES, WHO IS PRECEDED BY A THOUSAND
> ELEPHANTS; WHO LIVES IN A PALACE, THE ROOF OF WHICH
> GLITTERS WITH THE LUSTER OF A HUNDRED THOUSAND
> RUBIES, AND WHO POSSESSES IN HIS TREASURY
> TWENTY THOUSAND CROWNS ENRICHED
> WITH DIAMONDS, TO THE CALIPH
> HARUN-AL-RASHID

"'Although the present that we send you be inconsiderable, yet receive it as a brother and a friend, in consideration of the friendship we bear you in our heart. We feel happy in having an opportunity of testifying this friendship to you. We ask the same share in your affections, as we hope we deserve it, being of a rank equal to that you hold. We salute you as a brother. Farewell.'

"The present comprised, firstly, a vase made of one single ruby, pierced and worked into a cup of half a foot in height and an inch thick, filled with fine, round pearls, all weighing half a drachm each; secondly, the skin of a serpent which had scales as large as an ordinary coin, and which possessed the peculiar virtue of preserving those who lay on it from all disease; thirdly, fifty thousand drachms of the most exquisite aloe-wood, together with thirty pieces of camphor as large as pistachio-nuts; and lastly, a female slave of the most enchanting beauty, whose clothes were covered with jewels.

"The ship set sail, and after a long but fortunate voyage we landed at Balsora, from whence I returned to Bagdad. The first thing I did after my arrival was to execute the commission I had been intrusted with. I took the letter of the King of Serendid and presented myself at the gate of the Commander of the Faithful, followed by the beautiful slave, and some of my family, who carried the presents which had been committed to my care. I mentioned the reason of my appearance there, and was immediately conducted to the throne of the caliph. I prostrated myself at his feet, explained my errand, and gave him the letter and the present. When he read the contents, he inquired of me whether it was true that the King of Serendid was as rich and powerful as he reported himself to be in his letter.

"I prostrated myself a second time, and when I arose replied: 'Commander of the Faithful, I can assure your Majesty that the King of Serendid does not exaggerate his riches and grandeur; I have seen his wealth and magnificence. The splendor of his palace cannot fail to excite admiration. When this prince wishes to appear in public, a throne is prepared for him on the back of an elephant; on this he sits, and proceeds between two rows, composed of his ministers, favorites, and others belonging to the court. Before him, on the same elephant, sits an officer with a golden lance in his hand, and behind the throne another stands with a pillar of gold, on the top of which is placed an emerald about half a foot long and an inch thick. The king is preceded by a guard of a thousand men habited in silk and gold stuffs, and mounted on elephants richly caparisoned.

"'While the king is on his march, the officer who sits before him on the elephant proclaims from time to time with a loud voice: "This is the great monarch, the powerful Sultan of the Indies, whose palace is covered with an hundred thousand rubies, and who possesses twenty thousand diamond crowns. This is the crowned monarch, greater than ever was Solima, or the great Mihragè."

"'After he has pronounced these words, the officer who stands behind the throne cries, in his turn, "This monarch who is so great and powerful must die, must die, must die!" The first officer then resumes, "Glory be to him who lives and dies not."'

"The caliph was satisfied with my discourse, and dismissed me with a rich present."

"Sindbad here finished his discourse, and his visitors retired; but Hindbad, as usual, received his hundred sequins. The guests and the porter returned on the following day, and Sindbad began the relation of his seventh and last voyage in these terms:"

THE SEVENTH AND LAST VOYAGE OF SINDBAD
THE SAILOR

"ON my return from my sixth voyage I absolutely relinquished all thoughts of ever venturing again on the seas. I was past the prime of life, and at an age which required rest; and besides this, I had sworn never more to expose myself to the perils I had so often experienced. I prepared, therefore, to enjoy my life in quiet and repose.

"One day one of my servants came to tell me that an officer of the caliph wanted to speak to me. I left the table, and went to him. 'The caliph,' said he, 'has ordered me to acquaint you that he wishes to see you.' I followed the officer to the palace, and he presented me to the prince, whom I saluted by prostrating myself at his feet. 'Sindbad,' said the caliph, 'I want you to do me a service. You must go once more to the King of Serendib with my answer and presents; it is but right that I should make him a proper return for the civility he has shown me.'

[137]

ARABIAN NIGHTS

"This order of the caliph's was a thunderbolt to me. 'Commander of the Faithful,' replied I, 'I am ready to execute anything with which your Majesty may desire to intrust me; but I humbly entreat you to consider that I am worn down with the unspeakable fatigues I have undergone. I have even made a vow never to leave Bagdad.' I then took occasion to relate the long history of my adventures, which he had the patience to listen to attentively. When I had done speaking, the caliph said: 'I confess that these are extraordinary adventures; nevertheless, they must not prevent your making the voyage I propose for my sake; it is only to the island of Serendid. Execute the commission I intrust you with, and then you will be at liberty to return. But you must go, for you must be sensible that it would be highly derogatory to my dignity if I remained under obligation to the king of that island.'

"As I plainly saw that the caliph had resolved on my going, I signified to him that I was ready to obey his commands. He seemed much pleased, and ordered me a thousand sequins to pay the expenses of the voyage.

"In a few days I was prepared for my departure; and as soon as I had received the presents from the caliph, together with a letter written with his own hand, I set off and took the route of Balsora, from whence I embarked. After a pleasant voyage I arrived at the island of Serendid. I immediately acquainted the ministers with the commission I had come to execute, and begged them to procure me an audience as soon as possible.

"The monarch immediately recollected me, and evinced great joy at my visit. 'Welcome, Sindbad,' said he; 'I assure you I have often thought of you since your departure. Blessed be this day in which I see you again.' After thanking the king for his kindness, I delivered the letter and present of the caliph, which he received with every mark of satisfaction and pleasure.

"The caliph sent him a complete bed of gold tissue, estimated at a thousand sequins, fifty robes of a very rare stuff, a hundred more of white linen, the finest that could be procured from

ARABIAN NIGHTS

Cairo, Suez, Cufa, and Alexandria; a bed of crimson, and another of a different pattern and color. Besides this, he sent a vase of agate, greater in width than in depth, of the thickness of a finger—on the sides there was sculptured in bas-relief a man kneeling on the ground, and in his hand a bow and arrow with which he was going to shoot at a lion; and a richly ornamented table, which was supposed from tradition to have belonged to the great Solomon. The letter of the caliph ran thus:

"'HEALTH, IN THE NAME OF THE SOVEREIGN GUIDE OF THE RIGHT
ROAD, TO THE POWERFUL AND HAPPY SULTAN, FROM THE
PART OF ABDALLA HARUN-AL-RASHID, WHOM
GOD HAS PLACED ON THE THRONE OF
HONOR, AFTER HIS ANCESTORS
OF HAPPY MEMORY

"'We have received your letter with joy; and we send you this, proceeding from our council, the garden of superior minds. We hope that in casting your eyes over it you will perceive our good intention, and think it agreeable. Farewell.'

"The King of Serendid was rejoiced to find that the caliph reciprocated his own feelings of friendship. Soon after this audience I requested another, that I might ask leave to depart, which I had some difficulty to obtain. At length I succeeded, and the king at my departure ordered me a very handsome present. I re-embarked immediately, intending to return to Bagdad, but I had not the good fortune to arrive as soon as I expected, for Allah had disposed it otherwise.

"Three or four days after we had set sail we were attacked by corsairs, who easily made themselves masters of our vessel. Some persons in the ship attempted to make resistance, but their boldness cost them their lives. I and all those who had the prudence to submit quietly to the corsairs were made slaves. After they had stripped us, and clothed us in rags instead of our own garments, they bent their course toward a distant island, where they sold us.

"I was purchased by a rich merchant, who brought me to his house, gave me food to eat, and clothed me as a slave. Some

[139]

ARABIAN NIGHTS

days after, as he was not well informed who I was, he asked me if I knew any trade. I replied that I was not an artisan, but a merchant by profession, and that the corsairs who had sold me had taken from me all I possessed. 'But tell me,' said he, 'do you think you could shoot with a bow and arrow?' I replied that I had practised that sport in my youth and that I had not entirely lost my skill. He then gave me a bow and some arrows, and, making me mount behind him on an elephant, he took me to a vast forest at the distance of some hours' journey from the city. We went a great way into the forest, till the merchant came to a spot where he wished to stop, and made me alight. Then he showed me a large tree. 'Get up in that tree,' said he, 'and shoot at the elephants that pass under it, for there are many of those animals in this forest; if one should fall, come and let me know.' Thereupon he left me some provisions, and returned to the city. I remained in the tree on the watch the whole night.

"During the first night no elephants came; but the next day, as soon as the sun had risen, a great number made their appearance. I shot many arrows at them, and at last one fell. The others immediately retired and left me at liberty to go and inform my master of the success I had met with. To reward me for this good intelligence, he regaled me with an excellent repast, and praised my address. We then returned together to the forest, where we dug a pit to bury the elephant I had killed. It was my master's intention to let the carcass rot in the earth, and then to take possession of the teeth.

"I continued my new occupation for two months, and not a day passed in which I did not kill an elephant. One morning, when I was waiting for some elephants to pass, I perceived, to my great astonishment, that instead of traversing the forest as usual, they stopped and came toward me with a terrible noise, and in such numbers that the ground trembled under their footsteps. They approached the tree in which I had stationed myself, and surrounded it with their trunks extended, and their eyes all fixed upon me. At this surprising spectacle I remained

THE LARGEST ELEPHANT TWISTED HIS TRUNK
ROUND THE TREE AND TORE IT UP BY
THE ROOTS

motionless, and was so unnerved that my bow and arrows fell from my hands.

"My terror was not groundless. After the elephants had viewed me for some time, one of the largest twisted his trunk round the body of the tree and shook it with so much violence that he tore it up by the roots and threw it on the ground. I fell with the tree; but the animal took me up with his trunk and placed me on his shoulders, where I lay extended, more dead than alive. The huge beast now put himself at the head of his companions, who followed him in a troop, and he carried me to a retired spot, where he set me down, and then went away with the rest.

"At length, after I had waited some time, seeing no other elephants, I arose, and perceived that I was on a little hill of some extent, entirely covered with bones and teeth of elephants. I now felt certain that this was their cemetery or place of burial, and that they had brought me hither to show it me, that I might desist from destroying them, as I took their lives merely for the sake of possessing their teeth. I did not stay long on the hill, but turned my steps toward the city, and, after walking for a day and a night, at last arrived at my master's.

"As soon as my master saw me, he exclaimed: 'Ah, poor Sindbad! I was anxious to know what could have become of you. I have been to the forest, and found a tree newly torn up by the roots, and your bow and arrows on the ground; after seeking you everywhere in vain, I despaired of ever seeing you again. Pray tell me what has happened to you, and by what fortunate chance you are still alive.' I satisfied his curiosity, and the following day he accompanied me to the hill, and with great joy convinced himself of the truth of my history. We loaded the elephant on which we had come with as many teeth as it could carry, and when we returned my master thus addressed me: 'Brother—for I will no longer treat you as a slave, after the discovery you have imparted to me, and which cannot fail to enrich me—may God pour on you all sorts of blessings and prosperity! Before him I give you your liberty. The elephants of our forest destroy annually a great number of slaves, whom we send in search of ivory. Whatever advice we give them, they are sure, sooner or later, to lose their lives by the wiles of these animals. Providence has delivered you from their fury, and has conferred this mercy on you alone. It is a sign that you are especially protected, and that you are required in this world to be of use to mankind. You have procured me a surprising advantage; we have not hitherto been able to get ivory without risking the lives of our slaves, and now our whole city will be enriched by your means. I intend to give you considerable presents. I might easily move the whole city to join me in making your fortune, but that is a pleasure I will keep for myself alone.'

"To this obliging discourse I replied: 'Master, may Allah preserve you! The liberty you grant me acquits you of all obligation toward me; and the only recompense I desire for the service I have had the good fortune to perform for you and the inhabitants of your city, is permission to return to my country.' 'Well,' he replied, 'the monsoon will soon bring us vessels, which come to be laden with ivory. I will then send you away with a sufficient sum to pay your expenses home.' I again thanked him for the liberty he had given me. I remained with him till the season for the monsoon, and during this interval we made frequent excursions to the hill and filled his magazines with ivory. All the other merchants in the city filled their warehouses likewise, for my discovery did not long remain a secret.

"The ships at length arrived, and my master, having chosen the one in which I was to embark, loaded it with ivory, making over half the cargo to me. He did not omit an abundance of provisions for my voyage, and he also obliged me to accept some rare curiosities of his country. After I had thanked him, I embarked.

"We touched at several islands to procure supplies. Our vessel having originally sailed from a port of the mainland of India, we touched there; and, fearful of the dangers of the sea to Balsora, I took out of the ship the ivory which belonged to me, and resolved to continue my journey by land. I sold my

ARABIAN NIGHTS

share of the cargo for a large sum of money, and purchased a variety of curious things for presents; when I had finished my preparations I joined a caravan of merchants. I remained a long time on the road, and suffered a great deal; but all these fatigues being at last surmounted, I arrived happily at Bagdad. I went immediately and presented myself to the caliph and gave him an account of my embassy. The caliph told me that my long absence had occasioned him some uneasiness, but that he always hoped that Allah would not forsake me.

"I retired well satisfied with the presents and honors he conferred on me; and then resigned myself entirely to my family, my relations, and friends."

"Sindbad thus concluded the recital of his seventh and last voyage; and, addressing himself to Hindbad, added: 'Well, my friend, have you ever heard of one who has suffered more than I have, or been in so many trying situations? Is it not that after so many troubles I should enjoy an agreeable and quiet life?' As he finished these words, Hindbad, approaching him, kissed his hand and said: 'I must confess that you have encountered frightful perils; my afflictions are not to be compared with yours. You not only deserve a quiet life, but are worthy of all the riches you possess, since you make so good a use of them and are so generous. May you continue to live happily till the hour of your death!'

"Sindbad caused Hindbad to receive another hundred sequins. He admitted him to his friendship, told him to quit the calling of a porter and to continue to eat at his table, that he might all his life have reason to remember Sindbad the Sailor.

"To-morrow," continued Sheherazade, "I will narrate the wonderful history of Noureddin Ali and Bedreddin Hassan."

THE HISTORY OF NOUREDDIN ALI AND
BEDREDDIN HASSAN

"THERE was once a sultan in Egypt who was a great observer of justice. He was merciful, beneficent, and liberal, and his valor made him the terror of the neighboring states. The vizier of this sultan was a prudent, wise, and discerning man, skilled in literature and all the sciences. This minister had two sons, handsome in person and resembling their father in talents. The elder was named Schemseddin Mohammed, and the younger Noureddin Ali. On the death of the vizier, their father, the sultan sent for them and, having put on each the dress of an ordinary vizier, spoke thus: 'I regret your father's death, and feel sincerely for your loss; and as I wish to prove my sympathy to you, I invest each of you with equal dignity, for I know you live together and are perfectly united. Go and imitate your father.'

"The two new viziers thanked the sultan for the favor he had conferred on them, and returned home to order their father's

ARABIAN NIGHTS

funeral. When a month had expired they made their appearance in public, and went for the first time to the council of the sultan, after which they continued to attend regularly every day that it assembled. Whenever the sultan went out to hunt, one of the brothers accompanied him, and this honor was accorded to them alternately. One evening, when the eldest brother was to accompany the sultan to the chase on the morrow, the brothers were talking after supper on different subjects, Schemseddin Mohammed said to Noureddin Ali: 'Brother, as we are not yet married and live in such harmony, a thought has occurred to me. Let us both marry on the same day, and wed two sisters, whom we will choose out of some family whose rank is equal to our own. What think you of this proposal?' 'I think, brother,' replied Noureddin Ali, 'it is worthy of the friendship that unites us. You could not have proposed a better plan, and I am ready to do whatever you wish in this matter.' 'Oh,' resumed the elder, 'this is not all; my design goes much further. In the event that our marriage is blessed with offspring, and that your wife brings you a son, while mine presents me with a daughter, we will unite the two when they are of a proper age.' 'Ah!' exclaimed his brother, 'this is indeed an admirable project. This marriage will complete our union, and I readily give my consent. But, brother,' added he, 'if this marriage is indeed to take place, should you expect my son to settle a fortune on your daughter?' 'In that there is no difficulty,' replied the other, 'and I am persuaded that besides the usual agreements in a marriage contract, you would not object to give in your son's name at least three thousand sequins, three good estates, and three slaves.' 'That I cannot agree to,' returned Noureddin Ali. 'Are not we brothers and colleagues, each invested with the same dignity and title? And do not we both know what is just? Inasmuch as the man is more noble than the woman, ought not you to bestow a handsome marriage portion on your daughter? I perceive you are a man who wishes to enrich himself at the expense of others.'

"Although Noureddin Ali spoke these words in jest, his brother,

11   [147]

who was of a fiery temper, was highly offended. 'Woe to thy son!' said he, angrily, 'since you dare to prefer him to my daughter. Know that after such insolence I would not marry my daughter to your son, even if you were to give her more riches than you possess.' This strange quarrel between the brothers about the marriage of their children, who were not yet born, did not cease here. Schemseddin Mohammed went so far as to threaten his brother. 'If I were not obliged,' said he, 'to accompany the sultan to-morrow, I would treat you as you deserve; but on my return you shall learn that it does not become the younger brother to treat the elde with the insolence you have shown toward me.' With these words he retired to his apartment, and his brother followed his example.

"Schemseddin Mohammed rose very early the next morning, and repaired to the palace, from whence he went out with the sultan. As for Noureddin Ali, he passed the night in great distress, and, having well considered that it was not possible for him to remain any longer with a brother who treated him with such contempt, he formed the resolution of quitting his home. He caused a good mule to be caparisoned, provided himself with money, precious stones, and some eatables, and, having told his people that he was going on a journey of three or four days, he departed.

"On leaving Cairo, he went over the desert toward Arabia, but his mule became lame on the road and he was obliged to continue his journey on foot. He had the good fortune to be overtaken by a messenger who was going to Balsora, and who took him up behind him on his camel. When they were arrived at Balsora, Noureddin Ali alighted, thanking the messenger for his assistance. As he walked along the streets, seeking for a lodging, he saw a person of high rank coming toward him, accompanied by a numerous train. All the inhabitants paid great respect to this personage, waiting to let him pass; and Noureddin Ali stopped like the rest. It was the grand vizier of the Sultan of Balsora, parading the city to enforce peace and good order by his presence.

"This minister chanced to cast his eyes on the young man,

and was struck with his engaging countenance; he looked on Noureddin Ali with favor, and as he passed near him, perceiving that the stranger wore a traveler's garb, he stopped to ask him who he was and from whence he came. 'My lord,' replied Noureddin Ali, 'I come from Egypt, and am a native of Cairo. I have quitted my country on account of a quarrel with one of my relations, and I have resolved to travel over the whole world, and to die rather than return home.' When the grand vizier, who was a venerable old man, heard these words, he replied: 'My son, do not persevere in the project you have formed. In this world there is nothing but misery, and you little think what hardships you will have to endure. Come rather with me, and perhaps I can make you forget the cause which has induced you to quit your country.'

"Noureddin Ali followed the grand vizier of Balsora, who soon became acquainted with his good qualities and conceived a great affection for him, so that one day when they were alone together, the old man thus addressed him: 'My son, I am, as you see, so far advanced in years that there is no prospect of my living much longer. Heaven has given me an only daughter as handsome as yourself, and she is now of a marriageable age. Many of the most powerful lords of this court have already demanded her of me for their sons, but I never could bring myself to part with her. Now I love you, and think you so worthy of being allied to my family that I am willing to accept you as my son-in-law. If this proposal pleases you, I will inform the sultan that I have adopted you by this marriage, and I will entreat him to permit me to bestow upon you my appointment as grand vizier of Balsora; and as I require rest in my old age, I will resign to you all my possessions, with the administration of the affairs of state.'

"On hearing this speech, Noureddin Ali threw himself at the grand vizier's feet, and in terms which evinced the joy and gratitude that flowed from his heart, declared himself ready to do anything his patron should dictate. The grand vizier then called together the principal officers of his household, and ordered them to prepare the great hall in his house for a grand entertainment. He sent invitations to all the nobles of the court and to the great men of the city, to summon them to the feast. Noureddin Ali had made him acquainted with his rank, and when they were all assembled he thus addressed them: 'My friends, I am happy to inform you of a circumstance which I have hitherto kept secret. I have a brother who is grand vizier of the Sultan of Egypt, as I have the happiness to be grand vizier to the sultan of these dominions. This brother of mine has an only son, whom he would not marry at the court of Egypt, and he has sent him here to be united to my daughter, that the two branches of our family might be thus joined together. This young nobleman whom you see here, and whom I recognized as my nephew on his arrival, I am going to make my son-in-law. I trust you will do him the honor of being present at the nuptials which I intend shall be solemnized this day.' The grand vizier spoke thus because he thought that no one could be offended at his preferring his nephew to all those noblemen who had offered their alliance; and, indeed, they replied that he did right to conclude this marriage, that they would willingly be present at the ceremony, and that they hoped Allah would bless both uncle and nephew many years with the fruits of this happy union. When they had thus expressed their approbation of the marriage of the vizier's daughter with Noureddin Ali, they sat down to table and feasted for a considerable time. Toward the end of the repast the cadis entered with the marriage contract in their hands. The chief among the noblemen signed it, and the whole company retired.

"When all the guests were gone, the grand vizier desired the attendants who had the care of the bath to conduct Noureddin Ali thither. He found provided for him new linen of a beautiful fineness and whiteness, as well as every other necessary. When the bridegroom had enjoyed his bath he was going to resume his own dress, but another of the greatest magnificence was presented to him in its place. Thus adorned, and perfumed with the most exquisite odors, he returned to the grand vizier, his father-in-law, who was charmed with his appearance, and placed him by his side, saying: 'My son, you have disclosed to me who you are and the rank you held at the Egyptian court; you have also told me that you had a quarrel with your brother, and that this caused you to leave your country. I entreat you to relate to me the nature of this quarrel, for you must conceal nothing from me.'

"Noureddin Ali related all the circumstances connected with his dispute with his brother. The grand vizier could not refrain from laughing very heartily. 'This is indeed,' said he, 'the strangest thing I ever heard of! Is it possible that your quarrel was carried to such lengths merely for an imaginary wedding? I am sorry that you quarreled with your elder brother for such a trifle; however, I perceive that he was in the wrong to be offended with what you said merely in jest, and I ought to be thankful that this strife has been the means of procuring me a son-in-law such as you. But,' continued the old man, 'the night is advancing, and it is time for you to retire. Go; my daughter is expecting your arrival. To-morrow I will present you to the sultan, and I flatter myself he will receive you in a way that shall satisfy us both.'

"Noureddin Ali left his father-in-law to repair to the chamber of his bride. And it is a very remarkable thing that on the same day that these nuptials were celebrated at Balsora, Schemseddin Mohammed was married at Cairo in the following manner:

"After Noureddin Ali had left Cairo with the intention never to return, Schemseddin Mohammed, who was absent with the sultan on the hunting party, returned at the end of a month. Schemseddin Mohammed at once ran into the apartment of Noureddin Ali; but great was his surprise on being informed that his brother had left Cairo, under pretense of making a journey of four or five days; that he set off on a mule on the very day of the sultan's departure; and that since that time he had never been seen or heard of. Schemseddin Mohammed was the more chagrined at this intelligence as he accused himself of having caused his brother's flight by the harsh words he had used toward him. He despatched a courier, who passed through Damascus and went on to Aleppo; but Noureddin Ali was at that time at Balsora. When the messenger returned without bringing any tidings of him, Schemseddin Mohammed determined to send in other directions to seek for Noureddin Ali, but in the mean time he formed the design of marrying. He made choice of the daughter of one of the most powerful nobles of Cairo, and was united to her on the same day that his brother married the daughter of the grand vizier of Balsora.

"But this is not all," continued Sheherazade; "I will now tell you, my lord, what happened afterward. At the expiration of nine months the wife of Schemseddin Mohammed brought her husband a daughter, at Cairo, and on the same day the wife of Noureddin Ali, at Balsora, brought into the world a boy, who was named Bedreddin Hassan. The grand vizier of Balsora testified his joy by vast gifts to the poor and by instituting public rejoicings on the birth of his grandson. To prove his affection for Noureddin Ali, he afterward went to the palace to entreat the sultan to grant him leave to transfer his office, that he might have the satisfaction, before he died, of seeing his son-in-law in his place.

"The sultan readily granted to his vizier the wished-for favor, and he ordered Noureddin Ali to be clothed in his presence in the dress of a grand vizier.

"The happiness of the father-in-law was complete when he saw Noureddin Ali presiding at the council in his place. Noureddin Ali acquitted himself of his new duties so well that he appeared to have exercised the office all his life. He presided at the council whenever the infirmities of age would not allow his father-in-law to be present. The good old man died four years after this marriage, with the satisfaction of seeing a descendant firmly established, who promised to sustain the honor and credit of his family.

"Noureddin Ali performed the last duties to his dead father-in-law with the greatest tenderness and gratitude; and as soon as Bedreddin Hassan, his son, had reached the age of seven years, he placed him under the care of an excellent master, who began the boy's education in a way suitable to his birth.

"By the time Bedreddin Hassan had been two years with his tutor he had learned to read, and could write the Koran by heart. Noureddin Ali, his father, then procured him other masters, and he made such rapid progress in his studies that at the age of twelve years he was no longer in need of their assistance. By that time the features of his countenance had become so beautiful that he was the admiration of all who saw him.

"As his father wished to make him capable of one day filling the situation he himself held, he spared nothing to qualify him for it. In short, he neglected nothing that could tend to the advancement of his dearly beloved son; and he had begun to enjoy the fruits of his care when he was suddenly attacked by a disease so violent that he felt his end was approaching. He prepared to die like a good Mussulman. In these precious moments he did not forget his beloved son, Bedreddin Hassan; he caused him to be called to his bedside, and thus addressed him: 'My son, you see that this world is perishable; that world only to which I am shortly going is eternal. You must from this moment begin to prepare to take this journey without regret, your conscience acquitting you of having neglected any of the duties of a Mussulman, or of an honest man. With regard to your religion, you have been sufficiently instructed in that by the masters you have had, as well as by what you have read. As to your duty as an honest man, I will now give you some advice. As it is right you should know who you are, and you cannot possibly have that knowledge without knowing who I am, I will now inform you.

"'I was born in Egypt; my father was prime minister to the sultan of that country. I, too, had the honor of being one of the viziers of the same sultan, jointly with my brother, your uncle, who I believe is still alive, and is called Schemseddin Mohammed. I was compelled to separate from him, and I came into this country. But you will learn all these things more fully from a packet which I shall give you.'

[153]

"Noureddin Ali then took out a scroll, which he had written with his own hand, and gave it to Bedreddin Hassan. 'Take it,' he said; 'read it at your leisure; you will find in it, among other things, the date of my marriage, and that of your birth.' Bedreddin Hassan, truly grieved at seeing his father in such a state, and touched by his discourse, received the packet with tears in his eyes, promising never to let it go out of his possession.

"Noureddin Ali continued to give counsel to his son till the last moments of his life, and after his death he was interred with all the honors due to his rank and dignity. Bedreddin Hassan was inconsolable at the death of his father. Instead of mourning for one month, as is the custom, he passed two in retreat, overwhelmed by his sorrow, during which time he would not see any one, nor did he even go out to pay his respects to the sultan, who, displeased with this neglect, which he considered as a mark of contempt toward him, suffered his anger to rise to a great height. He summoned the new grand vizier whom he had elected in the place of Noureddin Ali, and ordered him to go to the house of the deceased minister, and to confiscate it, together with all Noureddin Ali's other houses, grounds, and effects; nor was anything to be left for Bedreddin Hassan, whose person also he ordered the officer to seize.

"The grand vizier immediately set out to execute his commission. One of the slaves of Bedreddin Hassan, who had by chance joined the crowd at the council, no sooner learned the intention of the grand vizier than he hastened to warn his master of the danger. He found him seated in the vestibule of his house, as full of affliction as if his father were but just dead. The slave threw himself at his master's feet, quite out of breath, and exclaimed, 'Fly, my lord, fly quickly!' 'What is the matter?' inquired Bedreddin Hassan, raising his head. 'What news hast thou?' 'My lord,' replied the slave, 'you have not a moment to lose. The sultan is enraged against you, and they are now coming by his order to confiscate all your possessions and even to seize your person.'

"This news brought by the faithful and affectionate slave

occasioned Bedreddin Hassan some perplexity. 'But,' said he, 'cannot I return and take even some money and jewels?' 'My dear lord,' replied the slave, 'the grand vizier will be here in a moment. Depart instantly and make your escape.' Bedreddin Hassan immediately got up from the sofa on which he was sitting, and put on his slippers; then, covering his head with one corner of his robe to conceal his face, he fled, without knowing whither to turn his steps to avoid the danger which threatened him. The first thought that occurred to him was to make for the nearest gate of the city. He ran without stopping till he came to the public cemetery, and, as evening was approaching, determined to pass the night near his father's tomb. This tomb was a large edifice of magnificent appearance, built in the shape of a dome, which Noureddin Ali had erected during his lifetime; but Bedreddin Hassan on his way met with a very rich Jew, a banker and merchant by profession.

"This Jew, who was called Isaac, knew Bedreddin Hassan, and he stopped and saluted him very respectfully; after kissing his hand, he said: 'My lord, may I take the liberty of asking you where you are going to at this hour alone, and seemingly so agitated? Is there anything that disturbs you?' 'Yes,' replied Bedreddin Hassan; 'I fell asleep just now, and my father appeared to me in a dream. His countenance was threatening, as if he had been very angry with me. I awoke much terrified, and I set off immediately to come and pray at his tomb.' 'My lord,' replied the Jew, who did not know the real cause of Bedreddin Hassan's quitting the city, 'as the late grand vizier your father, of happy memory, had several vessels laden with merchandise which are still at sea and now belong to you, I entreat you to grant me the preference over any other merchant. I am in a position to purchase for ready money the cargoes of all your vessels; and as a proof of what I say, if it please you, I will give you a thousand sequins for the first which arrives in port; I have the money here in a purse, and am ready to pay it.' Saying this, he drew out a large purse, which he showed to Bedreddin Hassan.

ARABIAN NIGHTS

"Forced from his home, and robbed of everything he possessed, Bedreddin Hassan looked upon this proposition of the Jew as a favor from Heaven, and accepted the offer with great joy. 'O my master,' said the Jew, 'you grant me then the cargo of the first of your vessels that arrives for one thousand sequins?' 'I do,' replied Bedreddin Hassan. 'The bargain is made.' The Jew then put the purse of sequins into his hands, at the same time offering to count them, but Bedreddin Hassan saved him the trouble by saying he trusted in his honor. 'Then, my lord,' resumed the Jew, 'will you have the goodness to write an acknowledgment of the bargain we have made?' He then pulled from his girdle an ink-horn, and, taking a cane prepared for writing, he presented it to the young man, with a leaf of paper which he found in his pocket-book, and while he held the ink, Bedreddin Hassan wrote these words:

"This writing is to witness that Bedreddin Hassan, of Balsora, has sold the cargo of the first of his ships which shall arrive at this port to the Jew Isaac, for the sum of one thousand sequins, received.

"BEDREDDIN HASSAN, OF BALSORA.

"This writing he gave to the Jew, who put it in his girdle, and they separated, Isaac pursuing his way to the city, while Bedreddin Hassan proceeded to the tomb of his father, Noureddin Ali. When he had reached it he prostrated himself, and with many tears began to lament his miserable fate. 'Alas!' said he, 'unfortunate Bedreddin, what will become of thee? Where wilt thou find refuge from the unjust prince who persecutes thee?' He remained a considerable time in this state; but at length he arose and, leaning his head on his father's sepulcher, he renewed his lamentations, and continued to weep and sigh until, overtaken by sleep, he fell into a gentle slumber.

"He had scarcely begun to taste the sweets of repose when a genie, who had chosen this cemetery as his retreat during the day, and who was about to set forth on his nightly excursions, perceived this young man in the tomb of Noureddin Ali. He entered, and, as Bedreddin Hassan lay with his face upward,

ARABIAN NIGHTS

the genie was struck with admiration at his beauty, and, after gazing at him for some time, he said to himself, 'To judge of this creature by his countenance, it can only be an angel sent by Allah from the terrestrial paradise to enchant the world with its beauty.' After he had contemplated the sleeper again, he rose into the air, where by chance he met a fairy. They saluted each other, and the genie said, 'I entreat you to descend with me to the cemetery where I live, and I will show you a prodigy of beauty who will awaken your admiration as he has excited mine.' The fairy consented, and they both instantly descended. When they came to the tomb, the genie, showing Bedreddin Hassan to her, exclaimed, 'Tell me, did you ever see so handsome a youth as this?'

"The fairy examined Bedreddin Hassan attentively, and then replied, turning toward the genie, 'I confess that he is very handsome, but I have just seen in Cairo an object still more wonderful, and will tell you something concerning it if you will attend to me.' 'That I will, with pleasure,' replied the genie. 'You must know, then,' resumed the fairy, 'that the Sultan of Egypt has a vizier named Schemseddin Mohammed, and this Schemseddin Mohammed has a daughter about twenty years of age. She is the most beautiful and perfect creature ever seen. A few days since, the sultan, hearing from every one of the extraordinary beauty of this young lady, sent for the vizier, her father, and said to him, "I understand you have a daughter who is marriageable, and I wish to make her my wife. Will not you give her to me?" The vizier was rather disconcerted, and instead of accepting the offer with joy he replied: "O sultan, I am not worthy of the honor your Majesty would confer on me; and I humbly entreat you not to be displeased that I should decline your offer. You know that I had a brother called Nouredd n Ali, who, like myself, had the honor of being one of your viziers. We had a quarrel, in consequence of which he suddenly disappeared, and I have never heard of him since that time till within these four days, when I learned that he had lately died at Balsora, where he enjoyed the dignity of grand vizier to the sultan. He has left one son; and as we formerly agreed that our children, if ever we had any, should marry each other, I am certain that when he died he had not abandoned his design. For this reason I wish, on my part, to perform my promise; and I supplicate your Majesty to permit me to do so."

"'The sultan was extremely irritated by this answer of Schemseddin Mohammed, and said to him: "Is it thus you return the condescension with which I proposed my alliance to your family? You dare to show preference to another over me? I swear to you that your daughter shall have for her husband the meanest and ugliest of my slaves." With these words he dismissed the vizier, who returned home much mortified.

"'To-day the sultan ordered to be brought to him one of his grooms, who is very much deformed, and so ugly it is impossible to look at him without terror; and, after commanding Schemseddin Mohammed to give his consent to the marriage of his daughter with this horrible slave, he had the contract drawn up, and signed by witnesses in his presence. The preparations for these strange nuptials are now completed, and at this moment all the slaves of the nobles of the Egyptian court are at the door of the bath, each with a torch in his hand; they are waiting for the humpbacked groom, who is in the bath, to come out, that they may lead him to his bride, who is already dressed to receive him. At the time I left Cairo the ladies were assembled to conduct her in her nuptial ornaments to the hall where she is to receive her deformed bridegroom, and where she is now expecting him.'

"When the fairy had ceased speaking, the genie replied that he could not believe it possible for the beauty of this damsel to surpass that of the youth who lay sleeping before them. 'I will not dispute with you,' said the fairy; 'I will only say that he deserves to marry the charming lady who is destined for the groom; and I think we should perform a good action were we to frustrate the injustice of the sultan and to substitute this young man for the slave.' 'You speak wisely,' resumed the genie. 'Let us disappoint the vengeance of the sultan, console an afflicted father, and make his daughter as happy as she now believes herself to be miserable. I take upon me to carry this youth to Cairo without waking him, and I leave to you the task of disposing of him after we have executed our enterprise.'

"After the genie and the fairy had decided together what they should do, the genie gently raised Bedreddin Hassan, transported him through the air with inconceivable swiftness, and placed him at the door of a public apartment adjoining the bath from whence the groom was to come.

"Awaking at this instant, Bedreddin Hassan was much astonished to find himself in a city quite unknown to him, and was going to inquire where he was when the genie gave him a gentle tap on the shoulder and warned him not to speak a word; then, putting a torch in his hand, he said to him: 'Go and join the people whom you see at the door of yonder bath, and walk with them till you come to a hall where a wedding is going to be celebrated. You will easily distinguish the bridegroom by his being deformed. Place yourself on his right hand when you enter, and from time to time open the purse of sequins which you have in your bosom and distribute the money among the musicians and dancers as you go along. When you have reached the hall, do not fail to give some also to the female slaves whom you will see about the bride. Be bold, and be not surprised at anything; fear no one, and trust for the consequence in the power of one who will dispose of everything as he thinks best for you.'

"The young Bedreddin Hassan, thus instructed in what he was to do, advanced toward the door of the bath. The first thing he did was to light his torch by that of a slave; then, mixing with the rest as if he had been sent by a nobleman of Cairo, he walked with them, and accompanied the groom, who came out of the bath and mounted one of the horses from the sultan's stable.

"Finding himself near the musicians and dancers who preceded the humpbacked groom, Bedreddin Hassan frequently drew from his purse handfuls of sequins, which he distributed among them. As he conferred these bounties with admirable grace and with a very liberal air, all those who received them cast their eyes on him and no sooner had they seen him than they were fascinated by him, so great was his beauty.

"At length the procession arrived at the palace of Schemseddin Mohammed, who little thought his nephew was so near him. To prevent confusion, some of the officers stopped all the slaves who carried torches, and would not suffer them to enter. They also wanted to exclude Bedreddin Hassan; but the musicians and dancers declared they would not proceed if he were not allowed to accompany them. 'He is not one of the slaves,' said they. 'He must be some young stranger who wishes from curiosity to see the ceremonies observed at weddings in this city.' Saying this, they placed him in their midst and made him go in, in spite of the officers. They took from him his torch, and when they had brought him into the hall they placed him on the right hand of the groom, who was seated on a magnificent throne, next to the daughter of the vizier.

"The bride was dressed in her richest ornaments, but her countenance displayed a melancholy the cause of which was easily divined by any one who saw by her side the humpbacked bridegroom. The throne of this ill-matched pair was erected in the middle of a large divan; the wives of the emirs, viziers, and officers of the sultan's chamber, together with many other ladies of the court, were seated a little below on each side, according to their rank.

"When they saw Bedreddin Hassan enter, they all fixed their eyes on him, and could not cease looking at him, so much were they struck with the beauty of his figure and countenance. 'This handsome youth,' exclaimed the ladies, 'ought to be married to our bride, and not this deformed wretch.' They went further than this, and even ventured to utter imprecations against the sultan, who was abusing his power by uniting deformity to beauty. At length the musicians began their concert, and the women who had dressed the bride approached her.

"Each time the bride changed her dress, which, according

to custom, she was obliged to do seven different times, she arose, and, followed by her women, passed before the groom without deigning to look at him, and went to present herself to Bedreddin Hassan, to show herself to him in her new ornaments. Remembering the instructions he had received from the genie, Bedreddin Hassan on each of these occasions put his hand into the purse and drew it out full of sequins, which he distributed to the women who attended the bride. They testified their gratitude, and told him by signs that they wished him to marry the bride instead of the humpbacked groom.

"When the ceremony of changing the dresses was completed, the musicians ceased playing and retired, making signs to Bedreddin Hassan to remain. The ladies also motioned him to stay, and took their leave, together with all those who did not belong to the house. The bride went into a closet, where her women followed to undress her, and there remained no one in the hall except the humpbacked groom, Bedreddin Hassan, and some servants. The hunchback, who was furiously enraged with Bedreddin Hassan, gave him a scowling look out of the corners of his eyes, and cried out: 'What art thou waiting for? Get thee gone! Why dost thou not depart with the rest?' As Bedreddin Hassan had no pretext for remaining, he retired somewhat out of countenance; but he had scarcely left the vestibule when the genie and the fairy appeared before him, and stopped him. 'Whither art thou going?' said the genie. 'Return, for the hunchback has left the hall; and proceed at once to the chamber of the bride. When you are alone with her tell her confidently that you are her husband, that the sultan only intended to put off a jest upon the hunchback, and that to appease this pretended husband you have ordered him a large dish of cream in his stable. Use all the arguments you can think of to persuade her of the truth of this. We will take proper precautions so that the hunchback shall not return to prevent you from visiting your bride, for she is yours, not his.'

"While the genie was thus encouraging Bedreddin Hassan, and instructing him in the part he was to play, the hunchback had really quitted the hall. The genie went and sought him out, and, assuming the figure of a large, black cat, began to mew in a terrific manner. The hunchback clapped his hands and made a noise to frighten the creature away; but the cat, instead of retreating, set up its back and fixed its fiery eyes fiercely on him, mewing louder than before. It then began to swell, increasing in size until it was larger than an ass. The hunchback was going to call for assistance, but he was so terrified that he could not utter a sound. To increase his terror, the genie suddenly changed himself into a large buffalo, and under this shape cried with a loud voice, 'O miserable hunchback!' At these words the frightened groom fell on the floor and replied, trembling, 'Sovereign prince of the buffaloes, what dost thou require of me?' 'Ill befall thee!' replied the genie; 'thou hast the temerity to dare to marry my mistress?' 'O my lord!' cried the hunchback, 'I entreat you to pardon me; if I have erred it is through ignorance alone. Command me in whatever you please, I swear I am ready to obey.' 'I swear to thee,' resumed the genie, 'that if thou quittest this spot or breakest silence before the sun rises, nay, if thou utterest but a syllable, I will crush thy head to atoms. At sunrise I permit thee to leave this house; but I command thee to fly quickly, and if thou hast ever the audacity to return, it shall cost thee thy life.' Thus saying, the genie transformed himself into a man, and took the hunchback by the heels; then, holding him against the wall with his head downward, he added, 'If thou darest to stir before the sun rises I repeat to thee that I will take thee by the feet and dash thy head against this wall.'

"Meanwhile Bedreddin Hassan, encouraged by the genie and the fairy, had re-entered the hall and proceeded privately into the nuptial chamber, where he seated himself, waiting with anxious expectation the issue of his adventure. After some time the bride arrived.

"The young bride was extremely surprised when, instead of the hunchback, she beheld Bedreddin Hassan. 'O my friend,' exclaimed she, 'how came you here at this hour? I suppose you are one of my husband's comrades?' 'No, madam,' replied

Bedreddin Hassan, 'I have nothing to do with that disgusting hunchback. Be undeceived; such beauty as yours will not be sacrificed to the most despicable of men. I am the happy mortal to whom you are married. The sultan chose to amuse himself by playing off this little jest on the vizier, your father, and has selected me for your real husband. We have dismissed the hunchback to his stable, where he is now regaling himself with a dish of cream; and you may be assured that he will never more appear before your beautiful eyes.'

"At this discourse the daughter of the vizier regained an air of cheerfulness, which added so much to her beauty that Bedreddin Hassan was quite charmed with her. 'I did not expect so agreeable a surprise,' said she; 'I considered myself condemned to pass the rest of my days in misery, but my happiness is so much the greater in being united to a man so worthy of my affection.' Bedreddin Hassan was delighted to find himself in possession of so beautiful a spouse. He undressed, putting his clothes on a chair, together with the purse which the Jew had given him, and which was still full, notwithstanding all the gold he had taken from it.

"When the two lovers were asleep the genie, who had sought out the fairy, told her it was now time to complete the task they had so well begun and so happily conducted thus far. 'Let us not,' said he, 'be surprised by daylight, which will now soon appear; go and take away the young man without waking him.'

"The fairy repaired to the chamber of the lovers, who were both sleeping profoundly, and stole away Bedreddin Hassan, dressed as he was in his shirt and drawers. Accompanied by the genie, she flew with wonderful swiftness to the gates of Damascus, in Syria. The fairy gently placed Bedreddin Hassan on the ground near the gate, and then flew away, the genie vanishing with her.

"Presently the gates were opened; and the people, who had assembled in great numbers to go out, were extremely surprised at seeing Bedreddin Hassan lying on the ground in only his shirt and drawers. A slight breeze which was beginning to rise blew

12   [163]

aside the cap which shaded his face. They were all surprised
at the whiteness of the skin and they exclaimed so loudly in
their admiration that they awakened the young man. His astonishment was not less than theirs on finding himself at the gate
of a city where he had never been, and on seeing a crowd of people
who were examining him attentively. He cried out, 'Friends, I
intreat you to inform me where I am, and what you want of me.'
One of the spectators replied, 'Young man, the gates of this city
are but just opened, and when we came out we found you lying
here, just as you now are; and we stopped to look at you. Have
you passed the night here, and do you know that you are at one
of the gates of Damascus?' 'At one of the gates of Damascus!'
exclaimed Bedreddin Hassan. 'You do but jest with me. When I
went to bed last night I was at Cairo.' At these words some of
the people, moved with compassion, said it was a pity that so
handsome a youth should have lost his senses; and so they passed
on.

"A venerable old man next addressed him. 'My son,' he said,
'you must be mistaken, for how could you be last night at Cairo
and this morning at Damascus? That cannot be.' 'It is very
true, notwithstanding,' replied Bedreddin Hassan; 'and I assure
you, moreover, that I passed the whole of yesterday at Balsora.'
He had scarcely uttered these words when they all burst into a
laugh, and cried, 'He is mad, he is mad!' Some, however, pitied
him on account of his extreme youth; and a man who was
looking on said: 'My son, you have lost your reason; you know
not what you say. How is it possible that a man should be in
one day at Balsora, in the same night at Cairo, and the next
morning at Damascus?' 'What I tell you,' persisted Bedreddin
Hassan, 'is as true as that I was last night married in the city
of Cairo.' All those who had laughed before burst into fresh
shouts at hearing this. 'Take care,' resumed the person who had
addressed him before, 'you must have dreamed all this, and the
illusion still remains impressed on your mind.' 'I know what
I am saying,' replied the youth, 'I have not dreamed I was at
Cairo, for I am persuaded I was there in reality. But can you

ARABIAN NIGHTS

tell me what is become of my robe, my turban, and the purse of sequins I had at Cairo?'

"Although he assured them that all this was true, yet the people who listened to him only laughed at what he said. At length he rose and walked into the city; but the crowd followed him, crying out, 'A madman! a madman!' On hearing this, some of the inhabitants ran to the windows, others came out at their doors, and some joined the throng who had surrounded Bedreddin Hassan, and joined in the cry, 'A madman!' without knowing why they shouted. Tormented by his pursuers, he came to the house of a pastry-cook, and entered to escape from the hooting of the mob who followed him.

"This pastry-cook had formerly been the chief of a troop of wandering Arabs who attacked caravans; and although he was now established at Damascus, yet he was feared by all who knew anything of his former life. His appearance soon dispersed the mob that followed Bedreddin Hassan. The pastry-cook began to question the young man, inquiring who he was, and what had led him to Damascus. Bedreddin Hassan related the story of his birth, and told of the death of the grand vizier, his father. He then proceeded to relate how he had left Balsora; how, after falling asleep on the tomb of his father, he had awaked to find himself at Cairo, where he married a lady. Lastly, he expressed his surprise at seeing himself in Damascus without being able to understand any of these miracles.

"'Your history is very astonishing,' said the pastry-cook; 'but if you will follow my advice, you will not disclose to any one the facts you have related to me. You may remain with me till your fortunes change; and, as I have no children, I will adopt you as my son, if you consent. You may then go freely about the city, and will no longer be exposed to the insults of the populace.'

"Although this proposal conferred no great honor on the son of a grand vizier, Bedreddin Hassan nevertheless accepted the pastry-cook's offer, judging very properly that it was the only step he could take in his present situation. The pastry-

[165]

cook procured him clothes, and, taking witnesses with him, went before a cadi to declare that he adopted the young man as his son. Bedreddin Hassan resided with him, and, only calling himself by the simple name of Hassan, soon learned the art of making pastry.

"Whilst this was passing at Damascus, the daughter of Schemseddin Mohammed awoke, and, not finding Bedreddin Hassan by her side, concluded that he had risen softly, not to interrupt her slumbers, and that he would soon return. She was still expecting him, when her father, the vizier Schemseddin Mohammed, came to the door of her apartment. He was much affected by the affront he conceived had been put upon him by the Sultan of Egypt, and came to bewail with her on the unhappy destiny to which she had been abandoned. He called her by her name; and she no sooner heard his voice than she rose up to open the door to him. She kissed his hand, and received him with an air of so much satisfaction that the vizier, who expected to find her bathed in tears and in grief equal to his own, was extremely surprised. 'Miserable one!' cried he, in an angry tone, 'is it thus you appear before me? Bearing the horrid fate to which you have been sacrificed, can you present yourself to me with a countenance which bespeaks content?' When the bride perceived her father's displeasure at the joy which brightened her features, she replied: 'My lord, I entreat you not to reproach me so unjustly. I have not been married to that monster the hunchback, who is more detestable in my eyes than death itself; all the company treated him with such derision and contempt that he was obliged to go away and hide himself and make room for a charming young man who is my real husband.' 'What story is this?' cried the grand vizier. 'Was not the hunchback married to you last night?' 'No, my lord,' returned she; 'my husband is the young man I was speaking of, who has large eyes and fine, black eyebrows.' At these words Schemseddin Mohammed lost all patience and put himself in a violent rage with his daughter. 'Ah, foolish girl!' said he. 'Will you make me lose my senses by the lies you tell?' 'It is you, father,' replied

she, 'who almost drive me out of my senses by your incredulity.'
'Is it not true,' persisted the vizier, 'that the hunchback—'
'Let us talk no more of the hunchback,' interrupted she; 'evil
befall the hunchback! I again tell you,' she continued, 'that he
has not passed the night in my chamber, but my dear husband,
whom I have mentioned to you; and indeed he cannot be now
at any great distance from hence.'

"Schemseddin Mohammed went out immediately to look
for this husband; but instead of finding him he was in the
greatest astonishment at seeing the humpbacked fellow standing
on his head with his feet in the air, and in the very position in
which the genie had left him. 'What is the meaning of all this?'
he asked him. 'Who placed you in that situation?' The hunchback, who instantly recognized the vizier, answered, 'You are
the man who wishes to give me in marriage to the mistress of a
buffalo; to one who is in love with a genie? But I won't be your
dupe, I promise you.'

"Schemseddin Mohammed thought the hunchback was out
of his senses. 'Get up,' he cried, 'and stand upon your legs.'
'I will beware how I do that,' answered he, 'unless, indeed, the
sun be risen. You must know that as I was coming here yesterday evening a large black cat suddenly appeared to me; and
it kept increasing in size till it was as large as a buffalo. I shall
never forget what it said to me; therefore leave me here.' Instead of complying, the vizier took hold of the hunchback by
the legs and obliged him to get up. As soon as he was on his legs
he ran away as fast as he could. He went directly to the palace,
and presented himself before the Sultan of Egypt, who was highly
amused at the account he gave of the manner in which the genie
had treated him.

"Schemseddin Mohammed then went back to his daughter's
apartment, quite uncertain how to think or act. 'Unhappy
girl,' he said to his daughter, 'can you give me no further account
of this adventure, which confuses and distracts me?' 'My father,'
she replied, 'I cannot tell you anything more than I have already
had the honor to relate to you. But see,' she added, 'here is

some part of my husband's dress, which he has left on this chair, and perhaps this may throw some light on what you wish to discover.' So saying, she presented the turban of Benreddin Hassan to the vizier, who examined it attentively. He then said, 'I should conjecture this to be a turban that belonged to a vizier if it were not made in the fashion of those of Moussoul.' As he was thus turning it over in his hand he felt something sewn up in the inside of the turban between the folds. He asked, therefore, for scissors, and on unripping the turban he discovered a paper folded up. This was the packet which Noureddin Ali on his death-bed had given to his son Bedreddin Hassan, who had concealed it in his turban. On opening the packet, Schemseddin Mohammed instantly knew the handwriting of his brother Noureddin Ali, and read the following direction: 'For my son, Bedreddin Hassan.' Before he had time to reflect on these circumstances, his daughter put into her father's hands the purse which she had found in Bedreddin Hassan's pocket. He immediately opened it, and saw it filled with sequins; for, through the care of the genie and fairy, it had remained full in spite of all the gold that Bedreddin Hassan had bestowed on those around him. Upon a sort of ticket attached to the purse the vizier read these words, 'A thousand sequins belonging to the Jew Isaac.' And under them was the following inscription, which the Jew had written before he had left Bedreddin Hassan: 'Delivered to Bedreddin Hassan, in payment for the cargo of the first vessel that arrives in port belonging to him, and which belonged to Noureddin Ali, his father, of happy memory.' The vizier had scarcely finished reading these words when he uttered a loud cry and fainted away.

"When Schemseddin Mohammed recovered from his fainting-fit, he exclaimed: 'My daughter, be not surprised at the accident which has just happened to me; so wonderful is the adventure which has caused it that you will hardly give credit to it. The husband who has passed the night with you is no other than your cousin, the son of Noureddin Ali. The thousand sequins in this purse remind me of the quarrel I had with my dear brother.

Doubt not this is the wedding-present he makes you. Allah be praised for all these things.' He then looked at the writing in his brother's hand, and kissed it many times, bathing it with his tears. 'Why cannot I see Noureddin Ali himself here,' he exclaimed, 'and be reconciled to him, as well as I see his handwriting, which causes me so much joy?'

"He read the packet through and found the dates of his brother's arrival at Balsora, of his marriage, and of the birth of Bedreddin Hassan; then, comparing these dates with those of his own marriage and of his daughter's birth at Cairo, he could not help wondering at the coincidence; and remembering that his nephew was his son-in-law, he gave himself up entirely to the emotions of pleasure to which all these circumstances gave rise.

"Nevertheless Schemseddin Mohammed could not understand why his nephew had disappeared; he expected him to arrive every moment, and awaited his coming with the greatest impatience. When seven days had passed and no Bedreddin Hassan appeared, he ordered him to be sought for in every part of Cairo, but he could hear no tidings of him, and this caused him much uneasiness. 'This is, indeed,' said he, 'a singular adventure; surely such a strange fate never befell mortal before.'

"Uncertain what might happen in the course of time, he thought proper himself to write the account of what had taken place, detailing the manner in which the nuptials were celebrated, and how the hall and the chamber of his daughter were furnished. He also carefully preserved the turban, the purse, and the rest of the dress of Bedreddin Hassan.

"After some time the daughter of Schemseddin Mohammed gave birth to a son. A nurse was provided for the child, with other women and slaves to attend upon him, and his grandfather named him Agib.

"When the young Agib had attained the age of seven years, the vizier Schemseddin Mohammed, instead of having him taught to read at home, sent him to school to a master who had a great reputation for his learning; and two slaves had the care of conducting him to school and bringing him back every day. Agib used to play with his comrades; and as they were all of much inferior condition to himself they treated him with great deference, and in this the schoolmaster set the example by excusing many faults in Agib which he did not pass over in other scholars. The blind submission with which Agib was treated completely spoiled him. He became proud and insolent; he expected his companions to bear everything from him, but would not in return comply with any of their wishes. At last he made himself so obnoxious to all the scholars that they complained of him to the master of the school. The master at first exhorted them to have patience; but, perceiving that by so doing he only increased the insolence of Agib, and being tired himself of the trouble that headstrong boy gave, he said to them: 'My boys, I see that Agib is an insolent fellow. I will tell you how to mortify him in a way that will prevent his tormenting you any longer; indeed, it may perhaps prevent his returning any more to school. To-morrow when he comes, and you are going to play together, place yourselves round him and let one of you say aloud: 'We are going to play, but every one who wishes to join in the game must tell his name, and that of his father and mother. Those who refuse to do so shall not play with us.' The master then explained to them how mortified Agib would be, and they all went home with the greatest satisfaction.

"The following day, when they were assembled, they did not fail to do as their master had instructed them. They surrounded Agib, and one of them said, 'Let us play at some game, but on condition that he who cannot tell his name, and that of his father and mother, shall not play with us.' Agib and all the rest agreed to these conditions. Then the boy who had spoken first interrogated them all, and each answered satisfactorily till Agib's turn came. The boy said, 'I am called Agib; my mother is named the Queen of Beauty, and my father is Schemseddin Mohammed, the vizier of the sultan.'

"At these words all the children cried, 'Agib, this is not true;

that is not the name of your father, but of your grandfather.'
'Woe to you!' replied he, angrily. 'Do you dare to say that
the vizier Schemseddin Mohammed is not my father?' The
scholars then all laughed at him, and cried out, 'No, no! he is
only your grandfather, and you shall not play with us; we will
take care not to come near you.' Then they left him and continued to laugh among themselves. Agib was so mortified that
he began to cry.

"The master, who had been listening and heard all that passed,
now made his appearance and said to Agib: 'Do not you know
yet, Agib, that the vizier Schemseddin Mohammed is not your
father? He is your grandfather and the father of your mother.
Like yourself, we are ignorant of the name of your father; we
only know that the sultan wished to marry your mother to one
of his grooms who was deformed, but that a genie took the
groom's place. This is unpleasant for you, but it ought to teach
you to treat your companions with less haughtiness than you have
hitherto shown.'

"Vexed at the jokes of his school-fellows, little Agib immediately left the school, and returned home in tears. He went
first to the apartment of his mother, who, alarmed at seeing
him in such grief, anxiously inquired the cause. When he had
told her his adventure, he cried out, 'In the name of God, mother,
tell me who is my father?' 'My son,' replied she, 'your father
is Schemseddin Mohammed, who embraces you every day.'
'You do not tell me the truth,' said Agib; 'he is not my father,
but yours. But whose son am I?' At this the Queen of Beauty,
recalling to her mind the night of her marriage, which had been
followed by so long a widowhood, began to weep bitterly, mourning the loss of a husband so amiable as Bedreddin Hassan.

"The Queen of Beauty and her son Agib were still weeping
when Schemseddin Mohammed entered and desired to know
the cause of their grief. His daughter related the mortification
her son had met with at school. This account very soon affected
the vizier, who joined his tears with theirs. Being very much
disturbed by this cruel reflection, he went to the palace of the

sultan, prostrated himself at his master's feet, and humbly entreated permission to take a journey to seek his nephew, Bedreddin Hassan, for he could not bear that the whole city should suppose his daughter had been married to a genie. The sultan felt for the grief of the vizier, approved his intention, and gave him leave to execute it; he even wrote a letter of recommendation in the most gracious manner to the princes and nobles in whose dominions Bedreddin Hassan might be, requesting them to authorize the young man's departure with the grand vizier.

"Schemseddin Mohammed immediately began to prepare for his departure, and at the end of four days he set off, accompanied by his daughter and by Agib, his grandson.

"They took the road to Damascus, and traveled for nineteen days without stopping; but on the twentieth they halted in a beautiful meadow, at a little distance from the gates of the city, and had their tents pitched on the banks of a river.

"The vizier Schemseddin Mohammed declared his intention of remaining two days in this spot, proposing to continue his journey on the third. He allowed the persons in his suite to visit Damascus. They almost all availed themselves of this permission.

"The Queen of Beauty, who wished that her son Agib should also have the gratification of walking about this celebrated city, ordered the black eunuch who held the office of governor to the child to take Agib into the town, admonishing him to be very careful that the boy did not meet with any accident.

"Agib, who was magnificently dressed, set out with the eunuch. Directly they entered the city, Agib, who was as beautiful as the morning, attracted the admiration of every one. Some ran out from their doors to see him nearer; others came to the windows; and people who were walking in the streets, not satisfied with stopping to look at him, ran by his side to have the pleasure of contemplating his beauty for a longer time. The eunuch and Agib came by chance to the shop where Bedreddin Hassan was; and, pressed by the throng that surrounded them, they were obliged to stop at his door.

ARABIAN NIGHTS

"The pastry-cook who had adopted Bedreddin Hassan as his son had been dead some years, and to this adopted son had left his shop and all his property. Bedreddin Hassan, therefore, was now master of the shop, and exercised the trade of a pastry-cook so successfully that he had acquired a great reputation in Damascus. Observing many people assembled round his door to look at Agib and the black eunuch, Bedreddin Hassan also began to examine them attentively.

"Directly he cast his eyes on Agib he felt himself agitated, without knowing why. He was not struck like the crowd with the extreme beauty of the boy; his emotion arose from another cause, which he could not understand. It was the force of nature which moved this tender father and caused him to approach Agib, and say to him with an engaging air, 'My little lord, you have won my heart; I beg you will do me the favor to walk into my shop and eat some of my pastry, that I may have the pleasure of admiring you at my leisure.' He pronounced these words with so much tenderness that the tears came into his eyes. Little Agib was affected by his manner, and, turning toward the eunuch, said, 'This good man has a countenance that pleases me, and he speaks to me in so affectionate a manner that I cannot avoid doing what he requests; let us go in and eat some of his pastry.' 'Not so,' replied the eunuch; 'it would be a pretty tale to tell that the son of a vizier had gone into a pastry-cook's shop to eat; do not think that I shall allow it.' 'Alas! my young master,' cried Bedreddin Hassan, 'those are very cruel who trust you with a man who treats you so harshly.' Then, addressing the eunuch, he continued: 'My good friend, do not prevent this young gentleman from doing me the favor I ask. Rather do me the favor of coming in with him, and thus you will evince that, although you are without as brown as the chestnut, you are as white as that nut within. Do you know,' continued he, 'that I have a secret which will change your color from black to white?' The eunuch began to laugh on hearing this, and asked Bedreddin Hassan what this secret was. 'I will tell you,' replied the pastry-cook; and immediately he recited some verses in praise of black eunuchs. The

[173]

eunuch was delighted with these verses, and no longer resisted the entreaties of Bedreddin Hassan. He suffered Agib to go into the pastry-cook's shop, whither he also accompanied him.

"Bedreddin Hassan was extremely pleased at having obtained his request; and, returning to his work, he said, 'I was making some cheese-cakes; you must, if you please, eat some, for I feel sure you will find them excellent.' Saying this, he drew a cheese-cake out of the oven, and, having strewed on it some grains of pomegranate and sugar, he served it to Agib, who found it delicious. The eunuch, to whom Bedreddin Hassan presented one likewise, was of the same opinion.

"Whilst they were both eating, Bedreddin Hassan examined Agib with the greatest attention; and, reflecting that perhaps the charming wife from whom he had been so soon and cruelly separated might have brought him such a son, he could not suppress some tears. He was preparing to question the little Agib on the reason of his journey to Damascus, but had not time to satisfy his curiosity, for the eunuch took him away as soon as he had done eating. Bedreddin Hassan was not satisfied with following him with his eyes only, but, immediately shutting up his shop, he went out and overtook them by the time they had reached the gate of the city.

"The eunuch, perceiving that he followed them, said to him, angrily: 'Importunate man! What do you want?' 'My good friend,' replied Bedreddin Hassan, 'do not be displeased; I have a little business just beyond the city which I have thought of, and I must go and give orders concerning it.' This answer did not satisfy the eunuch, who turned to Agib and said: 'See what you have brought on me. You would go into this man's shop, but indeed I was a fool to suffer it.' 'Perhaps,' said Agib, 'he may really have business beyond the city, and the road is free to all.' They then continued walking, without looking behind them, till they had reached the tents of the grand vizier; they then looked back and saw that Bedreddin Hassan still followed them closely. Agib, perceiving that the pastry-cook was within a few paces of him, feared that the vizier his grandfather would learn that he had been in a pastry-cook's shop to eat. Urged by this fear, he took up a large stone that lay at his feet and threw it at Bedreddin Hassan. It struck him in the middle of his forehead and covered him with blood. Agib then ran away as fast as he could into the tent of the eunuch.

"Bedreddin Hassan returned to the city, stanching the blood from his wound. 'I was wrong,' said he to himself, 'to leave my house and occasion so much trouble to the child, for he only treated me thus because he no doubt supposed that I had some bad design against him.' When he reached home he had his wound dressed, and consoled himself with the reflection that there were many people in this world more unfortunate than himself.

"Bedreddin Hassan continued to exercise the business of a pastry-cook at Damascus, and his uncle, Schemseddin Mohammed, left the city three days after his arrival. The vizier took the road to Emaus, and went from thence to Hamah, and thence to Aleppo, where he rested two days. From Aleppo he crossed the Euphrates, entered Mesopotamia, and after traversing Mardin, Moussoul, Sengira, Diarbekir, and several other towns, he arrived at last at Balsora, where he directly requested an audience of the sultan. That prince, who had been informed of the rank of Schemseddin Mohammed, immediately granted his request. He received him very favorably, and asked him the cause of his journey to Balsora. 'O King!' replied the vizier Schemseddin Mohammed, 'I am come to learn tidings of the son of Noureddin Ali, my brother, who had the honor of serving your Majesty.' 'It is a long time since Noureddin Ali died,' said the sultan; 'and as for his son, all that I can tell you is that, about two months after the death of his father, he suddenly disappeared, and no one has seen him since, notwithstanding the pains I have taken to discover him. But his mother, who was the daughter of one of my viziers, is still living.' Schemseddin Mohammed requested permission to see this lady, and to conduct her into Egypt. The sultan consented, and Schemseddin Mohammed inquired for the abode of this lady, and went to her immediately, accompanied by his daughter and her son.

ARABIAN NIGHTS

"The widow of Noureddin Ali lived in the same house which had been occupied by her deceased husband. On entering it he kissed the door, and a marble tablet on which the name of his brother was written in letters of gold. He desired to speak to his sister-in-law, whose servants informed him that she was in a small edifice built in the shape of a dome, which they showed him in the middle of a spacious court. This affectionate mother was accustomed to pass the greater part of the day and night in this building, which she had erected to represent the tomb of Bedreddin Hassan, whom she supposed to be dead, after she had long and vainly expected his return. She was then weeping for the loss of this dear son, and Schemseddin Mohammed found her plunged in the deepest affliction.

"He saluted her on entering, and informed her that he had the honor of being her brother-in-law; and also told her the reason which had caused him to leave Cairo and travel to Balsora. After he had made his sister-in-law acquainted with all that had happened at Cairo on the night of his daughter's nuptials, and the surprise which the discovery of the packet that was found sewn up in Bedreddin Hassan's turban had occasioned, he presented Agib and the Queen of Beauty to her.

"When the widow of Noureddin Ali understood that the dear son she so much regretted might still be alive she rose up and tenderly embraced the Queen of Beauty and little Agib, in whom she recognized the features of Bedreddin Hassan. She kissed the child again and again, and he received her embraces with every demonstration of joy. 'It is time, madam,' said Schemseddin Mohammed, 'to forget your sorrows and to dry your tears, for you must now arrange your affairs and go with us into Egypt. The Sultan of Balsora has given me permission to take you with me, and I trust you will not refuse to come. I hope we shall have the good fortune to meet with my nephew, your son.'

"The widow of Noureddin Ali listened to this proposal with great pleasure, and instantly began to make preparations for departure. Schemseddin Mohammed requested another audience of the sultan, to take leave of that monarch, who sent him

ARABIAN NIGHTS

back laden with honors. Intrusted with a present for the Sultan of Egypt, he left Balsora and again took the road to Damascus.

"As soon as they arrived in the vicinity of that city, Schemseddin Mohammed ordered his servants to pitch the tents just without the gate by which they were to enter. He told his people he should remain there three days, that he might rest himself, and also to purchase whatever things were most curious and worthy of being presented to the Sultan of Egypt. While he himself was occupied in selecting the most beautiful stuffs which the principal merchants brought to him, Agib entreated the black eunuch to go and walk with him in the city, declaring that he was desirous of seeing whatever he had not had time to visit when he was there before, and that he was also very anxious to get some news of the pastry-cook whom he had wounded with the stone. The eunuch agreed to the proposal, and walked into the city with him, having first obtained leave of Agib's mother, the Queen of Beauty.

"They entered Damascus, walked through the great squares, saw the public buildings and the covered market where the richest merchandise was sold. They then passed by the shop of Bedreddin Hassan, whom they found still engaged in making cheese-cakes. 'Hail to you!' said Agib to him. 'Look at me. Do you remember to have seen me before?' At these words Bedreddin Hassan cast his eyes upon the boy, and instantly recognized him. At the very same moment—oh, surprising effect of paternal love!—he felt the same emotion he had experienced at his first meeting with Agib. He was greatly troubled, and instead of answering him he stood for some time unable to speak a single word. At length he said: 'Do me the favor, my young lord, once more to come into my shop and eat a cheese-cake. I beg you will pardon me for the displeasure I caused you by following you out of the city. It was a sort of charm which drew me after you and which I could neither resist nor explain to myself.'

"Surprised at this speech of Bedreddin Hassan's, Agib replied: 'The friendship you profess toward me is carried to excess, and

ARABIAN NIGHTS

I will not come into your house unless you promise faithfully
not to follow me when I go away. If you pledge your word
and keep it, I will come again to-morrow.' 'My little master,'
answered Bedreddin Hassan, 'I will do anything you desire me.'
Agib and the eunuch then entered his shop.

"Bedreddin Hassan immediately set before them some cheese-
cakes. 'Come,' said Agib, 'sit down by me and eat with us.'
When Bedreddin Hassan was seated he was going to embrace
Agib, to express to him the joy he experienced at being near him;
but Agib pushed him back, saying: 'Be quiet; your friendship is
too tender. Be content with looking at and conversing with me.'
Bedreddin Hassan obeyed, and began to sing a song which he
composed at the moment in praise of Agib. He did not eat, but
was attentive to serve his guests. When they had finished eating
he took a vase of sherbet and prepared a large china bowlful, in
which he put some snow, and, presenting the bowl to little Agib,
'Take it,' cried he; 'it is rose sherbet, the most delicious that
this city can produce; you never tasted any so good.' Agib
drank some with great pleasure; Bedreddin Hassan then took
the bowl and offered it to the eunuch, who drained it to the last
drop.

"When Agib and the eunuch were satisfied they thanked the
pastry-cook for the good entertainment they had received, and
returned as quickly as they could, as it was late. They arrived
at the encampment of Schemseddin Mohammed, and went first
to the tent which the ladies occupied. The grandmother of Agib
was rejoiced to see him again; and as she had always her son
Bedreddin Hassan in her mind, she could not refrain from tears
on embracing the boy. 'Ah, my child,' cried she, 'my happiness
would be complete if I could have the pleasure of embracing
your father Bedreddin Hassan as I embrace you.' She was
just going to supper. She made him sit next her and asked
him many questions about his walk; then, saying that he
must be hungry, she helped him to a piece of cheese-cake
of her own making; and it was excellent, for she could make
these cakes better than any pastry-cook. She gave some to the

eunuch also; but they had both eaten so much that they could hardly touch it.

"Agib had scarcely begun to eat the cheese-cake before him when, pretending that it did not suit his palate, he put it back on his plate; and Schaban, for this was the name of the eunuch, did the same. Vexed at seeing her grandson so indifferent about her cheese-cake, the widow of Noureddin Ali said: 'What, my son! do you scorn the work of my hands in this way? Let me tell you that no one in the world can make such good cheese-cakes excepting your father Bedreddin Hassan, to whom I myself taught the curious art of making them.' 'Ah, my good grandmother,' cried Agib, 'if you cannot make them better than this, there is a pastry-cook in the city who surpasses you in skill; we have just been eating one in his shop which is a great deal better than this.'

"At these words the grandmother cast an angry look at the eunuch. 'How! Schaban,' said she, 'is my grandson intrusted to your care that you should take him to eat at a pastry-cook's like a beggar's child?' 'O lady,' replied the eunuch, 'it is true that we have been talking to a pastry-cook, but we did not eat at his house.' 'Indeed,' interrupted Agib, 'we went into his shop and ate a cheese-cake.' The lady, more angry than ever at the eunuch's deceit, left the table and ran to the tent of Schemseddin Mohammed, whom she informed of this misdemeanor of the eunuch in terms likely to exasperate the vizier against the delinquent.

"Schemseddin Mohammed, who was naturally of a warm temper, flew into a violent passion. He immediately repaired to the tent of his sister-in-law, and said to the eunuch, 'Wretch! hast thou the temerity to abuse the confidence I have placed in thee?' Schaban, although sufficiently convicted by the testimony of Agib, thought proper still to deny the fact. But the child maintained the contrary. 'Now, thou wicked slave,' cried the vizier, turning to the eunuch, 'after this wilt thou deny that you both went into a pastry-shop and ate there?' Schaban had the effrontery to swear that it was not true. 'Thou art a liar!'

13

said the vizier. 'I believe my grandson rather than thee. Nevertheless, if thou canst eat the whole of the cheese-cake which is on this table I shall be persuaded that thou speakest the truth.'

"Though he was full to the very throat, Schaban submitted to this trial and took a bit of the cheese-cake; but he was obliged to take it out of his mouth again, for his stomach turned against it. He, however, persisted in his falsehood. Irritated by the repeated falsities of the eunuch, and fully convinced that he was guilty, the vizier had him laid on the ground and ordered him to receive the bastinado. The unhappy wretch uttered loud cries on suffering this punishment, and confessed his fault. 'It is true,' cried he, 'that we did eat a cheese-cake at a pastry-shop; and it was an hundred times better than that which is on this table.'

"The widow of Noureddin Ali thought it was through spite to her and to mortify her that Schaban praised the pastry-cook's cheese-cake; therefore, addressing herself to him, she said: 'I cannot believe that the cheese-cakes of this pastry-cook are more excellent than mine. I will be satisfied on this point. Thou knowest where the man lives; go to him and bring me back a cheese-cake directly.' She then ordered some money to be given to the eunuch that he might buy the cheese-cake, and he set off. When he came to Bedreddin Hassan's shop he said: 'Here is some money for you. Give me one of your cheese-cakes; one of our ladies wishes to taste them.' There happened to be some hot cakes on the table, just out of the oven. Bedreddin Hassan chose the best, and, giving it to the eunuch, said, 'Take this; I warrant it to be excellent, and I can assure you that no one in the world can make such cheese-cakes excepting my mother, who perhaps is still living.'

"Schaban returned quickly to the tent with his cheese-cake. He placed it before the widow of Noureddin Ali, who was impatiently expecting it. She broke off a piece to taste it; but it had scarcely touched her lips when she uttered a loud cry and fainted away. Schemseddin Mohammed, who was present, was very much surprised at this accident, and did all in his power to restore her. As soon as she was recovered she exclaimed, 'By Allah! it must have been my son, my dear son Bedreddin Hassan, who made this cake.'

"When the vizier Schemseddin Mohammed heard his sister-in-law say that it was Bedreddin Hassan who had made the cheese-cake, he felt inexpressible joy; but then reflecting that this joy was altogether premature, he said to her: 'But, madam, what makes you think this? Cannot there be a pastry-cook in the world who is able to make cheese-cakes as well as your son?' 'I allow,' replied she, 'that there may be pastry-cooks capable of making them as good, but as I make them in a very peculiar manner, and as no one except my son possesses this secret, it must certainly have been he who made this. Let us rejoice, my dear brother,' added she, in a transport of joy, 'we have at length found him whom we have been so long and so anxiously seeking.' 'Madam,' said the vizier, 'I entreat you to moderate your impatience; we shall soon know what to think of this adventure. We have only to desire the pastry-cook to come here; if he be Bedreddin Hassan, you and my daughter will recollect him. But you must conceal yourselves, and see him without his seeing you, for I do not wish the discovery to take place at Damascus.'

"He then left the ladies in their tent and retired to his own. Then he summoned fifty of his people before him, and said to them: 'Take each of you a stick, and follow Schaban, who will conduct you to a pastry-cook's in the city. When you get there, break everything you find in his shop. If he inquires why you commit such an outrage, only ask if it was not he who made the cheese-cake that was bought of him by a eunuch; if he acknowledge the fact, seize him, bind him securely, and bring him to me, but take care that you do not strike or hurt him. Go, and lose no time.'

"The vizier was quickly obeyed; his people, armed with sticks and led by the black eunuch, repaired to the house of Bedreddin Hassan, where they broke in pieces the plates, the boilers, the saucepans, the tables, and all other furniture and utensils they could discover, so that Bedreddin Hassan's shop was deluged with sherbet, cream, and confectionery. At this sight Bedreddin Hassan was much astonished, and said to them in a pitiful tone: 'My good people, why do you treat me thus? What have I done?' 'Was it you,' asked they in return, 'who made the cheese-cake which you sold the eunuch who is with us?' 'Yes,' said Bedreddin Hassan, 'I made it myself. What fault have you to find with it? I defy any one to make a better!' Instead of answering him, they seized his person, and, having torn off the linen of his turban, they made use of it to tie his hands behind him; then they dragged him by force out of his shop.

"The populace, who had gathered round, were touched with compassion for Bedreddin Hassan. They took his part, and were inclined to oppose the designs of the people of Schemseddin Mohammed; but at this moment some officers of the governor of the city arrived, and, dispersing the mob, favored the carrying off of Bedreddin Hassan; for Schemseddin Mohammed had been to the governor of Damascus to acquaint him with the order he had given, and to request his assistance and guard; and this governor, who ruled over Syria in the name of the Sultan of Egypt, did not dare to refuse anything to the vizier of his master. Bedreddin Hassan was therefore dragged away.

"On his arrival, the vizier inquired for the pastry-cook. When he was brought before him, poor Bedreddin Hassan said, with tears in his eyes, 'Oh, my lord, my lord, do me the favor to tell me in what I have offended you?' 'How, wretch!' exclaimed the vizier, 'was it not thou who madest the cheese-cake thou sentest me?' 'I confess that it was,' replied Bedreddin Hassan, 'but what crime have I committed by doing so?' 'I will punish thee as thou deservest,' resumed Schemseddin Mohammed, 'and thou shalt pay with thy life for having made so bad a cake.' 'Woe is me!' cried Bedreddin Hassan; 'what do I hear? Is it a crime worthy of death to have made a bad cheese-cake?' 'Yes,' replied the vizier, 'and expect not from me any other treatment.'

"As Schemseddin Mohammed had resolved to set off that same night, he ordered the tents to be struck and all preparations to be made for the commencement of the journey. As

ARABIAN NIGHTS

for Bedreddin Hassan, the vizier gave instructions that he might be put in a well-fastened case, and carried on a camel. As soon as everything was in readiness the vizier and the people in his suite began their march. They traveled the whole of that night and the following day without resting; at the approach of night they stopped. They then took Bedreddin Hassan out of his case to give him some food; but they were careful to keep him at a distance from his mother and his wife, and during the twenty days occupied by their journey they treated him in the same manner.

"On reaching Cairo they encamped without the city walls, by order of the vizier, who desired his servants to bring Bedreddin Hassan before him. When the prisoner was come, Schemseddin Mohammed said to a carpenter whom he had sent for on purpose, 'Go and get some wood and cut me a large stake immediately.' 'Oh, my lord,' cried Bedreddin Hassan, 'what are you going to do with this stake?' 'To fasten you to it,' replied the vizier, 'and then have you carried through all the quarters of the city that every one may behold in thee a vile pastry-cook who makes cheese-cakes without putting pepper in them.' At these words Bedreddin Hassan exclaimed in so comic a manner that Schemseddin Mohammed had difficulty to refrain from laughter: 'Oh, Allah! is it then for not having put pepper in a cheese-cake that I am condemned to suffer a cruel and ignominious death? What!' said Bedreddin Hassan, 'was everything in my house to be broken and destroyed, myself imprisoned in a box, and at last a stake prepared for my execution—was all this done only because I did not put pepper in a cheese-cake? Powers of Heaven! who ever heard of such a thing?'

"As the night was now far advanced, Schemseddin Mohammed ordered Bedreddin Hassan to be put back into his case, and said to him, 'Remain there till to-morrow; the day shall not pass before I order thee to be put to death.' The case was taken away and placed on the camel that had brought it from Damascus; all the other camels were reladen, and the vizier, mounting his horse, ordered that the camel which carried his nephew should go before him; thus he entered the city, followed by all his equipage. After passing through several streets, he arrived at his house, where the case was deposited with strict charge not to open it till he should think proper.

"Whilst they were unloading the other camels, Schemseddin Mohammed took aside the mother of Bedreddin Hassan and his daughter, and, addressing the latter, said: 'God be praised, my dear daughter, that we have so happily met with your cousin and husband. I dare say you recollect the state in which your chamber was on the night of your nuptials? Go and have everything placed as it was then. If by chance you do not remember it, I can supply the defect in your memory by the description I wrote at the time. On my part, I will go and give orders for the rest.'

"The Queen of Beauty went joyfully to execute the commands of her father, who began to place all the things in the hall in the same position as when Bedreddin Hassan was there with the hump-backed groom of the Sultan of Egypt. As he read the writing, his servants put each piece of furniture in its place. The throne was not forgotten, nor the lighted torches. When everything was prepared in the hall, the vizier entered the chamber of his daughter, where he placed the clothes of Bedreddin Hassan, together with the purse of sequins. Then he said to the Queen of Beauty: 'Undress yourself, my daughter, and go to bed; and when Bedreddin Hassan comes into this chamber begin to complain of his long absence, and tell him that you were much surprised, when you awoke, not to find him by your side. Press him to return to bed, and to-morrow morning you will entertain your mother-in-law and me with the account of what he says.' At these words, he went out of his daughter's chamber and left her.

"Schemseddin Mohammed commanded all the servants, excepting only two or three, to go out of the hall, and to these he gave directions to take Bedreddin Hassan out of the case, to put him on a shirt and drawers, and thereupon to bring him into the hall, where they were to leave him alone and shut the door.

"MY LORD, WHAT ARE YOU DOING AT THE DOOR?"

ARABIAN NIGHTS

In spite of his unhappy condition, Bedreddin Hassan had fallen so soundly asleep that the servants of the vizier took him out of the case and put on his shirt and drawers without waking him; and then they carried him so quickly into the hall that they did not give him time to recollect himself. When he found himself alone in the hall, he looked round; and the things he saw reminding him of his marriage, he perceived with astonishment, on a closer inspection, that this was the same hall in which he had seen the humpbacked groom. His surprise increased when, drawing near to the door of a chamber which he found open, he saw his clothes in the same spot where he remembered to have placed them on the night of his nuptials. 'Good heavens!' said he, rubbing his eyes, 'am I asleep or awake?'

"The Queen of Beauty, who watched him, was much amused at his astonishment. She drew aside the curtain of the bed, and, advancing her head, said in a tender voice: 'My lord, what are you doing at the door? Come and lie down again. You have been absent a long time; I was much surprised, when I awoke, not to find you by my side.' Bedreddin Hassan's countenance changed when he perceived that the lady who spoke to him was the same charming person to whom he had been married years ago. He went into the chamber; but instead of going to bed, as his mind was full of the thoughts of what had passed during the last ten years, and he could not persuade himself that so many events had taken place in only one night, he approached the chair where his clothes and purse of sequins were. These he examined with great attention, and then exclaimed, 'By the great living God! these are things which I cannot understand.' The lady, who was diverted at his embarrassment, said to him: 'Once more, my dear lord, let me beg you to come to bed. What troubles you thus?' At these words he advanced toward the Queen of Beauty and said, 'I entreat you, madam, to acquaint me if it is long since I left you.' 'The question surprises me,' replied she. 'Did you not just now rise from the bed? Your mind must be strangely disturbed.' 'Madam,' resumed Bedreddin Hassan, 'my spirits certainly are not very composed. I remember to have been with

you, it is true; but I also remember to have lived ten years at
Damascus. If I have really slept with you this night, I cannot
have been absent so long.' 'Yes, my lord,' replied the Queen of
Beauty, 'you have no doubt dreamed that you were at Damascus.'
'What a ridiculous thing is this!' cried Bedreddin Hassan, bursting into a laugh; 'I assure you, madam, that this dream will
appear to you very laughable. I found myself at the gates of
Damascus in my shirt and drawers, just as I am at this moment;
I entered the city amidst the shouts and hisses of the populace,
who followed to insult me; I took refuge with a pastry-cook
who adopted me, taught me his business, and left me all his
property when he died. After his death I kept his shop. In
short, madam, a great number of adventures befell me which
would be too tedious to relate; all I can say is that I did well
to awake, for they were going to nail me to a stake.' 'And
why,' said the Queen of Beauty, pretending surprise, 'why
were you to suffer so cruelly? You must have committed some
heinous crime.' 'No indeed,' replied Bedreddin Hassan; 'it
was for the most ridiculous thing you can conceive. My only
crime was that I had sold a cheese-cake in which I had not put
any pepper.' 'I must confess,' said the lady, laughing heartily,
'that you were treated very unjustly.' 'O madam,' resumed he,
'this was not all; on account of this cursed cheese-cake, in which I
was accused of not having put any pepper, they broke and
destroyed everything in my shop; they bound me with cords
and shut me up in a case, where I was so closely confined that I
feel as if I were still in it. At last they sent for a carpenter
and ordered him to prepare a stake to crucify me. But God
be praised that all this is only a dream.'

"Bedreddin Hassan did not pass the night very quietly; he
awoke from time to time and asked himself whether he was
dreaming or awake. He doubted his good fortune, and, wishing
to ascertain the truth, he drew the curtains and cast his eyes
round the room. 'I am not deceived,' said he; 'this is the same
chamber into which I came instead of the hunchback, and where
I saw the beautiful lady who was destined for him.' Daylight,

ARABIAN NIGHTS

which now began to appear, had not removed his uneasiness when the vizier Schemseddin Mohammed, his uncle, knocked at the door and entered to wish him good day. Bedreddin Hassan was extremely surprised to see a man with whom he was so well acquainted appear immediately after; but the visitor no longer bore the appearance of the terrible judge who had pronounced the decree of his death. 'Ah!' cried he, 'it is you who have treated me so cruelly and condemned me to a death the thoughts of which still fill me with horror, for having made a cheese-cake without putting pepper in it!' The vizier laughed; and, to dispel Bedreddin Hassan's fears, related how, by the interference of a genie (for the account he had received from the hunchback made him suspect the truth), the young man had been conveyed to his house, and had married his daughter instead of the groom belonging to the sultan. He then acquainted him that it was by means of the packet written by Noureddin Ali that he had discovered him to be his nephew; and at last told him how, in consequence of this discovery, he had left Cairo and had gone to Balsora in search of him. 'My dear nephew,' added he, embracing Bedreddin Hassan with the greatest tenderness, 'I beg your pardon for all I have made you suffer since I have discovered you. I wished to bring you here before I acquainted you with your good fortune, which you must find so much the more pleasant as it has cost you so much pain. Console yourself for all your afflictions with the joy you must experience at being again with those who are most dear to you. Whilst you dress yourself I will summon your mother, who is all impatience to embrace you; and I will bring you your son, whom you saw at Damascus, and toward whom you felt so much affection without knowing him.'

"No words can give any idea of the joy of Bedreddin Hassan when he saw his mother and his son Agib. These three persons embraced one another with all the transports which nature and the tenderest affection can inspire.

"Whilst these things were passing in the house of Schemseddin the vizier himself had gone to the palace to give the sultan an account of the success of his journey. The sultan was so delighted at the account of this wonderful history, that he ordered it to be written and carefully preserved among the archives of his kingdom.

"But, my lord," added Sheherazade, "however entertaining the history I have related may have been, I know another which is far more wonderful; if your Majesty will but hear it to-morrow night, I am sure you will think so, too." Shahriar arose without making any reply, for he was doubtful what he should do. "This good sultana," said he to himself, "relates very long stories; and when she has once begun one, there is no possibility of refusing to hear the whole of it. I do not know whether I ought not to order her death to-day; yet no, I will not do anything precipitately. The story she promises me is, perhaps, the most amusing of any I have yet heard, and I must not deprive myself of the pleasure of hearing it. After she has finished it I will give orders for her execution."

Dinarzade did not fail on the following morning to wake the sultana before daybreak, according to her usual custom. And Sheherazade, having requested permission of Shahriar to relate the history she had promised him, began as follows:

THE HISTORY OF THE LITTLE HUNCHBACK

"IN the city of Casgar, which is situated near the confines of Great Tartary, there formerly lived a tailor who had the good fortune to possess a very beautiful wife, between whom and himself there existed the strongest mutual affection. One day, while this tailor was at work in his shop, a little hunchbacked fellow sat down at the door and began playing on a timbrel, and singing to the sound of this instrument. The tailor was much pleased with his performance and resolved to take him home and introduce him to his wife, that the hunchback might amuse them both in the evening with his pleasant and humorous songs. He proposed this to the hunchback, who readily accepted the invitation; and the tailor shut up his shop and took his guest home with him.

"So soon as they reached the tailor's house his wife put before them a very nice dish of fish which she had been dressing. Then all three sat down; but in eating his portion the little hunchback had the misfortune to swallow a large fish-bone, which stuck fast in his throat and almost instantly killed him before the tailor or his wife could do anything to assist him. They were both greatly alarmed at this accident; for, as the mishap had happened in their house, they had great reason to fear it might come to the knowledge of some of the officers of justice, who would punish them as murderers. The husband, therefore, devised an expedient to get rid of the dead body.

"He recollected that a Jewish physician lived in his neighborhood; and he formed a plan which he put in execution. He and his wife took up the body and carried it to the physician's house. They knocked at the door, at the bottom of a steep and narrow flight of stairs leading to the physician's apartment. A maidservant immediately came down without even staying for a light, and asked them what they wanted. 'Have the kindness to tell your master,' said the tailor, 'that we have brought him a patient who is very ill and for whom we request his advice.' Then he held out a piece of money in his hand, saying, 'Give him this in advance that he may be assured we do not intend he should give his labor for nothing.' While the servant went back to inform her master, the Jewish physician, of this good news, the tailor and his wife quickly carried the body of the little hunchback up-stairs, placed him close to the door, and returned home as fast as possible.

"In the mean time the servant went and told the physician that a man and a woman were waiting for him at the door, and that they had brought a sick person with them, whom they requested him to see. She then gave him the money she had received from the tailor. Pleased at the thought of being paid beforehand, the physician concluded this must be a most excellent patient, and one who ought not to be neglected. 'Bring a light directly,' cried he to the girl, 'and follow me.' So saying, he ran toward the staircase in a hurry, without even waiting for the light, and, stumbling against the little hunchback, he gave him such a blow with his foot as sent him from the top of the stairs to the bottom. He called out to the servant, bidding her

THE HUNCHBACK SINGS FOR THE TAILOR'S WIFE

come quickly with the light. She at last appeared, and they went down-stairs. When the physician found that it was a dead man who had rolled down-stairs, he was so alarmed at the sight that he invoked all the prophets of the law to his assistance. 'Wretch that I am!' exclaimed he, 'why did I not wait for the light? I have completely killed the sick man whom they brought to me. I am the cause of his death! I am a lost man! Alas! they will come and drag me hence as a murderer!'

"He immediately took up the body and carried it into the apartment of his wife, who almost fainted when she saw him come in with his fatal load. 'Alas!' she cried, 'we are quite ruined if we cannot find some means of getting rid of this dead man before to-morrow morning. We shall certainly be slain if we keep him till day breaks. What a misfortune! How came you to kill this man?' 'Never mind how it happened,' said the Jew; 'our only business at present is to remedy this dreadful calamity.'

"The physician and his wife then consulted together to devise means to rid themselves of the body during the night. At last his wife said: 'A thought occurs to me. Let us take the corpse up to the terrace of our house and lower it down the chimney into the warehouse of our neighbor the Mussulman.'

"This Mussulman was one of the sultan's purveyors; and it was his office to furnish oil, butter, and other articles of a similar kind for the sultan's household.

"The Jewish physician approved of his wife's plan. They took the little hunchback and carried him to the roof of the house; and, after fastening a cord under his arms, they let him gently down the chimney into the purveyor's apartment. They managed this so cleverly that he remained standing on his feet against the wall, exactly as if he were alive. As soon as they found they had landed the hunchback, they drew up the cords and left him standing in the chimney-corner. They then retired to their chamber. Presently the sultan's purveyor came home. He had just returned from a wedding-feast, and he had a lantern in his hand. He was very much surprised when he saw by the

14 [195]

light of his lantern a man standing up in the chimney; but, as he was naturally brave, and thought the intruder was a thief, he seized a large stick, with which he directly ran at the little hunchback. 'Oh, oh!' he cried, 'I thought it was the rats and mice that ate my butter and tallow, and I find you come down the chimney and rob me. I do not think you will ever wish to visit me again.' Then he attacked the hunchback and gave him many hard blows. The body at last fell down with its face on the ground. The purveyor redoubled his blows; but at length, remarking that the person he struck was quite motionless, he stooped to examine his enemy more closely. When he perceived that the man was dead his rage gave place to fear. 'What have I done, unhappy man that I am!' he exclaimed. 'Alas, I have carried my vengeance too far! May Allah have pity upon me, or my life is gone!' Thus he stood, pale and confounded. He imagined he already saw the officers of justice coming to conduct him to his punishment, and he knew not what to do.

"While the Sultan of Casgar's purveyor was beating the little hunchback he did not perceive his hump; the instant he noticed it he poured out a hundred imprecations on it. 'Oh, you rascal of a hunchback! You dog of deformity! Would to Heaven you had robbed me of all my fat and grease before I had found you here!' Hereupon he took the body of the hunchback upon his shoulders, went out of his chamber and walked into the street, where he set it upright against a shop; and then he made the best of his way back to his house without once looking behind him.

"A little before daybreak, a Christian merchant, who was very rich and who furnished the palace of the sultan with most things which were wanted there, after passing the night in revelry and pleasure, had just come from home on his way to a bath. He happened to stop at the corner of the street close to the shop against which the sultan's purveyor had placed the hunchback's body. He pushed against the corpse, which at the very first touch fell directly against the merchant's back. The latter fancied himself attacked by a robber, and therefore knocked the hunchback down with a blow of his fist on the head. He repeated his blows and began calling out, 'Thief! thief!'

"A guard stationed in that quarter of the city came directly on hearing his cries, and, seeing a Christian beating a Mussulman, asked him how he dared ill-treat a Mussulman in that manner. 'He wanted to rob me,' answered the merchant, 'and he came up behind me to seize me by the throat.' 'You have revenged yourself,' replied the guard, taking hold of the merchant's arm and pulling him away; 'therefore let him go.' As he said this he held out his hand to the hunchback to assist him in getting up; but, observing that he was dead, he cried, 'Is it thus that a Christian has the impudence to assassinate a Mussulman?' Hereupon he laid hold of the merchant and carried him before the magistrate, who sent him to prison till the judge had risen and was ready to examine the accused. In the mean time the merchant became completely sober, and the more he reflected upon his adventure the less could he understand how a single blow with the fist could have taken away the life of a man.

"Upon the report of the guard, and after examining the body which they had brought with them, the judge interrogated the merchant, who could not deny the crime imputed to him, although he in fact was not guilty of it. As the little hunchback was one of the royal jesters, the judge determined to put the Christian to death. The judge accordingly ordered a gibbet to be erected, and then sent criers through the city to make known that a Christian was going to be hanged for having killed a Mussulman.

"At last they took the merchant out of prison and brought him on foot to the gallows. The executioner had fastened the cord round the merchant's neck, and was just going to draw him up into the air when the sultan's purveyor forced his way through the crowd and, rushing straight toward the executioner, called out: 'Stop, stop! It is not he who has committed the murder, but I.' The judge immediately interrogated the purveyor, who gave him a minute account of the manner in which he had killed the hunchback; and he concluded by saying that he had carried the body to the place where the merchant had found it. 'You are going,' added he, 'to slay an innocent person, for he cannot have killed a man who was not alive. It is enough for me that I have slain a Mussulman; I will not further burden my conscience with the murder of a Christian, an innocent man.'

"When the purveyor of the Sultan of Casgar thus publicly accused himself of having killed the hunchback, the judge could not do otherwise than immediately release the merchant. 'Let the merchant go,' said he to the executioner, 'and hang in his stead this man, by whose own confession it is evident that he is the guilty person.' The executioner immediately unbound the merchant and put the rope round the neck of the purveyor; but at the very instant when he was going to put this new victim to death he heard the voice of the Jewish physician, who exclaimed that the execution must be stopped, that he himself might come and take his place at the foot of the gallows.

"'Sir,' said he, directly he appeared before the judge, 'this Mussulman whom you are about to deprive of life does not deserve to die; I alone am the unhappy culprit. About the middle of last night a man and woman, who are total strangers to me, came and knocked at my door. They brought with them a sick person; my servant went instantly to the door without waiting for a light, and, having first received a piece of money from one of the visitors, she came to me and said that they wished I would come down and look at the sick person. While she was bringing me this message they brought the patient to the top of the stairs, and went their way. I went out directly, without waiting till my servant had lighted a candle, and, falling over the sick man in the dark, I gave him an unintentional kick, and he fell from the top of the staircase to the bottom. I then discovered that he was dead. He was a Mussulman, the very same little hunchback whose murderer you now wish to punish. My wife and myself took the body and carried it to the roof of our house, whence we let it down into the warehouse of our neighbor, the purveyor, whose life you are now going to take away most unjustly. I alone am the perpetrator of the murder, and, although it was unintentional, I am resolved to expiate my crime rather than burden my conscience with the death of two Mussulmans by suffering you to take away the life of the sultan's purveyor. Therefore dismiss him and let me take his place.'

"Convinced that the Jewish physician was the true murderer, the judge now ordered the executioner to seize him and set the purveyor at liberty. The cord was placed round the neck of the physician and in another moment he would have been a dead man, when the voice of the tailor was heard entreating the executioner to stop; and presently the tailor pushed his way to the judge, to whom he said: 'You have very nearly caused the death of three innocent persons; but if you will have the patience to listen to me, you shall hear who was the real murderer of the hunchback. If his death is to be expiated by that of another person, I am the person who ought to die.

"'As I was at work in my shop yesterday evening, a little before dark, this little hunchback came to my door half tipsy, and sat down. He immediately began to sing, and I proposed to him to come and pass the evening at my house. He agreed, and I took him home with me. We sat down to table, and I gave him a little piece of fish. While he was eating it a bone stuck fast in his throat, and, in spite of everything that my wife and I could do to relieve him, he died in a very short time. We were grieved and alarmed at his death; and for fear of being called to account for it, we carried the body to the door of the Jewish physician. I knocked, and told the servant who let me in to go back to her master as soon as possible, and request him to come down to see a patient whom we had brought to him; and that he might not refuse, I charged her to put into his own hand a piece of money which I gave her. Directly she had gone I carried the hunchback to the top of the stairs, and, leaving him there, my wife and myself made the best of our way home. When the physician came out of his room to go down-stairs, he stumbled against the hunchback, and rolled him down from the top to the bottom; this made him suppose that he was the

ARABIAN NIGHTS

cause of the little man's death. But seeing how the case stands, let the physician go, and take my life instead of his.'

"The judge and all the spectators were filled with astonishment at the various strange events to which the death of the little hunchback had given rise. 'Let the physician then depart,' said the judge, 'and hang the tailor, since he confesses the crime.' When the executioner had set the physician at liberty, he put the cord round the tailor's neck.

"While all this was going on and the executioner was preparing to hang the tailor, the Sultan of Casgar, who never allowed any length of time to pass without seeing the hunchback, his jester, ordered that he should be summoned into his presence. One of the attendants replied: 'The little hunchback, whom your Majesty is so desirous to see, yesterday became tipsy and escaped from the palace, contrary to his usual custom, to wander about the city, and this morning he was found dead. A man was brought before the judge, accused of his murder. At the very moment they were going to hang the culprit another man came up to the gallows, and then a third. Each of these accused himself and declared the rest were innocent of the murder. All this took up some time, and the judge is at this moment in the very act of examining the third of these men, who says he is the real murderer.'

"On hearing this report, the Sultan of Casgar sent one of his attendants to the place of execution. 'Go,' he cried, 'with all possible speed, and command the judge to bring all the accused persons instantly before me, and order them also to bring the body of the poor little hunchback, whom I wish to see once more.' The officer instantly went, and arrived at the very moment when the executioner was beginning to draw the cord, in order to hang the tailor. The messenger called out to them as loud as he could to suspend the execution. As the hangman knew the officer, he desisted from hanging the tailor. The judge proceeded to the palace with the tailor, the Jew, the purveyor, and the Christian merchant, and ordered four of his people to carry the body of the hunchback.

ARABIAN NIGHTS

"As soon as they came into the presence of the sultan, the judge prostrated himself at the monarch's feet, and when he rose he gave a faithful and accurate detail of everything that related to the adventure of the hunchback. The sultan thought it so very singular that, addressing himself to those who were present, he said, 'Has any one of you ever heard a more wonderful adventure than this which has happened to my jester?'

"'Vouchsafe me a hearing,' cried the tailor; 'since your Majesty likes pleasant stories, I have one to tell which will not, I think, displease you.' 'I will listen to thee also,' replied the sultan; 'but do not entertain any hopes that I shall suffer thee to live if thy story be not more diverting than that of the hunchback.' Then the tailor boldly began his tale in the following words:

THE STORY TOLD BY THE TAILOR

"WO days since, a tradesman of this city did me the honor of inviting me to an entertainment which he purposed giving to his friends. I repaired to his house yesterday at an early hour, and found about twenty people assembled.

"We were waiting for the master of the house, who had gone out on some sudden business, when we saw him come, accompanied by a young stranger. This young man was handsomely dressed and of a good figure, but he was lame. We all rose, and, to do honor to the master of the house, we begged the young man to sit with us on the sofa. He was just going to sit down when, perceiving a certain barber among the company, he abruptly stepped back and turned as if to go. Surprised at this, the master of the house stopped him. 'Where are you going?' said he. 'I have brought you here that you may give me the honor of your company, and you scarcely enter before you want to depart!' 'In the name of Allah, sir,' replied the stranger, 'I entreat you not to detain me, but suffer me to go. I cannot without horror behold that abominable barber who is sitting yonder. Although he was born in a country where the complexion of the people is white, he looks like an Ethiopian; but his mind is of a dye deeper and more horrible than his visage.'

"We were all very much surprised at this speech, and began to form a very bad opinion of the barber, though we knew not what reason the young stranger had for speaking of him in such terms. The master of the house begged the stranger to let us know the cause of his hatred to the barber. 'My master,' said the young man, 'you must know that I am lame through this barber's fault, and he has, moreover, brought upon me the most cruel affair which is possible to be conceived. For this reason I have made a vow to quit any place where he may be. I will not even reside in any town where he lives; for this reason I left Bagdad, where he was, and undertook a long journey to come and settle in this city, where I flattered myself I should be secure of never beholding him again. However, contrary to my hopes, I find him here; this obliges me, my masters, to deny myself the honor of partaking of your feast. I will this day leave your city and go to hide myself, if I can, in some place where yonder barber can never again offend my sight.' With this speech he was going to leave us, but the master of the house still detained him, and entreated him to relate to us the cause of the aversion he had against the barber, who all this time had kept his eyes fixed on the ground, without speaking a word. The young man seated himself and, turning his back toward the barber, began his history in these words:

"My father, who lived in Bagdad, was entitled by his rank to aspire to the highest offices of state, but he preferred leading a quiet life to all the chances of gaining honor. I was his only child; and when he died I was old enough to manage the large possessions he had bequeathed me. I did not waste them in folly, but employed them in a way that procured me the esteem of every one.

ARABIAN NIGHTS

"I had not yet felt the tender emotions of love, and I carefully avoided the society of women. One day, as I was walking in a street I saw a great number of ladies coming toward me. To avoid them I turned into a little street that lay before me and sat down on a bench near a door. Opposite me, in a window, stood a number of very fine flowers, and my eyes were fixed on them when the window opened and a lady appeared whose beauty dazzled me. She cast her eyes on me; and as she watered the flowers she looked at me with a smile, which inspired me with as much love for her as I had hitherto felt aversion toward the rest of her sex. After she had tended her flowers she shut the window and left me in a state of perturbation which I cannot describe.

"I should have remained a considerable time in thought had not a noise I heard in the street brought me to my senses. I turned my head as I got up, and saw one of the first cadis of the city approaching, mounted on a mule, and accompanied by five or six of his people. He alighted at the door of the house where the young lady had opened the window; and from this I concluded he was her father.

"I returned home, agitated by a passion all the more violent from its being the first attack. I was seized with a raging fever, which caused great affliction in my household. My relations, who loved me, alarmed by my sudden illness, importuned me to tell them the cause, but I was very careful to keep my secret.

"My friends began to despair of my life, when an old lady who had been informed of my illness arrived. She looked at me with a great deal of attention, and at length discovered, I know not how, the cause of my disorder. She took my relations aside and begged them to leave her alone with me.

"When the room was cleared she seated herself near my pillow. 'My son,' said she, 'you have hitherto persisted in concealing the cause of your illness; nor do I require you to confess it now; I have sufficient experience to penetrate into this secret. You are lovesick. I can probably accomplish your cure, provided you will tell me the name of the happy lady who has been able to wound a heart so insensible as yours; for you have the reputation of a woman-hater.'

"In short, the good lady said so much to me that at length I described to her the street where I had seen the lady, and related all the circumstances of my adventure. 'If you succeed,' continued I, 'and procure me the happiness of seeing this enchanting beauty, and of expressing to her the love with which I burn, you may rely on my gratitude.' 'My son,' replied the old lady, 'I know the person you mention. You were quite right in supposing her to be the daughter of the principal cadi in this city. I am not surprised that you should love her. She is the most beautiful as well as the most amiable lady in Bagdad; but she is very haughty and difficult of access. Would to Heaven you loved any other lady! I should not have so many difficulties to surmount as I foresee here. I will, nevertheless, employ all my art, but I shall require time for my advances. Nevertheless, take courage, and place confidence in me.'

"The old lady left me, and the fear that she would not succeed took hold on me and increased my disease. My old friend came to visit me the following day, and I soon read in her countenance that she had no favorable intelligence to announce. She said: 'My son, I was not mistaken. You love one who delights in letting those burn with unrequited passion who suffer themselves to be charmed with her beauty. She listened to me with pleasure whilst I talked to her only of the pain she made you suffer; but as soon as I opened my mouth to persuade her to allow you an interview, she cast an angry look at me and said, "You are very insolent to attempt to make such a proposition; and I desire you will never see me more if you intend to hold such language as this!"

"'But let not that afflict you,' continued the old lady; 'I hope at last to accomplish my design.'

"Not to protract my narration," continued the young man, "I will only say that this good messenger made several fruitless attempts in my favor with the haughty enemy of my peace. The vexation I endured increased my disorder to such a degree that

ARABIAN NIGHTS

I was considered as a man at the point of death when the old lady came to give me new life.

"That no one might hear her, she whispered in my ear, 'Determine what present you will make me for the good news I bring you.' These words produced a wonderful effect upon me. I raised myself in my bed, and replied with transport: 'The gift shall be worthy of you. What have you to tell me?' 'My good friend,' resumed she, 'you will not die this time; and I shall soon have the pleasure of seeing you in perfect health. Yesterday I went to the lady with whom you are in love, and found her in very good humor. I at first put on a mournful countenance, uttered a number of sighs, and shed some tears. "My good mother," said the lady, "why are you in such affliction?" "Alas! my dear lady," replied I, "I have just come from the young gentleman of whom I spoke to you the other day. He is at the point of death, and all for love of you. Alas! you are very cruel." "I do not know," said she, "why you should accuse me of being the cause of his death. How can I be blamed for his illness?" "How!" replied I. "Did I not tell you that he seated himself before your window just as you opened it to water your flowers? He beheld this prodigy of beauty, these charms, which your mirror reflects every day. He has languished for you, and his disease has taken such a hold on him that he is now reduced to the pitiable state I have described to you. You may remember, lady," continued I, "how harshly you reproved me lately, when I was going to tell you of his illness, and propose to you a method of relieving him in his dangerous condition. I returned to him after I left you, and when he perceived that I did not bring a favorable report his malady at once increased. From that time he has been in the most imminent danger of death; and I do not know whether you could now save his life even if you were inclined to take pity on him."

"'The fear of your death startled her, and I saw her face change color. "Is what you say quite true?" said she, "and does his illness proceed only from his love for me?" "Ah, lady," replied I, "it is but too true. Would to Heaven it were false!"

"And do you really think," resumed she, "that the hope of seeing and speaking to me would diminish the peril in which he lies?" "Very probably," said I; "and if you desire me, I will try this remedy." "Then," replied she, sighing, "let him hope he may see me; but he must not expect my acceptance if he aspires to marry me, unless my father gives his consent." "O lady," said I, "you are very good. I will go and announce to him that he will have the delight of seeing and conversing with you." "I do not know," said she, "that I can fix a more convenient time for our interview than Friday next, during the midday prayer. Then let him come immediately to this house. I shall see him from my window, and will come down to let him in. We will converse together during the hour of prayer, and he will retire before my father returns.'"

"Whilst the good lady was talking I felt my disorder diminish, and by the time she had concluded her discourse I found myself quite recovered. 'Take this,' said I, giving her my purse full of gold; 'to you alone I owe my cure.'

"The lady left me, and presently I found myself sufficiently strong to get up.

"On the appointed morning the old lady came, whilst I was dressing, making choice of the handsomest garments my wardrobe contained. 'I do not ask you,' said she, 'how you feel; the business you are engaged in tells me what I am to think; but will not you bathe before you go to the principal cadi's?' 'That would consume too much time,' replied I. 'I shall content myself with sending for a barber to shave my head and beard.' I then ordered one of my slaves to seek a barber who was expert and expeditious in his business.

"The slave brought me this unlucky barber who is here present. After saluting me, he said, 'My master, to judge by your looks I should say you are unwell.' I replied that I was recovering from a very severe illness. 'May Allah preserve you from all kinds of evils,' continued he, 'and may His favor accompany you everywhere.' 'I hope He will grant this wish,' said I, 'and I am much obliged to you.' 'Now tell me what is your pleasure?'

asked the barber. 'I have brought my razors and my lancets. Do you wish me to shave or to bleed you?' 'Did I not tell you,' returned I, 'that I am recovering from an illness? I did not send for you to bleed me. Be quick and shave me, and do not lose time in talking, for I have an appointment precisely at noon.'

"The barber was very slow in spreading out his apparatus and preparing his razors. Instead of putting water into his basin, he drew out of his case a very neat astrolabe, went out of my room and walked with a sedate step into the middle of the court, to take the height of the sun. He returned as deliberately as he had gone out, and said, on entering the chamber: 'You will no doubt be glad to learn, sir, that this is the eighteenth day of the moon of Safar, in the year six hundred and fifty-three from the Hegira of our great Prophet from Mecca to Medina, and in the year seven thousand three hundred and twenty of the epoch of the great Iskander with the two horns; and that the conjunction of Mars and Mercury signifies that you cannot choose a better time to be shaved than the present day and the present hour. But on the other side, this conjunction carries with it a bad omen for you. It demonstrates to me that you will this day encounter a great danger; not, indeed, a risk of losing your life, but the peril of an inconvenience which will remain with you all your days. You ought to thank me for warning you to be careful of this misfortune; I should be sorry if it befell you.'

"I was sincerely vexed at having fallen into the hands of this chattering and ridiculous barber. How mortifying was this delay to a lover who was preparing for a tender meeting with his mistress! 'I care very little,' said I, angrily, 'for your advice or your predictions. You came here to shave me; therefore either perform your office or begone, that I may send for another barber.' 'My master,' replied he, in so unconcerned a tone that I could scarcely contain myself, 'what reason have you to be angry? Do not you know that all barbers are not like me, and that you would not find another like myself, even if you had him made expressly for you? You only asked for a barber, and in my person you see united the best barber of Bagdad,

"BE QUICK AND SHAVE ME, AND DO NOT LOSE TIME IN TALKING"

an experienced physician, a profound chemist, a never-failing astrologer, a finished grammarian, a perfect rhetorician, a subtle logician; a mathematician, thoroughly accomplished in geometry, arithmetic, astronomy, and in all the refinements of algebra; an historian, thoroughly versed in the history of all the kingdoms in the universe. Besides these sciences, I am well instructed in all the points of philosophy, and have my memory well stored with all our laws and all our traditions. I am, moreover, a poet, and an architect. There is nothing in nature concealed from me. Your late honored father, to whom I pay a tribute of tears every time I think of him, was fully convinced of my merit. My gratitude and friendship for him attach me to you, and urge me to take you under my protection and secure you from all misfortunes with which the planets may threaten you.'

"Notwithstanding my anger, I could not help laughing at this speech. 'When do you mean to have done, impertinent chatterer?' cried I, 'and when do you intend to begin shaving me?'

"'Indeed,' replied the barber, 'you do me an injury by calling me a chatterer, for you must know that I everywhere enjoy the honorable appellation of "Silent." I had six brothers whom you might with some reason have termed chatterers; and that you may be acquainted with them, I will tell you that the eldest was named Bacbouc, the second Bakbarah, the third Bakbac, the fourth Alcouz, the fifth Alnaschar, and the sixth Schacabac. These men were indeed most tiresome talkers; but I, who am the youngest of the family, am very grave and sparing of my words.'

"Think what a situation was mine! What could I do with so cruel a tormentor? 'Give him three pieces of gold,' said I to the slave who managed the expenses of my house, 'and send him away, that I may be rid of him; I will not be shaved to-day.' 'My master,' cried the barber at hearing this, 'what am I to understand by these words? It was not I who came to seek you; it was you who ordered me to come; and that being the case, I swear by the faith of a Mussulman I will not quit your house till I have shaved you.'

"He did not stop; he began another speech which lasted a full half-hour. At length I exclaimed, 'Indeed it is not possible that there can be in the whole world a man who takes a greater delight in making others mad.'

"I then thought I might succeed better by gentle means. 'In the name of Allah,' I said to him, 'leave off your fine speeches and despatch me quickly; I have an affair of the greatest importance which obliges me to go out, as I have already told you.' At these words he began to laugh. 'It would be very praiseworthy,' said he, 'if our minds were always calm and equable; however, I am willing to believe that when you put yourself in a passion with me it was your late illness which ruffled your temper; on this account, therefore, you are in need of some instructions, and you cannot do better than follow the example of your father and your grandfather. They used to come and consult me in all their affairs; and I may safely say, without vanity, that they were always the better for my advice. I am entirely at your service, and you have only to command me.'

"'Cannot I persuade you,' interrupted I, 'to desist from these long speeches, which only drive me mad and prevent me from keeping my appointment? Shave me directly, or leave the house.'

"When he saw that I was really exasperated with him, he said, 'O master, do not be angry; I will begin directly.' In fact, he washed my head and began to shave me; but he had not touched me four times with his razor, when he stopped to say, 'My master, you are hasty; you should abstain from these gusts of passion, which only come from the devil.'

"'Go on shaving me,' said I, interrupting him again, 'and speak no more.' 'You mean to tell me,' replied he, 'that you have some pressing affair on your hands. I'll lay a wager that I am not mistaken.' 'I told you this two hours ago,' returned I; 'you ought to have shaved me long since.' 'Moderate your impatience,' replied he; 'perhaps you have not considered well what you are going to do; what a man does precipitately is almost always a source of repentance. I wish you would tell me what this affair is about which you are in such haste, and I will

ARABIAN NIGHTS

give you my opinion on it. You have plenty of time, for you are not expected till noon, and it will not be noon these three hours.' 'That is nothing to me,' said I; 'men who keep their word are always before the time appointed. Finish shaving me at once.'

"The more anxious I was for despatch, the less willing was he to obey me. He put down his razor to take up his astrolabe; and when he put down his astrolabe he took up his razor.

"He seized his astrolabe a second time, and left me, half shaved, to go and see precisely what o'clock it was. When he returned, 'My master,' said he, 'I was certain I was not mistaken; it wants three hours to noon, I am well assured, or all the rules of astronomy are false.' 'Mercy of Allah!' cried I, 'my patience is exhausted; I can hold out no longer. Cursed barber! ill-omened barber! I can hardly refrain from falling upon thee and strangling thee.' 'Be calm, my master,' said he, coolly; 'you seem to have no fear of bringing on your illness again. Do not be so passionate, and you shall be shaved in a moment.' Saying this, he put the astrolabe in its case, took his razor, and began to shave me; but whilst he was shaving he could not help talking. 'If,' said he, 'you would inform me what this affair is that will engage you at noon, I would give you some advice which you might find serviceable.' To satisfy him, I told him that some friends expected me at noon to give me a feast and rejoice with me on my recovery.

"Directly the barber heard me mention a feast, he exclaimed: 'May Allah bless you on this day as well as on every other! You bring to my mind that yesterday I invited four or five friends to come and regale with me to-day; I had forgotten it, and have not made any preparations for them.' 'Let not that embarrass you,' said I; 'although I am going out, my table is always well supplied, and I make you a present of all that has been prepared for it to-day. I will also give you as much wine as you want. Only be quick and finish shaving me; and remember that, instead of making you presents to hear you talk, I give them to you for being silent.'

"He was not content to rely on my word. 'May Allah recompense you,' cried he, 'for the favors you do me. But show me

[213]

these provisions directly, that I may judge if there will be enough to regale my friends handsomely.' 'I have,' said I, 'a lamb, six capons, a dozen fowls, and sufficient meat for four courses.' I gave orders to a slave to produce the whole supply, together with four large jugs of wine. 'This is well,' replied the barber; 'but we shall want some fruit and some herbs for sauce to the meat.' I desired my slaves to give him what he wanted. He left off shaving me to examine each thing separately; and as this examination took up nearly half an hour, I stamped and cried out with impatience. But I might excite myself as I pleased; the rascal did not hurry the more. At length, however, he again took up the razor, and for a few minutes went on shaving me; then, stopping suddenly, he cried: 'I should never have supposed that you had been of so liberal a turn; I begin to discover that your late father, of honored memory, lives a second time in you. Certainly I did not deserve the favors you heap on me; and I assure you that I shall retain an eternal sense of my obligation; for I may as well tell you for your future information, that I have nothing but what I get from generous people like yourself. In this I resemble Zantout, who rubs people at the bath, and Sali, who sells little burnt peas about the streets, and Salouz, who sells beans, and Akerscha, who sells herbs, and Abou Mekares, who waters the streets to lay the dust, and Cassem, who belongs to the caliph's guard. All these people rigidly avoid melancholy. They are neither sorrowful nor quarrelsome. Better satisfied with their fortune than the caliph himself in the midst of his court, they are always gay, and ready to dance and sing; and each of them has his peculiar dance and song with which he entertains the whole city of Bagdad. But what I esteem most highly in them is, that they are not great talkers, any more than your slave who has the honor of speaking to you. Now, my master, I will give you the song and the dance of Zantout, who rubs the people at the bath; look at me, and you will see an exact imitation.'

"The barber sang the song and danced the dance of Zantout; and, notwithstanding all I could say, he would not stop till he

ARABIAN NIGHTS

had given a similar imitation of each of the men he had mentioned. After that he said, 'Sir, I am going to invite all these good people to my house; and, if you will take my advice, you will be of our party, and leave your friends, who are perhaps great talkers and will only disturb you by their tiresome conversation; whereas at my house you will enjoy only pleasure.'

"Notwithstanding my anger, I could not avoid laughing at his folly. 'I wish,' said I, 'that I had no other engagement; then I would gladly accept your proposal; but I must entreat you to excuse me; I am too much engaged to-day. Finish shaving me, and hasten away, for perhaps your friends are already waiting for you.' 'O my master,' replied he, 'do not refuse me the favor I ask of you. Come and amuse yourself with the good company I shall have.' 'Say no more about it,' said I; 'I cannot be present at your feast.'

"I gained nothing by gentleness. 'Since you will not come with me,' replied the barber, 'you must allow me to accompany you. I will carry home the provisions you have given me; my friends shall eat of them if they like, and I will return immediately.' 'Good heaven!' exclaimed I, on hearing this, 'am I then condemned to bear the tormenting of this creature for this whole day? In the name of Allah,' said I to him, 'make an end of your tiresome speeches; go to your friends, eat and drink and enjoy yourselves, and leave me at liberty to go to mine. I will go alone; and, indeed, if you must know the truth, the place where I am going is not one in which you can be received; I only can be admitted. You jest, my master,' replied he. 'If your friends have invited you to an entertainment, what reason can prevent me from accompanying you? You will very much oblige them, I am sure, by taking with you a man like me, who has the art of entertaining a company and making them merry. Say what you will, I am resolved to go in spite of you.'

"These words threw me into the greatest embarrassment. 'How can I possibly contrive to get rid of this horrible barber?' thought I to myself. 'If I continue obstinately to contradict him, our contest will be never-ending. The first call to noon

[215]

prayers has already sounded.' It was, indeed, now almost the moment to set out. I determined, therefore, to appear as if I agreed to everything my tormentor said. He finished shaving me, and, directly this was done, I said to him: 'Take some of my people with you to carry these provisions to your home; then return hither. I will not go without you.'

"He accordingly went out, and I finished dressing myself as quickly as possible. I only waited till I heard the last summons to prayers, and then set forth on my errand. But this malicious barber, who seemed aware of my intention, took care only to accompany my people to within sight of his own house. So soon as he had seen them go in he concealed himself at the corner of the street to observe and follow me. Accordingly, when I got to the door of the cadi, I turned round and perceived him at the end of the street. I was greatly enraged at this sight.

"The cadi's door was half-open, and when I went in I found the old lady waiting for me. As soon as she had shut the door she conducted me to the apartment of the young lady with whom I was in love. But I had hardly commenced a conversation with her when we heard a great noise in the street. The young lady ran to the window, and, looking through the blinds, perceived that the cadi her father was already returning from prayers. I looked out, and saw the barber seated exactly opposite the house.

"I had now two subjects for alarm—the arrival of the cadi, and the presence of the barber. The young lady quieted my fears on the one subject by telling me that her father very rarely came up into her apartment. Moreover, as she had foreseen that such a consequence might take place, she had prepared the means of my escape in case of necessity; but the presence of that unlucky barber caused me great uneasiness, and my anxiety was not without cause.

"As soon as the cadi had returned home he began beating a slave who had deserved punishment. The slave uttered loud cries which could be plainly heard in the street. The barber thought I was the person who was being ill-treated, and that these were my cries. Fully persuaded of this, he began to call out as loud as he could. He tore his clothes, threw dust upon his head, and shouted for help to all the neighbors, who soon ran out of their houses. They inquired what was the matter, and why he called for help. 'Alas!' exclaimed he, 'they are murdering my master, my dear lord.' And, without waiting for further details, he ran to my house and returned, followed by all my servants armed with sticks. They knocked furiously at the door of the cadi, who sent a slave to know what the noise meant. But the slave returned quite frightened to his master. 'My lord,' said he, 'more than ten thousand men are determining to come into your house by force and are already beginning to break open the door.'

"The cadi himself ran to the door and inquired what the people wanted. His venerable appearance did not inspire my people with any respect, and they shouted insolently: 'Cursed cadi! Why are you going to murder our master? What has he done to you?' 'My good friends,' replied the cadi, 'why should I murder your master whom I do not know, and who has never offended me? My door is open; you may come in and search my house.' 'You have been beating him,' said the barber; 'I heard his cries not a minute ago.' 'But how,' persisted the cadi, 'can your master have offended me, that I should ill-treat him thus? Is he in my house? And if he is here, how could he get in, or who could have admitted him?' 'You will not make me believe you, for all your great beard, you wicked cadi!' cried the barber. 'I know what I mean. Your daughter loves our master, and arranged to meet him in your house during the midday prayers. You must have found this out, and returned quickly; you surprised him here, and ordered your slaves to give him the bastinado. But your cruelty shall not remain unpunished. Set him free, and let him come out directly, or we will go in and take him from you to your shame.' 'There is no occasion,' said the cadi, 'to make such a riot. If what you say is true, you have only to go in and search for your master.' Directly the cadi had spoken these words, the barber and my servants burst into the house like madmen, and began to ransack every corner in search of me.

"As I heard every word the barber said to the cadi, I endeavored to find some place in which I might conceal myself. the only hiding-place I could discover was a large, empty chest, into which I immediately crept and shut the lid down upon myself. After the barber had searched every other place, he at last came into the apartment where I lay. He ran directly to the chest and opened it; and, finding me crouching there, he took it up and carried it away upon his head. He rushed down the staircase, into a court, through which he quickly passed, and at last reached the street.

"As he was carrying me along the lid of the chest unfortunately opened. I had not resolution enough to bear the shame and disgrace of my exposure to the populace who followed us, and jumped down so hastily into the street that I hurt myself seriously, and have been lame ever since. I did not at first feel the full extent of the injury I had suffered; I therefore made haste to get up, and ran away from the people who were laughing at me. I scattered among them a handful or two of gold and silver, and while they were stopping to pick up the prize I made my escape by hurrying through several quiet streets. But the wretched barber followed me closely and never once lost sight of me; and as he followed me he continued calling aloud: 'Stop, my master! Why do you run so fast? Did I not tell you truly that you would endanger your life through your obstinacy in not allowing me to accompany you? All this happened to you through your own fault, and I know not what would have become of you if I had not determined to follow you. I pray you, wait for me.'

"Thus the unlucky barber kept calling out to me all through the street. This put me into such a rage that I could have stopped and strangled him; but that would only have increased my difficulties. I therefore went another way to work. As I perceived that his calling out attracted the eyes of every one toward me, I went into a khan, the master of which was known to me. I found him at the door. 'In the name of Allah,' I cried, 'prevent that mad fellow from following me in here.' He promised me to do so, and he kept his word, although not without great difficulty. But the wretch would not retire without uttering a thousand abusive words; and all the way home he continued to tell every one he met the very great service he pretended to have done me.

"Thus I got rid of this tiresome man. The master of the khan asked me to give him an account of my adventure. I did so, and begged him in return to let me have an apartment in his house till I was quite cured. He replied, 'You will be much better accommodated in your own house.' 'I do not wish to return there,' I answered, 'for that detestable barber will be sure to find me out, and I shall be pestered with him every day, and to have him constantly before my eyes would absolutely kill me with vexation. Besides, after what has happened to me this day, I am determined not to remain any longer in this city. I will wander wherever my unhappy destiny may lead me.' Accordingly, as soon as I was cured I took as much money as I thought would be sufficient for my journey, and gave the remainder of my fortune to my relations.

"I set out from Bagdad, and arrived here. I had every reason to hope that I should be free from this mischievous barber in a country so distant from my own, and I now discover him in your company! You may judge of the pain I feel at the sight of this man by whose means I became lame and was reduced to the dreadful necessity of giving up my family, my friends, and my country.'

"After speaking thus the lame man rose and went out.

"When the young man was gone we sat in great astonishment, thinking of his history. We cast our eyes toward the barber and told him that he had done wrong, if what we had just heard was true. 'My masters,' answered he, 'the silence which I have imposed upon myself while this young man was telling you his story ought to prove to you that he has asserted nothing but the truth; but, notwithstanding all he has told you, I still maintain that I was right in acting as I did, and I shall leave you to judge. Was

ARABIAN NIGHTS

he not thrown into a position of great danger, and would he have
escaped from it but for my assistance? He may think himself
very fortunate to have endured nothing worse than lameness.
Did I not expose myself to a much greater danger to rescue
him from a house where I thought he was being ill-treated?
How, then, can he complain of me, and attack me with injurious
reproaches? This is the reward of the man who serves the ungrateful. He accuses me of being a chatterer; that is mere
calumny. Of the seven brothers who comprise our family, I
am the one who speaks least, and yet who possesses the most wit.
To convince you of this, my masters, I have only to relate to
you my history and that of my brothers. I entreat you to favor
me with your attention.'

THE HISTORY OF THE BARBER

"URING the reign of the Caliph Mostanser Billah there were ten robbers who infested the roads in the neighborhood of Bagdad, and for a long time made themselves famous by their great depredations and horrible cruelties. At last their crimes came to the ears of the caliph, and that prince summoned the chief of the police into his presence some days before the feast of Bairam and commanded him, under pain of death, to bring all the ten robbers to his throne. The chief of the police made great exertions, and sent out so many of his men into the country that the ten robbers were taken on the very day of the feast. I happened to be walking on the banks of the Tigris when I saw ten very handsomely dressed men embark on board a boat. I might have known they were robbers if I had noticed the guard who accompanied them; but I observed only the men themselves, and, thinking that they were a company going to enjoy themselves, I embarked in the boat with them in the hope that they would suffer me to accompany them. We rowed down the Tigris, and the guards made us land at the caliph's palace. By this time I perceived that I had formed a wrong opinion of my companions. When we quitted the boat we were surrounded by a fresh party of the guards belonging to the chief of the police. We were bound and carried before the caliph. I suffered myself to be pinioned like the rest without saying a word; for what would it have profited me had I remonstrated or made any resistance? I should only have been ill-treated by the guards, who would have paid no attention to my expostulations.

"As soon as we had come before the caliph, he ordered the immediate execution of the ten rascals. 'Strike off the heads of these ten robbers,' said he. The executioner immediately ranged us in a line within reach of his arm, and, fortunately, I stood last in the row. Then, beginning with the first, he struck off the heads of the ten robbers; but when he came to me he stopped. The caliph, observing that the executioner did not cut off my head, called out in anger: 'Have I not ordered thee to cut off the heads of the ten robbers? Why, then, hast thou executed only nine?' 'Commander of the Faithful,' replied the executioner, 'Allah forbid that I should neglect your Majesty's orders. Here are ten bodies on the ground, and ten heads which I have cut off,' and he counted the corpses at his feet. When the caliph himself saw that the executioner was right, he looked at me with astonishment; and, finding that I had not the appearance of a robber, he said, 'Good old man, by what accident were you found among these wretches who deserved a thousand deaths?' 'Commander of the Faithful,' I replied, 'I will tell you the entire truth. This morning I saw these ten persons get into a boat; considering they were people who were going to celebrate this day, the great festival of our religion, I embarked with them.'

"The caliph could not help laughing at my adventure; and (very different from the lame young man who treated me as a babbler) he admired my discretion and power of keeping silence. 'Commander of the Faithful,' said I, 'let not your Majesty be astonished that I have held my tongue in circumstances under

I EMBARKED IN THE BOAT WITH THEM IN THE HOPE THAT THEY WOULD SUFFER ME TO ACCOMPANY THEM

ARABIAN NIGHTS

which most persons would have been more anxious to speak. I make it my particular study to practise silence, and by the possession of this virtue I have acquired the glorious surname of the Silent. My friends call me thus to distinguish me from six brothers of mine.' 'I heartily rejoice,' answered the caliph, 'that you have earned a title to which you show so excellent a claim. But inform me what sort of men your brothers were. Did they at all resemble you?' 'Not in the least,' I answered; 'they were all of them chatterers, and in person not one of us resembled another. The first of my brothers was humpbacked; the second was toothless; the third had but one eye; the fourth was quite blind; the fifth had lost his ears; the sixth was hare-lipped. The various adventures which happened to them would enable your Majesty to judge of their characters, if I might have the honor to relate their stories.' As I thought the caliph evidently wished to hear the history of my brothers, I went on without waiting for his answer.

THE HISTORY OF THE BARBER'S FIRST BROTHER

"MY eldest brother was called Bacbouc, the Humpback, and was a tailor by trade. As soon as he had passed through his apprenticeship he hired a shop which happened to be opposite a mill; and as he had not at first a great deal of business, he found some difficulty in getting a livelihood. The miller, on the contrary, was very wealthy, and had also a very beautiful wife. As my brother was one morning working in his shop, he perceived the window of the mill open, and the miller's wife looking into the street. She seemed to him so very handsome that he was quite enchanted with her; but she paid not the least attention to him, but shut the window, and did not make her appearance any more that day.

"In the mean time the poor tailor continued looking toward the mill all the time he was at work. When the evening came, and he was forced to shut up his shop, he had hardly resolution to depart, because he still hoped he should see again the miller's wife. The next morning he rose very early and ran to his shop, so impatient was he to behold the mistress of his heart. But he was not more fortunate than the day before, for the miller's wife looked out of the window only for one instant. That moment, however, was quite sufficient to render him like a man bewitched. On the third day he had indeed more reason to be satisfied, for the miller's wife actually caught him gazing fervently at her, and she readily divined his secret thoughts.

"On making this discovery, instead of being angry, she resolved to amuse herself with my brother. She looked at him with a smiling air, and he returned her glances in so comical a manner that she was obliged to shut the window as quick as possible for fear her bursts of laughter should make him find out she was turning him into ridicule. Bacbouc was so innocent that he flattered himself that she had looked upon him with favor.

"The miller's wife then resolved to play off a jest at my brother's expense. She happened to have in her possession a piece of handsome stuff which she had for a long time intended to make up into a garment. She wrapped it up, therefore, in a beautiful handkerchief embroidered with silk, and sent it to the tailor by a young female slave. This slave came to my brother's shop, and said, 'My mistress desires you to make a robe out of this piece of stuff that I have brought according to the pattern she sends with it.' My brother did not for a moment doubt that the miller's wife was in love with him. He thought that she had given him this employment only to show that she understood the state of his heart; and he felt sure of the progress he had made in her affections. Impressed with this good opinion of himself, he desired the slave to tell her mistress that he would put aside all other work for hers, and that the dress should be ready by the next morning. He really worked with so much diligence that the dress was finished the same day.

"The next morning the young slave came to see how the dress was progressing. Bacbouc immediately gave it her, neatly folded up, and said, 'I am sincerely desirous of obliging your mistress, and I wish by my diligence to persuade her to employ no one else but myself.' The slave then took a few steps, as if she meant to go; but suddenly turning back, she said, in a low voice to my brother, 'I had nearly forgotten part of my errand. My mistress charged me to ask you how you had passed the night, for she, poor lady, is so much in love with you that she has not slept a moment.' 'Tell her,' answered my poor simpleton of a brother, 'that my passion for her is so violent I have not closed my eyes for these four nights.'

"The slave had not left my brother above a quarter of an hour before he saw her return with a piece of satin. 'My mistress,' said she, 'is quite satisfied with her dress, which fits her perfectly; but as it is very handsome, she is desirous of having a new under-garment also to wear with it, and she entreats you to make her one as soon as possible out of this piece of satin.' 'It is sufficient,' answered Bacbouc; 'it shall be done before I leave my shop to-day; and you have only to come and fetch it in the evening.' The miller's wife showed herself very often to my brother at the window, and used all her fascinations in order to encourage him to work. The clothes were soon made, and the slave came to take them away, but she brought the tailor no money for what he had laid out in the trimmings for both the garments he had made, or to pay him for his own work. Moreover, this unfortunate lover, who unconsciously made sport for his tormentors, had eaten nothing the whole of that day, and was obliged to borrow money to purchase a supper.

"The day following, as soon as my brother had entered his shop, the young slave came to him and told him the miller wished to speak to him. 'My mistress,' added she, 'has shown him your work, and has said so much in your favor that he also wants you to work for him. She has acted thus because she wishes to make use of every chance that may assist her in making your acquaintance.' My brother was easily persuaded to believe this, and went with the slave to the mill. The miller received him kindly, and showed him a piece of cloth. 'I require some shirts,' said he, 'and wish you to make me twenty out of this piece of cloth; if any of the material is left you can return it to me.'

"My brother had five or six days of hard work before he finished the twenty shirts for the miller, who immediately after gave him another piece of cloth to make him twenty pairs of

THE MILLER OBLIGED MY BROTHER TO TURN THE
MILL DURING THE REST OF THE NIGHT

trousers. When they were finished Bacbouc carried them to the miller, who asked him what he demanded for his trouble. My brother upon this said that he should be satisfied with twenty drachms of silver. The miller immediately called the young slave and ordered her to bring the scales that he might weigh the money. The slave, who knew what was expected of her, looked at my brother angrily to make him understand that he would spoil everything if he received the money. He understood her very well, and therefore refused to take any part of the sum, although he was so much in want of money that he had been obliged to borrow to purchase the thread with which he had made the shirts and trousers. On leaving the miller he came directly to me, and entreated me to lend him a trifle to buy some food, telling me that his customers did not pay him. I gave him some money which I had in my purse; and upon this he lived some days. It is true he ate nothing but broth, and had not even enough of that.

"My brother one day went to the miller's. This man was busy about his mill, and, thinking my brother might have come to ask for his money, he offered it to him; but the young slave, who was present, again prevented his accepting his due, and made him tell the miller in answer that he did not come for payment, but only to inquire after his health. The miller thanked him for his kindness, and gave him a cloak to make. Bacbouc brought it home the next day and the miller took out his purse, but the young slave came in at that moment and looked at my brother, who then said to the miller, 'There is no hurry, neighbor; we will settle the business another time.' Thus the poor dupe returned to his shop, burdened by three great evils: he was in love, he was hungry, and he was penniless.

"The miller's wife was both avaricious and wicked. She was not satisfied with preventing my brother from receiving his pay, but she excited her husband to revenge himself for the profession of love which the tailor had made, and to accomplish this they took the following means. The miller invited Bacbouc one evening to supper; and after having treated him with but

ARABIAN NIGHTS

indifferent fare, he thus addressed him, 'It is too late, brother, for you to return home; you will do better, therefore, to sleep here.' Thereupon he showed him a place where there was a bed, and, leaving his guest there, he returned and went with his wife to the room where they usually slept. In the middle of the night the miller came back to my brother and called out to him: 'Are you asleep, neighbor? My mule is taken suddenly ill, and I have a great deal of corn to grind; you will therefore do me a very great favor if you will turn the mill for my mule.' To prove his readiness to oblige his host, my brother undertook the strange duty required of him, asking him only to be informed how he should set about it. The miller then harnessed him by the middle of his body, like a mule, to make him turn the mill; and, immediately giving him a good cut upon his loins with the whip, cried out, 'Get on, neighbor.' 'Why do you strike me?' inquired my brother. 'It is only to encourage you,' replied the miller, 'for without the whip my mule would not stir a step.' Bacbouc was astonished at this treatment, but he dared not complain. When he had gone five or six rounds he wished to rest himself, but the miller immediately gave him a dozen sharp cuts with the whip, calling out: 'Courage, neighbor! Don't stop. You must go on without taking breath or you will spoil my flour.'

"The miller thus obliged my brother to turn the mill during the rest of the night, and as soon as daylight appeared he went away without unfastening him, and returned to his wife's chamber. Bacbouc remained for some time harnessed in the mill. At last the young slave came and untied him. 'Alas! how my good mistress and myself have pitied you!' cried the cunning slave. 'We are not at all to blame for what you have suffered; we have had no share in the wicked trick which her husband has played you.' The unfortunate Bacbouc answered not a word, for he was thoroughly exhausted. He got back to his own house, and firmly resolved to think no more of the miller's wife.

"The recital of this history," continued the barber, "made

the caliph laugh. 'Go,' said he to me; 'return home; you shall receive something by my order to console you for the loss of the festivities in which you expected to share.' 'Commander of the Faithful,' replied I, 'I entreat your Majesty not to think of giving me anything till I have related the histories of my other brothers.' I continued in the following words:

THE HISTORY OF THE BARBER'S SECOND BROTHER

"MY second brother, Bakbarah, called the Toothless, was walking one day through the city, when he met an old woman. She accosted him in the following terms, 'I have a word to say to you, if you will stay a moment.' He immediately stopped and asked her what she wished. 'If you have time to go with me,' she replied, 'I will take you to a magnificent palace where you shall see a lady more beautiful than the day. She will receive you with a great deal of pleasure; and will feast you royally and give you excellent wine. I do not think I need say more.' 'But is this true that you tell me?' asked my brother. 'I am not given to lying,' replied the old woman. 'But you must remember what I require you to do. You must be prudent, speak little, and comply with every request that is made.' Bakbarah agreed to the conditions. They arrived at the gate of a large palace where were a great number of officers and servants. Some of these men wished to stop my brother, but the old woman spoke to them and they let him pass. She then turned to my my brother and said: 'Remember that the young lady to whose

"YOU MUST BE PRUDENT, SPEAK LITTLE, AND COM-
PLY WITH EVERY REQUEST"

ARABIAN NIGHTS

house I have brought you likes to see mildness and modesty, and cannot bear to be contradicted. If you satisfy her in this there is no doubt but you will obtain from her whatever you wish.'

"She then led him into a very splendid apartment which formed part of a square building. There was a gallery all round it, and in the midst was a very beautiful garden. The old woman made him sit down on a gorgeously decorated sofa, and desired him to wait there while she went to inform the young lady of his arrival.

"As my brother had never before been in so superb a place, he immediately began to examine all the beautiful things he beheld; judging of his good fortune by the magnificence around him, he could hardly contain his joy. He almost immediately heard a great noise, which came from a long array of slaves who were in a state of much merriment, and who came toward him, bursting at intervals into violent fits of laughter. In the midst of the slaves he perceived a young lady of most extraordinary beauty whom he easily knew to be their mistress by the deference they paid her. Bakbarah, who expected to have had a private conversation with the lady, was very much surprised at the arrival of so large a company. The slaves put on a serious air as they approached him, and when the young lady was near the sofa my brother, who had risen, made a most profound reverence. She took her seat, and then, motioning him to be seated also, said to him, 'I am delighted to see you, and wish that your every desire may be fulfilled.' 'Lady,' replied Bakbarah, 'I cannot wish for a greater honor than that of appearing before you.'

"She immediately ordered the slaves to bring a collation, and they covered the table with baskets of various fruits and sweetmeats. The lady sat down at the table, with my brother and the slaves around her. As he happened to sit directly opposite to her she observed, as soon as he opened his mouth to eat, that he had no teeth. She remarked this circumstance to her slaves, and they all laughed immoderately. Bakbarah, who, from time to time, raised his head to look at the lady, and saw that she was laughing, imagined that her mirth arose from the

[237]

pleasure she felt at being in his company, and flattered himself
she would soon order the slaves to retire and that he should
enjoy her conversation in private. The lady guessed his thoughts,
and took a pleasure in continuing a delusion which seemed so
agreeable to him. She said a thousand soft and tender things
to him, and she presented him with some of the choicest dishes
with her own hand.

"When the collation was finished she rose from table. Ten
slaves instantly took some musical instruments and began to
play and sing while the rest danced. In order to make himself
agreeable, my brother also began dancing, and the young lady
herself joined in the amusement. After they had danced for some
time they all sat down to take breath. The lady called for a
glass of wine, and then cast a smile at my brother to intimate
that she was going to drink his health. He instantly rose up,
and stood while she drank. When she had emptied the glass,
instead of returning it, she had it filled again and presented it
to my brother, that he might pledge her.

"Bakbarah took the glass, and, as he received it from the young
lady, he kissed her hand. Then he drank to her. After this the
young lady made him sit down by her side and began to caress
him. She put her arm round his neck and patted him several
times gently with her hand. Delighted with these favors, he
thought himself the happiest man in the world. He felt tempted
to return the caress the charming lady lavished upon him, but
he dared not take this liberty before the slaves, who had their
eyes upon him, and who continued to laugh at this trifling.
The young lady had at first tapped him gently, but at last she
began to give him such forcible slaps that he grew angry. At
this moment the old woman who had brought my brother there
gave him a look which made him understand that he had forgotten the advice she had before given him. The young lady
then took hold of him by the arm and drew him toward her,
continuing to bestow on him a thousand pretended caresses.
Her slaves, whose only aim was to divert her, began to take
a part in the sport. One of them gave poor Bakbarah a

fillip on the nose with all her strength; another pulled his ears almost off, while the rest kept slapping him in a way that went beyond jesting.

"My brother bore all this ill-usage with the most exemplary patience. He even affected to be amused by it, and looked at the old woman with a forced smile. The young lady then said to my brother: 'You are a brave man, and I am delighted at finding in you so much kindness and forbearance for all my little whims. I see you possess a disposition conformable to mine.' 'O lady,' replied Bakbarah, who was delighted with this speech, 'I am no longer myself, but am entirely at your disposal; you have full power to do with me as you please.' 'You give me the greatest happiness,' said the lady, 'by showing so much submission to my will.' Then she called to the attendants to bring perfumes and rose-water. At these words two slaves went out and instantly returned. One carried a silver vase containing exquisite aloe-wood with which she perfumed my brother; the other bore a flagon of rose-water which she sprinkled over his face and hands.

"When this ceremony was finished the young lady commanded the slaves who had before sung and played to recommence their concert. They obeyed; and while the music was going on the lady called another slave and ordered her to take my brother with her. 'You know what you have to do,' she said, 'and when you have done it bring him back to me.' Bakbarah immediately got up, and, going toward the old woman, requested her to tell him what they wished him to do. 'Our mistress,' replied she in a whisper, 'is very eccentric. She wishes to see how you would look disguised as a female. This slave, therefore, has orders to take you with her, to paint your eyebrows, shave off your mustache, and dress you like a woman.' 'You may paint my eyebrows,' said my brother, 'but as to being shaved, that I will by no means allow. How can I appear in the streets without my mustache?' 'Beware,' answered the woman, 'how you refuse anything that is required of you. You will quite spoil your fortune, which is now prospering greatly. She loves you and wishes to make you happy. Will you, for the sake of a paltry mustache, forego the greatest happiness any man can possibly enjoy?'

"Bakbarah at length yielded to the old woman's arguments, and without further opposition he suffered the slave to lead him to an apartment, where they painted his eyebrows red. They shaved off his mustache, and were absolutely going to remove his beard. But the easiness of my brother's temper did not carry him quite so far as to make him suffer that. 'Not a single stroke,' he exclaimed, 'shall you make at my beard.' The slave represented to him that it was in vain he had parted with his mustache if he would not also agree to lose his beard—that a hairy countenance did not at all coincide with the dress of a woman; and she declared herself astonished that a man who was about to gain the hand of the most beautiful woman in Bagdad should care for his beard. The old woman sided with the slave, and adduced fresh reasons, threatening my brother with her mistress's displeasure. She said so much that Bakbarah at last permitted them to do what they wished.

"As soon as they had dressed him like a woman, they brought him back to the young lady, who burst into a violent fit of laughter at his appearance. The young lady then rose, still laughing, and said, 'After the good nature you have shown to me I should be wrong if I did not bestow my whole heart upon you; but you must do one thing more for love of me; it is only to dance before me in your present costume.' Bakbarah obeyed, and the young lady and the slaves danced with him, laughing all the while as if they were crazy. After they had danced for some time they all surrounded the poor dupe, and gave him so many blows and kicks that he fell down, almost fainting. The old woman came to his assistance and, without giving him time to express his indignation at such ill-treatment, whispered in his ear: 'Be comforted, for you have now reached the end of your sufferings and are about to receive your reward. You have only one thing more to do,' added she, 'and that is a mere trifle. You must know that my mistress is accustomed, whenever she is in a merry mood, like to-day, not to suffer any of her favorites to come near her unless they have run a race with her. You must be stripped to your shirt, and then she will start a few paces before you, and run through the gallery, and from room to room, till you have caught her. Therefore undress yourself quickly and do not make any difficulty about it.'

"My brother had already carried his compliance too far to stop. The young lady now took off her robe in order to run with greater ease. When they were both ready to begin the race the lady took a start of about twenty paces and then began running with wonderful swiftness. My brother followed her as fast as he could. Instead of losing any of the advantage she had first taken, the young lady kept continually gaining upon my brother. She then turned off down a long, dark passage, and escaped through a side door unperceived by my brother. Bakbarah, who kept constantly following her, had lost sight of her in this passage; moreover, he was obliged to slacken his pace on account of the darkness. At last he perceived a light, toward which he made with all possible haste; he passed through a door, which was instantly shut upon him.

"You may imagine what was his astonishment when he found himself in the middle of a street inhabited by curriers. They were equally surprised at seeing a man among them in his shirt, his eyebrows painted red, and without either beard or mustache. They began to hoot at him, and some even ran after him and beat him with strips of leather. They then seized him and set him on an ass, and led him through the city, exposed to the laughter of the mob.

"To complete his misfortunes, they led him through the street where the judge of the police lived, and this magistrate immediately sent to inquire the cause of the uproar. The curriers informed him that they had seen my brother come out, exactly in the state in which he then was, from the gate leading to the apartments of the women belonging to the grand vizier, which opened into their street. The judge immediately commanded that the unfortunate Bakbarah should receive a hundred strokes

ARABIAN NIGHTS

upon the soles of his feet, and that he should be thrust out of the
city and forbidden ever to enter it again.

"'This, O Commander of the Faithful,' said I to the caliph,
'is the history of my second brother. He knew not, poor man,
that the ladies of our great and powerful nobles amuse themselves
by playing off jests of this kind upon any young man who is
silly enough to trust himself in their hands.'

"The barber then proceeded at once to tell the history of his
third brother.

THE HISTORY OF THE BARBER'S THIRD BROTHER

"COMMANDER of the Faithful," the barber said to the caliph, "my third brother, who was called Bakbac, was quite blind; and his condition was so wretched that he was reduced to beg.

"He happened one day to knock at the door of a house when the master was sitting alone. 'Who is there?' he called out. My brother made no answer, but knocked a second time. Again the master of the house inquired who was at the door, but Bakbac did not answer. He then came down, opened the door, and asked my brother what he wanted. 'Bestow something upon me, for the love of God!' answered Bakbac. 'You seem to me to be blind,' said the master of the house. 'Alas! it is true,' replied my brother. 'Hold out your hand,' cried the other. My brother, who made sure of receiving something, immediately put his hand out, but the master of the house only took hold of it to assist him in going up-stairs to his apartment. Bakbac imagined that the master of the house would give him some food, for he often received provisions at other houses. When they had reached the upper chamber, the master of the house let go my brother's hand and sat down in his place; he then again asked him what he wanted. 'I have already told you,' replied Bakbac, 'that I beg you to give me something, for the love of God.' 'My good blind man,' answered the master, 'all I can do for you is to wish that Allah may restore your sight to you.' 'You might have told me that at the door,' said my brother, 'and spared me the labor of coming up-stairs.' 'The staircase is before you,' the master of the house answered, 'and if you wish it, you may go down alone.' My brother then began to descend, but, missing his footing about half-way down, he fell to the bottom of the stairs and bruised his head and strained his back cruelly. He got up with difficulty, and went away muttering curses at the master of the house, who did nothing but laugh at his fall.

"As he turned away from the house two of his companions, who were also blind, happened to pass by and knew his voice. They stopped to ask him what success he had met with. He told them what had just befallen him. 'I conjure you,' continued he, 'to accompany me home that I may in your presence take some of the money which we have in store to buy something for my supper.' The two blind men agreed to his proposal, and he conducted them home.

"It is necessary here to observe that the master of the house in which my brother had been so ill-treated was a thief, and a man of cunning and malicious disposition. He had overheard from his window what Bakbac had said to his comrades; he therefore came down-stairs and followed them, and passed with them unobserved into an old woman's house where my brother lodged. As soon as they were seated Bakbac said to the other two, 'We must shut the door, brothers, and take care that there is no stranger among us.' At these words the robber was very much embarrassed, but, perceiving a rope that hung from a beam in the middle of the room, he took hold of it and swung in the air

THE ROBBER HUNG FROM A BEAM WHILE THE
BLIND MEN FELT ALL ROUND THE ROOM
WITH THEIR STICKS

ARABIAN NIGHTS

while the blind men shut the door and felt all round the room with their sticks. When this was concluded, and they were again seated, he let go the rope and sat down by the side of my brother in perfect silence. The latter, thinking there was no one in the room but his blind companions, thus addressed them: 'O my comrades, as you have made me the keeper of all the money we three have collected for a long time past, I wish to prove to you that I am not unworthy of the trust. The last t me we reckoned, you remember, we had ten thousand drachms, and we put them into ten bags; I will now show you that I have not touched one of them.' Having said this, he groped about among some old rags and clothes, and drew out the ten bags, and, giving them to his companions, he continued, 'Here are all the bags, and you may count the money if you like.' They answered that they were perfectly satisfied with his honesty. He then opened one of the bags and took out ten drachms, and the other two blind men did the same.

"My brother replaced the bags in the spot from which he had taken them. One of the blind men then said there was no occasion to spend anything for supper that night, as he had received from the charity of some good people sufficient provisions for all three, and took out of his wallet some bread, cheese, and fruit, which he placed upon a table. They then began to eat, and the robber, who sat on the right hand of my brother, chose the best pieces, and ate of their provisions with them. But in spite of all the care he took to avoid making the least noise, Bakbac heard him chew, and instantly exclaimed: 'We are betrayed! There is a stranger among us!' As he said this he stretched out his hand and seized the robber by the arm. He then fell upon him, calling out, 'Thief!' and giving him many blows with his fist. The other blind men joined in the cry, and beat the robber, who defended himself as well as he could. As he was both strong and active, and had the advantage of seeing, he laid about him furiously, and called out, 'Thieves! robbers!' louder than his enemies.

"The neighbors assembled at the noise, broke open the door,

and with much difficulty separated the combatants. Having at last put an end to the fray, they inquired the cause of the disagreement. 'O my masters,' cried my brother, who had not yet let the robber go, 'this man whom I have got hold of is a thief; he came in here with us for the purpose of robbing us of the little money we possess.' Directly he saw the people enter, the robber had shut his eyes and pretended to be blind. He now exclaimed: 'He is a liar, my masters. I swear by the name of Allah that I am one of their companions and associates, and that they refuse to give me the share of our money which belongs to me. They all three have joined against me, and I demand justice.' The neighbors, who did not wish to interfere with the disputes of these blind men, carried them all four before the judge of the police.

"When they were come before this magistrate, the robber, who still pretended to be blind, began to speak. 'Since you, my lord, have been appointed to administer justice in behalf of the caliph,' he said, 'whose power may Allah prosper, I will declare to you that we are all equally guilty. But as we have pledged ourselves by an oath not to reveal anything except we receive the bastinado, you must order us to be beaten if you wish to be informed of our crime; and you may begin with me.' My brother now wished to speak, but the officers compelled him to hold his tongue. They then began to bastinado the robber.

"He had the resolution to bear twenty or thirty strokes; and then, pretending to be overcome with pain, he opened first one eye and then the other, calling out at the same time for mercy, and begging the judge to order a remission of his punishment. When he saw the robber with both his eyes open, the judge was very much astonished. 'Scoundrel!' he cried. 'What does this mean?' 'O my lord,' replied the robber, 'I will discover a most important secret if you will have the goodness to pardon me. Then I will reveal the whole mystery to you.'

"The judge ordered his people to stop beating the robber, and promised to pardon him. 'Trusting to your promise,' replied the robber, 'I now declare to you, my lord, that my companions and I can see perfectly well. We all four feign blindness in order that we may enter houses without molestation, and even penetrate into the apartments of the women, whose charity we sometimes take advantage of. I, moreover, confess to you that we have collected among us at least ten thousand drachms by this cunning trick. This morning I demanded of my companions two thousand five hundred drachms, which came to my share; but because I declared I would break off all connection with them they refused to give me my money. When I continued to insist on having it they all fell upon me and ill-treated me in a shameful manner. I wait here for you to do me justice, my lord, and expect that you will make them deliver up the two thousand five hundred drachms which are my due. If you wish that my comrades should acknowledge the truth of what I advance, order them to receive three times as many blows as you have given me, and you will see them open their eyes as I did.'

"My brother and the other two blind men began to exclaim loudly against this infamous imposture, but the judge would not hear a word. 'Rascals!' he cried. 'Is it thus that you counterfeit blindness and go about deceiving people?' 'He is an imposter!' exclaimed my brother. 'What he says is false!'

"But all my brother's protestations were useless. He and his companions each received two hundred strokes of the bastinado. The judge every moment expected them to open their eyes, and attributed to their great obstinacy the non-performance of what it was impossible for them to do. During the whole of this time the robber kept saying to the blind men, 'My good friends, open your eyes, and do not wait till you almost die under the punishment.' Then he added, addressing himself to the judge, 'I see very well, my lord, that they will be obstinate to the end and that they will never open their eyes. Would it not be better to pardon them now and send some one with me to take the ten thousand drachms they have concealed?'

"The judge did not intend to neglect securing the money. He therefore commanded one of his people to accompany the

ARABIAN NIGHTS

robber, and they brought the ten bags back with them. He then ordered two thousand five hundred drachms to be counted out and given to the robber, and kept the remainder for himself. With respect to my brother and his companions, he commanded them to quit the city and thought he had dealt very leniently with them.

"This is the conclusion of the melancholy adventure of my third brother.

"The caliph laughed as much at this story as he had done at those he had before heard, and I began the history of my fourth brother.

THE HISTORY OF THE BARBER'S FOURTH BROTHER

"THE name of my fourth brother was Alcouz. How he lost his eye I shall have the honor to relate to your Majesty. He was a butcher by trade; and as he had a particular talent in bringing up rams and teaching them to fight, he had the friendship of some of the principal people, who were much amused with combats of this kind, and who even kept fighting-rams at their own houses. He had, moreover, a very good business, and there was always in his shop the finest and freshest meat that was to be found.

"As he was one day in his shop, an old man came in to purchase six pounds of meat. He paid for his purchase and went away. My brother observed that the money the old man paid was very beautiful, new, and well coined. He resolved, therefore, to lay it by in a separate part of his closet. During five months the same old man came regularly every day for the same quantity

ARABIAN NIGHTS

of meat, and paid for it with the same sort of money, which my brother as regularly continued to lay by.

"At the end of the five months Alcouz, who wished to purchase a quantity of sheep, resolved to pay for them out of this particular money. He therefore went to his box and opened it; but great was his astonishment when he discovered, instead of his money, only a parcel of leaves of a round shape. He immediately began to beat his breast, and made so great a noise that he brought all his neighbors about him. Their surprise was as great as his own when he informed them of what had happened. 'Would to Allah,' cried my brother, with tears in his eyes, 'that this treacherous old man came here now with his hypocritical face!' He had hardly spoken these words when he saw the old man at a distance, coming toward him. My brother, having seized hold of him, vociferated with all his force: 'Mussulmans, assist me! Hear me tell the shameful trick that this infamous man has played me!' He then related to a large crowd of people who had gathered round him the story he had just told to his neighbors. When he had finished his tale the old man quietly answered: 'You will do best to let me go, and thus make amends for the affront you have offered me before so many people. Unless you do this I may revenge myself in a more serious manner, which I should be sorry to do.' 'And what have you to say against me?' replied my brother. 'I am an honest man in my business, and I fear you not.' 'You wish that I should make it public?' returned the old man. 'Listen,' added he, addressing himself to the people, 'and hear me tell you that, instead of selling the flesh of sheep, as he ought to do, this man sells human flesh!' 'You are an imposter!' cried my brother. 'No, no!' answered the other; 'at this very moment there is a man with his throat cut hanging up on the outside of your shop like a sheep! Let these people go there and we shall soon know whether I have spoken the truth.'

"That very morning, before my brother had opened the box in which the leaves were, he had killed a sheep, and had dressed and exposed it outside his shop as usual. He therefore declared

HE PAID FOR HIS PURCHASE AND WENT AWAY

that what the old man had said was false; but in spite of all his protestations the credulous mob wished to ascertain the fact on the spot. They therefore obliged my brother to let the old man go, and, seizing Alcouz himself, ran to his shop. There, indeed, they saw a man with his throat cut, hanging up exactly as the accused had stated; for this old man was a magician, and had blinded the eyes of all the people, as he had formerly done those of my brother when he made him take the leaves that were offered him for real money.

"At sight of this, one of the men who held Alcouz gave him a great blow with his fist, and at the same time cried: 'You wretch! Would you make us eat human flesh?' The old man also, who had followed them, immediately gave him another blow that knocked out one of his eyes. Every one who could get near my brother joined in beating him. They dragged him before the judge, carrying with them the corpse, which they had taken down as a proof of the criminal's guilt. 'O my lord,' said the old magician to the judge, 'you see before you a man who is so barbarous as to kill men and sell their flesh for that of sheep. The people expect that you will punish him in an exemplary manner.' The judge listened with great patience to what my brother had to say; but the story of the money that had been changed into leaves appeared so utterly incredible that he treated my brother as an imposter, and, choosing rather to believe his own eyes, he ordered that Alcouz should receive five hundred blows. After this he obliged him to reveal where his money was, confiscated the whole of it, and condemned him to perpetual banishment.

"At the time that this dreadful adventure happened to Alcouz, my fourth brother, I was absent from Bagdad. He retired to a very obscure part of the city, where he remained concealed till the wounds his punishment had produced were healed. It was on the back that he had been most cruelly beaten. As soon as he was able to walk he traveled, during the night and through unfrequented roads, to a city where no one knew him; there he took a lodging, from whence he hardly ever stirred. But tired

ARABIAN NIGHTS

at last of his exclusive life, he one day went to walk in the suburbs of the town. Suddenly he heard a great noise of horsemen coming along behind him. He happened just at this instant to be near the door of a large house; and as he was afraid of everybody after what had happened to him, he fancied that these horsemen were in pursuit of him in order to arrest him. He therefore opened the door for the purpose of concealing himself. After shutting it again he went into a large court; but directly he entered, two servants came up to him and seized him, saying: 'Allah be praised that you have come of your own free will to deliver yourself into our hands. You have disturbed us so much for these last three nights we have been unable to sleep; and you have spared our lives only because we have frustrated your wicked intention of taking them.'

"You may easily imagine that my brother was not a little surprised at this welcome. 'My good friends,' said he to the men, 'I know not what you would have with me; doubtless you mistake me for another person.' 'No, no,' replied they; 'we know well enough that you and your comrades are thieves. You were not satisfied with having robbed our master of all he possessed and reducing him to beggary; you wished to take his life. Let us see if you have not the knife about you which you had in your hand when we pursued you last night.' Hereupon they began to search him, and found that he had a knife. 'So, so,' cried they, as they snatched it from him; 'and have you the assurance still to deny that you are a robber?' 'How!' answered my brother, 'cannot a man carry a knife in his pocket without being a thief? Listen to my story,' he added, 'and instead of having a bad opinion of me you will pity me for my misfortunes.' But instead of listening to him they immediately fell upon him, pulled off his clothes, and then, observing the scars upon his back, they redoubled their blows. 'You scoundrel! Do you wish to make us believe you are an honest man when your back is so covered with scars?' 'Alas!' cried my brother, 'my sins must be very great since, after having been once most unjustly treated, I am served so a second time, without having committed the least fault.'

ARABIAN NIGHTS

"The two servants paid no attention to my brother's complaints. They carried him before the judge. 'How dare you,' said the judge, 'break into people's houses and pursue them with a knife in your hand?' 'O my lord,' answered poor Alcouz, 'I am one of the most innocent men in the world. I shall be undone if you will not do me the favor patiently to listen to me. No man is more worthy of compassion than I am.' 'O judge,' cried one of the servants, 'will you listen for a moment to a robber who breaks into people's houses, pillages them, and murders the inhabitants? If you refuse to believe, look at his back and that will prove the truth of our words.' When he had said this, they uncovered my brother's back and showed it to the judge, who, without inquiring any further into the matter, ordered that he should at once receive a hundred strokes with a leathern strap on his shoulders. He then commanded him to be led through the city upon a camel, while a crier going before him called out, 'THUS SHALL MEN BE PUNISHED WHO FORCIBLY BREAK INTO HOUSES.'

"When this punishment was over, they set Alcouz down outside the town and forbade him ever to enter it again.

"The Caliph Mostanser Billah did not laugh so much at this history as at the others, for he was kind enough to commiserate the unfortunate Alcouz. He then wished to give me something and send me away; but, without giving his servants time to obey his orders, I said: 'You may now have observed, most sovereign lord and master, that I speak very little. Since your Majesty has had the goodness to listen to me thus far, and as you express a wish to hear the adventures of my two other brothers, I hope and trust they will not afford you less amusement than the histories you have already heard.'

THE HISTORY OF THE BARBER'S FIFTH BROTHER

"THE name of my fifth brother was Alnaschar. While he lived with my father he was excessively idle Our father at last died at a very advanced age, and all he left us consisted of seven hundred drachms of silver. We divided it equally among us, and each took one hundred for his share. Alnaschar, who had never before possessed so much money at one time, found himself very much embarrassed how to dispose of it. He at last determined to lay out his hundred drachms in the purchase of glasses, bottles, and other glass articles. He put his whole stock into an open basket and chose a very small shop, where he sat down with his basket before him, and, leaning his back against the wall, waited till customers should come to buy his merchandise.

"As he sat thus he began to meditate, and in the midst of his reverie he pronounced the following speech so loud that a tailor who was his neighbor could hear him. 'This basket,' said he, 'cost me one hundred drachms, and that is all I had in the world. Selling its contents by retail, I shall manage to make two hundred drachms; these two hundred I shall employ again in purchasing glassware, so that I shall make four hundred

AS HE SAT THUS HE BEGAN TO MEDITATE

ARABIAN NIGHTS

drachms. By continuing this trade, I shall in time amass the sum of four thousand drachms. With these four thousand I shall easily make eight, and as soon as I have gained ten thousand I will leave off selling glassware and turn jeweler. When I have got together as much wealth as I wish to have I will purchase a beautiful house, large estates, eunuchs, slaves, and horses; I will entertain my friends handsomely and shall make some noise in the world. But I will not leave off trading till I have realized one hundred thousand drachms. And when I thus become rich I shall think myself equal to a prince, and I will send and demand the daughter of the grand vizier in marriage. I shall represent to him that I have heard most astonishing reports of the beauty, wisdom, wit, and every other good quality of his daughter; and, in short, that I will bestow upon her, the very night of our nuptials, a thousand pieces of gold. If the vizier should be so ill-bred as to refuse me his daughter, I will go and take her away in spite of him.

"'As soon as I have married the grand vizier's daughter I shall purchase ten very young and handsome black eunuchs for her. I will dress myself like a prince and ride in procession through the town, mounted on a fine horse, the saddle of which shall be of pure gold, and the caparisons of cloth of gold enriched with diamonds and pearls. I will be accompanied by slaves, and thus we shall proceed to the palace of the vizier, with the eyes of all fixed upon me, both nobles and common people, who will pay me the most profound reverence as I go along. When I have dismounted at the grand vizier's I will ascend the stairs, while my servants stand ranged in two rows to the right and left; and the grand vizier, rising to receive me as his son-in-law, will give me his place and seat himself before me to show me the greater respect. Two of my men shall have each a purse containing one thousand pieces of gold. I will take one of these purses and present it to the grand vizier with these words, "Behold the thousand pieces of gold which I have promised you on the first night of my marriage." Then, offering him the other purse, I will add, "To show you that I am a man of my word, and to

ARABIAN NIGHTS

prove that I will give more than I promise, receive this other purse of equal value." After such an act my generosity will be talked of by all the world.

"'I will then return home with the same pomp with which I set out. My wife must send an officer to compliment me on my visit to her father. I shall bestow a beautiful robe of honor on the officer, and send him back with a rich present. If she shall wish to make me a present in return, I will refuse it, and dismiss the person who brings it. I will not, moreover, permit her to leave her apartments upon any account whatever without first obtaining my permission; and whenever I visit her it shall always be in a way that shall impress her with the greatest respect for me. I will always appear magnificently dressed; and whenever I wish to pass the evening with my wife I will sit in the most honorable seat, where I will assume a grave and solemn air, not turning my head to the right or to the left. I will speak but little; and when my wife, beautiful as the full moon, presents herself before me in all her splendor, I will pretend not to see her. Her women, who will be standing round her, must say: "O our dear lord and master, behold before you your spouse, the humblest of your slaves. She waits for you to caress her, and is much mortified that you do not deign to take the least notice of her. She is greatly fatigued at standing so long before you; permit her, therefore, to sit down." I will not answer a word to this speech, and my continued silence will greatly augment their surprise and grief. They will then throw themselves at my feet, and, after they have remained prostrate before me a considerable time, entreating and begging me to notice them, I will at last lift up my head and, casting upon my wife a careless glance, will resume my former attitude. Thinking perhaps that my wife may not be dressed or adorned to my taste, they will lead her back to her room to change her habit, and in the mean time I will return to my apartment and put on a more magnificent dress than I wore before. They will then return a second time and renew their entreaties, and I shall again have the pleasure of disregarding my wife till they have prayed and besought me

[262]

as long and earnestly as before. And I will thus begin, on the very first day of my marriage, to teach her how she may expect to be treated during the remainder of her life.

"'After the various ceremonies of our nuptials are over,' continued Alnaschar, 'I will take from the hands of one of the attendants a purse containing five hundred pieces of gold, which I will give to the female attendants, and then they will leave me alone with my spouse. After they have retired I will treat my wife with such utter indifference that she will not fail to complain to her mother, the lady of the grand vizier, of my pride and neglect. Her mother will then come to visit me. She will kiss my hands respectfully, and say to me: "My master" (for she will not dare to call me son-in-law, for fear that her familiarity should displease me), "I entreat you not to despise my child in such a manner. I know her whole heart is devoted to you." Although my mother-in-law addresses me so respectfully and kindly, I will not answer her a word, but remain as grave and solemn as ever. She will then throw herself at my feet and, kissing them repeatedly, will say: "My lord, you surely have no fault to find with my daughter? Forbear to inflict so great a mortification upon her, and do her the favor to look at and speak to her, and thus strengthen her good intention of endeavoring to satisfy and please you in everything."

"'All this shall have no effect upon me; and my mother-in-law, observing my indifference, will take a glass of wine and, putting it into my wife's hand, will say, "Go and offer him this glass of wine yourself; he will not have the cruelty to refuse it from so beautiful a hand." My wife will then take the glass and stand before me, trembling. When she observes that I do not relent toward her she will address me thus, with her eyes bathed in tears, "My heart, my dear soul, my amiable lord, I conjure you to have the goodness to take this glass of wine from the hand of the humblest of your slaves." I shall, however, neither look at her nor speak. At last, tired and annoyed with her solicitations and prayers, I will throw a terrible glance at her, and give her a blow on her cheek, and push

ARABIAN NIGHTS

her so violently from me with my foot that she will fall down beside the sofa.'

"My brother was so entirely absorbed in these chimerical visions that he thrust out his foot as if the whole scene were a reality, and he unfortunately struck his basket of glassware so violently that it fell from his shopboard into the street, where it was all broken to pieces.

"His neighbor the tailor, who had heard the whole of Alnaschar's extravagant speech, burst into a fit of laughter when he saw the basket overturned. 'O cruel wretch!' said he to my brother, 'ought you not to die with shame for thus ill-treating a young wife when she has given you no reason for complaint? If I were your father-in-law, the grand vizier, I would order you a hundred blows with a leathern strap, as you deserve.'

"This most unfortunate accident brought my brother to his senses; and, knowing that it had been caused by his own insufferable pride, he beat his breast, tore his garments, and shrieked so violently that all the neighbors came running up to inquire what was the matter. Some pitied Alnaschar; others laughed at his folly. But the vanity which he had before shown was now entirely subdued by the loss of his property; and he continued bewailing his hard and cruel fate when a lady of considerable rank passed by, mounted on a mule richly caparisoned. The sight of my brother's distress excited her compassion. She asked who he was and the reason of his violent grief. The people replied that he was a poor man who had laid out the little money he possessed in a basket of glassware, and that the basket had fallen down and all his glass was broken. The lady immediately turned to a eunuch who accompanied her, and ordered him to give my brother what money he had with him. The eunuch obeyed, and put a purse containing five hundred pieces of gold into my brother's hand. Alnaschar was ready to expire with joy at sight of this wealth. He bestowed a thousand blessings on the lady, and, after shutting up his shop, he went home.

"He made many serious reflections on the good fortune which had so unexpectedly come to him; and while he was thus employed he heard some person knock at his door. He asked who was there and, perceiving that his visitor was a female, he admitted her. 'My son,' said she, addressing my brother, 'I have a favor to request of you. It is now the time for prayers, and I wish to wash myself that I may be fit to perform my devotions. Suffer me, I entreat you, to come into your house, and bestow on me a basin of water.' My brother looked at her and saw she was somewhat advanced in years, and, although he did not know her, he nevertheless acceded to her request. He again fell to thinking of his adventure; he took his gold and put it into a sort of long and narrow purse which he could easily carry at his girdle. The old woman in the mean time said her prayers; and when she had done she wished Alnaschar all manner of prosperity, and thanked him for his kindness.

"As she was very meanly dressed, my brother thought that she meant to ask charity; he therefore offered her two pieces of gold. The old woman drew back with as great an appearance of surprise as if my brother had done her an injury. 'O Allah!' cried she, 'what do you mean by this? Is it possible, my master, that you can take me for one of those poor wretches who make a practice of impudently going into men's houses and begging? Put back your money, for I have no need of it, Allah be praised! I belong to a young lady in this city whose beauty is incomparable, and she is so rich that she does not let me want for anything.'

"My brother was not wise enough to see through the cunning of the old woman, who refused the two pieces of gold only to dupe him the more. He asked her if she could not procure him the honor of seeing this lady. 'Certainly,' answered she; 'and you may even succeed in marrying her; and, in becoming her husband, you will get possession of all her fortune. Take your money and follow me.' Delighted that his singular good fortune in receiving such a large sum of money should be followed by the acquisition of a beautiful and rich wife, Alnaschar forgot every thought of prudence. He took his five hundred pieces of gold and suffered the old woman to lead him away.

"He followed her till they came to the door of a large house, at which she knocked. A young female Greek slave opened the door. The old woman made Alnaschar enter first. He passed through a well-paved court, and she then brought him into a hall whose handsome furniture confirmed him in the high opinion he had conceived of the mistress of the house. While the old woman went to inform the young lady of his arrival he sat down. The lady of the house presently made her appearance, and he was much more struck with her beauty than with the magnificence and richness of her dress. He rose up the moment he saw her. The lady requested him to resume his seat, and placed herself by his side. She expressed great pleasure at seeing him, and after some kind speeches she said to him: 'We are not here sufficiently at our ease. Come, give me your hand.' So she led him to a distant apartment, where they remained some time in conversation; she then left him, with a promise to return in a few moments. He had waited some time when, instead of the lady, a large black slave entered, with a scimitar in his hand; and he cried, casting a terrible look at my brother, 'What do you here?' Alnaschar was seized with so violent a fright he could not make any answer. The black immediately stripped him, took away his gold, and gave him several wounds with his scimitar. Poor Alnaschar fell down on the ground, where he remained motionless, though he did not lose his senses. The black slave, thinking he had killed my brother, called for some salt, and the Greek slave brought him a large dishful. They rubbed the salt over my brother's wounds, and, although the pain he felt was almost intolerable, he had the presence of mind to show no signs of life. The black slave and the young Greek now went away, and the old woman who had caught my brother in this snare came in. She took him by the legs and drew him toward a trap-door, which she opened. She then threw him in, and he found himself in a subterraneous vault, surrounded by the bodies of different people who had been murdered. It was some time, however, before he knew this, as the violence of the fall had stunned him and taken away his senses. The salt with which his wounds had been rubbed had preserved his life. He soon felt himself sufficiently strong to sit up. At the end of two days he opened the trap-door in the night, and, observing a place in a courtyard in which he could conceal himself, he remained there till daybreak. He then saw the wicked old woman come out; she opened the street door and went away in search of more prey. As soon as she was out of sight he escaped out of this den of murderers and fled to my house. He then informed me of the adventures he had encountered in the last few days.

"At the end of a month he was quite cured of his wounds, and then resolved to avenge himself on the old woman who had so cruelly deceived him. For this purpose he took a purse large enough to hold five hundred pieces of money; but instead of putting gold in it, he filled it with pieces of glass.

"My brother then tied the purse to his girdle and disguised himself as an old woman, taking with him a scimitar concealed under his dress. He went out early one morning, and soon met the old hag, who was already prowling about the city, seeking to entrap some unwary passenger. Alnaschar accosted her, and, in a feigned woman's voice, he said: 'Can you do me the favor to lend me some scales for weighing money? I am a Persian, and have just arrived in this city. I have brought five hundred pieces of gold from my own country, and I wish to see if they are the proper weight.' 'My good woman,' replied the old hag, 'you could not have addressed yourself to a more proper person than myself. You need only follow me, and I will take you to the house of my son, who is a money-changer, and he will be glad to weigh the gold for you himself.' My brother followed her to the same house whither she had led him the first time, and the door was opened by the Greek slave.

"The old woman conducted my brother into the hall, where she bade him wait a moment while she went to find her son. The pretended son then appeared in the form of the villainous black slave. 'Come, my old woman,' he called out; 'get up and follow me.' Having spoken this, he walked on before to the place where he committed his murders. Alnaschar rose and followed the black slave; but as he went he drew his scimitar from under his robe and struck the slave such a blow on the hinder part of the neck that he cut his head completely off. He then took the head up in one hand, and with the other he drew the body after him to the entrance of the subterraneous vault, into which he cast both head and body. The Greek slave, who was used to this business, quickly appeared with a basin of salt; but when she saw Alnaschar with the scimitar in his hand, and without the veil that had concealed his face, she let the basin fall and ran away, but my brother soon overtook her and struck her head from her shoulders. Hearing the noise they made, the wicked old woman ran to see what was the matter, but Alnaschar seized her before she had time to make her escape. 'Wretch!' he exclaimed, 'dost thou not know me?' 'Alas! my master,' she tremblingly answered, 'I do not remember to have ever seen you before. Who are you?' 'I am the man into whose house you came the other day to request leave to wash yourself and say your hypocritical prayers.' She instantly fell down on her knees and begged for mercy, but he cut her into four pieces.

"Now the lady alone remained, and she knew nothing at all of what was passing. My brother went to look for her, and discovered her in a chamber. When she saw him enter she nearly fainted. She begged him to spare her life, and he had the generosity to grant her prayer. Then he said, 'How can you, lady, live with such wretches as those on whom I have even now so justly revenged myself?' She answered: 'I was the wife of a very worthy merchant, and that wicked old woman, whose treacherous character I did not know, sometimes came to see me. She said to me one day, "O lady, we are going to have a merry and splendid wedding at our house, and you will be well entertained there if you will honor us with your company." I suffered myself to be prevailed upon to go, and I took a hundred pieces of gold with me. I followed her till she came to this house, where I saw the black, who detained me here by force; and it is now three years since I have been kept here as a prisoner.' My brother replied, 'To judge by the time he has continued his proceedings, this black must have amassed great wealth.' 'So

ARABIAN NIGHTS

much,' she answered, 'that if you could carry it away you would never be poor again. Follow me and I will show it you.' She conducted Alnaschar into a room, where he really saw so many coffers filled with gold that he could not conceal his astonishment. The lady said to him, 'Go and bring here a sufficient number of persons to carry all this away.'

"My brother needed no second bidding. He went away and had quickly collected ten men together. He brought them back with him, and was much astonished to find the door of the house open; but his astonishment was still greater when, on going into the room where he had left the coffers, he could not find a single one. The lady had been more cunning and more diligent than he, and she and the coffers had vanished during my brother's absence. That he might not return with empty hands, he ordered the men to take whatever movables they could find in the chambers and different apartments, whence he carried off much more than sufficient to repay him the value of the five hundred pieces of gold of which he had been robbed. But when he left the house my brother forgot to shut the door, and the neighbors, who knew Alnaschar, went and gave information to the judge.

"Alnaschar passed the night quite comfortably; but early the next morning, as he was going out, he encountered twenty men belonging to the police, who immediately seized him. 'You must come with us,' they cried; 'our master wants to speak with you.' My brother begged them to have patience, but they compelled him to go with them and carried him before the judge.

"As soon as he came into the judge's presence, that officer said to him, 'I desire you to inform me from what place you got all that furniture you caused to be brought home yesterday.' 'O judge,' replied Alnaschar, 'I am ready to tell you the whole truth; but permit me in the first place to implore your favor, and to beg that you will pledge me your word that nothing shall happen to me.' 'I promise it,' said the judge. My brother then related, without disguise, every circumstance that had happened to him from the time when the old woman first came to his

[269]

ARABIAN NIGHTS

house till his return to the chamber in which he had left the young lady, after having killed the black, the Greek slave, and the old woman. With regard to what he had carried home, he entreated the judge to suffer him to keep at least a part of it as amends for the five hundred pieces of gold of which he had been robbed.

"The judge immediately sent some of his people to my brother's house to bring away everything, without promising to let Alnaschar keep any part of the spoil; and as soon as the things were deposited in his own warehouse he ordered my brother instantly to leave the city, and forbade him to return again on pain of death; because he was fearful that if my brother remained in the city he would go and complain to the caliph of the judge's injustice. Alnaschar obeyed the order without a murmur. He departed from the city and fled for refuge to another town. But on the road he fell among robbers, who took from him everything he had and stripped him naked."

THE HISTORY OF THE BARBER'S SIXTH BROTHER

"THE history of my sixth brother is the only one that now remains to be told. He was called Schacabac, the Hare-lipped. He was at first sufficiently industrious to employ the hundred drachms of silver which came to his share in a very advantageous manner; but at length he was reduced by reverse of fortune to the necessity of begging his bread. His chief aim was to procure admission into the houses of the great by bribing the officers and domestics; and when he had once managed to get admitted to them, he failed not to excite their compassion.

"He one day passed by a very magnificent building, through the door of which he could see a vast number of servants. He went up to one of them and inquired of him to whom the house belonged. 'My good man,' answered the servant, 'where can you come from, that you ask such a question? Any one you met would tell you it belonged to a Barmecide.' My brother, who well knew the liberal and generous disposition of the Barmecides, addressed himself to the porters, and requested them to bestow some charity upon him. 'Come in,' answered they,

ARABIAN NIGHTS

'no one prevents you, and speak to our master; he will send you back well satisfied.'

"My brother did not expect so much kindness; and after returning many thanks to the porters he entered the palace, which was so large that he spent some time in seeking out the apartment belonging to the Barmecide. He at length came to a large, square building very handsome to behold, into which he entered by a vestibule that led to a fine garden.

"My brother advanced still farther, and entered a hall, where he perceived a venerable old man, whose beard was long and white, sitting on a sofa in the most distinguished place. It was the Barmecide himself, who told him in an obliging manner that he was welcome, and asked him what he wished. 'My lord,' answered my brother, 'I am a poor man who stands very much in need of the assistance of such powerful and generous persons as yourself.' He could not have done better than address himself to the person to whom he spoke, for this man possessed a thousand amiable qualities.

"The Barmecide was much astonished at my brother's answer, and exclaimed: 'Is it possible that in Bagdad such a man as you should be so much distressed as you say you are? I cannot suffer this to be.' At this exclamation my brother, thinking the Barmecide was going to give him a singular proof of his liberality, wished him every blessing. 'It shall never be said,' replied the Barmecide, 'that I leave you unsuccored. I intend that you shall not leave me.' 'O my master,' cried my brother, 'I swear to you that I have not even eaten anything this day.' 'Alas! poor man,' cried the Barmecide, 'you will die of hunger! Here, boy,' added he, raising his voice, 'bring us instantly a basin of water that we may wash our hands.'

"Although no boy appeared, and my brother could see neither basin nor water, the Barmecide began to rub his hands, as if some one held the water for him, and said to my brother, 'Come hither, and wash with me.' Schacabac supposed that the Barmecide loved his jest; and as he knew the submission the rich expected from the poor, he imitated all the movements of his host.

[272]

ARABIAN NIGHTS

"'Come,' said the Barmecide, 'now bring us something to eat, and do not keep us waiting.' When he had said this, although nothing had been brought to eat, he pretended to help himself from a dish, and to carry food to his mouth and chew it, while he called out to my brother: 'Eat, I entreat you, my guest. Eat, I beg of you; you seem, for a hungry man, to have but a poor appetite.' 'Pardon me, my lord,' replied Schacabac, who was imitating the motions of his host very accurately, 'you see I lose no time.' 'What think you of this bread?' said the Barmecide. 'Don't you find it excellent?' 'In truth, my lord,' answered my brother, who in fact saw neither bread nor meat, 'I never tasted anything more white or delicate.' 'Eat your fill, then,' rejoined the Barmecide. Presently he said: 'Boy, bring us another dish. Come, my friend,' he continued to my brother, though no boy appeared, 'taste this and tell me if you have ever eaten boiled mutton and barley better dressed than this.' 'Oh, it is admirable,' answered my brother; 'and you see that I help myself very plentifully.' 'I am rejoiced to see you,' said the Barmecide. He presently called for a goose with sweet sauce, and dressed with vinegar, honey, dried raisins, gray peas, and dried figs. This was brought in the same imaginary manner as the mutton. But the dish the Barmecide praised most highly of all was a lamb stuffed with pistachio nuts, and which was served in the same manner as the other dishes. 'Now this,' said he, 'is a dish you never met with anywhere but at my table, and I wish you to eat heartily of it.' As he said this he pretended to take a piece in his hand and put it to my brother's mouth. My brother opened his mouth and pretended to take the piece of lamb, and to chew and swallow it with the greatest pleasure. 'I was quite sure,' said the Barmecide, 'you would think it excellent.' 'Nothing can be more delicious,' replied Schacabac. 'Indeed, I have never seen a table so well furnished as yours.' 'Now bring me the ragout,' said the Barmecide, 'and I think you will like it as much as the lamb. What do you think of it?' 'It is wonderful,' answered my brother; 'in this ragout we have at once the flavor of amber, cloves, nutmegs, ginger, pepper,

[273]

and sweet herbs; and yet they are all so well balanced that the presence of one does not destroy the flavor of the rest. How delicious it is!' 'Do justice to it, then,' cried the Barmecide, 'and I pray you eat heartily. Ho! boy,' cried he, raising his voice, 'bring us a fresh ragout.' 'Not so, my master,' said Schacabac, 'for in truth I cannot indeed eat any more.'

"'Then let the dessert be served,' said the Barmecide. 'Bring in the fruit.' He then waited a few moments, to give the servants time to change the dishes; then, resuming his speech, he said, 'Taste these almonds; they are just gathered, and very good.' They then both pretended to peel the almonds and eat them. The Barmecide after this invited my brother to partake of many other things. 'You see here,' he said, 'all sorts of fruits, cakes, dried comfits, and preserves; take what you like.' Then, stretching out his hand, as if he was going to give my brother something, he said, 'Take this lozenge; it is excellent to assist digestion.' Schacabac pretended to take the lozenge and eat it. He still continued to persuade my brother to eat, and said, 'For a man who was almost starving when he came here, you have really eaten hardly anything.' 'O my master,' replied Schacabac, whose jaws were weary of moving with nothing to chew, 'I assure you I am so full that I cannot eat a morsel more.'

"'Then,' cried the Barmecide, 'after a man has eaten so heartily he should drink a little. You have no objection to good wine?' 'My master,' replied my brother, 'I pray you to forgive me—I never drink wine, because it is forbidden me.' 'You are too scrupulous,' said the Barmecide. 'Come, come; do as I do.' And he ordered some wine to be brought. But the wine, like the dinner and dessert, was imaginary. The Barmecide then pretended to pour some out, and drank the first glass. Then he poured out another glass for my brother, and, presenting it to him, he cried, 'Come, drink my health, and tell me if you think the wine good.'

"My brother pretended to take the glass. He held it up, and looked to see if the wine were of a good bright color; he put it to his nose to test its perfume; then, making a most profound reverence to the Barmecide, he drank it off, pretending that the draught gave him the most exquisite pleasure. 'My master,' he said, 'I find this wine excellent; but it does not seem to me quite strong enough.' 'You have only to command,' replied the other, 'if you wish for a stronger kind. We will see if this will suit you better.' He then pretended to pour out wine of another kind for himself and for my brother. He repeated this action so frequently that Schacabac pretended that the wine had got into his head and feigned intoxication. He raised his hand and gave the Barmecide such a violent blow that he knocked him down. He was going to strike him a second time, but the Barmecide called out, 'Are you mad?' My brother then pretended to recollect himself, and said: 'O my master, you had the goodness to receive your slave into your house, and to make a great feast for him; you should have been satisfied with making him eat, but you compelled him to drink wine. I am very sorry, and humbly ask your pardon.'

"When Schacabac had finished this speech, the Barmecide, instead of putting himself in a great passion and being very angry, burst into a violent fit of laughter. 'For a long time,' said he, 'I have sought a person of your disposition. I not only pardon the blow you have given me, but from this moment I look upon you as one of my friends and desire that you make my house your home. You have had the good sense to accommodate yourself to my humor, and the patience to carry on the jest to the end; but we will now eat in reality.' So saying, he clapped his hands, and this time several slaves appeared, whom he ordered to set out the table and serve the dinner. His commands were quickly obeyed, and my brother was now in reality regaled with all the dishes he had before partaken of in imagination. As soon as the table was cleared, wine was brought, and a number of beautiful and richly attired female slaves appeared and began to sing some pleasant airs to the sound of instruments. Schacabac had in the end every reason to be satisfied with the kindness and hospitality of the Barmecide, who took a great fancy to him.

"The Barmecide found my brother possessed of so much

knowledge of various sorts that in the course of a few days he intrusted to him the care of all his house and affairs; and my brother acquitted himself of his charge, during a period of twenty years, to the complete satisfaction of his employer. At the end of that time the Barmecide paid the common debt of nature; and as he did not leave any heirs, all his fortune fell to the state; my brother was even deprived of all his savings. Finding himself thus reduced to his former state of beggary, he joined a caravan of pilgrims going to Mecca. During the journey the caravan was attacked and plundered by a party of Bedouin Arabs, who were more numerous than the pilgrims.

"My brother thus became the slave of a Bedouin, who for many days in succession gave him the bastinado in order to induce him to get himself ransomed. Schacabac protested that it was useless to ill-treat him in this manner. 'I am your slave,' said he, 'and you may dispose of me as you like, but I declare to you that it is not in my power to ransom myself.' My brother tried every expedient to convince the Bedouin of his wretched condition. But the Bedouin was inexorable, and through revenge at finding himself disappointed of a considerable sum of money which he had fully expected to receive, he took his knife and slit my brother's lips. By this inhuman act he endeavored to revenge himself for the loss he considered he had suffered.

"This Bedouin had a wife who was rather handsome, and her husband soon after left my brother with her when he went on his excursions. At such times his wife left no means untried to console Schacabac for the rigor of his situation. She even gave him to understand she was in love with him; but he took every precaution to avoid being alone with her, whenever she seemed to wish it. At length she became so much accustomed to joke and amuse herself with the hard-hearted Schacabac whenever she met him that she one day forgot herself, and jested with him in the presence of her husband. As ill-luck would have it, my poor brother, without in the least thinking he was observed, returned her pleasantries. The Bedouin immediately imagined his slave and his wife loved each other. This suspicion put him into the greatest rage. He sprang upon my brother, and, after mutilating him in a barbarous manner, he carried him on a camel to the top of a high, rugged mountain, where he left him. This mountain happened to be on the road to Bagdad, and some travelers, who found my brother there, informed me of his situation. I made all the haste I could to the place, and I found the unfortunate Schacabac in the most deplorable condition. I afforded him every aid, and brought him back with me into the city.

"This was what I related to the caliph Mostanser Billah," said the barber, in conclusion. "The caliph very much applauded my conduct, and expressed his approval by reiterated fits of laughter. He said to me, 'They have given you with justice the name of the Silent, and no one can say you do not deserve it. Nevertheless, I have some private reasons for wishing you to leave the city; I therefore order you immediately to depart. Go, and never let me hear of thee again.' I yielded to necessity, and traveled for many years in distant lands. At length I was informed that the caliph was dead; I therefore returned to Bagdad, where I did not find one of my brothers alive. It was on my return to this city that I rendered to this lame young man the important service of which you have heard. You are also witnesses of his great ingratitude, and of the injurious manner in which he has treated me. Instead of acknowledging his great obligations to me, he has chosen rather to quit his own country in order to avoid me. As soon as I discovered that he had left Bagdad, I did not hesitate a moment, but instantly set out to seek him. I passed on from province to province, and I met him to-day when I least expected it. And least of all did I expect to find him so irritated against me."

"Having in this manner related to the Sultan of Casgar the history of the lame young man, and of the barber of Bagdad, the tailor went on as follows:

"'When the barber had finished his story, we plainly perceived the young man was not wrong when he called him a great chatterer. We sat down to table and continued to enjoy ourselves till the time of the sunset prayers. All the company then separated, and I returned to my shop, where I remained till it was time to shut it up and go to my house.

"'It was then that the little hunchback, who was half drunk, came to my shop, in front of which he sat down and sang to the sound of his timbrel. I thought that by taking him home with me I should afford some entertainment to my wife, and it was for this reason only that I invited him. My wife gave us a dish of fish for supper. I gave some to the little hunchback, who began to eat without taking sufficient care to avoid the bones, and presently he fell down senseless before us. We tried every means in our power to relieve him, but without effect; and then, in the great terror of the moment, we did not hesitate to carry the body out of our house and induce the Jewish physician to receive it in the manner your Majesty has heard told. The Jewish physician let it down into the apartment of the purveyor, and the purveyor carried it into the street, where the merchant thought he had killed the poor man. This, O Sultan,' added the tailor, 'is what I have to say in my justification. It is for you to determine whether we are worthy of your clemency or anger—whether we deserve to live or die.'

"The Sultan of Casgar's countenance expressed so much satisfaction that it gave new courage to the tailor and his companions. 'I cannot deny,' said the monarch, 'that I am more astonished at the history of the lame young man and of the barber, and the adventures of his brothers than at anything in the history of my buffoon. But before I send you all four back to your own houses, and order the hunchback to be buried, I wish to see this barber who has been the cause of your pardon. And since he is now in my capital, it will not be difficult to produce him.' He ordered one of his attendants to go and find the barber out and to take with him the tailor, who knew where the *silent* man was.

"The officer and the tailor soon returned, and brought back with them the barber, whom they presented to the sultan. He appeared a man of about ninety years of age. His beard and eyebrows were as white as snow; his ears hung down to a considerable length, and his nose was very long. The sultan could scarcely refrain from laughter at the sight of him. 'Man of silence,' said he to the barber, 'I understand that you are acquainted with many wonderful histories. I desire that you will relate one of them to me.' 'O Sultan!' replied the barber, 'for the present, if it please your Majesty, we will not speak of the histories which I can tell; but I most humbly entreat permission to ask one question, and to be informed for what reason this Christian, this Jew, this Mussulman, and this hunchback whom I see extended on the ground, are in your Majesty's presence.' The sultan smiled at the freedom of the barber, and said, 'What can that matter to thee?' 'O Sultan!' returned the barber, 'it is of importance that I should make this inquiry in order that your Majesty may know that I am not a great talker, but, on the contrary, a man who had very justly acquired the title of the Silent.'

"The Sultan of Casgar graciously satisfied the barber's curiosity. He desired that the adventures of the little hunchback should be related to him, since the old man seemed so very anxious to hear it. When the barber had heard the whole story he shook his head as if there were something in the tale which he could not well comprehend. 'In truth,' he exclaimed, 'this is a very wonderful history; but I should vastly like to examine this hunchback a little more attentively.' He then drew near to him and sat down on the ground. He took the hunchback's head between his knees, and, after examining him very closely, he suddenly burst out into a violent fit of mirth. 'You may very well say,' he at length cried, 'that no man dies without a cause. If ever a history deserved to be written in letters of gold, it is this of the hunchback.'

"At this speech every one looked upon the barber as an old madman, and the sultan said:

"'Man of silence, answer me. What is the reason of your clamorous laughter?' 'O Sultan!' replied the barber, 'I swear by your Majesty's good nature that this hunchback fellow is not

ARABIAN NIGHTS

dead; there is still life in him, and you may consider me a fool and a madman if I do not instantly prove it to you.' Hereupon he produced a box in which there were various medicines. He opened it, and, taking out a phial containing a sort of balsam, he rubbed it thoroughly and for a long time into the neck of the hunchback. He then drew out of a case an iron instrument of peculiar shape with which he opened the hunchback's jaws; and thus he was enabled to put a small pair of pincers into the patient's throat, and drew out the fish-bone, which he held up and showed to all the spectators. Almost immediately the hunchback sneezed, stretched out his hands and feet, opened his eyes, and gave many other proofs that he was alive.

"The Sultan of Casgar, and all who witnessed this operation, were less surprised at seeing the hunchback brought to life, although he had passed a night and almost a whole day without the least apparent sign of animation, than delighted with the merit and skill of the barber, whom they now began to regard as a very great personage in spite of all his faults. The sultan was so filled with joy and admiration that he ordered the history of the hunchback and that of the barber to be instantly committed to writing, that a story which so well deserved to be preserved might never be forgotten. Nor was this all. In order that the tailor, the Jewish physician, the purveyor, and the Christian merchant might ever remember with pleasure the adventures which the hunchback's accident had caused them, he gave to each of them a very rich robe, which he made them put on in his presence before he dismissed them. And he bestowed upon the barber a large pension, and kept him ever afterward near his own person."

Thus the Sultana Sheherazade finished the story of the long series of adventures to which the supposed death of the hunchback had given rise. Her sister Dinarzade said to her: "My dear princess, I am much the more delighted with the story you have just finished from the unexpected incident by which it was brought to a conclusion. I really thought the little hunch-

THE BARBER EXTRACTS THE FISH-BONE FROM THE
HUNCHBACK'S THROAT

back was quite dead." "This surprise has also afforded me pleasure," said Shahriar. "I have also been entertained by the adventures of the barber's brothers." "I am highly satisfied, my dear sister," replied Sheherazade, "that I have been able thus to entertain you and the sultan our lord and master; and since I have had the good fortune not to weary his Majesty, I shall have the honor, if he will have the goodness to prolong my life still further, to relate to him the history of Aladdin, or the Wonderful Lamp.

THE HISTORY OF ALADDIN, OR THE WONDERFUL LAMP

"IN the capital of one of the richest and most extensive provinces of the great empire of China there lived a tailor whose name was Mustapha. The profits of his trade barley sufficed for the subsistence of himself, his wife, and the one son whom Heaven had sent him.

"This son, whose name was Aladdin, had been brought up in a very negligent manner, and had been so much left to himself that he had contracted many very bad habits. He was obstinate, disobedient, and mischievous, and regarded nothing his father or mother said to him.

"When he was old enough to learn a trade, his father, who was too poor to have him taught any other business than his own, took him to his shop and began to show him how to use his needle. But neither kindness nor the fear of punishment could restrain Aladdin's volatile and restless disposition, nor could his father succeed in making him attend to his work.

[284]

ARABIAN NIGHTS

No sooner was Mustapha's back turned than Aladdin was off, and returned no more during the whole day. His father frequently chastised him, but Aladdin remained incorrigible; and with great sorrow Mustapha was obliged at last to abandon him to his idle course. This conduct of his son's gave him great pain; and the vexation of not being able to induce young Aladdin to pursue a proper and reputable course of life brought on a virulent disease that put a period to Mustapha's existence.

"As Aladdin's mother saw that her son would never follow the trade of his father, she shut up Mustapha's shop and sold off all his stock. Upon the sum thus realized, added to what she could earn by spinning cotton, she and her son subsisted.

"Aladdin was now no longer restrained by the dread of his father's anger, and so regardless was he of his mother's advice that he even threatened her whenever she attempted to remonstrate with him. He gave himself completely up to idleness. He pursued this course of life till he was fifteen years old, without showing the least token of good feeling of any sort, and without making the slightest reflection upon what was to be his future lot. Affairs were in this state when, as he was one day playing with his companions in one of the public places, a stranger who was going by stopped and looked attentively at him.

"This stranger was a magician, so learned and famous for his skill that by way of distinction he was called the *African* Magician.

"Whether this African Magician, who was well skilled in physiognomy, thought he saw in the countenance of Aladdin signs of a disposition well suited to the purpose for which he had undertaken a long journey, or whether he had any other project in view, is uncertain; but he very cleverly obtained information concerning Aladdin's family, discovered who he was, and ascertained the sort of character and disposition he possessed. When he had made himself master of these particulars he went up to the youngster, and, taking him aside, asked him if his father was not called Mustapha, and whether he was not a tailor by trade. 'Yes, sir,' replied Aladdin; 'but he has been dead a long time.'

[285]

ARABIAN NIGHTS

"On hearing this the African Magician threw his arms round Aladdin's neck, and embraced and kissed him repeatedly, while the tears ran from his eyes. Aladdin, who observed his emotion, asked him what reason he had to weep. 'Alas! my child,' replied the magician, 'how can I refrain? I am your uncle; your father was my most excellent brother. I have been traveling hither for several years; and at the very instant of my arrival in this place, when I was congratulating myself upon the prospect of seeing him, you inform me of his death. How can I be so unfeeling as not to give way to the most violent grief when I thus find myself deprived of all my expected pleasure?' He then asked Aladdin where his mother lived; and when Aladdin had informed him, the African Magician gave him a handful of small money, saying to him, 'My son, go to your mother; make my respects to her, and tell her that I will come and see her to-morrow, that I may have the consolation of seeing the spot where my good brother lived so many years and where his career closed at last.'

"As soon as the African Magician had quitted him, Aladdin ran to his mother, highly delighted with the money that had been given him. 'Pray tell me, mother,' he cried, as he entered the house, 'whether I have an uncle.' 'No, my child,' replied she, 'you have no uncle, either on your poor father's side or on mine.' 'For all that,' answered the boy, 'I have just seen a man who told me he was my father's brother and my uncle. He even wept and embraced me when I told him of my father's death. And to prove to you that he spoke the truth,' added he, showing her the money which he had received, 'see what he has given me! He bade me also be sure and give his kindest greeting to you, and to say that he would come and see you himself to-morrow, as he was very desirous of beholding the house where my father lived and died.' 'It is true, indeed, my son,' replied Aladdin's mother, 'that your father had a brother once; but he has been dead a long time, and I never heard your father mention any other.'

"The next day the African Magician again accosted Aladdin while he was playing with three other boys. He embraced him as before, and, putting two pieces of gold in his hand, said

[286]

to him: 'Take this, my boy, and carry it to your mother. Tell her that I intend to come and sup with her this evening, and that I send this money that she may purchase what is necessary for our entertainment; but first inform me in what quarter of the city I shall find your house.' Aladdin gave him the necessary information, and the magician took his departure.

"Aladdin carried home the two pieces of gold to his mother, and, when he had told her of his supposed uncle's intention, she went out and purchased a large supply of good provisions. And as she did not possess a sufficient quantity of china or earthenware to hold all her purchases, she went and borrowed what she wanted of her neighbors. When everything was ready she desired Aladdin to go out into the street, and, if he saw his uncle, to show him the way.

"Although Aladdin had pointed out to the magician the exact situation of his mother's house, he was nevertheless very ready to go; but just as he reached the door he heard some one knock. Aladdin instantly opened the door, and saw the African Magician, who had several bottles of wine in his hands that they might all regale themselves.

"When the visitor had given to Aladdin all the things he had brought, he paid his respects to the boy's mother and requested her to show him the place where his brother Mustapha had been accustomed to sit upon the sofa. She pointed it out, and he immediately prostrated himself before it and kissed the sofa several times. 'Alas, my poor brother!' he exclaimed, 'how unfortunate am I not to have arrived in time to embrace you once more before you died!' The mother of Aladdin begged this pretended brother to sit in the place her husband used to occupy. 'No,' he cried, 'I will do no such thing. Give me leave, however, to seat myself opposite, that if I am deprived of the pleasure of seeing him here in person, I may at least look at the spot and try to imagine him present.' Aladdin's mother pressed him no further, but permitted him to take whatever seat he chose.

"When the African Magician had seated himself, he began to enter into conversation with Aladdin's mother. 'Do not be surprised, my good sister,' he said, 'that you have never seen me during the whole time you have been married to my late brother Mustapha, of happy memory. It is full forty years since I left this country, of which, like my brother, I am a native. In the course of this long period I have traveled through India, Persia, Arabia, Syria, and Egypt; and, after passing a considerable time in all the finest and most remarkable cities in those countries, I went into Africa, where I resided for many years. At last, as it is the most natural disposition of man never to forget his native country, or lose the recollection of his family, his friends, and the companions of his youth, the desire of seeing mine took so powerful a hold on my mind, that I felt sufficiently bold once more to undergo the fatigue of this long journey. I therefore began my travels. It is useless to say how long I was thus employed, or to enumerate the various obstacles I had to encounter before I came to the end of my labors. But nothing so much mortified me or gave me so much pain as the intelligence of the death of my poor brother, whom I tenderly loved. I have recognized almost every feature of his countenance in the face of my nephew.'

"The magician, who perceived that Aladdin's mother was very much affected at this conversation about her husband, now changed the subject, and, turning toward Aladdin, asked him his name. 'I am called Aladdin,' he answered. 'And pray, Aladdin,' said the magician, 'what is your occupation? Have you learned any trade?'

"At this speech Aladdin was much disconcerted; but his mother, seeing this, answered for him. 'Aladdin,' she said, 'is a very idle boy. His father did all he could to make him learn his business, but could not get him to work; and since my husband's death, in spite of everything I can say, Aladdin will learn nothing, but leads the idle life of a vagabond. He knows very well that his father left us nothing to live upon; he can see that, though I pass the whole day in spinning cotton, I can hardly get bread for us to eat. In short, I am resolved soon to turn him out of doors, and make him seek a livelihood where he can find it.'

ARABIAN NIGHTS

"As she spoke these words, the woman burst into tears. 'This is not right, Aladdin,' said the African Magician. 'Dear nephew, you must think of supporting yourself and working for your bread. There are many trades you might learn; consider if there be not any one you have an inclination for in preference to the rest. Perhaps the business which your father followed displeases you and you would rather be brought up to some other calling. If you have any objection to learning a trade, and yet wish to grow up as a respectable and honest man, I will procure you a shop and furnish it with rich stuffs and fine linens. You shall sell the goods, and with the profits that you make you shall buy other merchandise; and in this manner you will pass your life very respectably. Consult your own inclinations, and tell me candidly what you think of the plan.'

"This offer greatly flattered the vanity of Aladdin; and he was the more averse to any manual industry because he knew well enough that the shops which contained goods of this sort were much frequented, and the merchants themselves well dressed and highly esteemed. He therefore hinted to the magician that he thought very favorably of this plan. 'Since this employment is agreeable to you,' replied the magician, 'I will take you with me to-morrow and have you properly and handsomely dressed, as becomes one of the richest merchants of this city; and then we will procure a shop of the description I have named.'

"Aladdin's mother, who till now had not been convinced that the magician was really the brother of her husband, no longer doubted the truth of his statement when she heard all the good he promised to do her son. She thanked him most sincerely for his kind intentions, and, charging Aladdin to behave himself so as to prove worthy of the good fortune his uncle had led him to expect, she served up the supper. During the meal the conversation turned on the same subject, and continued till the magician, perceiving that the night was far advanced, took leave of Aladdin and his mother, and retired.

"The magician did not fail to return the next morning according to promise. He took Aladdin away with him and brought the lad to a merchant's where ready-made clothes were sold, suited to every description of people, and made of the finest stuffs. He made Aladdin try on such as seemed to fit him, and said, 'Dear nephew, choose such as please you best out of this number.' Delighted with the liberality of his new uncle, Aladdin made choice of a garment. The magician bought it, together with everything that was necessary to complete the dress.

"When Aladdin saw himself thus handsomely dressed he overwhelmed his uncle with thanks; the magician on his part again promised to continue to aid and protect him. He then conducted Aladdin to the most frequented parts of the city, particularly to the quarter where the shops of the most opulent merchants were situated; and when he had come to the street where fine stuffs and linens were sold in the shops, he said to Aladdin, 'You will soon become a merchant like those who keep these shops. It is proper that you should frequent this place and become acquainted with them.' After this he took him to the largest and most noted mosques, to the khans where the foreign merchants lived, and through every part of the sultan's palace where he had leave to enter. When they had thus visited all the chief parts of the city they came to the khan where the magician had hired an apartment. They found several merchants with whom he had made some slight acquaintance since his arrival, and whom he had invited to partake of a repast, that he might introduce his pretended nephew to them.

"The entertainment was not over till the evening. Aladdin then wished to take leave of his uncle and go home. The magician, however, would not suffer him to go alone. He went himself, and conducted Aladdin back to his mother's. When she saw her son so handsomely dressed the good woman was transported with joy. She invoked a thousand blessings on the magician, who had been at so great an expense on her dear child's account. 'O generous relation,' she exclaimed, 'I know not how to thank you for your great liberality. I thank you with my whole soul. May you live many happy years.'

ARABIAN NIGHTS

"'Aladdin,' replied the magician, 'is a good boy. He seems to pay attention to what I say. I have no doubt that we shall make him what we wish. I am sorry for one thing, and that is, that I shall not be able to perform all my promises to-morrow. It is Friday, and on that day all the shops are shut. We will, however, settle all this business the day after to-morrow, and I will come here to-morrow to take Aladdin away with me and show him the public gardens.' The magician then took his leave and departed. Aladdin, who was delighted at seeing himself so well dressed, was still more pleased at the idea of going to the gardens in the suburbs of the city. He had never been beyond the gates, nor had he seen the neighboring country, which was really very beautiful and attractive.

"The next morning Aladdin got up very early in order to be ready to set out the very moment his uncle called for him. The moment he saw the magician coming he went to inform his mother of the fact; then he took leave of her and ran to meet his uncle.

"The magician received Aladdin in the most affectionate manner. 'Come, my good boy,' said he, with a smile, 'I will to-day show you some very fine things.' He led the boy out at a gate that led to some palaces, to each of which there was a beautiful garden wherein they had the liberty of walking. In the mean time they were advancing into the country, and the cunning magician, who wanted to go still farther, for the purpose of putting into execution a design which he had in his head, went into one of these gardens and sat down by the side of a large basin of pure water which received its supply through the jaws of a bronze lion. He then pretended to be very tired, in order to give Aladdin an opportunity of resting. 'My dear nephew,' he said, 'like myself, you must be fatigued. Let us rest ourselves here a little while, and get fresh strength to pursue our walk.'

"When they had seated themselves, the magician took out from a piece of linen cloth which hung from his girdle various sorts of fruits and some cakes. He divided a cake between himself and Aladdin, and gave the youth leave to eat whatever fruit he liked best. While they were refreshing themselves he gave his pretended nephew much good advice, desiring him to associate with intelligent and prudent men, to pay every attention to them, and to profit by their conversation. When they had finished their slight repast they rose and pursued their way by the side of the gardens. The magician insensibly led Aladdin far beyond the last of these gardens; and they walked on through the country till they came into the region of the mountains.

"Aladdin, who had never in his whole life before taken so long a walk, felt very tired. 'Where are we going, my dear uncle?' said he. 'We have got much farther than the gardens, and I can see nothing but hills and mountains before us. And if we go on any farther I know not whether I shall have strength enough to walk back to the city.' 'Take courage, nephew,' replied his pretended uncle; 'I wish to show you another garden that far surpasses in magnificence all you have hitherto seen.' Aladdin was persuaded to proceed, and the magician led him on a considerable distance, amusing him all the time with entertaining stories.

"At length they came to a narrow valley, situated between two mountains of nearly the same height. This was the very spot to which the magician wished to bring Aladdin, in order to put in execution the grand project that was the sole cause of his journey to China from the extremity of Africa. Presently he said to Aladdin: 'We need go no farther. I shall here unfold to your view some extraordinary things hitherto unknown to mortals; when you shall have seen them you will thank me a thousand times for having made you an eye-witness of such marvels. I am now going to strike a light, and do you in the mean time collect all the dry sticks and leaves that you can find in order to make a fire.'

"So many pieces of dried sticks lay scattered about this place that Aladdin had collected more than sufficient for his purpose by the time the magician had lighted his match. He then set them on fire; and as soon as they blazed up the African threw upon them a certain perfume. A thick and dense smoke immediately arose, which seemed to unfold itself at some mysterious words pronounced by the magician, and which Aladdin did not in the least comprehend. A moment afterward the ground shook slightly and, opening near the spot where they stood, discovered a square stone of about a foot and a half across, with a brass ring fixed in the center, by which it could be lifted up.

"Aladdin was dreadfully alarmed at these doings, and was about to run away when the magician stopped him in an angry manner, at the same moment giving him a violent blow that felled him to the ground and very nearly knocked some of his teeth out, as appeared from the blood that ran from his mouth. Poor Aladdin, with tears in his eyes and trembling in every limb, got up and exclaimed, 'What have I done to deserve so severe a blow?' 'I have my reasons for it,' replied the magician. 'I am your uncle, and consider myself as your father, therefore you should not question my proceedings. Do not, however, my boy,' added he, in a milder tone of voice, 'be at all afraid; I desire nothing of you but that you obey me most implicitly; and this you must do if you wish to render yourself worthy of the great advantages I mean to afford you.' These fine speeches in some measure calmed the frightened Aladdin; and when the magician saw him less alarmed he said: 'You have observed what I have done by virtue of my perfumes and the words that I pronounced. I must now inform you that under the stone which you see here there is concealed a treasure which is destined for you, and which will one day render you richer than the most powerful potentates of the earth. It is moreover true that no one in the whole world but you can be permitted to touch or lift up this stone and go into the region that lies beneath it. Even I myself am not able to approach it and take possession of the treasure which is below it. And, in order to insure your success, you must observe and execute in every respect the instructions I am going to give you. This is a matter of the greatest consequence both to you and to myself.'

ARABIAN NIGHTS

"Overwhelmed with astonishment at everything he had seen and heard, and full of the idea of this treasure which the magician said was to make him forever happy, Aladdin forgot everything that had happened. 'Well, my dear uncle,' he exclaimed as he got up, 'what must I do? Tell me, and I am ready to obey you in everything.' 'I heartily rejoice,' replied the magician, 'that you have made so good a resolution. Come to me, take hold of this ring and lift up the stone.' 'I am not strong enough, uncle,' said Aladdin; 'you must help me.' 'No, no,' answered the magician, 'you have no occasion for my assistance. You must lift up the stone entirely by yourself. Only pronounce the name of your father and your grandfather, take hold of the ring and lift it; it will come up without any difficulty.' Aladdin did exactly as the magician told him; he raised the stone without any trouble, and laid it aside.

"When the stone was taken away a small excavation was visible, at the bottom of which there appeared a small door, with steps to go down still lower. 'You must now, my good boy,' said the magician to Aladdin, 'observe exactly every direction I am going to give you. Go down into this cavern; and when you have come to the bottom of the steps you will perceive an open door, which leads into a large, vaulted space divided into three successive halls. In each of these you will see on both sides of you four bronze vases, full of gold and silver; but you must take particular care not to touch any of this treasure. When you get into the first hall, take up your robe, and bind it closely round you. Then be sure you go on to the second without stopping, and from thence in the same manner to the third. Above everything, be very careful not to go near the walls, or even to touch them with your robe; for if any part of your dress comes in contact with them, your instant death will be the consequence. At the end of the third hall there is a door which leads to a garden, planted with beautiful trees, all of which are laden with fruit. Go straight forward and pursue a path which you will perceive, and which will bring you to the foot of a flight of fifty steps, at the top of which there is a terrace. When

ARABIAN NIGHTS

you have ascended to the terrace you will observe a niche before you in which there is a lighted lamp. Take the lamp and extinguish it. Then throw out the wick and the liquid that is in it and put the lamp in your bosom. When you have done this, bring it to me. If you should feel desirous of gathering any of the fruit in the garden you may do so; there is nothing to prevent your taking as much as you please.'

"When the magician had given these directions to Aladdin, he took off a ring which he had on one of his fingers, and put it on the hand of his pretended nephew, telling him at the same time that it was a preservative against every evil that might otherwise happen to him. 'Go,' added he, 'descend boldly. We shall now both of us become immensely rich for the rest of our lives.'

"Aladdin jumped into the opening, and then went on down the steps. He found the three halls, which exactly answered the description the magician had given of them. He passed through them with the greatest precaution possible. He went on to the garden, and without stopping ascended to the terrace. He took the lamp which stood lighted in the niche, threw out its contents, and put it into his bosom. He then came back down the terrace and stopped in the garden to look at the fruit, which he had only seen for an instant as he passed along. The trees of this garden were all laden with the most extraordinary fruit. Each tree bore large balls, and the fruit of each tree had a separate color. Some were white, others sparkling and transparent like crystal; some were red and of different shades; others green, blue, or violet; and some of a yellowish hue; in short, there were fruits of almost every color. The white globes were pearls; the sparkling and transparent fruits were diamonds; the deep red were rubies; the green, emeralds; the blue, turquoises; the violet, amethysts; those tinged with yellow, sapphires; and all the other colored fruits, varieties of precious stones; and they were all of the largest size, and the most perfect ever seen in the whole world. Aladdin, who knew neither their beauty nor their value, was not at all struck with their appearance, which did not suit his taste, as the figs, grapes, and other excellent fruits common in China would have done. As he was not yet of an age to be acquainted with the value of these stones, he thought they were only pieces of colored glass, and did not, therefore, attach any importance to them. Yet the variety and contrast of so many beautiful colors, as well as the brilliancy and extraordinary size of these fruits tempted him to gather some of each kind; and he took so many of every color that he filled both his pockets as well as the two new purses that the magician had bought for him at the time he made him a present of his new dress; and as his pockets, which were already full, could not hold his two purses, he fastened them one on each side of his girdle or sash. He also wrapped some stones in its folds, as it was of silk and made very full. In this manner he carried them so that they could not fall out. He did not even neglect to fill his bosom quite full, putting many of the largest and handsomest between his robe and shirt.

"Laden in this manner with the most immense treasure, but ignorant of its value, Aladdin made his way hastily through the three halls, that he might not make the magician wait too long. Having traversed them with the same caution he had used before, he began to ascend the steps he had come down, and presented himself at the entrance of the cave, where the magician was impatiently waiting for him. As soon as Aladdin perceived him he called out, 'Give me your hand, uncle; help me up.' 'My dear boy,' replied the magician, 'you will do better first to give me the lamp, as that will only embarrass you.' 'It is not at all in my way,' said Aladdin, 'and I will give it you when I am out of the cave.' The magician still persisted in demanding the lamp before he helped Aladdin out of the cave; but the latter had in fact so covered it with the fruit of the trees that he could not readily get at it, and absolutely refused to give it up till he had got out of the cave. The magician was then in such despair at the obstinate refusal of the boy, that at length he fell into the most violent rage. He threw a little perfume on the fire, which he had taken care to keep up; and he

THE MAGICIAN PERSISTED IN DEMANDING THE LAMP
BEFORE HE HELPED ALADDIN OUT OF THE CAVE

had hardly pronounced two magic words when the stone, which served to shut up the entrance to the cavern, returned of its own accord to its place, and the earth covered it exactly in the same way as when the magician and Aladdin first arrived there.

"There is no doubt that this magician was not the brother of Mustapha the tailor, as he had pretended to be, and consequently not the uncle of Aladdin. He was most probably a native of Africa, as that is a country where magic is more studied than in any other. He had given himself up to it from his earliest youth, and after nearly forty years spent in enchantments, he had at length discovered that there was in the world a certain wonderful lamp the possession of which would make him the most powerful monarch of the universe, if he could succeed in laying hands on it. By a late experiment in geomancy he discovered that this lamp was in a subterranean cave in the middle of China, in the very spot that has just been described. Thoroughly convinced of the truth of this discovery, he had come from the farthest part of Africa, and after a long and painful journey had arrived in the city that was nearest the depository of this treasure. But though the lamp was certainly in the place which he had found out, yet he was not permitted to take it away himself, nor to go in person into the cave where it was. It was absolutely necessary that another person should go down to take it, and then put it into his hands. For this reason he had addressed himself to Aladdin, who seemed to him to be an artless youth, well adapted to perform the service he required of him; and he had resolved as soon as he had got the lamp from the boy to raise the last fumigation, pronounce the two magic words which produced the effect already seen, and sacrifice poor Aladdin to his avarice and wickedness, that no witness might exist who could say he was in possession of the lamp. The blow he had given Aladdin, as well as the authority he had exercised over him, were only for the purpose of accustoming the youth to fear him, and obey his orders without hesitation, so that when Aladdin had possession of the wonderful lamp he might instantly deliver it to him. But the event disappointed his hopes and expectations, for he was in such haste to sacrifice poor Aladdin, for fear that while he was contesting the matter with him some person might come and make that public which he wished to be kept quite secret, that he completely defeated his own object.

"When the magician found all his hopes and expectations forever blasted there remained but one thing that he could do, and that was to return to Africa; and, indeed, he set out on his journey the very same day. He was careful to travel the by-paths, in order to avoid the city where he had met Aladdin. He was also afraid to meet any person who might have seen him walk out with the lad, and come back without him.

"To judge from all these circumstances, it might naturally be supposed that Aladdin was hopelessly lost; and, indeed, the magician himself, who thought he had thus destroyed the boy, had quite forgotten the ring which he had placed on his finger, and which was now to render Aladdin the most essential service, and to save his life. Aladdin knew not the wonderful qualities either of the ring or of the lamp; and it is indeed astonishing that the loss of both these prizes did not drive the magician to absolute despair.

"Aladdin, who did not expect to be thus wickedly deceived by his pretended uncle, after all the kindness and generosity which the latter had shown to him, was in the highest degree astonished at his position. When he found himself thus buried alive, he called aloud a thousand times to his uncle, telling him he was ready to give up the lamp. But all his cries were useless, and, having no other means of making himself heard, he remained in perfect darkness, bemoaning his unhappy fate. His tears being at length exhausted, he went down to the bottom of the flight of stairs, intending to go toward the light in the garden where he had before been. But the walls, which had been opened by enchantment, were now shut by the same means. He groped along the walls to the right and left several times, but could not discover the smallest opening. He then renewed his cries and tears, and sat down upon the steps of his dungeon, without the least hope that he should ever again see the light of day, and with the melancholy conviction that he should only pass from the darkness he was now in to the shades of an inevitable and speedy death.

"Aladdin remained two days in this hopeless state, without either eating or drinking. On the third day, regarding his death as certain, he lifted up his hands and, joining them as in the act of prayer, he wholly resigned himself to the will of Heaven. In this action of joining his hands he happened, quite unconsciously, to rub the ring which the magician had put upon his finger and of the virtue of which he was as yet ignorant. When the ring was thus rubbed, a genie of enormous stature and a most horrid countenance instantly rose as it were out of the earth before him. This genie was so tall that his head touched the vaulted roof, and he addressed these words to Aladdin: 'What dost thou command? I am ready to obey thee as thy slave—as the slave of him who has the ring on his finger—both I and the other slaves of the ring.'

"On any other occasion Aladdin would have been so frightened at the sight of this startling figure that he would have been unable to speak; but he was so entirely taken up with the danger and peril of his situation that he answered without the least hesitation. 'Whoever you are, take me, if you can, out of this place.' He had scarcely pronounced these words when the earth opened and he found himself outside the cave, at the very spot to which the magician had brought him. It will easily be understood that, after having remained in complete darkness for so long a time, Aladdin had at first some difficulty in supporting the brightness of open day. By degrees, however, his eyes became accustomed to the light; and, on looking round him, he was surprised to find not the smallest opening in the earth. He could not comprehend in what manner he had so suddenly emerged from it. But he could recognize the place where the fire had been made. Looking round, he descried the city in the distance, surrounded by the gardens, and thus he knew the road he had come with the magician. He returned the same way, thanking Heaven for having again suffered him to behold and revisit the face of the earth, which he had quite despaired of ever seeing more. He arrived at the city, but it was only with great difficulty that he got home. When he was within the door, the joy he experienced at again seeing his mother, added to the weak state he was in from not having eaten anything for the space of three days, made him faint, and it was some time before he came to himself. His mother, who had already mourned for him as lost or dead, used every possible effort to restore him to life. At length he recovered, and the first thing he said to his mother was: 'O my dear mother, bring me something to eat before you do anything else. I have tasted nothing these three days.' His mother instantly set what she had before him. 'My dear child,' said she as she did so, 'do not hurry yourself, for that is dangerous. Eat but little, and that slowly, and you must take great care what you do in your exhausted state.'

"Aladdin followed his mother's advice. He ate slowly and sparingly, and drank with equal moderation. When he had done he said: 'I have great reason, my dear mother, to complain of you for putting me in the power of a man whose object was to destroy me, and who at this very moment supposes my death so certain that he cannot doubt either that I am no longer alive, or at least that I shall not survive another day. But you took him to be my uncle, and I was also equally deceived. Indeed, how could we suspect him of any treachery when he almost overwhelmed me with his kindness and generosity and made me so many promises of future advantage? But I must tell you, mother, that he was a traitor, a wicked man, a cheat. He was so good and kind to me only that, after answering his own purpose, he might destroy me. For my part, I can assure you I have not given him the least cause for the bad treatment I have received; and you will yourself be convinced of this from the account I am going to give you of everything that has happened from the moment when I left you till he put his wicked design in execution.'

"Aladdin then related to his mother all that had happened to him. He took the lamp out of his bosom and showed it to his mother, as well as the transparent and different colored fruits that he had gathered as he returned. He gave the two purses that contained these fruits to his mother, who did not set much value upon them. The fruits were, in fact, precious stones; and the luster which they threw around them by means of a lamp that hung in the chamber ought to have shown her they were of the greatest value; but the mother of Aladdin knew no more of their value than her son. Aladdin therefore put them all behind one of the cushions of the sofa on which they were sitting.

"Aladdin had no sooner concluded the recital of his adventures than his mother began to abuse the pretended uncle in the strongest terms. She called him a traitor, an assassin, magician, the enemy and destroyer of the human race. 'Yes, my child,' she cried, 'he is a magician; and magicians are public evils! They hold communication with demons by means of their sorceries and enchantments. Blessed be Heaven that has not suffered the wickedness of this wretch to have its full effect upon you! You, too, ought to return thanks for your deliverance.'

"As Aladdin had not been able to take any repose in the subterraneous place in which he had been buried, it is no wonder that he passed the whole of that night in the most profound sleep, and that it was even late the next morning before he awoke. He at last rose, and the first thing he said to his mother was, that he was very hungry and that she could not oblige him more than by giving him something for breakfast. 'Alas! my child,' replied his mother, 'I have not a morsel of bread to give you. Last night you finished all the trifling store of food there was in the house. But have a little patience, and it shall not be long before I will bring you some. I have here a little cotton I have spun; I will go and sell it and purchase something for our dinner.' 'Keep your cotton, mother,' said Aladdin, 'for another time, and give me the lamp which I brought with me yesterday. I will go and sell that; and the money it will bring will serve us for breakfast and dinner too—nay, perhaps also for supper.'

"Aladdin's mother took the lamp from the place where she had deposited it. 'Here it is,' she said to her son; 'but it seems to me to be very dirty. If I were to clean it a little perhaps it might sell for something more.' She then took some water and a little fine sand to clean the lamp, but she had scarcely begun to rub it when instantly, and in the presence of her son, a hideous and gigantic genie rose out of the ground before her, and cried with a voice as loud as thunder: 'What are thy commands? I am ready to obey thee as thy slave, and the slave of those who have the lamp in their hands; both I and the other slaves of the lamp!' The mother of Aladdin was too much startled to answer this address. She was unable to endure the sight of an apparition so hideous and alarming; and her fears were so great that as soon as the genie began to speak she fell down in a fainting-fit.

"Aladdin had once before seen a similar appearance in the cavern. He did not lose either his presence of mind or his judgment; but he instantly seized the lamp, and supplied his mother's place by answering for her in a firm tone of voice, 'I am hungry; bring me something to eat.' The genie disappeared, and returned a moment after with a large silver basin, which he carried on his head, and twelve covered dishes of the same material filled with the choicest meats, and six loaves as white as snow upon as many plates. He carried two bottles of the most excellent wine and two silver cups in his hands. He placed all these things upon the sofa, and instantly vanished.

"All this had occurred in so short a time that Aladdin's mother had not recovered from her fainting-fit before the genie had disappeared the second time. Aladdin, who had before thrown some water over her without any effect was about to renew his endeavors, but at the very instant she quite recovered.

"'My dear mother,' cried Aladdin, 'there is nothing the matter. Come and eat; here is something that will put you in good spirits again, and at the same time satisfy my hunger.'

"His mother was extremely astonished when she beheld the large basin, the twelve dishes, the six loaves, the two bottles of wine and two cups, and perceived the delicious odor that exhaled from them. 'O my child!' she cried, 'how came all this abundance here? And whom have we to thank for such liberality? The sultan surely cannot have been made acquainted with our poverty and have had compassion upon us?' 'My good mother,' replied Aladdin, 'come and sit down, and begin to eat; you are as much in want of food as I am. I will tell you everything when we have broken our fast.' They then sat down, and both of them ate with the greater appetite, as neither mother nor son had ever seen a table so well supplied.

"During the repast the mother of Aladdin could not help stopping frequently to look at and admire the basin and dishes, although she was not quite sure whether they were silver or any other metal. Nor, indeed, was her son better informed on the subject than herself. When they had made an end of their repast, they found that enough remained, not only for supper, but even for two meals the next day as plentiful as those they had just made.

"When Aladdin's mother had taken away the things and put aside what they had not consumed, she came and seated herself on the sofa near her son. 'I now expect, my dear son,' she said, 'that you will satisfy my impatient curiosity, and let me hear the account you have promised me.' Aladdin then related to his mother everything that had passed between him and the genie. At this discourse of her son, and his account of the appearance of the genie, Aladdin's mother was in the greatest astonishment. 'What is this you tell me, child, about your genie?' she exclaimed. 'Never since I was born have I heard of any person of my acquaintance who has seen one. How comes it, then, that this villainous genie should have accosted me? Why did he not rather address himself to you, to whom he had before appeared in the subterraneous cavern?'

"'Mother,' replied Aladdin, 'the genie who appeared just now to you is not the same who appeared to me. In some things, indeed, they resemble each other, being both as large as giants; but they are very different both in their countenance and dress, and they belong to different masters. If you recollect, he whom I saw called himself the slave of the ring which I had on my

[305]

finger, and the genie who appeared to you was the slave of the lamp you had in your hand; but I believe you did not hear him, as you seemed to faint the instant he began to speak.' 'What!' cried his mother, 'was your lamp the reason why this cursed genie addressed himself to me rather than to you? Ah, my son, take the lamp out of my sight, and put it where you please, so that I never touch it again. Indeed, I would rather that you should throw it away or sell it than run the risk of being killed with fright by again touching it. And if you will follow my advice, you will put away the ring as well. We ought to have no commerce with genii.'

"'With your permission, however, my dear mother,' replied Aladdin, 'I shall beware of parting with this lamp, which has already been so useful to us both. Do you not see what it has procured us, and that it will also continue to furnish us with enough for our support? You may easily judge, as I do, that it was not for nothing my wicked pretended uncle gave himself so much trouble and undertook so long and fatiguing a journey. He did all this merely to get possession of this wonderful lamp, which he preferred to all the gold and silver which he knew was in the three halls. And since chance has discovered its virtues to us, let us avail ourselves of them; but we must be careful not to make any parade, lest we draw upon ourselves the envy and jealousy of our neighbors. I will take the lamp out of your sight, and put it where I shall be able to find it whenever I have occasion for it, since you are so much alarmed at the appearance of genii. Again, I cannot make up my mind to throw the ring away. But for this ring you would never have seen me again. You must permit me, therefore, to keep and to wear it always very carefully on my finger. Who can tell if some danger may not again happen to me which neither you nor I can now foresee, and from which the ring may deliver me?' As the arguments of Aladdin appeared very reasonable, his mother had no further objections to make.

"At supper the next evening, the remainder of the provisions the genie had brought was consumed. The following morning,

ARABIAN NIGHTS

Aladdin, who did not like to wait till hunger pressed him, took one of the silver plates under his robe, and went out early in order to sell it. He addressed himself to a Jew whom he happened to meet. Aladdin took him aside and, showing him the plate, asked if he would buy it.

"The Jew, a clever and cunning man, took the plate and examined it. Directly he had satisfied himself that it was good silver, he desired to know how much the seller expected for it. Aladdin, who knew not its value, merely said that he supposed the Jew knew what the plate was worth, and that he would depend upon the purchaser's honor. Uncertain whether Aladdin was acquainted with its real value or not, the Jew took out of his purse a piece of gold which was exactly one seventy-second part of the value of the plate, and offered it to Aladdin. The latter eagerly took the money, and, without staying to say anything more, went away so quickly that the Jew was very sorry he had not foreseen Aladdin's ignorance of the value of the plate, and in consequence offered him much less for it.

"On his way home, Aladdin stopped at a baker's shop, where he bought enough bread for his mother and himself, paying for his purchase out of his piece of gold, and receiving the change. When he came home he gave the rest of the money to his mother, who went to the market and purchased as much provision as would last them for several days.

"They thus continued to live quietly and economically till Aladdin had sold all the twelve dishes, one after the other, to the same Jew, exactly as he had sold the first; and then they found they wanted more money. The Jew, who had given Aladdin a piece of gold for the first, dared not offer him less for the other dishes, for fear he might lose so good a customer. He therefore bought them all at the same rate. When the money for the last plate was expended, Aladdin had recourse to the basin, which was at least ten times as heavy as any of the plates. He wished to carry this to his merchant, but its great weight prevented him; he was obliged, therefore, to seek out the Jew and bring him to his mother's. After ascertaining the weight of the basin, the

ARABIAN NIGHTS

Jew counted out ten pieces of gold, with which Aladdin was satisfied.

"While these ten pieces lasted they were devoted to the daily expenses of the house. In the mean time Aladdin spent his days in walking about, or conversing with men whose acquaintance he made.

"When his ten pieces of gold were spent, Aladdin had recourse to the lamp. He took it up and looked for the particular spot that his mother had rubbed. As he easily perceived the place where the sand had touched the lamp, he applied his hand to the same spot, and the genie whom he had before seen instantly appeared. But as Aladdin had rubbed the lamp more gently than his mother had done, the genie spoke to him in a softened tone. 'What are thy commands,' said he, in the same words as before. 'I am hungry,' cried Aladdin; 'bring me something to eat.' The genie disappeared, and in a short time returned, loaded with a service similar to that which he had brought before. He placed it upon the sofa, and vanished in an instant.

"Aladdin and his mother immediately took their seats at the table, and after they finished their repast there still remained sufficient food to last them two whole days.

"When Aladdin again found that all his provisions were gone, and he had no money to purchase any, he took one of the silver dishes, and went to look for the Jew who had bought the former dishes of him, intending to deal with him again. As he walked along he happened to pass the shop of a goldsmith, a respectable old man, whose probity and general honesty were unimpeachable. The goldsmith, who perceived him, called to him to come into the shop. 'My son,' said he, 'I have often seen you pass this way, loaded as you are now, and each time you have spoken to a certain Jew; and then I have seen you come back again empty-handed. It has struck me that you went and sold him what you carried. But perhaps you do not know that this Jew is a very great cheat, and that no one who knows him will have any dealings with him? Now I have merely a proposition to make to you. If you will show me what you are now carrying,

ARABIAN NIGHTS

and if you are going to sell it, I will faithfully give you what it is worth, if it be anything in my way of business; if not, I will introduce you to other merchants who will deal honestly with you.'

"The hope of getting a better price for his silver plate induced Aladdin to take it out from under his robe and show it to the goldsmith. The old man, who knew at first sight that the plate was of the finest silver, asked him if he had sold any like this to the Jew, and if so, how much he had received for them. Aladdin plainly told him that he had sold twelve, and that the Jew had given him a piece of gold for each. 'Out upon the thief!' cried the merchant. 'However, my son, what is done cannot be undone, and let us think of it no more; but I will let you see what your dish, which is made of the finest silver we ever use in our shops, is really worth, and then you will understand to what extent the Jew has cheated you.'

"The goldsmith took his scales, weighed the dish, and after explaining to Aladdin how much a mark of silver was he made him observe that, valued according to weight, the plate was worth seventy-two pieces of gold, which he immediately counted out to him. 'This,' said he, 'is the exact value of your plate; if you doubt what I say, you may go to any of our goldsmiths, and if you find that he will give you more for it, I promise to forfeit double the sum. We make our profit by the fashion or workmanship of the goods we buy in this manner.' Aladdin thanked the goldsmith for the good and profitable advice he had given him; and for the future he carried his dishes to no one else. He took the basin also to this goldsmith's shop, and received the value according to its weight.

"Although Aladdin and his mother had an inexhaustible source of money in their lamp, and could procure what they wished whenever they wanted anything, they continued to live with the same frugality they had always shown, except that Aladdin devoted a small sum to innocent amusements and to procuring some things that were necessary in the house. Thus mother and son lived very happily together for many years, with the profitable assistance which Aladdin occasionally procured from the lamp.

"During this interval Aladdin resorted frequently to those places where persons of distinction were to be met with. He visited the shops of the most considerable merchants in gold and silver stuffs, in silks, fine linens, and jewelry; and, by sometimes taking part in their conversation, he insensibly acquired the style and manners of good company. By frequenting the jewelers' shops he learned how erroneous was the idea he had formed that the transparent fruits he had gathered in the garden whence he took the lamp were only colored glass; he now knew their value, for he was convinced that they were jewels of inestimable price. He had acquired this knowledge by observing all kinds of precious stones that were bought and sold in the shops; and as he did not see any stones that could be compared with those he possessed, either in brilliancy or in size, he concluded that he had really procured a most invaluable treasure. He had, however, the prudence not to mention this discovery to any one, not even to his mother, and doubtless it was in consequence of his silence that he afterward rose to the great good fortune to which we shall in the end see him elevated.

"One day as he was walking abroad in the city, Aladdin heard the criers reading a proclamation of the sultan, ordering all persons to shut up their shops and retire into their houses, until the Princess Badroulboudour,[1] the daughter of the sultan, had passed by on her way to the bath and had returned to the palace.

"The casual hearing of this order created in Aladdin a curiosity to see the princess unveiled; but this he could only accomplish by going to some house whose inmates he knew, and by looking through the lattices. This plan, however, by no means satisfied him, because the princess usually wore a veil as she went to the bath. He thought at last of a scheme which proved completely successful. He went and hid himself behind the door of the

---

[1] The name *Badroulboudour* signifies "The Full Moon among full moons."

WHEN SHE HAD COME WITHIN THREE OR FOUR
PACES OF THE DOOR OF THE BATH SHE
LIFTED UP THE VEIL

bath, which was so constructed that he could not fail to see the face of every one who passed through it.

"Aladdin had not waited long in his place of concealment before the princess made her appearance; and he saw her perfectly well without being himself seen. The princess was accompanied by a great crowd of women and eunuchs, who walked on either side of her, while others followed her. When she had come within three or four paces of the door of the bath she lifted up the veil which had concealed her face, and thus gave Aladdin an opportunity of seeing her quite at his ease as she approached the door.

"Till this moment Aladdin had never seen any woman without her veil, except his mother, who was rather old, and who, even in her youth, had not possessed any beauty. He was therefore incapable of forming any judgment respecting the attractions of women.

"The appearance of the Princess Badroulboudour dispelled the notion Aladdin had entertained that all women resembled his mother. His opinions underwent an entire change, and his heart could not help surrendering itself to the object whose appearance had captivated him. The princess was, in fact, the most beautiful brunette ever seen. Her eyes were large, well shaped, and full of fire; yet the expression of her countenance was sweet and modest. Her nose was pretty and properly proportioned; her mouth small; her lips were like vermilion and beautifully formed; in short, every feature of her face was perfectly lovely and regular. It is, therefore, by no means wonderful that Aladdin was dazzled at beholding a combination of charms to which he had hitherto been a stranger. Besides all these perfections, this princess had an elegant figure and a most majestic air.

"Long after she had passed him and entered the bath Aladdin stood still like a man entranced, retracing and impressing more strongly on his own mind the image by which he had been charmed, and which had penetrated to the very bottom of his heart. At last he came to himself, and, recollecting that the princess was gone, and that it would be perfectly useless for him to linger in the hope of seeing her come out, as she would then be veiled, he determined to quit his post and retire.

"When he came home, Aladdin was unable to conceal his disquietude from the observation of his mother. She was very much surprised to see him appear so melancholy and to notice the embarrassment of his manner. She asked him if anything had happened to him, or if he were unwell. He gave her no answer whatever, but continued sitting on the sofa, entirely taken up in retracing in his imagination the lovely image of the Princess Badroulboudour.

"Aladdin passed a wakeful night, occupied by thoughts of the beauty and charms of the Princess Badroulboudour; but the next morning, as he was sitting upon the sofa opposite his mother, he addressed her in the following words: 'O my mother, I will now break the long silence I have kept since my return from the city yesterday morning. I was not ill, as you seemed to think, nor is anything the matter with me now; yet I can assure you that the pain I at this moment feel, and which I shall ever continue to feel, is much worse than any disease.

"'It was not proclaimed in this quarter of the city,' continued Aladdin, 'and therefore you of course have not heard that the Princess Badroulboudour, the daughter of our sultan, went to the bath after dinner yesterday. As I was not far from the bath at the time, the desire I felt to see the face of the princess made me take it into my head to place myself behind the door of the bath, supposing that she might take off her veil just before she went into the building. She did take off her veil as she passed in, and I had the supreme happiness and satisfaction of seeing this beautiful princess. This, my dear mother, is the true cause of the state you saw me in yesterday, and the reason of the silence I have hitherto kept. I feel such a violent affection for this princess that I know no terms strong enough to express it; and, as my ardent love for her increases every instant, I am convinced it can only be satisfied by the possession of the amiable Princess Badroulboudour, whom I have resolved to ask in marriage of the sultan.'

ARABIAN NIGHTS

"Aladdin's mother listened with great attention to this speech of her son's till he came to the last sentence; but when she heard that it was his intention to demand the Princess Badroulboudour in marriage, she could not help bursting into a violent fit of laughter. 'Alas! my son,' she cried, 'what are you thinking of? You must surely have lost your senses to talk thus.' 'Dear mother,' replied Aladdin, 'I do assure you I have not lost my senses. I foresaw very well that you would reproach me with folly and madness; but whatever you may say, nothing will prevent me from again declaring to you that my resolution to demand the Princess Badroulboudour of the sultan in marriage is absolutely unchangeable.'

"'In truth, my son,' replied his mother, very seriously, 'I cannot help telling you that you seem entirely to have forgotten who you are; and even if you are determined to put this resolution in practice, I do not know who will have the audacity to carry your message to the sultan.' 'You yourself must do that,' answered he, instantly, without the least hesitation. 'I!' cried his mother, with the strongest marks of surprise. 'I go to the sultan!—not I, indeed. Nothing shall induce me to engage in such an enterprise. Have you forgotten that you are the son of one of the poorest tailors in this city? Do you not know that sultans do not deign to bestow their daughters even upon the sons of other sultans unless the suitors have some chance of succeeding to the throne?'

"'My dear mother,' replied Aladdin, 'neither your reasons nor remonstrances will in the least change my resolution. I have told you that I would demand the Princess Badroulboudour in marriage, and that you must impart my wish to the sultan. It is a favor which I entreat at your hands, and I beg you not to refuse me, unless you would see me die, whereas by granting it you will give me life, as it were, a second time.'

"Aladdin's mother was very much embarrassed when she saw with what obstinacy her son persisted in his mad design. 'My dear son,' she said, 'I am your mother, and I am ready to do anything that is reasonable and suited to your situation

ARABIAN NIGHTS

in life and my own, and to undertake anything for your sake. If this business were merely to ask in marriage the daughter of any of our neighbors whose condition was similar to yours, I would not object. But to hope for success, even with the daughter of one of our neighbors, you ought to possess some little fortune, or at least to be master of some business. But you, regardless of the lowness of your birth, and of your want of merit or fortune, at once aspire to the highest prize, and pretend to nothing less than to ask in marriage the daughter of your sovereign, who has but to open his lips to blast all your designs and destroy you at once.

"'I will not,' continued Aladdin's mother, 'speak of the probable consequences of this business to you; you ought to reflect upon them if you have any reason left; but I will only consider my own position. Now, suppose that I have the impudence to present myself before his Majesty and make such a mad request of him, to whom should I in the first place address myself to obtain admission to his presence? Do you not see that the very first person I spoke to would treat me as a madwoman, and drive me back with all the indignity and contempt I should so justly merit? But even if I overcame this difficulty, and procured an audience of the sultan, what should I do then? Are you in a position to bring forward your request? Do you think that you deserve the favor which you wish me to ask for you? How can I even open my lips to propose such a thing to the sultan? His illustrious presence and the magnificence of his whole court will instantly strike me dumb with shame. But there is another reason, my son, which you have not yet thought of; and that is, that no one ever appears before the sultan without offering him some present when a favor is sought at his hands. Presents have at least this advantage, that if the monarch refuses your request he will listen patiently to what you have to say. But what present have you to offer him? Be reasonable, and reflect that you aspire to a thing it is impossible to obtain.'

"Aladdin listened with the greatest patience to all these rep-

[316]

resentations by which his mother sought to dissuade him from his purpose, and addressed her in these words: 'I readily acknowledge to you, my dear mother, that it is a great piece of rashness in me to dare to aspire so high as I do; and that it is also very inconsiderate in me to request you with so much earnestness and warmth to go and propose this marriage to the sultan. I love the Princess Badroulboudour far beyond anything you can possibly conceive, and shall forever persevere in my wish and intention of marrying her. I thank you sincerely for the hints you have given me.

"'You say that it is not customary to request an audience of the sultan without carrying a present in your hand, and tell me that I have nothing worthy of offering him. I agree with you about the present, and indeed I never once thought of it. But when you tell me I have nothing worthy of his acceptance, I must say you are wrong. Do you not suppose, mother, that the colored fruits I brought home with me on the day when I was saved from an almost inevitable death would be an acceptable present to the sultan? I mean those things which we thought were pieces of colored glass. I know their value better now, and can inform you that they are precious stones of inestimable worth, and worthy the acceptance of a great sovereign. All the gems which I have seen at our jewelers' are not to be compared with those we have either for size or beauty, and yet they are very highly valued. As I can judge from the little experience I have, I feel assured the present cannot but be very agreeable to the sultan. You have a porcelain dish of a very good shape and size for holding them. Bring it to me, and let us see how the stones will look when we have arranged them according to their different colors.'

"Aladdin's mother brought the dish, and he took the precious stones out of the two purses and arranged them upon it. The effect they produced in broad daylight, by the variety of their colors, their luster, and brilliancy, was so great that both mother and son were absolutely dazzled and astonished.

"When they had for some time admired the beauty of the

present, Aladdin resumed the conversation in these words: 'You cannot now excuse yourself any longer from going and presenting yourself to the sultan upon the plea that you have nothing to offer him. Here is a present which, in my opinion, will procure for you a most favorable reception.'

"Notwithstanding its great beauty and brilliancy, Aladdin's mother had no high opinion of the value of her son's present; still she supposed it would be very acceptable. She was, therefore, aware that she could make no further objection on this score. She again recurred to the nature of the request which Aladdin wished her to make to the sultan. 'I cannot, my son,' she said, 'possibly believe that this present will produce the effect you wish and that the sultan will look upon you with a favorable eye. Then, if you choose me for your messenger, it becomes necessary for me to acquit myself with propriety in the business you wish me to undertake. I shall be struck quite dumb, and thus not only lose all my labor, but the present also, and after all I shall have to come back and inform you of the destruction of all your hopes and expectations.'

"Aladdin's mother continued to urge upon her son many other reasons which should have made him change his mind; but the charms of the Princess Badroulboudour had made too strong an impression upon Aladdin to suffer him to alter his intentions. He persisted in requiring his mother to perform her part in his scheme; and the affection she had for him at length conquered her repugnance, and she promised to do as he bade her.

"Aladdin and his mother talked of nothing else during the rest of the day. Next day Aladdin rose at daybreak, and went immediately to call his mother. He was anxious that she should dress herself as soon as possible, that she might repair to the gate of the sultan's palace, and enter when the grand vizier and all the officers of state went into the hall of audience, where the sultan always presided in person.

"Aladdin's mother did exactly as her son wished. She took the porcelain dish in which the present of jewels had been arranged, and folded it up in a very fine white-linen cloth. Thereupon she set out, to the great joy of Aladdin, and took the road toward the palace of the sultan. The grand vizier, accompanied by the other officers of the court, had already gone into the hall of audience before she arrived at the gate. The crowd was very great. The doors were opened, and Aladdin's mother went into the divan with the rest. Aladdin's mother stopped, and placed herself so that she was opposite the sultan, the grand vizier, and other officers who formed the council. The different applicants were called up one after the other, according to the order in which their petitions had been presented; and their different cases were heard, pleaded, and determined till the usual hour for breaking up the council. The sultan then rose, saluted the court, and went back to his apartment, followed by the grand vizier. The other viziers and officers who formed the council then went their various ways. All the applicants whose private business had brought them there did the same.

"Aladdin's mother, who saw the sultan get up and retire, rightly imagined that he would not appear any more that day; and, as she observed that every one was going away, she determined to return home. When Aladdin saw her come back with the present in her hand he knew not at first what to think of the success of her journey. The good woman, who had never before set her foot within the walls of a palace, and who of course knew nothing of the customs of such places, very soon relieved her son from his embarrassment by saying, with a satisfied air: 'I have seen the sultan, my son, and I am certain he has seen me also. I placed myself directly opposite to him, and there was no person in the way to prevent his seeing me; but he was so much engaged in speaking with those who stood around him that I really felt compassion when I saw the patience and kindness with which he listened to them. This lasted so long that I believe at length he was quite worn out, for he got up before any one expected it and retired very suddenly, without staying to hear a great number of persons who were all ranged in readiness to address him in their turn. But do not lose heart. I will not fail to go again to-morrow; the sultan will not then, perhaps, have so much business on his hands.'

"However violent Aladdin's passion was, he felt compelled to be satisfied with this answer and to summon up all his patience. He had at least the satisfaction of knowing that his mother had got over a most difficult part of the business, and had penetrated into the presence of the sultan; and he therefore hoped that she would not hesitate to acquit herself of the commission with which she was intrusted when the favorable moment for addressing the sultan should arrive.

"The next morning Aladdin's mother set out for the sultan's palace, carrying with her the present of jewels; but again her journey was useless. She returned again to the palace six different times on the appointed days, always placing herself opposite the sultan. But she was each time as unsuccessful as at first; and she would have gone probably a hundred times with as little result if the sultan, who saw her standing opposite him every day the divan sat, had not taken notice of her.

"One day, however, when the council had broken up and the sultan had retired to his apartment, he said to his grand vizier: 'For some time past I have observed a certain woman who comes regularly every day when I hold my council, and who carries something in her hand wrapped in a linen cloth. She always takes care to place herself opposite to me. Do you know what she wants?'

"The grand vizier, who did not wish to appear ignorant of the matter, though in fact he knew no more about it than the sultan himself, replied: 'Your majesty must be aware that women often make complaints upon the most trivial subjects. Probably she has come to your Majesty with some complaint against a person who has sold her some bad meat, or on some equally insignificant matter.' This answer, however, did not satisfy the sultan. 'The very next day the council sits,' said he to the grand vizier, 'if this woman returns, do not fail to call her, that I may hear what she has to say.'

ARABIAN NIGHTS

"The mother of Aladdin returned to the palace the next day the council met, and placed herself opposite the sultan.

"The grand vizier had scarcely begun to make his usual report when the sultan perceived Aladdin's mother. Touched with compassion at the great patience she had shown, he said to the grand vizier: 'In the first place, do you not observe the woman whom I mentioned to you the other day? Order her to come here, and we will begin by hearing what she has to say, and giving her an answer.' The grand vizier immediately pointed out the woman in question to the chief of the ushers, and desired him to go and bring her before the sultan. The officer went directly to the mother of Aladdin, and at a sign he made she followed him to the foot of the throne.

"Following the example set her by many others whom she had seen approach the sultan, Aladdin's mother prostrated herself, and she remained in that position till the sultan commanded her to rise. She obeyed, and he then addressed her in these words: 'For this long time past, good woman, I have seen you regularly attend my divan, and remain near the entrance from the time the council begins to assemble till it breaks up. What is the business that brings you here?' Aladdin's mother answered thus: 'O gracious monarch, before I inform your Majesty of the extraordinary and almost incredible cause that compels me to appear before your sublime throne, I entreat you to pardon the boldness of the request I am about to make. It is of so uncommon a nature that I tremble, and feel almost overcome with shame, to think that I should have to propose it to my sultan.' To give the applicant full liberty to explain herself, the sultan commanded every one to leave the divan, and remained with only his grand vizier in attendance. He then told her she might speak, and exhorted her to tell the truth without fear.

"The kindness of the sultan, however, did not perfectly satisfy Aladdin's mother. She was still anxious to screen herself from the indignation which she could not but dread the proposal she had to make would excite. 'O mighty sovereign,' said she, again addressing the sultan, 'I once more entreat your Majesty to assure me of your pardon beforehand, in case you should think my request at all injurious or offensive.' 'Whatever it may be,' replied the sultan, 'I pardon you in advance. Speak, therefore, with confidence.'

"Aladdin's mother faithfully related to the sultan by what means Aladdin had seen the Princess Badroulboudour, and with what a violent passion the sight of the princess had inspired him. She told how he had declared this attachment to her, and repeated every remonstrance she had urged to avert his thoughts from this passion. 'A passion,' added she, 'as injurious to your Majesty as to the princess your daughter. But,' she went on to say, 'my son would not listen to anything I could say, nor acknowledge his temerity. And once more I entreat your Majesty to pardon not only me for making such a request, but also my son Aladdin, for having conceived the rash and daring thought of aspiring to so illustrious an alliance.'

"The sultan listened to this speech with the greatest patience and good humor, and showed not the least mark of anger at the extraordinary r quest of Aladdin's mother. Before he returned any answer, he asked her what she had with her tied up in a cloth. Upon this Aladdin's mother took up the porcelain dish, which she had set down at the foot of the throne. She removed the linen cloth and presented the dish to the sultan.

"It is impossible to express the utter astonishment of the monarch when he saw collected together in that dish such a quantity of the most precious, perfect, and brilliant jewels, greater in size and value than any he had ever seen. When he began to recollect himself, he took the present from the hand of Aladdin's mother, and exc'aimed, in a transport of joy, 'Ah! how very beautiful, how glorious is this!' And then, after admiring the jewels separately, he turned to his grand vizier and, showing him the dish, asked him if jewels so perfect and valuable had ever been seen before. The vizier was himself delighted with the jewels. 'Tell me,' added the sultan, 'what do you say to such a present? Is not the donor worthy of the princess my daughter? and must not I give her to him who comes and demands her at such a price?'

"This speech of the sultan's was very disagreeable to the grand vizier, because the monarch had some time before given that minister to understand that he had an intention of bestowing the hand of the princess upon the vizier's only son. There-

THE VIZIER WAS HIMSELF DELIGHTED WITH THE JEWELS

fore the vizier was fearful that the sultan would be dazzled by the rich and extraordinary present, and would, in consequence, alter his mind. He therefore approached the sultan and whispered the following words in his ear: 'O great monarch, every one must allow that this present is not unworthy of the princess, but I entreat you to grant me three months before you absolutely determine to bestow her hand. I hope that long before that time my son, for whom you have the condescension to express to me great inclination, will be able to offer a much more considerable present than that of Aladdin, who is an entire stranger to your Majesty.' Although the sultan in his own mind was quite convinced that it was not possible for his grand vizier's son to make so valuable a present to the princess, he nevertheless granted the delay requested. Thereupon he turned toward Aladdin's mother, and said to her: 'Go, my good woman. Return home, and tell your son that I agree to the proposal he has made through you, but that I cannot bestow the princess my daughter in marriage until I have ordered and received certain furniture and ornaments, which will not be ready for three months. At the end of that time you may return here.'

"The mother of Aladdin went home in a very joyful mood. When Aladdin saw his mother enter the house, he noticed two circumstances that led him to suppose she brought him good news. In the first place, she had returned that morning much sooner than usual; and, secondly, her countenance expressed pleasure and good humor. 'Tell me, mother,' said Aladdin, 'do you bid me hope, or am I doomed to die in despair?' When his mother had taken off her veil and had seated herself on the sofa by his side, she said, 'O my son, not to keep you any longer in suspense, I will in the first place tell you that you have every reason to be satisfied.' She then went on to explain to him in what manner she had obtained an audience before any one else was heard. She described the precautions she had taken to make her request to the sultan in such a way that he might not be offended when he came to know that she asked nothing less than the hand of the Princess Badroulboudour in marriage for her son; and lastly, she repeated the favorable answer the sultan had given her with his own mouth. She then added that, as far as she could judge from the words and behavior of the sultan, it was the present that had such a powerful effect upon his mind as to induce him to return so favorable an answer. 'This is my belief,' added she, 'because, before the sultan returned me any answer at all, the grand vizier whispered something in his ear, and I was afraid it would lessen the good intentions he had toward you.'

"When Aladdin heard this good news he thought himself the happiest of mortals. He thanked his mother for all the pains she had taken in managing this business, and for the happy success with which her perseverance had been rewarded. Impatient as he was to possess the object of his affection, the three months that were to elapse seemed to him an age. He nevertheless endeavored to wait with patience, as he relied upon the word of the sultan, which he considered irrevocable.

"It happened one evening, when about two months of the time had gone, that as Aladdin's mother was going to light her lamp she found that she had no oil in the house. Accordingly she went out to buy some, and on going into the city she soon perceived signs of great festivity and rejoicing. All the shops, instead of being shut up, were open and ornamented with green branches and decorations, and every preparation was being made for an illumination. The people also showed evident signs of pleasure and rejoicing. The streets were crowded with the different officers in their dresses of ceremony, mounted on horses most richly caparisoned, and surrounded by a great number of attendants and domestics on foot, who were going and coming in every direction. On seeing all this, Aladdin's mother asked the merchant of whom she bought the oil what it all meant. 'Where do you come from, my good woman,' said he, 'that you do not know that the son of the grand vizier is this evening to be married to the Princess Badroulboudour, the daughter of our sultan? The princess is just now coming from the bath, and the officers whom you see have assembled here to escort her back to the palace, where the ceremony is to be performed.'

"Aladdin's mother did not wait to hear more. She returned home with all possible speed, and arrived quite out of breath. She found her son not in the least prepared for the bad news she brought him. 'All is lost, my son!' she exclaimed. 'You depended upon the fair promises of the sultan, and have been deceived.' Aladdin instantly replied: 'My dear mother, why should not the sultan keep his word? How do you know anything about it?' 'This very evening,' answered Aladdin's mother,

ARABIAN NIGHTS

'the son of the grand vizier is to marry the Princess Badroulboudour at the palace.' She then related to him in what way she
had heard the news.

"Aladdin was greatly astonished at this intelligence. It came
upon him like a thunder-stroke. Any person but himself would
have been quite overwhelmed, but a sort of secret jealousy prevented him from remaining long inactive. He quickly bethought
himself of the lamp, which had hitherto been so useful to him;
and then, without indulging in vain reproaches, he only said:
'This bridegroom, mother, shall not be so happy to-night as he
expects. While I am gone for a few moments into my chamber,
do you prepare supper.'

"His mother easily understood that Aladdin intended to
make use of the lamp in order, if possible, to prevent the completion of the marriage of the grand vizier's son with the Princess
Badroulboudour. In this conjecture she was right, for as soon
as he was in his own room he took the wonderful lamp, rubbed
it, and the genie instantly appeared before him. 'What are
thy commands?' said he to Aladdin. 'Attend to me,' answered
Aladdin. 'You have hitherto supplied me with food and drink
when I needed it. I have now a business of more importance for
you. I have demanded of the sultan the Princess Badroulboudour, his daughter, in marriage. He promised her to me, stipu-
lating for a delay of three months; but, instead of keeping his
word, he has this very evening, when the three months have not
yet elapsed, given his daughter in marriage to the son of his grand
vizier. What I order you to do is this: as soon as the bride
and bridegroom have retired to rest, take them up and instantly
bring them both here in their bed.' 'O master,' replied the genie,
'I will obey thee. Hast thou any further commands?' 'None
at present,' said Aladdin. The genie instantly disappeared.

"Aladdin then went back to his mother, and supped with her
in the same tranquil manner as usual. After supper he returned
to his chamber and left his mother to betake herself to bed.
He, of course, did not retire to rest, but waited till the genie
should return and report the execution of his orders.

ARABIAN NIGHTS

"In the mean time every preparation was made in the sultan's palace to celebrate the nuptials of the princess, and the whole evening was spent in ceremony and rejoicing till the night was far advanced. When the proper time came, the son of the grand vizier retired, unperceived, at a sign that the chief of the eunuchs belonging to the princess privately gave him; and this officer then introduced him into the apartment of the princess, his wife, and conducted him to the chamber where the nuptial couch was prepared. The vizier's son retired to bed first; and in a short time the sultana, accompanied by her own women and those of her daughter, brought the bride into the room. The sultana assisted in undressing her; and, wishing her a good night, she retired with all the women.

"Scarcely had this taken place, when the genie, the faithful slave of the lamp, took up the bed with the bride and bridegroom in it; and, to the great astonishment of them both, in an instant transported them to Aladdin's chamber, where he set them down.

"Aladdin, who was awaiting the genie's arrival with the greatest impatience, did not long suffer the son of the grand vizier to retain his place. 'Take this bridegroom,' said he to the genie, 'and shut him up in the lumber-room, and return again in the morning just at daybreak.' The genie instantly took the grand vizier's son and transported him in his shirt to the place Aladdin had designated, where he left him, after first breathing upon him in such a way that he became paralyzed in every limb, and could not stir.

"Though Aladdin felt a deep and fervent affection for the princess, he did not enter into any long conversation with her when he was with her alone. 'Fear nothing, most adorable princess,' he exclaimed, with an air of deep respect; 'you are here in safety; and however violent the love which I feel for you may be—with whatever ardor I adore your beauty and charms—be assured that I will never exceed the limits of the profound veneration I have for you. I have been forced,' he added, 'to proceed to this extremity; but what I have done has not been with the intention of offending you, but to prevent an unjust rival from

[327]

calling you his, contrary to the promise which the sultan your father has made to me.'

"The princess, who knew nothing of all these particulars, paid very little attention to what Aladdin said. The alarm and astonishment caused by this surprising and unexpected adventure had such an effect upon her that Aladdin could not get a single word from her in reply. Presently he laid himself down in the place of the grand vizier's son, with his back turned toward the princess, having first taken the precaution to place a drawn saber between the princess and himself, as a sign that he deserved to be punished if he offended her in any way.

"Satisfied with having thus deprived his rival of the beauteous princess who had been promised to him, Aladdin slept very tranquilly. But very different was the case with the princess. Never in her whole life had she passed so unpleasant and disagreeable a night; and we need only remember in what a place and situation the genie had left the son of the grand vizier to judge that the bridegroom spent his time in still greater discomfort.

"Aladdin had no occasion to rub his lamp the next morning to call the genie, who appeared punctually at the appointed hour, and found Aladdin dressing himself. 'I am here,' said he to Aladdin. 'What commands hast thou for me?' 'Go,' answered Aladdin, 'and bring back the son of the grand vizier from the place where you have put him. Place him again in his bed, and transport it to the palace of the sultan, whence you have brought it.' The genie instantly went to release the grand vizier's son from his imprisonment, and as soon as he appeared Aladdin took away the saber. He placed the bridegroom by the side of the princess, and in one moment the bed was carried back to the very same chamber of the sultan's palace whence it had been taken.

"During all these transactions the genie was invisible to the princess and the son of the grand vizier. They did not even hear a single word of the conversation that passed between Aladdin and him, and perceived only by the agitation of the bed that they were being transported from one place to another.

ARABIAN NIGHTS

"The genie had just replaced the nuptial couch in the princess's chamber when the sultan came to visit his daughter and wish her good morning. The son of the grand vizier, who was half dead with the cold he had suffered all night, and who not yet had time enough to warm himself, jumped out of bed as soon as he heard the door open, and went into the dressing-room where he had undressed himself the evening before.

"The sultan came up to the bedside of the princess, and kissed her between her eyes, as is the usual custom in wishing any one a good morning. He asked her, with a smile upon his face, how she had slept, but when he looked at her he was extremely surprised to observe that she was in the most dejected and melancholy state. She cast upon him very sorrowful looks, and showed by her whole manner that she was in a state of great alarm and grief. The sultan again spoke to her; but, as he could not get a word from her in reply, he retired. He could not, however, but suspect from her continued silence that something very extraordinary had happened. He therefore went immediately to the apartment of the sultana his wife, to whom he mentioned the state in which he had found the princess, and the reception she had given him. 'O my lord,' replied the sultana, 'I will go and see her. I shall be very much surprised if she will receive me in the same manner.'

"As soon as the sultana was dressed, she went to the apartment of the princess. She approached the bed and, wishing her daughter a good morning, embraced her; but her surprise was great when she found that the princess was in the greatest distress. Therefore she said, affectionately: 'My dear daughter, what is the reason that you do not return the caresses I bestow upon you? Something surely has occurred which I do not understand. Tell me candidly what it is, and do not suffer me to remain long in an uncertainty that distresses me beyond measure.'

"At length, with a deep sigh, the Princess Badroulboudour broke silence. 'Alas! my most honored mother,' she cried, 'pardon me if I have failed in the respect that is due to you. My mind is so entirely absorbed by the strange and extraordinary things which happened to me last night that I have not yet recovered from my fears, and can scarcely summon courage to speak to you.' She then related in the greatest agitation how on the previous night the bed had been taken up and transported into an ill-furnished and dismal chamber, where she found herself quite alone, and separated from her husband without at all knowing what had become of him; and that she found in this apartment a young man who, after addressing a few words to her which her terror prevented her from understanding, lay down in her husband's place, having first put his saber between them; and that when morning approached her husband was restored to her and the bed again brought back to her own chamber in a single instant. 'This second removal,' she added, 'was but just completed when the sultan my father came into my chamber. I was then so full of grief and distress that I could not answer him a single word.'

"The sultana listened with great attention to everything the princess had to relate, but she could not give full credit to her daughter's story. 'You have done well, my child,' she said to the princess, 'not to inform the sultan your father of this matter. Take care that you mention it to no one, unless you wish to be considered a madwoman.' 'O my mother,' replied the princess, 'I assure you that I am in my right senses, and know what I say; you may ask my husband, and he will tell you the same thing.' 'I will take care to question him,' answered the sultana; 'but even if he gives me the same account as you have done, I shall not be convinced of its truth. In the mean time, however, I beg you will rise and drive this fantasy from your mind.' The sultana then called her women; and after she had made her daughter get up and seen her at her toilet, she went to the sultan's apartment and told him that some fancy seemed to have got into the head of his daughter, but that it was a mere trifle. She then ordered the son of the grand vizier to be called, in order to question him about what the princess had told her. But he felt himself so highly honored by this alliance with the sultan, that he determined to feign ignorance. 'Tell me, my dear son-in-law,' said the sultana, 'have you the same strange ideas in your head that your wife has taken into hers?' 'Honored madam,' he replied, 'may I be permitted to ask the meaning of this question?' 'This is sufficient,' answered the sultana; 'I do not wish to know more. I see you have more sense than she has.'

"The festivities in the palace continued throughout the day; and the sultan, who loved the princess tenderly, omitted nothing that he thought might inspire her with joy. He endeavored to interest her in the diversions and various exhibitions that were going on, but the recollection of what had happened the preceding night made such a strong impression on her mind that it was very clear her thoughts were unpleasantly occupied. The son of the grand vizier was equally mortified at the wretched night he had passed; but his ambitious views made him dissemble, and therefore, to judge from his appearance, any one would have thought him the happiest bridegroom in the world.

"Aladdin, who was well informed of everything that had occurred in the palace, did not doubt that the newly married pair would again sleep together, notwithstanding the adventure that had happened to them the night before. He did not, therefore, leave them to repose in quiet; a short time before night came on he again had recourse to his lamp. The genie instantly appeared and addressed Aladdin with the accustomed speech. 'The grand vizier's son and the Princess Badroulboudour,' replied Aladdin, 'are again to sleep together this night. Go, and as soon as they have retired, bring the bed hither as you did yesterday.'

"The genie obeyed Aladdin with the same fidelity he had shown on the previous night, and the vizier's son passed this second night in as cold and unpleasant a situation as he had passed the former, while the princess had the mortification of having Aladdin for a bedfellow, with the saber, as before, placed between them. In the morning the genie came to carry off the bed, and took it back to the chamber of the palace whence he had taken it.

ARABIAN NIGHTS

"The extraordinary reception which the Princess Badroulboudour had given to the sultan on the preceding morning had made him very anxious to learn how she had passed the second night, and whether she would again receive him in the same manner as before. He therefore went to her apartment early in the morning. The grand vizier's son, still more mortified and distressed at the misfortune that had befallen him on the second night than he had been at the first, no sooner heard the sultan than he rose as fast as possible, and ran into the dressing-room. The sultan came to her bedside and wished the princess a good morning. 'Well, my daughter,' he said, 'are you as ill-humored this morning as you were yesterday? Tell me how you slept last night.' The princess made no reply, and the sultan perceived that she was still more dejected and distressed than she had been the morning before. He could not but believe that something very extraordinary had happened to her. Irritated at the mystery she maintained with him, he drew his saber and exclaimed, in an angry voice, 'O daughter, tell me what you thus conceal, or I will instantly strike off your head.'

"Terrified at the menaces of the sultan and at the sight of the drawn saber, the princess at length broke silence. 'My dear father,' she exclaimed, with tears in her eyes, 'if I have offended your Majesty, I most earnestly entreat your pardon. Knowing your goodness, I trust I shall change your anger into compassion by relating to you the occasion of the distressing and melancholy situation in which I have been placed both last night and the night before.' This appeased and softened the sultan. The princess went on to relate what had happened to her on both these horrible nights, and spoke in so affecting a manner that the sultan was penetrated with grief for the sufferings of his beloved daughter. She concluded her narrative by saying, 'If your Majesty has the least doubt of the truth of any part of what I have said, you can easily inquire of the husband you have bestowed upon me; he will corroborate me in everything I have related.'

"The sultan sympathized very fully with the distress this surprising adventure must have excited in his daughter's mind.

ARABIAN NIGHTS

'My child,' said he, 'you were wrong not to divulge to me yesterday the strange story which you have just related, and in which I am not less interested than yourself. I have not bestowed you in marriage to render you unhappy, but, on the contrary, to increase your happiness and to afford you every enjoyment you so well deserve. Banish from your memory, then, the melancholy remembrance of what you have been relating to me; I will take care that you shall experience no more such nights as those which you have now suffered.'

"When the sultan got back to his apartment he immediately sent for the grand vizier. 'Have you seen your son?' he asked him, 'and has he made any communication to you?' On the reply of the minister that he had not seen his son, the sultan reported to him everything he had heard from the Princess Badroulboudour. He then added: 'I have no doubt that my daughter has told me the truth. I wish, nevertheless, to have this matter confirmed by the testimony of your son. Go and question him.'

"The grand vizier immediately went to his son, informed him of what the sultan had said, and commanded him to tell everything that had happened. 'I will conceal nothing from you, my father,' replied the son. 'Everything the princess has told the sultan is true; but she was unable to give an account of the bad treatment which I in particular have experienced. Since my marriage I have spent two of the most dreadful nights you can possibly conceive. But you yourself can judge of the dreadful state I was in when I tell you that I passed both nights standing upright in a sort of narrow lumber-room, with nothing upon me but my shirt, and deprived of the power of moving from the spot where I was placed, or of making the least movement, although I could not see the obstacle that rendered me thus powerless. Let me add that all this has by no means lessened the respect and affection which I had for the princess my wife; though I confess to you most sincerely that, in spite of all the honor and glory that I derive from having the daughter of my sovereign for my wife, I would much sooner die than continue

[333]

to enjoy this high alliance if I must continue to undergo the severe and horrible treatment I have already suffered. I am sure the princess must be of the same opinion as myself, and that our separation is as necessary for her comfort as for my own. I entreat you, therefore, my dear father, to procure the consent of the sultan to have our marriage declared null and void.'

"Great as had been the ambition of the grand vizier to have his son so nearly allied to the sultan, the fixed resolution which he found the young man had formed of dissolving his union with the princess made him think it necessary to request his son to have patience for a few days before the matter was finally settled, in order to see whether this unpleasant business might not settle itself. He then left his son and returned to the sultan, to whom he acknowledged that everything the princess had said was true. And then, without waiting till the sultan himself spoke to him about annulling the marriage, he requested permission for his son to leave the palace, giving his reason that it was not just that the Princess Badroulboudour should be exposed for one instant longer to so terrible a persecution through the marriage she had contracted.

"The grand vizier had no difficulty in obtaining his request. The sultan, who had already settled the matter in his own mind, immediately gave orders that the rejoicings should be stopped, not only in his own palace, but throughout the whole extent of his dominions; and in a short time every mark of public joy and festivity within the kingdom ceased. This sudden and unexpected change gave rise to a variety of different conjectures. Every one was inquiring why these strange orders were issued, and all affirmed that the grand vizier had been seen coming out of the palace and going toward his own house accompanied by his son, and that they both seemed very much dejected. Aladdin was the only person who knew the real reason of the change, and he rejoiced most sincerely at the happy success arising from the use of the lamp. And now that he knew for a certainty that his rival had left the palace, and that the marriage between the princess and the vizier's son was absolutely annulled, he had no further occasion to rub his lamp and have recourse to the genie in order to prevent the completion of the marriage.

"Aladdin allowed the three months which the sultan wished to elapse before the marriage of the Princess Badroulboudour and himself to pass without making any application. On the very morning after the whole period had expired he did not fail to send his mother to the palace, to put the sultan in mind of his promise. She went accordingly and stood at her usual place near the entrance of the divan. As soon as the sultan cast his eyes that way and beheld her, he recollected her, and she instantly brought to his mind the request she had made. As the grand vizier approached to make some report to him, the sultan stopped him by saying, 'I perceive yonder that good woman who presented us with the beautiful collection of jewels some time since; order her to come forward.' The grand vizier directly turned his head toward the entrance of the divan and perceived the mother of Aladdin. He immediately called to the chief of the ushers and, pointing her out to him, desired him to conduct her forward.

"Aladdin's mother advanced to the foot of the throne, where she prostrated herself in the usual manner. After she had risen the sultan asked her what she wished. 'O mighty monarch,' she replied, 'I again present myself before the throne of your Majesty to announce to you, in the name of my son Aladdin, that the three months during which you have desired him to wait have expired, and to entreat that you will have the goodness to recall that circumstance to your remembrance.'

"When, on a former occasion, the sultan had desired a delay of three months before he acceded to the request of this good woman, he thought he should hear no more of a marriage which appeared to him entirely unsuited to the princess his daughter. He naturally judged of the suitor's position from the apparent poverty and low situation of Aladdin's mother, who always appeared before him in a very coarse and common dress. The application, therefore, which she now made to him to keep his word embarrassed him greatly, and he did not think it prudent to give her an immediate and direct answer. He consulted his grand vizier, and acknowledged the repugnance he felt at concluding a marriage between the princess and an unknown man, whom fortune, he conjectured, had not raised much above the condition of a common citizen.

"The grand vizier did not hesitate to give his opinion on the subject. 'O my lord,' said he to the sultan, 'it seems to me that there is a very easy and yet very certain method to avoid this unequal marriage—a method of which this Aladdin, even if he were known to your Majesty, could not complain. It is, to set so high a price upon the princess your daughter that all his riches, however great they may be, cannot amount to the value. Then he will be obliged to desist from his bold design, which he certainly does not seem to have considered well before he engaged in it.'

"The sultan approved of the advice of his grand vizier, and, after some little reflection, he said to Aladdin's mother: 'Good woman, it is right that a sultan should keep his word, and I am ready to adhere to mine and to render your son happy by marrying him to the princess my daughter; but as I cannot bestow her in marriage till I have seen proofs that she will be well provided for, tell your son that I will fulfil my promise as soon as he sends me forty large basins of massive gold quite full of jewels, like those which you have already presented to me from him. These basins must be carried by forty black slaves, each of whom shall be conducted by a white slave, young, handsome, and richly dressed. These are the conditions upon which I am ready to give him the princess my daughter for his wife. Go, my good woman, and I will wait till you bring me his answer.'

"Aladdin's mother again prostrated herself at the foot of the throne, and retired. On her way home she smiled within herself at the foolish projects of her son. 'Where, indeed,' said she, 'is he to find so many golden basins, and such a great quantity of colored glass as he will require to fill them? Will he attempt to go back into the subterraneous cavern, the entrance of which is shut up, that he may gather them off the trees? And where can he procure all the handsome slaves whom the sultan demands? He is far enough from having his wishes accomplished, and I believe he will not be very well satisfied with the result of my embassy.' Thus she entered the house with her mind occupied by these thoughts. 'My son,' said she, 'I advise you to think no more of your projected marriage with the Princess Badroulboudour. The sultan, indeed, received me with great kindness, and I believe that he was well inclined toward you. It was the grand vizier who, if I am not mistaken, made him alter his opinion. After I had represented to his Majesty that the three months had expired, and that I came on your behalf to request he would recollect his promise, I observed that he did not make me the answer I am going to repeat to you until he had spoken for some time in a low tone of voice to the grand vizier.' Aladdin's mother then gave her son a very exact account of everything the sultan had said, and of the conditions upon which he consented to the marriage of the princess his daughter with Aladdin. 'He is even now, my son,' she continued, 'waiting for your answer; but between ourselves,' she said, with a smile, 'he may wait long enough.' 'Not so long as you may think, mother,' replied Aladdin; 'and the sultan deceives himself if he supposes that by such exorbitant demands he can prevent my thinking any more of the Princess Badroulboudour. I am very well satisfied, for what he requires is a trifle in comparison to what I would give him to possess such a treasure as the princess. While I am taking measures to satisfy his demands, do you go and prepare something for dinner and leave me awhile to myself.'

"As soon as his mother was gone out to purchase provisions, Aladdin took the lamp. When he rubbed it, the genie instantly appeared, and demanded to know what was required of him. 'The sultan agrees to give me the princess his daughter in marriage,' said Aladdin, 'but he demands of me forty large basins of massive gold, filled to the very top with the various fruits of the garden from which I took the lamp of which you are the slave.

ARABIAN NIGHTS

He requires also that these forty basins should be brought to him by forty black slaves, preceded by an equal number of young and handsome white slaves very richly dressed. Go and procure me this present as soon as possible, that I may send it to the sultan before the sitting of the divan is over.' The genie said that his master's commands should be instantly executed, and disappeared.

"In a very short time the genie returned with forty black slaves, each carrying upon his head a large golden basin of great weight, full of pearls, diamonds, rubies, and emeralds, which might compete for brilliancy and size with those which had already been presented to the sultan. Each basin was covered with a cloth of silver embroidered with flowers of gold. The forty black slaves with their golden basins and their white companions entirely filled the house, which was but small, as well as the court in front and a garden behind it. The genie asked Aladdin if he was satisfied, and on being told that nothing further was required he immediately disappeared.

"Aladdin's mother now returned from market, and great was her surprise on coming home to see so many persons and such vast wealth. When she had set down the provisions she had brought with her, she was going to take off her veil, but Aladdin prevented her, and exclaimed: 'There is no time to lose. It is of consequence that you should return to the palace before the divan breaks up, that you may at once deliver to the sultan the present and dowry which he demands for the Princess Badroulboudour, that he may judge of my ardent and sincere zeal to procure the honor of being received into alliance with his family.'

"Without waiting for his mother's answer, Aladdin opened the door that led into the street and ordered all the slaves to go out one after the other. He then posted a white slave in front of each of the black ones, who carried the golden basins on their heads. When his mother, who followed the last black slave, had gone out, he shut the door and remained quietly in his chamber, fully convinced that the sultan, after receiving such a present as he had required, would now readily consent to accept him as his son-in-law.

"The first white slave who went out of Aladdin's house caused all the passers-by to stop; and before all the eighty slaves had emerged from the courtyard the street was filled with a great crowd of people who collected from all parts to see this grand and extraordinary sight. The dress of each slave was made of a rich stuff, and so studded with precious stones that those who thought themselves the best judges reckoned the value of each suit at many thousand gold pieces. The graceful manner and elegant form of the slaves, and their great similarity to one another, together with their staid and solemn march, and the dazzling luster that the different jewels, which were set in their girdles of massive gold, shed around—all this, added to the branches of precious stones fastened to their head-dresses, produced in the multitude of spectators such astonishment and admiration that they could not take their eyes from them so long as any of the slaves remained in sight.

"When the first of the eighty slaves arrived at the outer court of the palace, the porters were in the greatest haste to open the door, as they took the first slave for a king, so richly and magnificently was he dressed. They were advancing to kiss the hem of his robe when the slave, instructed by the genie, prevented them, and in a grave tone of voice said, 'Our master will appear at the proper time.'

"The first slave, followed by all the rest, advanced as far as the second court, which was very spacious, and contained those apartments used for the holding of the sultan's divan. The officers who were at the head of the sultan's guards were very handsomely clothed, but they were completely eclipsed by the eighty slaves who were the bearers of Aladdin's present, in which they themselves were included. Nothing throughout the sultan's whole palace appeared so brilliant as they; and however magnificently dressed the different nobles of the court might be, they dwindled into insignificance in comparison with these splendid strangers.

"As the sultan had been informed of the march and arrival of these slaves, he had given orders to have them admitted. Accordingly, when they presented themselves at the hall of council, they found the door of the divan open. They entered in regular order, one half going to the right and the other to the left. After they were all within the hall and had formed a large semicircle before the throne, each of the black slaves placed upon the carpet the basin which he carried. They then all prostrated themselves so low that their foreheads touched the ground. The white slaves also performed the same ceremony. Then they all rose, and in doing so the black slaves skilfully uncovered the basins which were before them, and then remained standing in an attitude of profound respect.

"The mother of Aladdin, who had in the mean time advanced to the foot of the throne, prostrated herself and thus addressed the sultan: 'O mighty ruler, my son Aladdin is well aware that this present which he has sent your Majesty is very much beneath the inestimable worth of the Princess Badroulboudour. He nevertheless hopes that your Majesty will graciously accept it and that it may find favor in the eyes of the princess.'

"This complimentary address of Aladdin's mother was entirely lost upon the sultan, who paid no attention to her words. The forty golden basins, heaped up with jewels of the most brilliant luster, the finest water, and greatest value he had ever seen, and the appearance of the eighty slaves, who seemed like so many kings, both from the magnificence of their dress and their splendid appearance, made such an impression upon him that he could not restrain his admiration. Instead, therefore, of making any answer to the compliments of Aladdin's mother, he addressed himself to the grand vizier, who could not himself imagine whence such an immense profusion of riches could possibly have come. 'Tell me, vizier,' he exclaimed, in the hearing of all, 'what do you think of the person who has now sent me this rich and marvelous present? Do you not think that he is worthy of the princess my daughter?'

"Whatever jealousy and pain the grand vizier might feel at

thus seeing an unknown person become the son-in-law of the sultan in preference to his own son, he was afraid to dissemble his real opinion on the present occasion. It was very evident that Aladdin had by his unbounded magnificence become in the eyes of the sultan very deserving of being honored with the high alliance to which he aspired. He therefore answered the sultan in the following words: 'Far be it from me, mighty king, to suppose that he who makes your Majesty so worthy a present should himself be undeserving the honor you wish to bestow upon him. I would even say that he deserved still more, if all the treasures of the universe could be put in competition with the princess your daughter.'

"The sultan hesitated no longer. The mere sight of such immense riches, and the wonderful celerity with which Aladdin had fulfilled his request without making the least difficulty about the exorbitant conditions for which he had stipulated, easily persuaded him that Aladdin must possess every necessary quality. He determined, therefore, to send back Aladdin's mother as well satisfied as she could possibly expect, and accordingly he said to her, 'Go, my good woman, and tell your son that I am waiting with open arms to receive and embrace him; and that the greater diligence he uses in coming to receive from my hands the gift I am ready to bestow upon him, in my daughter, the greater pleasure he will afford me.'

"When Aladdin's mother had departed, as happy as a woman could be, the sultan put an end to the audience and ordered the eunuchs of the princess's household to be called. On their arrival he commanded them to take up the basins and carry them to the apartment of their mistress, whither he himself went in order to examine them with her at leisure.

"The eighty slaves were not forgotten. They were conducted into the interior of the palace; and when the sultan was speaking to the princess of their magnificent appearance, he ordered them to come opposite to her apartment that she might see them and be convinced that so far from having given an exaggerated account of them he had said much less than they deserved.

ARABIAN NIGHTS

"In the mean time Aladdin's mother reached home, and instantly showed by her manner that she was the bearer of excellent news. 'You have every reason, my dear son,' she said, 'to be satisfied. Contrary to my expectations, I have now to announce to you that you have gained your suit. I must inform you that the sultan, amid the applause of his whole court, has announced that you are worthy to possess the Princess Badroulboudour, and he is now waiting to embrace you and to conclude the marriage. The sultan waits for you with the greatest impatience, and therefore you must lose no time in making your appearance before him.'

"Aladdin was so delighted at this intelligence, and so enraptured with the thought of the enchanting object of his love, that he hardly answered his mother, but instantly retired to his chamber. He then took up the lamp that had thus far been so friendly to him. He rubbed it, and immediately the genie again showed his ready obedience to its power by appearing to execute his commands. 'O genie,' said Aladdin to him, 'I have called thee to take me immediately to a bath; and when I have bathed, I command thee to have in readiness for me, if possible, a richer and more magnificent dress than was ever worn by any monarch.' So soon as Aladdin had concluded his speech, the genie rendered him invisible, took him in his arms, and transported him to a bath formed of the finest marble of the most beautiful and diversified colors. Aladdin immediately felt himself undressed by invisible hands in a large and handsome saloon. From thence he was conducted into a moderately heated bath, and was there washed and rubbed with various sorts of perfumed waters. He emerged completely altered in appearance. His skin was white and fresh, his countenance blooming, and his whole body felt light and active. He then went back to the saloon, where, instead of the dress he had left, he found the one he had desired the genie to procure. Assisted by the genie, he dressed himself, and in doing so could not refrain from expressing the greatest admiration at each part of his costume as he put it on. As soon as this business was over, the genie transported him back into the same chamber of his own house whence he had brought him. He then inquired if Aladdin had any other commands. 'Yes,' replied Aladdin; 'I command thee to bring me as quickly as possible a horse which shall surpass in beauty and excellence the most valuable horse in the sultan's stables; the saddle, bridle, and other furniture shall be worth many thousands of gold pieces. I also order thee to get me at the same time twenty slaves, as splendidly and richly clothed as those who carried the present, to march beside and behind me, and twenty more to march in two ranks before me. Thou must also procure six females to attend upon my mother, and these slaves must be as tastefully and richly clothed as those of the Princess Badroulboudour, and each of them must carry a complete dress, fit in point of splendor and magnificence for any sultana. I also want ten thousand pieces of gold in each of ten separate purses. Go and be diligent.'

"When Aladdin had given his orders the genie disappeared, and a moment afterward returned with the horse, the forty slaves, ten of whom had each a purse with ten thousand pieces of gold, and the six female slaves, each carrying a dress for Aladdin's mother wrapped up in a piece of silver tissue.

"Aladdin took only four out of the ten purses, and made a present of them to his mother, as he said that she might want them. He left the other six in the hands of the slaves who carried them, desiring them to keep the money and throw it out by handfuls to the populace as they went along the streets on their way to the palace of the sultan. He ordered them also to march before him with the other slaves. He then presented the six female slaves to his mother, telling her that they were for her, and would in future consider her as their mistress, and that the dresses they had in their hands were for her use.

"When Aladdin had thus arranged everything for his progress to the palace, he told the genie that he would call him when he had any further occasion for his services. The genie instantly vanished. Aladdin then sent to the palace one of the forty slaves, who might have been considered the handsomest had they not all been equally well-favored. This slave was ordered to address himself to the chief of the ushers, and inquire of him when his master might have the honor of throwing himself at the feet of the sultan. The slave soon delivered this message, and brought word back that the sultan was waiting for his son-in-law with the greatest impatience.

"Aladdin immediately mounted his horse and began his march in the order that has been mentioned. The streets through which he passed were soon filled with crowds of people who made the air resound with their acclamations and with shouts of admiration, particularly when the six slaves who carried the purses threw handfuls of gold on all sides. When the report spread around that the sultan had bestowed upon Aladdin the hand of the Princess Badroulboudour, no one ever thought about the meanness of his birth, or envied him his great fortune, so entirely did he appear to deserve it.

"He at length arrived at the palace, where everything was ready for his reception. When he came to the second gate he wished to alight, according to the custom observed by the grand vizier, the generals of the army, and the governors of provinces; but the chief of the ushers, who attended him by the sultan's order, prevented him from dismounting, and accompanied him to the hall of audience, where he assisted him from his horse. In the mean time all the ushers formed a double row at the entrance into the hall; and their chief, placing Aladdin on his right hand, went up through the midst of them, and conducted him to the foot of the throne.

"When the sultan saw Aladdin coming he was not more surprised at finding him more richly and magnificently clothed than he was himself, than he was delighted and astonished at the propriety of his manner, his graceful figure, and a certain air of grandeur. His astonishment, however, did not prevent him from rising and descending two or three steps of his throne in order to prevent Aladdin from throwing himself at his feet, and to embrace him with the most evident marks of friendship and affection. Aladdin again endeavored to cast himself at the sultan's feet, but the sultan compelled him to ascend the steps and sit between him and his grand vizier.

"Aladdin then addressed the sultan in these words: 'I receive the honors which your Majesty has the goodness to bestow upon me because it is your pleasure to bestow them; nevertheless, I have not forgotten that I was born your slave. If there can be the shadow of a reason,' he continued, 'to which I can in the least attribute the favorable reception which has been granted me, I candidly avow that I am indebted for it to a boldness which chance alone brought about, and in consequence of which I have raised my eyes, my thoughts, and my aspirations to the divine princess, who is the sole object of my eager hopes. I request your Majesty's pardon for my rashness, but my grief would be the death of me if I should lose the hope of seeing my wishes accomplished.'

"'My son,' replied the sultan, 'you would do me injustice to doubt even for an instant the sincerity of my word. Your life is so dear to me that I shall endeavor to preserve it forever by presenting you with the object for which you pine.'

"As he concluded this speech the sultan made a sign, and the air was immediately filled with the sound of trumpets, hautbois, and timbrels. The sultan then conducted Aladdin into a magnificent saloon, where a great feast had been prepared. The sultan and Aladdin sat down together to eat; the grand vizier and nobles of the court, each according to his dignity and rank, waited upon them during their repast. The sultan entered into conversation on a variety of different topics; and while they thus discoursed, whatever the subject happened to be, Aladdin spoke with so much information and knowledge that he completely confirmed the sultan in the good opinion the latter had at first formed of him.

"When the repast was over, the sultan ordered the chief judge to attend, and commanded him to draw up a contract of marriage between the Princess Badroulboudour and Aladdin.

"When the judge had drawn out the contract with all the requisite forms, the sultan asked Aladdin if he wished to remain in the palace and conclude all the ceremonies that day. 'O mighty monarch,' he replied, 'however impatient I may be to receive the gift that your Majesty's bounty destines for me, I request you to permit me to defer my happiness until I have built a palace for the princess that shall be worthy even of her merit and dignity. And for this purpose I entreat your Majesty to have the goodness to point out a suitable place near your own for its situation, that I may always be ready to pay my court to your Majesty. I will neglect nothing to get it finished with all possible diligence.' 'My son,' answered the sultan, 'take whatever spot you think proper to choose. There is a large open space in front of my palace, and I have intended for some time to build upon it; but remember, that to have my happiness complete, I cannot too soon see you united to my daughter.' With these kind words he again embraced Aladdin, who now took leave of the sultan.

"Aladdin then mounted his horse and returned home in the same order in which he had come, and receiving acclamations from the people, who wished him all happiness and prosperity. As soon as he had entered the court and alighted from his horse he retired to his own chamber. He instantly rubbed the lamp, and called the genie, who appeared directly and offered his services. 'O genie,' said Aladdin to him, 'I have hitherto had every reason to praise the precision and promptitude with which thou hast executed whatever I have required of thee, by means of the power of thy mistress, this lamp; but now, if possible, thou must show even greater zeal and despatch than thou hast yet shown. I command thee, therefore, to build me a palace as quickly as possible, opposite to that belonging to the sultan, and at a short distance from it; and let this palace be in every way worthy to receive the Princess Badroulboudour, my bride. I leave the choice of the materials to thee. Thou shalt decide whether it shall be of porphyry, of jasper, of agate, of lapis lazuli, or of the finest and rarest kinds of marble. The form of the palace also I leave to thy judgment; I only expect that at the top of the palace there shall be erected a large saloon, with a dome in the center, and four equal sides, the walls of which shall be formed of massive gold and silver, in alternate layers, with twenty-four windows, six on each side. The lattices of each window, except one, which is to be purposely left unfinished, shall be enriched with diamonds, rubies, and emeralds, set with the greatest taste and symmetry, and in a style unequaled by anything in the whole world. I wish this palace to have a large court in the front, another at the back, and a garden. But, above everything, be sure that there is a room well filled with money, both in gold and silver. There must also be kitchens, offices, and receptacles for rich and valuable furniture, suited to the different seasons. Stables I must likewise have, filled with the most beautiful horses, also grooms and attendants; and the appliances for hunting must be there. I must have attendants for the kitchen and offices, and female slaves for the service of the princess. Go, and return as soon as thy task is completed.'

"The sun had already gone down when Aladdin finished giving his orders to the genie respecting the construction of the palace. The very next morning when the day broke, Aladdin had scarcely risen before the genie presented himself. 'O master,' said he, 'thy palace is finished. Come and see if it is built as thou didst wish.' Aladdin signified his assent, and the genie transported him to the palace in an instant. He found it exceed his utmost expectation, and could not sufficiently admire it. The genie conducted him through every part of it, and he everywhere found the greatest wealth applied with the utmost propriety. There were also the proper officers and slaves all dressed according to their rank and ready to engage in their different employments. Amongst other things the genie remembered to show Aladdin the treasury, the door of which was opened by the treasurer. Aladdin here observed large vases filled to the very brim with purses of different sizes, each containing a sum of money. The genie now led Aladdin to the stables, where he made him take notice of the most beautiful horses in the world, with servants and grooms busily employed about them.

"When Aladdin had examined the whole palace, and had

particularly inspected the saloon with the four-and-twenty windows, and had seen all the riches and magnificence it contained, he exclaimed: 'O genie, no one can be more satisfied than I am, and I should be very wrong to make the least complaint. There is one thing only which I did not mention to thee, because it escaped my recollection; it is, to have a carpet of the finest velvet laid from the gate of the sultan's palace to the door of the apartment in this which is appropriated to the princess, that she may walk upon it when she leaves the sultan's palace.' 'I will return in an instant,' replied the genie; and he had not been gone a moment before Aladdin saw the carpet he had ordered rolled out by invisible hands. The genie again made his appearance, and carried Aladdin back to his own house just as the gates of the sultan's palace were about to be opened.

"The sultan's porters who came to open the gates, and who were accustomed to see an open space where Aladdin's palace now stood, were much astonished at observing that space occupied by a building, and at seeing a velvet carpet, which seemed to stretch from that part directly opposite to the gate of the sultan's abode. The news of this wonder soon spread throughout the palace, and the grand vizier was no less astonished than were the rest. The first thing he did was to go to the sultan; but he tried to represent the whole business as enchantment. 'Why do you endeavor, O vizier,' replied the sultan, 'to make this appear as the effect of enchantment? You know as well as I that it is the palace of Aladdin, which I in your presence yesterday gave him permission to build for the reception of the princess my daughter. After the immense display of riches which we have seen, can you think it so very extraordinary that he should be able to build one in this short time? He wished, no doubt, to surprise us, and we every day see what miracles riches can perform. Confess that you wish, through motives of jealousy, to make this appear as the effect of sorcery.' The hour had now come for entering the council-hall, and this conversation was consequently broken off.

"When Aladdin had returned home and dismissed the genie,

he found that his mother was up and had begun to put on one of the dresses which he had ordered for her the day before. About the time when the sultan usually left the council Aladdin requested his mother to go, attended by the female slaves whom the genie had procured for her use. He desired her also, if she should see the sultan, to inform him that she came in the hope of having the honor of accompanying the Princess Badroulboudour in the evening, when the time came for the princess to go to her own palace. She accordingly set forth. Aladdin himself mounted his horse and left his paternal house never more to return; but he did not forget to take with him his wonderful lamp, which had been the cause of all his happiness. He went to his superb residence with all the pomp with which he had presented himself to the sultan on the preceding day.

"As soon as the porters of the sultan's palace perceived the mother of Aladdin, they gave notice of her approach to the sultan himself. He immediately sent orders to the bands who were already placed in different parts of the terrace, and in a moment the air re-echoed with festive sounds which spread pleasure throughout the city. All the people thronged to the great square that intervened between the palaces of the sultan and Aladdin. Aladdin's palace first attracted their admiration, not merely because they had been accustomed to see only that of the sultan, which could not be put in comparison with Aladdin's; but their greatest surprise arose from their not being able to comprehend by what unheard-of means so magnificent a palace could have been reared in a spot where the day before there had been no materials, nor any foundation laid.

"Aladdin's mother was received with great honor, and was introduced by the chief of the eunuchs into the apartment of the Princess Badroulboudour. As soon as the princess perceived her, she ran and embraced her, and made her sit down upon her own sofa. And while the Princess Badroulboudour's women were dressing their mistress, and adorning her with the most valuable of the jewels which Aladdin had presented to her, she entertained her visitor with a most magnificent collation. The sultan paid great honor and respect to Aladdin's mother. She had often seen the sultan in public, but he had never yet seen her without her veil. The sultan, too, had always seen her very plainly dressed, and he was therefore the more struck at finding her as magnificently attired as the princess his daughter.

"When the evening approached, the princess took leave of the sultan her father. Their parting was tender and accompanied by tears, and the princess at last left her apartment and began her progress to her new dwelling, with Aladdin's mother on her left hand, followed by a hundred female slaves, all magnificently dressed. All the bands of instruments, whose strains had been incessantly heard since the arrival of Aladdin's mother, united at once and marched with them. These were followed by a hundred attendants and an equal number of black eunuchs in two rows, with their proper officers at their head. Four hundred young pages belonging to the sultan, marching in two troops on each side, with flambeaux in their hands, spread a great light around.

"In this order did the princess proceed, walking upon the carpet which extended from Aladdin's palace to that of the sultan. And as she continued her progress the musicians went forward and mingled with those who were placed on the terrace of Aladdin's palace; and with their help they formed a concert which augmented the general joy.

"The princess at length arrived at her destination, and Aladdin ran with every expression of joy to the entrance of the apartments appropriated to her, in order to welcome her. 'O adorable princess,' cried Aladdin, 'if I should have the misfortune to have displeased you by the temerity with which I have aspired to the great honor of being allied to the daughter of my sultan, please to consider that it was to your beautiful eyes and to your charms alone that you must attribute my rashness, and not to myself.' 'O prince, for thus I must now call you,' replied the princess, 'I obey the will of the sultan my father; and now that I have seen you, I freely own that I obey him without reluctance.'

"Aladdin was delighted at this satisfactory and charming

answer. He took the princess's hand, which he kissed with the greatest demonstrations of joy. Then he conducted her into a large saloon. Here, through the attention of the genie, there was a table spread with everything rare and excellent. The dishes were of massive gold and filled with the most delicious viands. The vases, the basins, and the goblets with which the sideboard was amply furnished, were also of gold. The princess, enchanted at the sight of such a collection of riches, said to Aladdin, 'O prince, I thought nothing in the whole world was more beautiful than the palace of the sultan my father; but the appearance of this saloon tells me I was deceived.'

"The Princess Badroulboudour, Aladdin, and his mother sat down to table, and instantly a band of the most harmonious instruments, played upon by women of great beauty, who accompanied the sweet strains with their voices, began a concert which lasted till the repast was finished. The princess was so delighted with the music that she said she had never heard anything to equal it in the palace of her father. But she knew not that these musicians were fairies, chosen by the slave of the lamp.

"When supper was concluded and everything had been removed with the greatest diligence, a troop of dancers of both sexes took the places of the musicians. They performed dances with various figures, as was the custom of the country, and concluded by one executed by a male and female who danced with the most surprising activity and agility. It was near midnight when, according to the custom at that time observed in China, Aladdin rose and presented his hand to the Princess Badroulboudour, that they might dance together and thus finish the ceremony of their nuptials. They both danced with such grace that they were the admiration of all present. When this ceremony was over, Aladdin did not let the hand of the princess go, but they went into the chamber together in which the nuptial bed had been prepared. In this manner did the ceremonies and rejoicings at the marriage of Aladdin and the Princess Badroulboudour conclude.

"The next morning when Aladdin arose, his chamberlains appeared to dress him. They clothed him in a new habit, but one as rich and magnificent as the dress he wore on the day of his marriage. They then brought him one of the horses appropriated to his use. He mounted it and rode to the palace of the sultan, surrounded by a large troop of slaves. The sultan received him with the same honors he had before shown him. He embraced him, and, after placing him on the throne close by his side, ordered breakfast to be served up. 'O great King,' said Aladdin to the sultan, 'I beseech your Majesty to withhold from me this honor to-day. I come for the express purpose of entreating you to come and partake of a repast in the palace of the princess, with your grand vizier, and the nobles of your court.' The sultan readily granted his son-in-law's request. He rose immediately and proceeded with Aladdin on his right hand and the grand vizier on his left, followed by the nobles, the principal officers going before them.

"The nearer the sultan came to the palace of Aladdin, the more was he struck with its beauty; yet this impression was faint compared with the astonishment he felt on entering. His expressions of surprise and pleasure were renewed in all the apartments through which he passed. But when the company came to the hall of the twenty-four windows, to which Aladdin had requested them to ascend; when the sultan had seen its ornaments, and had above all things cast his eyes on the lattices enriched with diamonds, rubies, and emeralds, all of the finest sort and most superb size; and when Aladdin had made him observe that the outside and inside of each window was decorated with equal magnificence, the sultan was so much astonished that he stood absolutely motionless. After remaining some time in that state, he at length said to his vizier, 'O vizier, is it possible there should be in my kingdom, and so near my own, so superb a palace, and yet that I should till this moment be ignorant of its existence?' 'Your Majesty,' replied the grand vizier, 'may remember that the day before yesterday you gave permission to Aladdin, whom you then acknowledged as your son-in-law, to build a palace opposite your own. On the same day when the sun went down not the smallest part of this palace was on this spot; and yesterday I had the honor to announce to your Majesty that it was built and finished.' 'I remember,' replied the sultan, 'but I never imagined that this palace would be one of the wonders of the world. Where throughout the universe will you find walls thus built of alternate layers of massive gold and silver instead of stone or marble, and windows with lattices studded with diamonds, rubies, and emeralds? Never in the whole world has such a thing been heard of.'

"The sultan wished to examine everything more closely, and observe the beauty of the twenty-four lattices. On looking at them separately he found only twenty-three that were equally rich, and he was therefore greatly astonished that the twenty-fourth should remain imperfect. 'Vizier,' said he, 'I am very much surprised that so magnificent a hall as this should remain unfinished in this particular.' 'O mighty Monarch,' replied the grand vizier, 'Aladdin apparently was pressed for time, and therefore was unable to finish this window like the rest.'

"Aladdin, who had quitted the sultan to give some orders, came and joined them during this conversation. 'My son,' said the sultan, 'this truly is a hall worthy the admiration of all the world. There is, however, one thing at which I am astonished, and that is, to observe this lattice unfinished. Is it through forgetfulness, or neglect, or because the workmen have not had time to put the finishing strokes to this beautiful specimen of architecture?' 'My lord,' answered Aladdin, 'it is not for any of these reasons that this lattice remains as your Majesty now sees it. It is left unfinished on purpose; and it was by my orders that the workmen have not touched it. I wish that your Majesty may have the glory of putting the finishing stroke to this saloon and palace, and I entreat you to believe that my intention in this is that I may have a memento of the favor I have received from you.' 'If you have done it with that view,' replied the sultan, 'I take it in good part; I will give the necessary orders about it.' He accordingly ordered the jewelers, who were best furnished with precious stones, and the most skilful goldsmiths in his capital to be sent for.

"When the sultan came down from the saloon, Aladdin conducted him into the chamber where he had entertained the Princess Badroulboudour on the evening of their nuptials. The princess herself entered a moment after, and received her father in such a manner as made it very evident that she was quite satisfied with her marriage. In the saloon two tables were set out with the most delicious viands, all served up in dishes of gold. The sultan sat down at the first table, and ate with his daughter, Aladdin, and the grand vizier. All the nobles of the court were regaled at the second, which was of great size. The repast highly pleased the sultan's taste, and he confessed that he had never partaken of so magnificent a feast.

"When the sultan rose from the table, he was informed that the jewelers and goldsmiths whom he had caused to be summoned were come. He then went up to the hall of the twenty-four windows, and there he pointed out to the jewelers and goldsmiths who followed him that window which was imperfect. 'I have ordered you to come here,' said the sultan, 'to finish this window, and make it quite perfect like the rest. Examine these windows, and lose no time in completing the unfinished one.'

"The jewelers and goldsmiths examined all the lattices with the closest attention; and after they had decided among themselves what each could contribute toward its completion, they presented themselves before the sultan, and the chief jeweler thus addressed him: 'We are ready, great King, to employ all our diligence to obey your Majesty; but amongst our whole craft we have not jewels sufficient in number or in value to complete so great a work.' 'I have enough,' cried the sultan, 'and more than you want. Come to my palace and you shall choose those you like best.'

"When the sultan came back to his palace, he caused all his jewels to be shown to the jewelers, and they took a great quantity of them, particularly of those which had been presented by Aladdin. They used up all these, without appearing to have made much progress in their work. They went back several times for more, and in the course of a month they had not finished more than half their task. They had used all the sultan's jewels, with as many of the grand vizier's as he could spare, and with all these they could not more than half finish the window.

"Aladdin was well aware that all the sultan's endeavors to make the lattice of this window like the others were vain, and that the jewelers would never complete their task. He therefore spoke to the workmen, and not only made them stop working, but even undo all they had yet finished, and carry back all the jewels to the sultan and the grand vizier.

"Thus all the work which the jewelers had been four weeks in performing was destroyed in a few hours. Then they went away and left Aladdin alone in the hall. He took out the lamp which he had with him and rubbed it. The genie instantly appeared. 'O genie,' said Aladdin to him, 'I ordered you to leave one of the twenty-four lattices of this hall imperfect, and you obeyed me. I now inform you I wish it to be completed like the rest.' The genie disappeared, and Aladdin went out of the saloon. He entered it again in a few moments and found the lattice finished as he wished, and similar to the others.

"In the mean time the jewelers and goldsmiths arrived at the palace, and were admitted to the presence of the sultan in his own apartment. The first jeweler then produced the precious stones he had brought with him, and in the name of the rest spoke thus: 'O mighty King, your Majesty knows for what length of time and how diligently we have worked in order to finish the business on which you deigned to employ us. It was already very far advanced when Aladdin obliged us not only to leave off, but even to destroy what we had already done, and to bring back your jewels, as well as those that belonged to the grand vizier.' The sultan asked whether Aladdin had given them any reason for this proceeding; and when they replied that he had said nothing, the sultan immediately ordered his horse to be brought. As soon as it came, he rode away to Aladdin's palace. When he arrived there, he dismounted at the foot of the flight of stairs that led to the hall of the twenty-four windows.

ARABIAN NIGHTS

Aladdin happened to be in the hall, and had just time to receive the sultan at the door.

"Without giving Aladdin time to chide him for not sending word of his intention to pay him a visit, and thus causing him to appear deficient in the respect he owed him, the sultan said, 'I have come, my son, purposing to ask why you wished to leave this very rare and magnificent hall in an unfinished state?'

"Aladdin dissembled the true reason, namely, that the sultan was not sufficiently rich in jewels to go to the necessary expense. But to let the monarch see how the palace itself surpassed not only his, but also every other palace in the whole world, since he was unable to finish even a very small part of it, Aladdin replied, 'It is true, great King, that your Majesty did behold this saloon unfinished, but I entreat you to look again and tell me if at this moment there is anything wanting?'

"The sultan immediately went to the window where he had observed the unfinished lattice, but when he saw it was like the rest he could hardly believe his eyes. When he was convinced that the lattice upon which his people had so long employed themselves, and which had cost the jewelers and goldsmiths so many days, was now suddenly finished, he embraced Aladdin and kissed him between the eyes. 'My dear son,' he cried, in astonishment, 'what a man you are, who can do such wonderful things almost instantaneously! There is not your equal in the world.'

"Aladdin received the sultan's praises with great modesty, and made the following reply, 'O King, it is my greatest glory to deserve the kindness and approbation of your Majesty.'

"The sultan returned to his palace in the way he had come, and found the grand vizier waiting his arrival. Full of admiration at the wonders which he had witnessed, the sultan related everything to his minister in such terms that the vizier did not doubt for a moment the accuracy of the sultan's account. But this still more confirmed him in the belief which he already entertained, that the palace of Aladdin had been built by enchantment. He attempted to repeat his suspicions, but the sultan interrupted him with these words, 'O vizier, you have before said the same thing, but I very plainly perceive you have not forgotten the marriage of my daughter, the Princess Badroulboudour, with your son.'

"The grand vizier clearly saw that the sultan was prejudiced. He did not, therefore, attempt to enter into any dispute with him, but suffered him to retain his own opinion.

"Aladdin did not remain shut up in his palace, but took care to make a progress through different parts of the city at least once every week. Sometimes he went to attend prayers at various mosques; at others, to visit the grand vizier, who regularly came on stated days under pretense of paying his court; and sometimes he honored with his presence the houses of the principal nobles, whom he frequently entertained at his own palace. Whenever he went out, he ordered two of the slaves who attended him as he rode to throw handfuls of gold in the streets through which he passed, and where the people always collected in crowds to see him.

"Aladdin so arranged his different occupations that not a week elapsed in which he did not once, at least, enjoy the diversion of the chase. Sometimes he hunted in the neighborhood of the city, and at others he went to a greater distance; and he gave proofs of his liberality in every town and village through which he passed. His generous disposition made the people load him with blessings; and it became the common custom to swear by his head. Indeed, Aladdin in a short time won the regard and affection of all classes, and, generally speaking, he was more beloved than even the sultan himself. To all his good qualities he joined a great degree of valor and an ardent desire for the good of the state. He had an opportunity of giving the strongest proofs of his patriotism in a revolt that took place on the confines of the kingdom. So soon as he became aware that the sultan meant to levy an army to quell the insurrection, he requested to have the command of the expedition. This he had no difficulty in obtaining. He instantly put himself at the head of his troops to march against the rebels, and conducted the whole enterprise with so much judgment and activity that the sultan had the news of the defeat, punishment, and dispersion of his enemies quite as soon as he heard of the arrival of the army at its point of destination. This action, which made Aladdin's name celebrated throughout the whole extent of the empire, did not in the least alter his disposition. He returned victorious, but as affable and modest as ever.

"Many years passed, and Aladdin still continued by his own good conduct to advance in popularity; but during this period the African Magician, who had unintentionally procured for him the means by which he was raised to his exalted situation, frequently thought in Africa, whither he had returned, of the poor lad he had duped. Although he was well persuaded that Aladdin had met a miserable death in the subterranean cavern where he had left him, he nevertheless thought it advisable to gain certainty on the subject. As he had a complete knowledge of the science of astrology, he sat down on the sofa and placed a square instrument before him. He uncovered it, and, after making the sand with which it was filled quite smooth and even, he arranged the points, drew the figures, and formed Aladdin's horoscope, with the view of discovering whether he had died in the subterranean cave. On examining it, in order to form his judgment, instead of finding Aladdin dead in the cave, he discovered that the youth had escaped out of it, that he was living in the greatest splendor, and that he had married a princess.

"When the magician learned by his diabolical art that Aladdin was in the enjoyment of these honors, the blood rushed into his face. 'This miserable son of a tailor,' he exclaimed in a rage, 'has discovered the secret and virtues of the lamp! I thought his death certain; but I find he enjoys all the fruits of my long and laborious exertions. I will prevent his enjoying them long, or perish in the attempt!' The magician soon made up his mind as to the method he should pursue. Early the next morning he mounted a Barbary horse which he had in his stable, and began his journey. Traveling without stopping longer than was necessary to rest his horse, he at last arrived in China, and soon reached the capital where the sultan lived whose daughter Aladdin had married. He alighted at a public khan and remained there in order to recover from the fatigue of his journey.

"The first step the African Magician took the next morning toward fulfilling his enterprise was to inquire in what repute Aladdin stood, and to ascertain how the people spoke of him. In walking about the city, he went into one of the most frequented and most celebrated houses of entertainment, where people of the greatest consequence and distinction assembled to drink a warm beverage of which he had himself partaken when he was there before. He accordingly seated himself, and an attendant poured some into a cup, and presented it to him. As he took the cup he heard some persons speaking of Aladdin's palace. When he had finished, he approached those who were conversing on that subject, and, taking his opportunity, he inquired what was the peculiar feature of this palace of which they spoke so highly. 'Surely you must be a total stranger,' said one of those to whom he addressed himself, 'and you can have arrived but lately in this city, if you have not seen or even heard of the palace of Prince Aladdin,' for by this title Aladdin, since his union with the Princess Badroulboudour, had always been called. 'I do not say,' continued the speaker, 'that it is *one* of the wonders of the world, but I maintain it is the *greatest* wonder of the world. Nothing so rich, so grand, or so magnificent has ever been seen. Only behold it, and you will acknowledge that I have spoken nothing but the truth.' 'Pardon my ignorance, I beseech you,' replied the magician; 'I arrived here only yesterday, and I have come from a great distance, even from the farthest part of Africa; the fame of this marvel had not reached that spot when I left it. I was, therefore, quite ignorant of what you have been telling me. I shall not, however, fail to go and see this palace. My impatience, indeed, is so great that I would at once proceed to satisfy my curiosity if you would do me the favor to show me the way.'

"The person to whom the magician addressed himself was

quite willing to point out to him the way he should go in order to see Aladdin's palace, and he and the magician immediately set out. When the magician arrived at the spot, and had accurately examined the palace on all sides, he felt fully convinced that Aladdin had availed himself of the power of the lamp in building it. He was quite aware how impossible it would be for Aladdin, the son of a tailor, to raise such a structure; but he well knew it was in the power of the genii, the slaves of the lamp, to produce such wonders—and this wonderful lamp he had once almost gained! Stung to the very soul by this evidence of the fortune and greatness of Aladdin, he determined at all hazards to obtain possession of the lamp which had wrought all these wonders.

"His first object was to discover the whereabouts of the lamp—whether Aladdin carried it about with him, or where he kept it; and this discovery he was able to make by a certain operation in geomancy. As soon, therefore, as he got back to his lodging, he took his square box and his sand. His magic art informed him that the lamp was in Aladdin's palace, and his joy was so great on ascertaining this that he could hardly contain himself. 'I shall get this lamp,' he cried, 'and I defy Aladdin to prevent my having it; and I will fling him back into that native obscurity and poverty from which he has taken so high a leap.'

"It happened, most unfortunately for Aladdin, that he was absent upon a hunting expedition. This excursion was to last eight days, and only three of them had elapsed. Of this the magician got information in the following way: When he had finished the operation whose result had afforded him so much joy, he went to see the master of the khan where he had taken up his abode, and, beginning to converse with him, soon turned the talk into the desired channel. He told him that he had just returned from the palace of Aladdin, and after giving him an enthusiastic account of all the remarkable and surprising things he had seen he continued, 'My curiosity goes still further, and I shall not be satisfied till I have seen the fortunate owner of this wonderful building.' 'That will not be at all a difficult

"WHO WILL EXCHANGE OLD LAMPS FOR NEW ONES?"

ARABIAN NIGHTS

matter,' replied the keeper of the khan, 'for hardly a day passes without affording you an opportunity of seeing him when he is at home; but he has been gone these three days on a grand hunting party, which is to last for some days longer.'

"The magician did not want to know more; he hurriedly took leave of the master of the khan and returned to his own apartment. 'This is the time for action,' said he to himself, 'and I must not let the opportunity escape.' He then went to the shop of a man who made and sold lamps. 'I want,' said he to the manufacturer, 'a dozen copper lamps,' The man replied that he had not quite so many in his shop, but if his customer would wait till the next day he would have them ready for him. The magician agreed to wait. He desired the dealer to be careful and have them very well polished.

"The next morning the magician received the twelve lamps, and paid the price demanded without asking for any abatement. He put them into a basket which he had provided for the purpose, and went with this on his arm to the neighborhood of Aladdin's palace. Here he walked to and fro, crying with a loud voice, 'Who will exchange old lamps for new ones?' As he continued thus calling, the children who were at play in the open square heard him. They ran and collected round him, hooting at him, as they took him for a madman. All who passed laughed at his apparent folly. 'That man,' said they, 'must surely have lost his senses, to offer to exchange new lamps for old ones.'

"The magician was not at all surprised at the shouts of the children, nor at the ridicule with which he was assailed. He seemed only intent on disposing of his merchandise, and continued to cry, 'Who will exchange old lamps for new ones?' He repeated this so often, while he walked to and fro on all sides of the palace, that at last the Princess Badroulboudour, who was in the saloon of the twenty-four windows, heard his voice; but as she could not distinguish what he said, she sent one of her female slaves to ascertain what was the reason of all the noise and bustle.

"The slave presently returned, and entered the saloon, laughing very heartily. 'Well, thou silly one,' said the princess, 'why do you not tell me what you are laughing at?' 'O Princess,' replied the slave, 'who can possibly help laughing at seeing yonder fool with a basket on his arm full of beautiful new lamps, which he will not sell, but offers to exchange for old ones?'

"Another of the female slaves hereupon said: 'Now you speak of old lamps, I know not whether the princess has noticed one that stands on the cornice; whoever the owner may be, he will not be very much displeased at finding a new lamp instead of that old one. If the princess will give me leave, she may have the pleasure of trying whether this fellow is fool enough to give me a new lamp for an old one.'

"This lamp of which the slave spoke was the very wonderful lamp which had been the cause of Aladdin's great success and fortune, and he had himself placed it upon the cornice before he went to the chase, for fear of losing it. Except when he hunted, Aladdin always carried the lamp about him. His precaution, it may be said, was certainly insufficient, for he should have locked the lamp up.

"The princess, who was ignorant of the value of the lamp and of its importance both to Aladdin and to herself, consented to make the trial, and ordered an eunuch to go and get it exchanged. The eunuch accordingly went down from the saloon, and no sooner came out of the palace gate than he perceived the magician. He immediately called to him, and when he came showed him the old lamp, and said, 'Give me a new lamp for this.'

"The magician at once conjectured that this was the lamp he was seeking, because he thought there would not be any other such lamp in Aladdin's palace, where everything of the kind was of gold or silver. He eagerly took the lamp from the eunuch, and after having thrust it as far as he could ,into his bosom he presented his basket, and bade him take which he liked best. The eunuch chose one, and carried the new lamp to the princess.

"The magician at once stole quietly to a distance, ceased his calling, and no longer invited people to exchange old lamps for new ones.

"As soon as he had traversed the square between the two palaces, he went through the most unfrequented streets and, as he had no further occasion either for his purchased lamps or his basket, he put his load down in the middle of a street where he thought himself unobserved. He then made all the haste he could to get to one of the gates of the city. When he was at last in the open country he turned down a by-road, and here he remained till he thought a good opportunity occurred to execute the design he had in view.

"The magician passed the remainder of the day in that retired spot, lingering there until the night was far advanced. He then drew the lamp out of his bosom and rubbed it. The genie instantly obeyed the summons. 'What are thy commands?' cried the genie; 'I am ready to obey thee as thy slave, and the slave of those who have the lamp in their hands, both I and the other slaves of the lamp.' 'I command you,' replied the magician, 'instantly to take the palace which you and the other slaves of the lamp have erected in this city; take it, exactly as it is, with everything in it, both dead and alive, and transport it, and me also, into the utmost confines of Africa.' Without making any answer the genie, assisted by the other slaves of the lamp, took him and the whole palace, and transported both to the spot he had pointed out.

"Having thus seen the African Magician, the Princess Badroulboudour, and Aladdin's palace transported to Africa, let us notice what happened in the sultan's capital.

"When that monarch rose the next morning he did not fail to go as usual to his cabinet and look out, that he might have the pleasure of contemplating and admiring Aladdin's palace. He cast his eyes in the direction where he was accustomed to see it, but saw only the open space that had been there before the palace was built. He thought he must be deceived. He rubbed his eyes, but still he could see' nothing more than at first. His astonishment was so great that he remained for some time rooted to the spot. He could by no means comprehend in what manner so large a place should so suddenly and completely vanish that not the smallest vestige remained. 'I cannot be deceived,' he said to himself; 'it was in this very place that I beheld it. If it had fallen down, the materials at least would lie strewn around; and if the earth had swallowed it up, we should perceive some marks of the devastation.' The sultan returned to his apartment and ordered the grand vizier to be summoned.

"The grand vizier quickly obeyed the sultan's call. He came, indeed, in so much haste, that neither he nor his attendants observed, as they passed, that the palace of Aladdin was no longer where it had stood.

"'O great King,' said the grand vizier, 'the eagerness and haste with which your Majesty has sent for me leads me to suppose that something very extraordinary has happened.' 'What has happened is indeed very extraordinary,' replied the sultan. 'Tell me, where is Aladdin's palace?' 'I have just now passed it,' replied the vizier, with the utmost surprise, 'and it seemed to me to be where it stood before.' 'Go into my cabinet,' answered the sultan, 'and come and tell me if you can see the palace.'

"The grand vizier went as he was ordered, and was as much amazed as the sultan had been. When he was quite sure that the palace of Aladdin had really disappeared, he returned to the sultan. 'Tell me,' demanded the latter, 'have you seen Aladdin's palace?' 'Your Majesty may remember,' replied the grand vizier, 'that I had the honor to tell you that this palace was the work of magic, but your Majesty did not think fit to give heed to my words.'

"The sultan, who could not deny the former representations of the grand vizier, was the more angry against Aladdin because he was also unable to answer the vizier's words. 'Where is this impostor, this wretch,' he exclaimed, 'that I may strike off his head?' 'It is some days since he came to take leave of your Majesty,' answered the grand vizier; 'we must send to him, to inquire about the disappearance of his palace; he cannot be ignorant of it.' 'This would be treating him with too great indulgence!' exclaimed the monarch. 'Go, and order thirty of my horsemen to bring him before me in chains.' The grand vizier instantly gave the order, and instructed the officer how he should prevent Aladdin's escape. The horsemen set out, and met Aladdin, who was returning from the chase, about five or six leagues from the city. The officer, when he first accosted him, declared that the sultan was so impatient to see his son-in-law that he had sent this party of horse out to meet him and to accompany him on his return.

"Aladdin had not the least suspicion of the true cause that had brought out this detachment of the sultan's guard. He continued hunting on his way home; but when he was within half a league from the city, the soldiers surrounded him, and the officer said: 'Prince Aladdin, it is with the greatest regret that I must inform you of the orders we have received from the sultan. We are to arrest you, and bring you to the palace like a state criminal. We entreat you not to be angry with us for doing our duty.' This declaration astonished Aladdin beyond measure. He felt himself innocent, and asked the officer if he knew of what crime he was accused, but the officer replied that neither he nor his men could give him any information.

"As Aladdin perceived that his own attendants were much inferior in number to the detachment of soldiers, he dismounted, and said to the officer: 'I submit; execute whatever orders you have received. I must, however, declare that I am guilty of no crime, either toward the person of the sultan or the state.' His captors immediately put a large and long chain about his neck, binding it tightly round his body, so that he had not the use of his arms. When the officer had put himself at the head of the troop one of the horsemen took hold of the end of the chain, and dragged forward Aladdin, who was obliged to follow on foot.

"When the guards entered the suburbs, all the people they met, and who saw Aladdin led along in this way like a state criminal, felt sure that he was going to lose his head. As he was generally beloved, some seized sabers, others whatever arms they could find, and those who had no weapons whatever took up stones and tumultuously followed the guards. The soldiers who rode in the rear wheeled about, as if they wished to disperse the crowd, but the people increased so fast in number that the guards thought it better to dissemble, well satisfied if they could conduct Aladdin safe to the palace without his being rescued. In due time they arrived in the open square before the palace, where the soldiers all formed into one line and faced about to keep off the armed multitude, while the officer and guard who led Aladdin entered the palace.

"Aladdin was brought before the sultan, who waited for him, with the grand vizier by his side, in a balcony; and as soon as the prisoner appeared, the sultan angrily commanded the executioner, who was already present by his orders, to strike off his head, as he wished not to hear a word or any explanation whatever.

"The executioner accordingly seized Aladdin, took off the chain, and after laying down on the ground a large piece of leather stained with the blood of the many criminals he had executed, desired Aladdin to kneel down, and then tied a bandage over his eyes. Then he drew his saber, and waited only for the sultan's signal, to separate Aladdin's head from his body.

"At that critical instant the grand vizier perceived how the populace, who had overpowered the guards and filled the square, were in the act of scaling the walls of the palace in many places, and had even begun to pull them down in order to open a passage. Before, therefore, the sultan could give the signal for Aladdin's death, he said to him: 'I beseech your Majesty to think maturely of what you are going to do. You will run the risk of having your palace torn to the ground; and if this misfortune should happen, the consequences cannot but be dreadful.' 'My palace torn down!' replied the sultan. 'Who will dare attempt it?' 'If your Majesty will cast your eyes toward the walls yonder,' observed the vizier, 'you will acknowledge the truth of what I say.'

"When the sultan saw the eager and violent commotion among the people his fear was very great. He instantly ordered the executioner to sheathe his saber, to take the bandage off Aladdin's eyes, and set him at liberty. He also commanded an

ARABIAN NIGHTS

officer to proclaim that he pardoned Aladdin, and that every one might retire.

"As all those who had mounted on the walls of the palace could see what occurred in the sultan's cabinet, they gave over their design and almost directly descended; and, highly delighted at having thus been the means of saving the life of one whom they really loved, they instantly published this news to those that were near them, and it quickly spread among all the populace. The justice the sultan had thus rendered Aladdin by pardoning him, disarmed the populace and quieted the tumult, so that presently every one returned home.

"When Aladdin found himself at liberty, he lifted up his head toward the balcony, and, perceiving the sultan there, he addressed him with the most pathetic gestures. 'I entreat your Majesty,' he said, 'to add a new favor to the pardon you have just granted me by informing me of my crime!' 'Thy crime, O perfidious wretch!' replied the sultan. 'Dost thou not know it? Come up hither and I will show thee.'

"Aladdin ascended to the terrace, and when he presented himself, the sultan walked on before, saying, 'Follow me.' He led the way to the cabinet that opened toward the place where Aladdin's palace had stood. When they came to the door: 'Enter here,' the sultan said; 'assuredly you ought to know where your own palace is. Look around, and tell me what has become of it.' Aladdin looked, but saw nothing. He perceived the space which his palace had lately occupied; but as he could not conceive how it had disappeared, this extraordinary event so confused and astonished him that he could not answer the sultan a single word. 'Tell me,' said the latter, 'where is your palace, and what has become of my daughter?' 'O mighty King,' replied Aladdin, 'I plainly see and must acknowledge that the palace which I built is no longer in the place where it stood. I see it has disappeared, but I can assure your Majesty that I had no share whatever in removing it.'

"'I care not what has become of your palace; that gives me no concern,' replied the sultan; 'I esteem my daughter a million

[369]

times beyond your palace, and unless you discover and bring her back to me, be assured that your head shall answer for it.' 'Great King,' said Aladdin, 'I entreat your Majesty to grant me forty days to make the most diligent inquiries; and if I do not within that period succeed in my search, I give you my promise that I will lay my head at the foot of your throne that you may dispose of me according to your pleasure.' 'I grant your request,' answered the sultan; 'but think not to abuse my favor, nor endeavor to escape my resentment. In whatever part of the world you are, I shall know how to find you.'

"Aladdin then left the sultan's presence in the deepest humiliation. He passed, with downcast eyes, through the courts of the palace, and the principal officers of the court, not one of whom he had ever offended, instead of coming to console him or offer him a retreat at their house, turned their backs upon him, alike unwilling to make it appear that they saw him, or that he should recognize them. His mind seemed unhinged by his great calamity; and of this he gave evident proofs when he was out of the palace, for, without thinking of what he did, he asked at every door, and of all he met, if they had seen his palace, or could give him any intelligence concerning it.

"These questions made every one think that Aladdin had lost his senses. Some even laughed at him, but those who had been on friendly terms with him compassioned him most sincerely. He remained three days in the city, eating only what was given him in charity, and unable to come to any decision.

"At length, as Aladdin could not in his wretched condition remain any longer in a city where he had hitherto lived in splendor, he departed and bent his steps toward the country. He soon turned out of the highroad, and, after walking a great distance in the most dreadful state of mind, he came, toward the close of day, to the bank of a river. He now gave himself up entirely to despair. 'Whither shall I go to seek my palace?' he murmured to himself. 'In what part of the world shall I find either my dwelling or my dear princess? Never shall I be able to succeed! It is much better, then, that I at once put an end to the woes that distract me.' He was going to throw himself into the river in pursuance of this resolution, but, being faithful to his religion, he thought he ought not to quit life without first repeating his prayers. In performing this ceremony, he went close to the bank to wash his face and hands, as was the custom of his country; but, as this spot was rather steep, he slipped down, and would have fallen into the river had he not been stopped by a piece of stone, or rock, that projected about two feet from the surface. Happy was it for him, too, that he still had on his finger the ring which the magician had given him when he made him go down into the subterranean cavern to bring away the precious lamp which had so nearly been buried with him. In grasping at the piece of rock he rubbed the ring strongly, and the same genie instantly appeared whom he had before seen in the subterranean cavern. 'What are thy commands?' cried the genie.

"Aladdin was most agreeably surprised by the sight of this unexpected succor that came to him in his despair. He directly replied, 'Save my life, genie, a second time, by informing me where the palace is which I have built, or by replacing it where it was.' 'What you require of me,' answered the genie, 'is beyond my power; I am only the slave of the ring; you must address yourself to the slave of the lamp.' 'If that be the case, then,' said Aladdin, 'at least transport me to the spot where my palace is, let it be in what part of the world it will; and place me under the window of the Princess Badroulboudour.' So soon as he said this the genie took him up and transported him to Africa, in the neighborhood of a great city. In the midst of a large meadow in which the palace stood he set him down directly under the windows of the apartment of the princess, and there left him.

"Notwithstanding the darkness of the night, Aladdin very readily recognized both his own palace and the apartment of the princess; but as the night was far advanced, and everything in the palace was still, he retired from before it, and seated himself at the foot of a tree. Full of hope, and reflecting on the good fortune which chance had procured him, he felt more calm and collected than he had been since he was arrested by the sultan's order and placed in such imminent peril.

"The next morning, as soon as the sun appeared above the horizon, Aladdin was most agreeably awakened by the songs of the birds, which had perched for the night upon the tree under which he lay and also among the other thick trees in the garden of his palace. He feasted his eyes upon the beautiful building, and felt an inexpressible joy at the thought of being again master of it, and once more possessing his dear princess. He got up and approached the apartment of the Princess Badroulboudour. He walked to and fro under the window, waiting till she rose, in hopes that she might observe him. While he thus waited he tried to conjecture what could have been the cause of his misfortune; and, after reflecting for some time, he felt convinced that this mishap arose from his having left his lamp about. He accused himself of negligence and carelessness in allowing the lamp to be out of his possession a single moment. He was, however, at a loss to conjecture who could be so jealous of his happiness. He would at once have understood the case if he had known that both he and his palace were in Africa, but the slave of the ring had not informed him of this fact. The very name of Africa would have brought to his recollection his declared enemy, the magician.

"The Princess Badroulboudour rose that morning much earlier than she had risen since she had been transported into Africa by the artifice of the magician, whose hated presence she was compelled to endure once every day, as he was master of the palace; but she constantly treated him so disdainfully that he had never yet had the boldness to remain there long. When she was dressed, one of her women, looking through the lattice, perceived Aladdin, and instantly ran and told her mistress who was there. The princess, who could scarcely believe the fact, immediately went to the window and saw him herself. She opened the lattice, and at the noise she made Aladdin raised his head. He saluted her with every demonstration of joy. 'Lose not a moment!' cried the princess; 'they are gone to open the secret door. Come to me instantly.' She then shut the lattice.

"This secret door was directly below the apartment of the princess. It was opened, and Aladdin entered his wife's apartment. It is impossible to express the joy they both felt at this meeting, after having concluded they were forever separated. They embraced over and over again and gave way to transports of the tenderest affection. At length Aladdin said, 'Before you speak of anything else, my Princess, tell me, in the name of Heaven, what has become of that old lamp which I placed upon the cornice of the saloon of the twenty - four windows before I went on the hunting party?' 'Alas! my dear husband,' replied the princess, 'I greatly fear that our misfortunes are connected with that lamp; and what the more distresses me is that it was I who meddled with it.' 'Do not, my beautiful Princess,' resumed Aladdin, 'attribute any fault to yourself; I only am to blame, for I ought to have been more careful in preserving it. But let us only think of how we may regain it; and for this purpose inform me, I beg of you, of everything that has happened, and tell me into whose hands the lamp has fallen.'

"The princess then gave Aladdin an account of all that had happened relative to the exchange of the old lamp for a new one. Then she told him how, on the following night, she had felt that the palace was flying through the air, and had found herself the next morning in the unknown country where she now was. She told him that this country was Africa, a fact she had learned from the traitor who by his magic art had transported her thither.

"'O Princess,' replied Aladdin, interrupting her, 'in telling me that we are in Africa you have at once unmasked the wretch who has betrayed us. He is the most infamous of men. But this is neither the time nor the place to enter into a detail of his crimes. I entreat you only to tell me what he has done with the lamp and where he has put it.' 'He constantly carries it wrapped up in his bosom,' replied the princess; 'I am sure of this, because he once took it out in my presence, showing it as a sort of trophy.'

"'Do not be offended, my Princess,' resumed Aladdin, 'at the questions I put to you; they are of the highest importance to us both. But to come at once to the point that most interests me, tell me, I conjure you, how have you been treated by this infamous wretch?' 'Since I have been in this place,' answered the princess, 'he has presented himself before me only once each day, and I am convinced that the disdain with which I have received his visits makes him repeat them less often. He has on many occasions tried to persuade me to be faithless to you, and to take him for my husband, striving to convince me that I ought never to expect to see you again; asserting that you were no longer alive, and that the sultan my father had caused your head to be cut off. He tried, moreover, to prove to me that you were an ungrateful wretch, and said that you owed all your good fortune to him. But he never had any answer from me but complaints and tears, and was therefore obliged to retire. I feel certain, nevertheless, that he means to suffer my first affliction to subside, with the hope and expectation that I shall change my mind with respect to him. What might have been the result of my continued resistance I know not; but your presence, my dear husband, at once dissipates all my fears.'

"'My Princess,' interrupted Aladdin, 'I trust I am not deceived when I tell you I have discovered the means of delivering you from our enemy. For this purpose, however, I must go into the town; I will return about noon and communicate to you the nature of my design. Let me, however, warn you not to be astonished if you see me return in a disguise; and be sure you give orders that I may not be kept waiting at the private door, but cause me to be admitted the instant I knock.' The princess promised that a slave should be ready to open the door on his arrival.

"When Aladdin left the palace he looked about on all sides, and at last discovered a peasant who was going into the country. Aladdin hastened to overtake him; and when he came up with the peasant proposed that they should exchange clothes, accompanying his offer with such a gift that the peasant readily agreed. The exchange was effected, and Aladdin took the road that led to the town. When he got there he went into a lane appropriated to druggists, and, entering the shop which appeared the best supplied, he asked the owner if he could sell him a certain powder.

"The merchant, who, from Aladdin's dress, conceived that his customer had not money enough to pay for the powder, replied that he kept it, but that it was very dear. Aladdin readily divined what was passing in the dealer's mind; he therefore took out his purse, and, showing him the gold it contained, desired to have half a dram of the powder. The merchant weighed it, wrapped it up, and, giving it to Aladdin, demanded a piece of gold as the price. Aladdin immediately paid him, and, without stopping any longer in the town, returned to the palace. He had no occasion to wait at the secret door. It was instantly opened, and he went up to the apartment of the Princess Badroulboudour. 'My beloved Princess,' said Aladdin as soon as he came in, 'the natural aversion you have expressed for this wicked magician may probably occasion you some pain in complying with the instructions I am going to give you. But permit me, in the first place, to tell you that it is absolutely necessary you should dissemble, and even offer some violence to your own feelings if you wish to be delivered from his persecution and if the sultan your father is to have the satisfaction of again beholding you. But if you follow my advice,' continued Aladdin, 'you will this moment proceed to attire yourself in one of your most elegant dresses; and when the magician comes, make no difficulty in receiving him with all the affability you can assume without appearing to act a part. Try to speak to him with an appearance of frankness, yet still with some remains of grief, which he may easily conceive will soon be entirely dissipated. In your conversation with him give him to understand that you are making the greatest efforts to forget me; and that he may be the more convinced of your sincerity, invite him even to sup with you, and tell him that you wish to taste some of the best wine this country can produce. On hearing this, he will leave you for a time in order to procure some. In his absence you must go to the sideboard and put this powder into one of the cups from which you usually drink. Put the cup on one side, and tell one of your women to fill it and bring it to you at a certain signal on which you must agree. On the magician's return, when you are again seated at table, after having eaten and drunk as much as you think proper, make your woman bring you the particular goblet in which the powder has been put, and then exchange cups with the magician. He will find the flavor of the wine you give him so excellent that he will not refuse it, but drink up the last drop. Scarcely shall he have emptied the cup when you will see him fall backward.'

"When Aladdin had thus proposed his plan, the princess answered: 'I must confess that I shall do great violence to my own feelings in agreeing to make these advances to the magician, although I am aware they are absolutely necessary. But what would I not resolve to undertake against such a cruel enemy? I will do as you direct, since your happiness, as well as mine, depends upon it.' Aladdin took his leave, and passed the remainder of the day in the neighborhood of the palace; and when the night came on he presented himself at the secret door.

"The princess, who had been inconsolable, not only at her separation from her husband, whom from the very first she had loved more through inclination than duty, but also at being separated from the sultan her father, had hitherto completely neglected her personal appearance from the first moment of this distressful separation. She had not felt in spirits to dress with anything like care, particularly since the first visit of the magician and when she had learned from her women that he was the person who had exchanged the old lamp for a new one; for, after the infamous deception he had practised, she could not look upon him without horror. But the opportunity of taking that vengeance upon him he so justly deserved made her resolve to satisfy Aladdin.

"As soon, therefore, as he was gone, she went to her toilet, and made her women dress her in the most becoming manner. She put on some of her richest attire, choosing those ornaments which set off her beauty to the best advantage.

"The magician did not fail to make his appearance at his usual hour. As soon as the princess saw him come into the saloon of the twenty-four windows, where she was waiting to receive him, she rose up in all the splendor of her beauty and her gorgeous array. She pointed to the most honorable seat, and remained standing while he approached it, that she might sit down at the same time with him. Altogether she treated him with a civility she had never before shown him.

"The magician, more dazzled by the splendid luster of her eyes than by the brilliancy of the jewels she wore, was struck with admiration. Her majestic air, and the gracious manner she put on, so opposite to the disdain he had hitherto met with from her, absolutely confused him.

"When he had taken his seat, the princess, in order to free him from the embarrassment which oppressed him, looked at him with an air of kindness which made him suppose she no longer beheld him with the aversion she had till now evinced, and then said to him: 'You are doubtless astonished at seeing me appear to-day so different from what I have been; but you will no longer be surprised at it when I tell you that my natural disposition is so much averse to grief, melancholy, vexation, and distress that I endeavor to drive them from me by every means in my power as soon as the cause of them has departed. I have reflected upon what you said respecting the fate of Aladdin, and from the disposition of the sultan my father, which I well know, I agree with you that my late husband could not possibly escape the terrible effects of the sultan's rage. I concluded, therefore, that even if I were to weep and lament for the rest of my life, my tears would not bring Aladdin to life. Accordingly, after having paid him, even to the tomb, every respect and duty which my affection required, I thought I ought at length to admit feelings of comfort and consolation. These are the thoughts which have produced the change you see. In order, then, to drive away all sorrow, and being convinced that you will assist me in these endeavors, I have ordered a supper to be prepared; but as the only wine I have is the produce of China, and as I am now in Africa, I have a great desire to taste what is made here, and I thought that, if there were any good wine to be had, you would be most likely to have the best.'

"The magician, who had never flattered himself that he should so soon and so easily acquire the good graces of the princess, hastened to tell her that he was unable sufficiently to express his sense of her goodness; he adverted to the wine of Africa, and told her that among the many advantages which that country possessed, the principal boast was that of producing excellent wine. He told her he had some wine seven years old that was not yet broached, and it was not saying too much to aver that it surpassed the produce of the whole world. 'If my Princess,' added he, 'will permit me, I will go and bring two bottles of this wine, and will return immediately.' 'The longer you are gone the more impatient shall I be to see you again,' replied the princess: 'remember that we sit down to the table on your return.'

"Full of the anticipation of his expected happiness, the magician hastened to bring the wine, and was back almost instantly. The princess felt sure that he would make haste, and therefore at once threw the powder which Aladdin had given her into a goblet, and set it aside until she should call for it. They then sat down opposite to each other, the magician's back being toward the sideboard. The princess helped him with her own hands to what appeared the best on the table, and said to him, 'If you have any inclination for music, I will give you some; but as we are by ourselves I think conversation will afford us more pleasure.' The magician regarded this speech as a fresh mark of her favor, and was almost intoxicated with delight.

"After they had feasted for some little time, the princess called for wine, and drank to the magician's health. 'You are right,' she cried, when she had drunk, 'in praising your wine;

ARABIAN NIGHTS

I have never tasted any so delicious.' 'O charming Princess,' replied the magician, holding in his hand the goblet they had given him, 'my wine acquires a fresh flavor by the approbation you have bestowed upon it.' 'Drink to my health,' resumed the princess; 'you must confess I can appreciate good wine.' He did as she ordered him.

"When they had continued eating some time longer, and had taken three cups each, the princess, who had most completely fascinated the magician, gave the signal to her woman to bring some wine, at the same time desiring her to bring her a goblet full, and also to fill the cup of the magician. When they had received the goblets, 'I know not,' the princess said to the magician, 'what is your custom here when two good friends drink together as we are doing now. At home in China, the gentleman presents his own goblet to the lady, who at the same time presents hers to the gentleman, and the lovers then drink to each other's health.' With these words she presented to her companion the goblet she held and put out her other hand to receive his. The magician hastened to make the exchange, with which he was the more delighted as he looked upon this favor as the surest token that he had made an entire conquest of the heart of the princess; and this thought completed his happiness. 'O lovely Princess,' he exclaimed, holding the goblet in his hand before he drank, 'never shall I forget that in drinking out of your goblet I have regained that life which your cruelty, had it continued, would most infallibly have destroyed.'

"The Princess Badroulboudour was almost worn out with the magician's absurd and tiresome compliments. 'Drink,' she cried, interrupting him; 'you may then say what you please to me.' At the same time she carried the goblet she held to her mouth, but barely suffered it to touch her lips, while the magician emptied his to the last drop. In draining the cup, he held his head quite back, and remained in that position till the princess, who kept the goblet to her lips, observed that his eyes were turned up, and presently he fell upon his back, dead, without the least struggle.

ARABIAN NIGHTS

"The princess had no occasion to order her people to go and open the secret door to admit Aladdin. Her women, who were stationed at different parts of the staircase, gave the word one to the other from the saloon, so that directly after the African Magician had fallen backward the door was opened.

THE PRINCESS OBSERVED THAT HIS EYES WERE
TURNED UP, AND PRESENTLY HE FELL UPON
HIS BACK, DEAD

"Aladdin went up to the saloon; and as soon as he saw the African Magician extended on the sofa, he stopped Princess Badroulboudour, who had risen to congratulate him on the joyful event. 'My Princess,' he cried, 'there is at this moment no time for rejoicing. Do me the favor to retire to your apartment, and to leave me alone, while I prepare to carry you back to China as quickly as you departed thence.' So soon as the princess, her women, and the eunuchs had quitted the hall, Aladdin shut the door; and then, going up to the body of the African Magician, he opened his vest and took out the lamp, which was wrapped up exactly in the manner the princess had described. He took it out and rubbed it. The genie instantly presented himself and made his usual profession of service. 'O genie,' said Aladdin, 'I have called you to command you in the name of this lamp, your mistress, immediately to take this palace and transport it to the same spot in China whence it was brought.' The genie testified his obedience by an inclination of his head, and forthwith vanished. The journey was made immediately, and only two slight shocks were perceptible—one when the palace was taken up from the place where it stood in Africa, and the other when it was set down in China, opposite to the sultan's palace; and this was all the work of an instant.

"Aladdin then went down to the apartment of the Princess Badroulboudour. 'O my Princess,' he exclaimed, embracing her, 'our joy will be complete by to-morrow morning.' As the princess had not finished her supper, and as Aladdin was greatly in want of refreshment, she ordered the attendants to bring the banquet from the saloon of the twenty-four windows where the supper had been served. The princess and Aladdin drank together, and found the old wine of the magician most excellent. Then, full of the pleasure of this meeting, they retired to their apartment.

"Since the disappearance of Aladdin's palace, and the loss of the Princess Badroulboudour, whom he did not hope to see again, the sultan had been inconsolable. He slept neither night nor day; and instead of avoiding everything that could increase his affliction, he, on the contrary, cherished every thought that was likely to remind him of it. Thus not only did he go every morning to the cabinet to indulge his grief by gazing on the spot where the vanished palace had stood, but he went several times during the day to renew his tears. The sun had not yet risen when the sultan entered his cabinet as usual on the very morning on which Aladdin's palace had been brought back to its place. When he first came in his mind was so much absorbed by his own feelings, and so penetrated with sorrow, that he cast his eyes toward the accustomed spot with the expectation of beholding nothing but a vacant space. But when he first found this void filled up he conjectured that it was only a deluding vision. He then looked with greater attention, and at length could no longer doubt that it was the palace of Aladdin which he saw. Grief and sorrow were succeeded in his heart by the most delightful sensations of joy. He instantly ordered his attendants to saddle him a horse. Directly it came he mounted it and rode away, thinking he could not arrive soon enough at Aladdin's palace.

"Aladdin, who conjectured that such a thing might happen, had risen at daybreak; and as soon as he had dressed himself in one of his most magnificent robes he went up to the hall of the twenty-four windows. Looking through the casement he perceived the sultan as he came along. He descended, and was just in time to receive the monarch at the foot of the grand staircase. 'O Aladdin!' cried the sultan, 'I cannot speak to you till I have seen and embraced my dear daughter.'

"Aladdin accordingly conducted the sultan to the apartment of the princess, whom Aladdin had informed, when he rose, that she was no longer in Africa, but in China, at the capital of the sultan her father, and close to his palace. She had just finished dressing when the sultan entered. He eagerly embraced her, bathing her face with his tears, while the princess, on her part, showed the greatest delight at again beholding him. For some time the sultan could not utter a syllable, so great was his emotion at recovering his daughter, while the princess shed tears of joy at the sight of her beloved father. 'My dear daughter,' exclaimed the sultan, 'I am glad to perceive that the joy you feel at again seeing me makes you appear so little changed that no one would imagine what sorrows you have had. No one could have been suddenly transported with a whole palace, as you have been, without feeling the greatest alarm and most dreadful anxiety. Relate to me every circumstance exactly as it happened, and do not conceal anything from me.'

"The princess felt a pleasure in satisfying the affectionate curiosity of the sultan. 'O my father,' said she, 'if I appear so little altered, I beg your Majesty to consider that my expectations and hopes were raised yesterday morning by the appearance of my dear husband and liberator, Aladdin, whom I had till then mourned as forever lost to me. The happiness I experienced in again embracing him restored me to my former state. Strictly speaking, my whole sorrow consisted in finding myself torn from your Majesty and my husband; not only out of my affection for him, but lest he should perish from the dreadful effects of your Majesty's rage, to which I did not doubt that he would be exposed, however innocent he might be; and no one could be less guilty than he in this matter. Aladdin himself had not the least share in my removal, of which I was alone the cause, although the innocent one.'

"To convince the sultan that she spoke the truth, the princess gave him a detailed account of how the African Magician had disguised himself like a seller of lamps, and offered to exchange new lamps for old ones. She related the jest she had intended to practise in exchanging Aladdin's lamp, the important and secret qualities of which she did not know. Then she told of the instant removal of the palace and herself in consequence of this exchange, and their being transported into Africa with the magician himself, who had been recognized by two of her women and also by the eunuch who had made the exchange, and she spoke of the proposal he made to marry her. She then informed him of the persecution she continued to suffer until the arrival of Aladdin; of the measures they conjointly took to get possession of the lamp which the magician constantly carried about him; in what manner they had succeeded with everything that happened till she presented to him the goblet in which she had privately put the powder Aladdin had given her. 'With respect to the rest,' added she, 'I leave Aladdin to inform you of it.'

"Aladdin had but little to add to this account. 'When they opened the private door,' he said, 'I immediately went up to the hall of the twenty-four windows and saw the traitor lying dead on the sofa from the effects of the powder. As it was not proper that the princess should remain there any longer, I requested her to go to her apartment with her women and eunuchs. When I was alone I took the lamp out of the magician's bosom and made use of the same secret he had employed to remove the palace and steal away the princess. I have brought the palace back to its place, and have had the happiness of restoring the princess to your Majesty as you commanded me. I have not deceived your majesty in this matter; and if you will take the trouble to go up to the saloon you will see the magician has been punished as he deserved.'

"In pursuance of this invitation the sultan rose and went up; and when he had seen the dead body of the magician, whose face had already become livid from the strength of the poison, he embraced Aladdin with the greatest tenderness. 'Do not be angry with me, my son,' cried he, 'for having used you harshly; paternal affection drove me to it, and I deserve to be pardoned for my fault, in consideration of the cause.' 'O great King,' replied Aladdin, 'I have not the least reason to complain of your Majesty's conduct; you have done only what was your duty. This magician was the sole cause of my disgrace. When your Majesty has leisure to hear me I will give you an account of another piece of treachery, not less infamous than this, which he practised toward me, from which the peculiar providence of Heaven has preserved me.' 'I will take care to find an opportunity,' said the sultan, 'and that quickly. But let us now think of rejoicing in this happy change.'

"Aladdin ordered that the magician's body should be thrown out as a prey for the beasts and birds. In the mean time the sultan had a festival of ten days' continuance proclaimed in honor of the return of the Princess Badroulboudour and Aladdin, and of the restoration of the palace.

"It was thus that Aladdin a second time escaped an almost inevitable death.

"A few years after the sultan died at a good old age, and as he left no male issue, the Princess Badroulboudour succeeded to the throne as his legitimate heir, and of course shared the

supreme power with Aladdin. They reigned together many
years and left an illustrious and numerous posterity.

"O great King," said the Sultana Sheherazade, when she had
finished the account of the adventures of Aladdin with the wonderful lamp, "your Majesty has doubtless remarked in the
African Magician the character of a man who has abandoned
himself to the inordinate passion of acquiring wealth by the
most unjustifiable methods, and one who, though he had the
cleverness to gain wealth, was not suffered to enjoy it, because he
was unworthy. In Aladdin, on the contrary, you see a man who
from the lowest origin rose to a throne by making use of the
treasures which he had accidentally acquired, as they were
intended to be used, namely, as means to attain the end he had
in view. In the sultan you must have observed that even a good,
just and equitable monarch runs the risk of being dethroned
when, by an act of injustice, and contrary to every rule of equity,
he dares with unreasonable haste to condemn an innocent man
without pausing to hear his defense. Your Majesty must feel
horror, too, at the crimes of the infamous magician, who sacrificed his life in the attempt to acquire treasures, a villain who
received the reward due to his crimes."

The Sultan of the Indies gave Sheherazade to understand
that he was very much pleased with the marvelous adventures
of the fortunate Aladdin, and that the other stories she had each
morning told him afforded him equal satisfaction. In fact, these
stories were always diverting, and each contained a good lesson.
It was very evident that the sultana made them succeed one
another so skilfully that the sultan was not sorry to have this
excuse for delaying the fulfilment of the oath he had so solemnly
taken, namely, to have a wife for but one night, and the next
morning to cause her to be put to death. He now only thought
whether he should not in the end absolutely exhaust the sultana's
store. With this intention, after hearing the conclusion of the
history of Aladdin and the Princess Badroulboudour, which was
very different from any tale he had yet heard, he even got the

ARABIAN NIGHTS

start of Dinarzade, and himself awoke the sultana with the inquiry if she had exhausted her supply of tales.

"O my lord," replied Sheherazade, smiling at this question, "I have many yet in store; the number of my tales is so great that it would be almost impossible to give your Majesty a list of them. But I fear that your Majesty will grow tired of hearing me much sooner than I shall want materials to go on with." "Do not be afraid of that," replied Shahriar, "but let me hear what you have next to relate."

Encouraged by this speech, the sultana immediately began—

THE HISTORY OF ALI BABA, AND OF THE FORTY
ROBBERS WHO WERE KILLED BY ONE SLAVE

"IN a certain town of Persia there lived two brothers, one of whom was named Cassim and the other Ali Baba. Their father at his death left them a very moderate fortune, which they divided equally.

"Cassim married a woman who very soon after her nuptials inherited a well-furnished shop, a warehouse filled with good merchandise, and some considerable property in land. Her husband thus found himself suddenly quite a prosperous man, and became one of the richest merchants in the whole town.

"Ali Baba, on the other hand, who had taken to wife a woman no better off for worldly goods than himself, lived in a very poor house, and had no other means of gaining his livelihood and supporting his wife and children than by going to cut wood in a neighboring forest and carrying it about the town to sell on three asses, which were his only possession.

"Ali Baba went one day to the forest, and had very nearly

26   [387]

ARABIAN NIGHTS

finished cutting as much wood as his asses, could carry when he perceived a thick cloud of dust which rose very high into the air and appeared to come from a point to the right of the spot where he stood. It was advancing toward him. He was soon able to distinguish a numerous company of men on horseback who were approaching at a quick pace.

"Although that part of the country had never been spoken of as being infested with robbers, Ali Baba nevertheless conjectured that these horsemen were thieves. Therefore without considering what might become of his asses, his first and only care was to save himself. He instantly climbed up into a large tree, the branches of which spread out so close and thick that only one small opening was left. He hid himself among the thick branches, with great hope of safety, as he could see everything that occurred without being observed. The tree itself also grew at the foot of a sort of isolated rock, considerably higher than the tree, and so steep that it could not be easily ascended.

"The men, who appeared stout, powerful, and well mounted, came up to this very rock and alighted at its foot. Ali Baba counted forty of them, and was very sure, from their appearance and mode of equipment, that they were robbers. They were, in fact, a band of robbers who abstained from committing any depredations in the neighborhood, but carried on their system of plunder at a considerable distance, and only had their place of rendezvous at that spot. Presently each horseman took the bridle off his horse and hung over its head a bag filled with barley, which he had brought with him; and when all had fastened their horses to bushes and trees they took off their traveling-bags, which appeared so heavy that Ali Baba thought they must be filled with gold and silver.

"The robber who was nearest to him, and whom Ali Baba took for the captain of the band, came with his bag on his shoulder close to the rock, beside the very tree in which Ali Baba had concealed himself. After making his way among some bushes and shrubs that grew there, the robber very deliberately pronounced these words, 'Open, sesame!' which Ali Baba distinctly heard.

ARABIAN NIGHTS

The captain of the band had no sooner spoken than a door opened; and, after making all his men pass before him and go in through the door, the chief entered also, and the door closed.

"The robbers continued within the rock for a considerable time; and Ali Baba was compelled to remain in the tree and wait with patience for their departure, as he was afraid to leave his place of refuge and endeavor to save himself by flight, lest some of the horsemen should come out and discover him.

"At length the door opened and the forty robbers came out. The captain, contrary to his former proceeding, made his appearance first. After he had seen all his troops pass out before him, Ali Baba heard him pronounce these words, 'Shut, sesame!' Each man then returned to his horse, put on its bridle, fastened his bag, and mounted. When the captain saw that they were all ready to proceed he put himself at their head and they departed on the road by which they had come.

"Ali Baba followed them with his eyes till he could see them no longer, and in order to be more secure delayed his descent till a considerable time after he had lost sight of them. As he recollected the words the captain of the robbers had used to open and shut the door, he had the curiosity to try if the same effect would be produced by his pronouncing them. He therefore made his way through the bushes till he came to the door which they concealed. He went up to it, and called out, 'Open, sesame!' and the door instantly flew wide open.

"Ali Baba expected to find only a dark and gloomy cave, and was much astonished at seeing a large, spacious, well-lighted and vaulted room, dug out of the rock, and so high that he could not touch the roof with his hand. It received its light from an opening at the top of the rock. He observed in it a large quantity of provisions, numerous bales of rich merchandise, a store of silk, stuffs, and brocades, and besides all this great quantities of money, both silver and gold, partly piled up in heaps and partly stored in large leather bags placed one on another. At the sight of all these things it seemed to him that this cave must have been used for centuries as a retreat for successive generations of robbers.

"Ali Baba did not hesitate long as to the plan he should pursue. He went into the cave, and as soon as he was there the door shut; but as he knew the secret by which to open it, this circumstance gave him no sort of uneasiness. He paid no attention to the silver, but made directly for the gold coin, and particularly that portion which was in the bags. He took up in several journeys as much as he could carry, and when he had got together what he thought sufficient for loading his three asses he went and collected them together, as they had strayed to some distance. He then brought them as close as he could to the rock and loaded them; and in order to conceal the sacks he so covered the whole over with wood that no one could perceive that his beasts had any other load. When he had finished his task he went up to the door, and pronounced the words, 'Shut, sesame!' The portal instantly closed; for although it shut of itself every time he went in, it remained open on his coming out till he commanded it to close.

"Ali Baba now took the road to the town; and when he got to his own house he drove his asses into a small courtyard and shut the gate with great care. He threw down the faggots of brushwood that covered the bags and carried the latter into his house, where he laid them down in a row before his wife.

"His wife felt the sacks to find out what might be their contents; and when she found them to be full of money she suspected her husband of having stolen them; and when he laid them all before her, she could not help saying, 'Ali Baba, is it possible that you should—?' He immediately interrupted her. 'Peace, my dear wife,' exclaimed he; 'do not alarm yourself; I am not a thief, unless it be robbery to deprive thieves of their plunder. You will change your opinion of me when I have told you my good fortune.' Hereupon he emptied the sacks, the contents of which formed a great heap of gold that quite dazzled his wife's eyes; and when he had done he related his whole adventure, and in conclusion he entreated her to keep it secret.

"Recovering from her alarm, his wife began to rejoice with Ali Baba on the good fortune which had befallen them, and was

THE CAPTAIN OF THE ROBBERS PRONOUNCED THESE
WORDS, "OPEN, SESAME!"

about to count over the money that lay before her, piece by piece. 'What are you going to do?' said he. 'You are very foolish, O wife; you would never have done counting this mass. I will immediately dig a pit to bury it in—we have no time to lose.' 'But it is only right' replied the wife, 'that we should know nearly what quantity there may be. I will go and borrow a small measure from some one of our neighbors, and whilst you are digging the pit I will ascertain how much we have.' 'What you want to do, wife,' replied Ali Baba, 'is of no use. However, you shall have your own way; only remember not to betray the secret.'

"Persisting in her design, the wife of Ali Baba set off, and went to her brother-in-law, Cassim, who lived at a short distance from her house. Cassim was from home; so she addressed herself to his wife, whom she begged to lend her a measure for a few minutes. Cassim's wife inquired if she wanted a large or a small one, to which Ali Baba's wife replied that a small one would suit her. 'That I will lend you with pleasure,' said the sister-in-law. 'Wait a moment and I will bring it you.' She went to bring a measure; but, knowing the poverty of Ali Baba, she was curious to know what sort of grain his wife wanted to measure. She bethought herself, therefore, of putting some tallow under the measure, in such a way that it could not be observed.

"The wife of Ali Baba returned home and, placing the measure on the heap of gold, filled and emptied it at a little distance on the sofa, till she had measured the whole mass. Her husband having by this time dug the pit for its reception, she informed him how many measures there were, and both rejoiced at the magnitude of the treasure. While Ali Baba was burying the gold his wife carried back the measure to her sister-in-law without observing that a piece of gold had stuck to the bottom of it. 'Here, sister,' said she, on returning it, 'you see I have not kept the measure long; I am much obliged to you for lending it me.'

"So soon as the wife of Ali Baba had taken her departure, Cassim's wife looked at the bottom of the measure, and was inexpressibly astonished to see a piece of gold sticking to it.

ARABIAN NIGHTS

Envy instantly took possession of her breast. 'What!' said she to herself, 'has Ali Baba such an abundance of gold that he measures instead of counting it? Where can that miserable wretch have got it?' Her husband Cassim was from home; he had gone, as usual, to his shop, from whence he would not return till evening. The time of his absence appeared an age to her, for she was burning with impatience to acquaint him with a circumstance which, she concluded, would surprise him as much as it had astonished her.

"On Cassim's return home, his wife said to him: 'Cassim, you think you are rich, but you are deceived; Ali Baba has infinitely more wealth than you can boast. He does not count his money as you do; he measures it.' Cassim demanded an explanation of this enigma, and his wife unraveled it by acquainting him with the expedient she had used to make this discovery, and showing him the piece of money she had found adhering to the bottom of the measure.

"Far from feeling any pleasure at the good fortune which had rescued his brother from poverty, Cassim conceived an implacable jealousy. The next morning before sunrise he went to Ali Baba. 'O Ali Baba,' said he, 'you are very reserved in your affairs; you pretend to be poor and wretched and a beggar, and yet you have so much money that you must measure it.' 'O my brother,' replied Ali Baba, 'I do no understand; pray explain yourself.' 'Do not pretend ignorance,' resumed Cassim; and, showing Ali Baba the piece of gold his wife had given him, he continued, 'How many pieces have you like this that my wife found sticking to the bottom of the measure which your wife borrowed of her yesterday?'

"From this speech Ali Baba at once understood that, in consequence of his own wife's obstinacy, Cassim and his wife were already acquainted with the fact he was so anxious to conceal from them, but the discovery was made and nothing could now be done to remedy the evil. Without showing the slightest sign of surprise or vexation, he frankly owned to his brother by what chance he had found out the retreat of the thieves and where it was situated; and he offered, if Cassim would agree to keep the secret, to share the treasure with him.

"'This I certainly expect you will do,' replied Cassim, in a haughty tone; and he added, 'but I demand to know also the precise spot where this treasure lies concealed, and the signs which may enable me to visit the place myself. If you refuse this information I will go and inform the police, and you will not only be deprived of all hope of obtaining any more money, but you will even lose that you have already taken, whereas I shall receive my portion for having informed against you.'

"Actuated more by his natural goodness of heart than intimidated by the insolent menaces of this cruel brother, Ali Baba gave him all the information he demanded, and even told him the words he must pronounce both on entering the cave and on quitting it. Cassim made no further inquiries of Ali Baba; he left him with the determination of being beforehand with him in any further views he might have on the treasure. Full of the hope of possessing himself of the whole mass, he set off the next morning before break of day with ten mules furnished with large hampers which he proposed to fill. He took the road which Ali Baba had pointed out, and arrived at the rock and the tree which from description he knew to be the one that had concealed his brother. He looked for the door and soon discovered it; and to cause it to open he pronounced the words, 'Open, sesame!' The door obeyed, he entered, and it immediately closed behind him. On examining the cave, he felt the utmost astonishment on seeing so much more wealth than the description of Ali Baba had led him to expect; and his admiration increased as he examined each department separately. Avaricious and fond of money as he was, he could have passed the whole day in feasting his eyes with the sight of so much gold, but he reflected that he had come to load his ten mules with as much of the treasure as he could collect. He took up a number of sacks and, coming to the door, his mind distracted by a multitude of ideas, found that he had forgotten the important words, and, instead of pronouncing, 'sesame,' he said, 'Open, barley.' He was thunderstruck on perceiving that the door, instead of flying open, remained closed. He named the various other kinds of grain, all but the right description, but the door did not move.

"Cassim was not prepared for an adventure of this kind. Fear took entire possession of his mind. The more he endeavored to recollect the word sesame, the more was his memory confused, and he remained as far from any recollection of it as if he had never heard of the word mentioned. He threw to the ground the sacks he had collected, and paced with hasty steps backward and forward in the cave. The riches which surrounded him had no longer any charms for his imagination.

"Toward noon the robbers returned to their cave, and when they saw the mules belonging to Cassim standing about the rock laden with hampers they were greatly surprised. They immediately drove away the ten mules, which Cassim had neglected to fasten, and which, therefore, dispersed in the forest. The robbers did not give themselves the trouble to run after the mules, for their chief object was to discover the owner of the beasts. While some were employed in searching the exterior recesses of the rock, the captain, with the rest, alighted and, drawing their sabers, the party went toward the door, pronounced the magic words, and it opened.

"Cassim, who from the inside of the cave had heard the noise of horses trampling on the ground, felt certain that the robbers had arrived and that his death was inevitable. Resolved, however, to make one effort to escape and reach some place of safety, he posted himself near the door, ready to run out as soon as it should open The word 'sesame,' which he had in vain endeavored to recall to his remembrance, was scarcely pronounced when the portal opened and he rushed out with such violence that he threw the captain to the ground. He could not, however, avoid the other thieves, who cut him to pieces on the spot.

"The next proceeding of the robbers after this execution was to enter the cave. They found, near the door, the bags which Cassim, after filling with gold, had removed there for the convenience of loading his mules, and they put them in their places again without observing the absence of those which Ali Baba had previously carried away. Conjecturing and consulting upon this event, they could easily account for Cassim's inability to effect his escape, but they could not in any way imagine how he had been able to enter the cave. They supposed that he might have descended from the top of the cave, but the opening which admitted the light was so high and the summit of the rock so inaccessible on the outside, that they all agreed such a feat was impossible. They could not suppose he had entered by the door, unless he had discovered the password which caused it to open, but they felt quite secure that they alone were possessed of this secret, for they were ignorant of having been overheard by Ali Baba.

"But as the manner in which this entry had been effected remained a mystery, and their united riches were no longer in safety, they agreed to cut the corpse of Cassim into four quarters and place them in the cave near the door, two quarters on one side, and two on the other, to frighten away any one who might have the boldness to hazard a similar enterprise, resolving themselves not to return to the cave for some time. This determination they put into immediate execution, and when they had nothing further to detain them they left their place of retreat well secured, mounted their horses, and set off to scour the country and, as before, to infest the roads most frequented by caravans, which afforded them favorable opportunities of plundering.

"The wife of Cassim in the mean time began to feel very uneasy when she observed night approach and yet her husband did not return. She went in the utmost alarm to Ali Baba, and said to him: 'O brother, I believe you are well aware that Cassim is gone to the forest and for what purpose. He has not yet come back, and I fear that some accident may have befallen him.'

"Ali Baba suspected his brother's intention after the conversation he had held with him, and for this reason he had abstained from visiting the forest on that day, that he might not offend Cassim. However, he replied that she need not yet feel any uneasiness, for that Cassim most probably thought it prudent not to return to the city until the daylight had entirely vanished. The wife of Cassim felt satisfied with this reason, and was the more easily persuaded of its truth when she considered how important it was that her husband should use the greatest secrecy for the accomplishment of his purpose. She returned to her house, and waited patiently till midnight, but after that hour her fears returned with twofold strength, and her grief was the greater, as she could not proclaim it, nor even relieve it by cries, which might have caused suspicion and inquiry in the neighborhood. She then began to repent of the silly curiosity which, heightened by envy, had induced her to endeavor to pry into the private affairs of her brother and sister-in-law. She spent the night in weeping, and at break of day she ran to Ali Baba and announced the cause of her early visit less by her words than by her tears.

"Ali Baba did not wait till his sister entreated him to go and seek for Cassim. After advising the disconsolate wife to restrain her grief, he immediately set off with his three asses and went to the forest. As he drew near the rock he was much astonished on observing that blood had been shed near the door, and, not having met in his way either his brother or the ten mules, he looked on this as an unfavorable omen. He reached the door, and on his pronouncing the words it opened. He was struck with horror when he discovered the body of his brother cut into four quarters, yet, notwithstanding the small share of fraternal affection he had received from Cassim during his life, he did not hesitate on the course he was to pursue in rendering the last act of duty to his brother's remains. He found materials in the cave wherein to wrap up the body, and, making two packets of the four quarters, he placed them on one of his asses, covering them with sticks to conceal them. The other two asses he expeditiously loaded with sacks of gold, putting wood over them as on the preceding occasion; and, having finished all he had to do and commanded the door to close, he took the road to the city, taking care to wait at the entrance of the forest until night had closed, that he might return without being observed. When he got home he left the two asses that were laden with gold, desiring his wife to take care to unload them; and, after telling her in a few words what had happened to Cassim, he led the third ass away to his sister-in-law.

"Ali Baba knocked at the door, which was opened to him by a female slave named Morgiana. This Morgiana was crafty, cunning, and Ali Baba knew her abilities well. When he had entered the courtyard he unloaded the wood and the two packages from the ass, and, taking the slave aside, he said: 'Morgiana, the first thing I have to request of you is inviolable secrecy. These two packets contain the body of your master, and we must endeavor to bury him as if he had died a natural death. Let me speak to your mistress, and take good heed of what I shall say to her.'

"Morgiana went to acquaint her mistress that Ali Baba had returned, and Ali Baba followed her. 'Well, brother,' inquired his sister-in-law, in an impatient tone, 'what news do you bring of my husband?' 'O my sister,' replied Ali Baba, 'I cannot answer you unless you first promise to listen to me from the beginning to the end of my story without interruption. It is of no less importance to you than to me, under the present circumstances, to preserve the greatest secrecy. Discretion is absolutely necessary for your repose and security.' 'Ah,' cried the sister in a mournful voice, 'this preamble convinces me that my husband is no more; but at the same time I feel the necessity of the secrecy you require.'

"Ali Baba then related to her all that had happened during his journey until he had brought away the body of Cassim. 'Sister,' added he, 'here is a great and sudden affliction for you. The evil is without remedy, but nevertheless, if my good offices can afford you consolation, I offer to join the small property Heaven has granted me to yours by marrying you. I can assure you my wife will not be jealous, and you will live comfortably together. If this proposal meets your approbation, we must contrive to bury my brother as if he had died a natural death; and this is an office which I think you may safely intrust to Morgiana, and I will on my part contribute all in my power to assist her.'

"The widow of Cassim reflected that she could not do better than consent to this offer, for Ali Baba now possessed greater riches than she could boast, and besides, by the discovery of the treasure, might increase them considerably. She did not, therefore, refuse his proposal, but on the contrary regarded it as a reasonable source of consolation. She wiped away her tears and testified to Ali Baba that she accepted his offer.

"Ali Baba, having strongly recommended to Morgiana to use the utmost discretion in the difficult part she was to perform, returned home with his ass.

"Morgiana did not belie her character for cunning. She went out with Ali Baba and betook herself to an apothecary who lived in the neighborhood. She knocked at the shop door, and when it was opened asked for a particular kind of lozenge, supposed to possess great efficacy in dangerous disorders. The apothecary gave her as much as the money she offered would pay for, asking who was ill in her master's family. 'Alas!' exclaimed she, with a deep sigh, 'it is my worthy master, Cassim himself. No one can understand his complaint; he can neither speak nor eat.' So saying, she carried off the lozenges which Cassim would never need more.

"On the following day Morgiana again went to the same apothecary, and with tears in her eyes inquired for an essence which it was customary only to administer when the patient was reduced to the last extremity, and when no other remedy had been left untried. 'Alas!' cried she, as she received it from the hands of the apothecary, 'I fear this remedy will not be of more use than the lozenges. I shall lose my beloved master!'

"Moreover, as Ali Baba and his wife were seen going to and from the house of Cassim in the course of the day, no one was surprised when, toward evening, the piercing cries of the widow and Morgiana announced the death of Cassim. At a very early hour the next morning Morgiana, knowing that a good old cobbler lived some distance off who was one of the first to open his shop, went out to visit him. Coming up to him, she wished him a good day, and put a piece of gold into his hand.

"Baba Mustapha, a man well known throughout all the city, was naturally of a gay turn, and had always something laughable to say. He examined the piece of money, and, seeing that it was gold, he said: 'This is good wage. What is to be done? I am ready to do your bidding.' 'Baba Mustapha,' said Morgiana to him, 'take all your materials for sewing and come directly with me; but I insist on this condition, that you let me put a bandage over your eyes when we have got to a certain place.' At these words Baba Mustapha began to make objections. 'Oh, ho!' said he, 'you want me to do something against my conscience or my honor.' But Morgiana interrupted him by putting another piece of gold into his hand. 'Allah forbid,' she said, 'that I should require you to do anything that would stain your honor; only come with me and fear nothing.'

"Baba Mustapha suffered himself to be led by the slave, who bound a handkerchief over his eyes and brought him to her deceased master's; nor did she remove the bandage until he was in the chamber where the body was deposited, the severed quarters having been put together. Taking off the covering, she said: 'Baba Mustapha, I have brought you hither that you might sew these pieces together. Lose no time, and when you have done I will give you another piece of gold.'

"When Baba Mustapha had finished his work, Morgiana bound his eyes again before he left the chamber, and, after giving him the third piece of money according to her promise, and earnestly recommending him to keep her secret, she conducted him to the place where she had first put on the handkerchief. Here she took the bandage from his eyes and left him to return to his house, watching him, however, until he was out of sight lest he should have the curiosity to return and notice her movements.

"Morgiana had heated some water to wash the body of Cassim; and Ali Baba, who entered just as she returned, washed it, perfumed it with incense, and wrapped it in the burying-clothes with the customary ceremonies. The joiner also brought the coffin which Ali Baba had taken care to order. In order that he might not observe anything particular, Morgiana received the coffin at the door, and, having paid the man and sent him away, she assisted Ali Baba to put the body into it. When he had nailed down the lid of the coffin, she went to the mosque to give notice that everything was ready for the funeral.

"Morgiana had scarcely returned before the Iman and the other ministers of the mosque arrived. Four of the neighbors took the coffin on their shoulders and carried it to the cemetery, following the Iman, who repeated prayers as he went along. Morgiana, as slave to the deceased, walked next, with her head uncovered. She was bathed in tears, and uttered the most piteous cries from time to time. Ali Baba closed the procession, accompanied by some of the neighbors.

"As for the widow of Cassim, she remained at home to lament and weep with the women of the neighborhood, who, according to the usual custom, had repaired to her house during the ceremony of the burial. In this manner the fatal end of Cassim was so well dissembled and concealed by Ali Baba and the rest that no one in the city had the least suspicion of the manner in which he had come by his death.

"Three or four days after the interment of Cassim, Ali Baba removed the few goods he possessed, together with the money he had taken from the robbers' store, which he conveyed by night into the house of the widow of Cassim, in order to establish himself there and thus announce his marriage with his sister-in-law; and as such matches are by no means extraordinary in our religion, no one showed any marks of surprise on the occasion.

"Ali Baba had a son who had passed a certain time with a merchant of considerable repute, who had always bestowed the highest commendations on his conduct. To this son he gave the shop of Cassim, with a further promise that if the young man continued to behave with prudence he would ere long marry him advantageously.

ARABIAN NIGHTS

"Leaving Ali Baba to enjoy his newly acquired fortune, we will now return to the forty thieves. They came back to their retreat in the forest when the time they had agreed to be absent had expired; but their astonishment was indescribable when they found the body of Cassim gone, and it was greatly increased on perceiving a visible diminution of their treasure. 'We are discovered,' said the captain, 'and entirely ruined if we are not very careful, or neglect to take immediate measures to remedy the evil; we shall by degrees lose all these riches which our ancestors, as well as we, have amassed with so much trouble and fatigue. All that we can at present judge concerning the loss we have sustained is that the thief whom we surprised at the fortunate moment when he was going to make his escape knew the secret of opening the door. But he was not the only one who possessed that secret; another must have the same knowledge. The removal of his body and the diminution of our treasure are incontestable proofs of the fact. And, as we have no reason to suppose that more than two people are acquainted with the secret, having destroyed one, we must not suffer the other to escape. What say you, my brave comrades? Are you not of my opinion?'

"This proposal of the captain's was thought so reasonable that the whole troop approved it, and agreed that it would be advisable to relinquish every other enterprise and occupy themselves solely with this affair, which they should not abandon until they had succeeded in detecting the thief.

"'I expected this decision, from your own courage and bravery,' resumed the captain; 'but the first thing to be done is that one of you who is bold, courageous, and cunning should go to the city unarmed and in the dress of a traveler, and employ all his art to discover if the singular death we inflicted on the culprit whom we destroyed is the common topic of conversation. Then he must find out who this man was and where he lived. It is absolutely necessary we should be acquainted with this, that we may not do anything of which we may have to repent by making ourselves known in a country where we have been so long forgotten, and

27   [403]

where it is so much to our interest to remain undisturbed. But in order to inspire with ardor him who shall undertake this commission, and to prevent his bringing us a false report which might occasion our total ruin, I propose that he should consent to submit to the penalty of death in case of failure.'

"Without waiting till his companions should speak, one of the robbers said: 'I willingly agree to these terms, and glory in exposing my life in the execution of such a commission. If I should fail you will at least remember that I have displayed both courage and readiness in my offer to serve the whole troop.'

"Amid the commendations of the captain and his companions the robber disguised himself in such a way that no one could have suspected him of belonging to the nefarious trade he followed. He set off at night, and entered the city just as day was beginning to appear. He went toward the public bazaar, where he saw only one shop open, and that was the shop of Baba Mustapha.

"The jovial cobbler was seated on his stool, ready to begin work. The robber went up to him and wished him a good morning, saying: 'My good man, you rise betimes to your work. How is it possible that an old man like you can see clearly at this early hour? Even if it were broad day I doubt whether your eyes are good enough to see the stitches you make.'

"'Whoever you are,' replied Baba Mustapha, 'you do not know much about me. Notwithstanding my age, I have excellent eyes; and you would have confessed as much had you known that not long since I sewed up a dead body in a place where there was not more light than we have here.'

"'The robber felt greatly elated at having on his arrival addressed himself to a man who of his own accord entered upon the very subject on which he ardently wished to gain information. 'A dead body!' replied he, with feigned astonishment, to induce the other to proceed. 'Why should you want to sew up a dead body? I suppose you mean that you sewed the shroud in which he was buried.' 'No, no,' said Baba Mustapha, 'I know what I mean; you want me to tell you more about it, but you shall not hear another syllable.'

ARABIAN NIGHTS

"The robber required no further proof to be fully convinced that he was on the right road to discover what he wished to know. He produced a piece of gold, and, putting it into Baba Mustapha's hand, he said: 'I have no desire to cheat you of your secret, although I can assure you I should not divulge it even if you intrusted me with it. The only favor I beg is that you will have the goodness to direct me to the house where you sewed up the dead body or that you will come with me and show me the way.'

"'Should I feel inclined to grant your request,' replied Baba Mustapha, holding the piece of money in his hand as if ready to return it, 'I assure you that I could not do it. And I will tell you why I must refuse. My employers took me to a particular place, and there they bound my eyes; and from thence I suffered myself to be led to the house; and when I had finished what I had to do I was brought back to my own house in the same manner. You see, therefore, how impossible it is that I should serve you in this matter.' 'But at least,' resumed the robber, 'you must nearly remember the way you went after your eyes were bound. Pray come with me; I will put a bandage over your eyes at the place where you were blindfolded, and we will walk together along the same streets, and follow the same turnings, which you will probably recollect to have taken; and, as all labor deserves a reward, here is another piece of gold. Come, grant me this favor.' And as he spoke he put another piece of money into the cobbler's hand.

"The two pieces of gold were a sore temptation to Baba Mustapha. At length he drew his purse from his bosom and, putting the gold into it, replied, 'I cannot positively assure you that I remember exactly the way they took me; but since you will have it so, come along; I will do my best to satisfy you.'

"To the great satisfaction of the robber, Baba Mustapha conducted the robber to the spot where Morgiana had put the bandage over his eyes. 'This is the place,' said he, 'where my eyes were bound; and then my face was turned in this direction.' The robber, who had his handkerchief ready, tied it over

Mustapha's eyes, and walked by his side, partly leading him and partly led by him, till Baba Mustapha stopped.

"'I think,' said he, 'I did not go farther than this'; and he was in fact exactly before the house which had once belonged to Cassim, and where Ali Baba now resided. Before taking the

MORGIANA MARKED THE OTHER DOORS IN THE SAME MANNER

bandage from the cobbler's eyes, the robber quickly made a mark on the door with some chalk he had brought for the purpose; and when he had taken the handkerchief off he asked Baba Mustapha if he knew to whom the house belonged. The cobbler replied that he did not live in that quarter of the town and therefore could not tell. As the robber found that he could gain no further intelligence from Baba Mustapha, he thanked him for the trouble he had taken; and when he had seen the cobbler turn away to go to his shop, he took the road to the forest, where he felt certain he should be well received.

"Soon after the robber and Baba Mustapha had separated Morgiana had occasion to go out on some errand, and when she returned she observed the mark which the robber had made on the door of Ali Baba's house. She stopped to examine it. 'What can this mark signify?' thought she. 'Has any one a spite against my master, or has it been made only for diversion? Be the motive what it may, I may as well use precautions against the worst that may happen.' She therefore took some chalk; and as several of the doors on each side of her master's house were of the same appearance, she marked them in the same manner, and then went in without saying anything of what she had done either to her master or mistress.

"In the mean time the thief made the best of his way back into the forest, where he rejoined his companions. He related the success of his journey. They all listened to him with great satisfaction, and the captain, after praising his diligence, thus addressed the rest: 'Comrades,' said he, 'we have no time to lose; let us arm ourselves and depart; and when we have entered the city (whither we had best go separately, not to create suspicion), let us all assemble in the great square—some on one side of it, some on the other—and I will go and find out the house with our companion who has brought us this good news, and then I shall be able to judge what method will be most advantageous to pursue.'

"The robbers all applauded their captain's proposal, and they were very soon equipped for their departure. They went in small parties of two or three together, and, walking at a certain distance from one another, they entered the city without occasioning any suspicion. The captain and the robber who had been there in the morning were the last to enter it; and the latter conducted the captain to the street in which he had marked the house of Ali Baba. When they reached the first door that had been marked by Morgiana, the thief pointed it out, saying that was the one he had marked. But as they continued walking, the captain perceived that the next door was marked in the same manner, and pointed out this circumstance to his guide, inquiring whether this was the house, or the one they had passed? His guide was quite confused, and knew not what to answer; and his embarrassment increased when, on proceeding with the captain, he found that four or five doors successively had the same mark. He assured the captain, with an oath, that he had marked but one. 'I cannot conceive,' added he, 'who can have imitated my mark with so much exactness; but I cannot now distinguish my mark from the others.'

"The captain, who found that his design was frustrated, returned to the great square, where he told the first of his people whom he met to inform the rest that they had made a fruitless expedition, and that now there was nothing to be done but to return to their place of retreat. He set the example and they all followed.

"When the troop had reassembled in the forest the captain explained to them the reason why he had ordered them to return. The spy was unanimously declared deserving of death, and he acquiesced in his condemnation, owning that he should have been more cautious in taking his measures; and, advancing with a serene countenance, he submitted to the stroke of a companion who was ordered to strike his head from his body.

"As it was necessary for the safety and preservation of the whole band, that the great injury they had suffered should not pass unavenged, another robber, who flattered himself with the hopes of better success than had attended the first, presented himself and requested the preference. It was granted him. He went to the city, corrupted Baba Mustapha by the same artifice that the first robber had used, and the cobbler led him to the house of Ali Baba with his eyes bound.

"The thief marked the door with red chalk in a place where it would be less noticed, thinking that would be a sure method of distinguishing it from those that were marked with white. But a short time afterward Morgiana went out as on the preceding day, and on her return the red mark did not escape her piercing eye. She immediately made a similar red mark on the neighboring doors.

"When he returned to his companions in the forest, the thief boasted of the precautions he had taken, which he declared to be infallible, to distinguish the house of Ali Baba from the others. The captain and the rest agreed with him, and all thought themselves sure of success. They repaired to the city in the same order and with as much care as before, armed also in the same way, ready to execute the blow they meditated. The captain and the robber went immediately to the street where Ali Baba resided, but the same difficulty occurred as on the former occasion. The captain was irritated, and the thief as utterly confounded as he who had preceded him in the same business.

"Thus was the captain obliged to return a second time with his comrades, as little satisfied with his expedition as he had been on the preceding day. The robber who was the author of the disappointment underwent the punishment which he had agreed to suffer as the penalty of non-success.

"The captain, seeing his troop diminished by two brave associates, feared it might decrease still more if he continued to trust to others the discovery of the house where Ali Baba resided. Experience convinced him that his companions did not excel in affairs that depended on cunning, as in those in which strength of arm only was required. He therefore undertook the business himself. He went to the city, and with the assistance of Baba Mustapha, who was ready to perform the same service for him which he had rendered to the other two, he found the house of Ali Baba; but not choosing to trust to the stratagem of making marks on it, which had hitherto proved so fallacious, he imprinted it so thoroughly on his memory by looking at it attentively that at last he was certain he could not mistake it.

"The captain returned to the forest, and when he had reached the cave where the rest of the robbers were waiting his return he said, 'Comrades, nothing now can prevent our taking full revenge of the injury that has been done us. I know with certainty the house of the culprit who is to experience our wrath, and on the road I have meditated a way of quitting scores with him so privately that no one shall be able to discover where our treasure is deposited. I have hit upon a plan to obtain this end, and when I have explained the plan to you, if any one can propose a better expedient, let him speak.' He then told them in what manner he intended to conduct the affair, and as they all gave their approbation he charged them to divide into small parties and go into the neighboring towns and villages, and to buy nineteen mules and thirty-eight large, leathern jars for carrying oil, one of which jars must be full, and all the others empty.

"In the course of two or three days the thieves had completed their purchases, and as the empty jars were rather too narrow at the mouth for the purpose to which he intended to apply them, the captain had them enlarged. Then he made one of the men, thoroughly armed, enter each jar. He closed the jars, so that they appeared full of oil, leaving, however, that part open which had been unsewed, to admit air for the men to breathe; and the better to carry on the deception, he rubbed the outside of each jar with oil which he took from the full one.

"Things being thus prepared, the mules were laden with the thirty-seven robbers, each concealed in a jar, and with the jar that was filled with oil. Then the captain, as conductor, took the road to the city at the hour that had been agreed on, and arrived about an hour after sunset, as he proposed. He went straight to the house of Ali Baba, intending to knock and request shelter for the night for himself and his mules. He was, however, spared the trouble of knocking, for he found Ali Baba at the door enjoying the fresh air after supper. He stopped his mules, and, addressing himself to Ali Baba, said: 'My good friend, I have brought the oil which you see here from a great distance to sell to-morrow in the market, and at this late hour I do not know where to obtain shelter for the night. If it would not occasion you much inconvenience, do me the favor to take me in, and you will confer a great obligation on me.'

"Although in the forest Ali Baba had seen the man who now spoke to him, and had even heard his voice, yet he had no idea that this was the captain of the forty robbers, disguised as an oil merchant. 'You are welcome,' he said, and immediately made room for the visitor and his mules to go in. At the same time Ali Baba called a slave and ordered him, when the mules were unladen, not only to put them under cover in the stable, but to give them some hay and corn. He also took the trouble of going into the kitchen to desire Morgiana to get supper quickly for a guest who had just arrived, and to prepare him a chamber and a bed.

"Ali Baba went still further in his desire to receive his guest with all possible civility. Observing that, after he had unladen his mules, and they had been taken into the stables as he had wished, the new-comer seemed making preparations to pass the night with them, he went to him to beg him to come into the room where he received company. The captain of the robbers endeavored to excuse himself from accepting the invitation, alleging that he was loath to be troublesome, but in reality that he might have an opportunity of executing his meditated project with more ease; and it was not until Ali Baba had used the most urgent persuasions that he complied with his request.

"Ali Baba remained with his perfidious guest, who sought his life in return for his hospitality, till he had finished the repast provided for him. He then said, 'You are at liberty to do as you please; you have only to ask for whatever you may want, and all I have is at your service.'

"The captain of the robbers rose at the same time with Ali Baba, and accompanied him to the door; and while Ali Baba went into the kitchen to speak to Morgiana, he went into the court under the pretext of going to the stable to see after his mules.

"Ali Baba, having again enjoined Morgiana to be attentive to his guest, added: 'To-morrow before daybreak I shall go to the bath. Take care that my bathing linen is ready, and give it to Abdalla'—this was the name of the slave—'and make me some good broth to take when I return.' After giving these orders he went to bed.

"The captain of the robbers in the mean time, on leaving

the stable went to give his people the necessary orders for what they were to do. Beginning at the first jar, and going through the whole number, he said to the man in each: 'When I throw some pebbles from the chamber where I am to be lodged to-night, do not fail to rip open the jar from top to bottom with the knife you are furnished with, and come out. I shall be with you immediately afterward.' The knife he spoke of was pointed and sharpened for the purpose of cutting the leathern jars. After giving these directions, he returned, and when he got to the kitchen door Morgiana took a light and conducted him to the chamber she had prepared for him, and there left him. Not to create any suspicion, he put out the light a short time after and lay down in his clothes, to be ready to rise as soon as he had taken his first sleep.

"Morgiana did not forget Ali Baba's orders. She prepared her master's linen for the bath, and gave it to Abdalla, who was not yet gone to bed. Then she put the pot on the fire to make the broth; but while she was skimming it the lamp went out. There was no more oil in the house, and she had not any candle, so she knew not what to do. She wanted a light to see to skim the pot, and mentioned her dilemma to Abdalla. 'Why are you so much disturbed at this?' said he. 'Go and take some oil out of one of the jars in the court.'

"Morgiana thanked Abdalla for the hint, and while he retired to bed she took the oil-can and went into the court. As she drew near to the jar that stood first in the row, the thief who was concealed within said in a low voice, 'Is it time?'

"Any other slave but Morgiana would, in the first moment of surprise at finding a man in the jar instead of the oil she expected, have made a great uproar which might have produced terrible consequences. But Morgiana was superior to the position she held. She was instantly aware of the importance of secrecy and caution, and understood the extreme danger in which Ali Baba and his family, as well as herself, were placed; she also saw the urgent necessity of devising a speedy remedy that should be silently executed. She collected her thoughts

MORGIANA POURED INTO EACH JAR SUFFICIENT
BOILING OIL TO SCALD THE ROBBERS TO DEATH

and, without showing any emotion, assumed the manner of the captain, and answered, 'Not yet, but presently.' She approached the next jar, and the same question was asked her. She went on to all the vessels in succession, making the same answer to the same question till she came to the last jar, which was full of oil.

"Morgiana by this means discovered that her master, who supposed he was giving a night's lodging to an oil merchant, had afforded shelter to thirty-eight robbers, and that the pretended merchant was their captain. She quickly filled her oil-can from the last jar and returned into the kitchen; and, after having put some oil in her lamp and lighted it, she took a large kettle and went again into the court to fill it with oil from the jar. This kettle she immediately put upon the fire, and made a great blaze under it with a quantity of wood; for the sooner the oil boiled the sooner her plan for the preservation of the whole family would be executed, and it required the utmost despatch. At length the oil boiled. She took the kettle and poured into each jar, from the first to the last, sufficient boiling oil to scald the robbers to death, a purpose she effectually carried out.

"When Morgiana had thus silently, and without disturbing any one, performed this intrepid act exactly as she had conceived it, she returned to the kitchen with the empty kettle and shut the door. She then blew out the lamp and remained perfectly silent, determined not to go to bed until, from a window of the kitchen which overlooked the court, she had observed what would ensue.

"Morgiana had scarcely waited a quarter of an hour when the captain of the robbers awoke. He got up, opened the window, and looked out. All was dark, and a profound silence reigned around; he gave the signal by throwing the pebbles, many of which struck the jars, as the sound plainly proved. He listened, but heard nothing that could lead him to suppose his men obeyed the summons. He became uneasy at this delay, and threw some pebbles a second, and even a third time. They all struck the jars, yet nothing appeared to indicate that the signal was answered. In the utmost alarm, he descended into the court and, approaching the first jar, intending to ask if the robber contained in it, and whom he supposed still living, was asleep, he smelt a strong scent of hot and burning oil issuing from the jar. Then he began to suspect that his enterprise against Ali Baba—to destroy him, pillage his house, and carry off, if possible, all the money which he had taken from him and the community, had failed. He proceeded to the next jar, and to all in succession, and discovered that all his men had shared the same fate; and by the diminution of the oil in the vessel which he had brought full, he guessed the means that had been used to deprive him of the assistance he expected. Mortified at having thus missed his aim, he jumped over the garden gate which led out of the court, and, going from one garden to another by getting over the walls, he made his escape.

"When Morgiana perceived that all was silent and still, and that the captain of the thieves did not return, she suspected the truth: namely, that he had decamped by the gardens instead of attempting to escape by the house door, which was fastened with double bolts. Fully satisfied he was gone, and overjoyed at having succeeded in securing the safety of the whole family, she at length retired to bed and soon fell asleep.

"Ali Baba went out before daybreak and repaired to the bath, followed by his slave, totally ignorant of the surprising event which had taken place in his house during the night, for Morgiana had not thought it necessary to wake him.

"When he returned from the bath, the sun had risen. Ali Baba was surprised to see the jars of oil still in their places, and to find that the merchant had not taken them to the market with his mules. He inquired the reason of Morgiana, who let him in, and who had left everything in its original state that she might impress him with the greatest sense of the effort she had made for his preservation.

"'My good master,' said Morgiana to Ali Baba, 'may Heaven preserve you and all your family. You will be better informed of what you wish to know when you have seen what I am going to show you.' Ali Baba followed Morgiana; and when she had shut the door she took him to the first jar and bade him look into it and see if it contained oil. He did as she desired, and, perceiving a man in the jar, he hastily drew back and uttered a cry of surprise. 'Do not be afraid,' said she; 'the man you see there will not do you any harm; he will never hurt either you or any one else again, for he is now a corpse.' 'Morgiana!' exclaimed Ali Baba, 'what does all this mean? I command you to explain this mystery.' 'I will explain it,' replied Morgiana, 'but moderate your astonishment and do not awaken the curiosity of your neighbors, or let them hear what is of the utmost importance that you should keep secret and concealed. Look first at all the other jars.'

"Ali Baba examined the jars, one after the other, from the first till he came to the last, which contained the oil; and he remarked that its contents were considerably diminished. When his survey was completed he stood motionless with astonishment, sometimes casting his eyes on Morgiana, then looking at the jars, but without speaking a word, so great was his surprise. At length he said, 'And what has become of the merchant?'

"'The merchant,' replied Morgiana, 'is no more a merchant than I am. I can tell you who he is and what is become of him.'

"In obedience to Ali Baba's request, Morgiana told him of all the events of the preceding night, of how she discovered and killed the thirty-seven thieves and of the escape of the captain of the band.

"When she had finished her narrative, Morgiana added: 'I am convinced that this is the conclusion of a scheme of which I observed the beginning two or three days ago, but with the particulars of which I did not think it necessary to trouble you. One morning as I returned from the city at an early hour I perceived the street door marked with white, and on the following day there was a red mark near the white one. Each time, without knowing for what purpose these marks were made, I made the same kind of mark, in the same part, on the doors of three or four of our neighbors on each side of this house. If you connect that fact with what has happened, you will find that the whole is a scheme, contrived by the thieves of the forest, whose troop, I know not wherefore, seems to be diminished by two. But be that as it may, the band is now reduced to three at most. This proves that the robbers had determined on your death, and you will do right to be on your guard against them so long as you are certain that one still remains. On my part, I will do all in my power toward your safety.'

"When Morgiana ceased speaking, Ali Baba, filled with gratitude for the great obligation he owed her, replied: 'I will recompense you as you deserve before I die. I owe my life to you; and to give you an immediate proof of my feelings, I give you your liberty from this moment, and will soon reward you in a more ample manner. I am as thoroughly convinced as you are that the forty robbers laid this snare for me. Through your means Allah has delivered me from the danger. What we have now to do is to use the utmost despatch in burying the bodies of this pest of the human race. Yet we must do so with so much secrecy that no one can entertain the slightest suspicion of their fate; and for this purpose I will instantly go to work with Abdalla.'

"Ali Baba's garden was of considerable size, and terminated in a clump of large trees. He went without delay with his slave to dig under these trees a ditch or grave of sufficient length and breadth to contain the bodies he had to inter. The ground was soft and easy to remove, so that they were not long in completing their work. They took the bodies out of the jars and removed the weapons with which the robbers had furnished themselves. They then carried the bodies to the bottom of the garden and placed them in the grave, and after having covered them with the earth they had previously removed, they spread about what remained to make the surface of the ground appear even, as it was before. Ali Baba carefully concealed the oil-jars and the arms; as for the mules, he sent them to the market at different times and disposed of them by means of his slave.

"Whilst Ali Baba was taking these precautions to prevent it being publicly known by what means he had become rich in so short a space of time, the captain of the forty thieves had returned to the forest mortified beyond measure; and in the agitation and confusion which he experienced at having met with such a disaster, he reached the cavern without coming to any resolution on what he should or should not do respecting Ali Baba.

"The dismal solitude of this gloomy habitation appeared to him insupportable. 'O ye brave companions,' cried he, 'ye

THE DISMAL SOLITUDE OF THIS GLOOMY HABITATION
APPEARED TO HIM INSUPPORTABLE

partners of my labors and my pains, where are you? What can I accomplish without your assistance? My regret for your loss would not have been so great had you died with your sabers in your hands, like valiant men. When shall I be able to collect together another troop of intrepid men like you? And even should I wish to assemble a new troop, how could I undertake it without exposing all our treasures of gold and silver to the mercy of him who has already enriched himself with a part of our possessions?

ARABIAN NIGHTS

I cannot, I must not, think of such an enterprise until I have put a period to his existence. What I have not been able to accomplish with your assistance I am determined to perform alone; and when I have secured this immense property from the danger of pillage I will endeavor to provide owners and heirs for it after my decease, that it may be not only preserved, but augmented to posterity.'

"The next morning the captain of the robbers awoke at an early hour, and, putting on a dress which was suitable to the design he meditated, repaired to the city, where he took a lodging in a khan. As he supposed that the events which had happened in the house of Ali Baba might have become generally known, he asked the host if there were any news stirring; in reply to which the host talked on a variety of subjects, but never mentioned the subject the captain had nearest at heart. By this the latter concluded that the reason why Ali Baba kept the transaction so profoundly secret was that he did not wish to divulge the fact of his having access to so immense a treasure. This idea excited the captain to neglect nothing that could hasten his enemy's destruction, which he intended to accomplish by means as secret as those Ali Baba had adopted toward the robbers.

"The captain provided himself with a horse, which he made use of to convey to his lodging several kinds of rich stuffs and fine linens, bringing them from the forest at various times. In order to dispose of this merchandise, he sought for a shop. Having found one that suited him, he hired it, stocked it with his goods, and established himself in it. The shop that was exactly opposite to his had belonged to Cassim, and was now occupied by the son of Ali Baba.

"The captain of the robbers, who had assumed the name of Cogia Houssain, took an early opportunity of offering those civilities to the merchants his neighbors which new-comers were expected to show. The son of Ali Baba being young and of a pleasing address, and the captain having more frequent occasion to converse with him than with the others, the two men soon formed an intimacy. This friendship the robber soon resolved to cultivate with greater assiduity and care when he recognized Ali Baba, who came to see his son, as he was in the habit of doing; and, on inquiring of the son, Cogia Houssain discovered that his foe was the young man's father. He now increased his attentions to him; he made him several presents, and often invited him to his table, where he regaled him very handsomely.

"The son of Ali Baba did not choose to receive so many attentions from Cogia Houssain without returning them; but his lodging was small, and he had no convenience for regaling a guest as he wished. He mentioned his intention to his father, adding that it was not proper that he should delay any longer to return the favors he had received from Cogia Houssain.

"Ali Baba very willingly undertook to provide an entertainment. 'My son,' said he, 'to-morrow is Friday; and as it is a day on which the most considerable merchants, such as Cogia Houssain and yourself, keep their shops shut, invite him to take a walk with you after dinner. On your return, contrive matters that you may pass my house, and then beg him to come in. It will be better to manage thus than to invite him in a formal way. I will give orders to Morgiana to prepare a supper by the time you come.'

"On the Friday Cogia Houssain and the son of Ali Baba met in the afternoon to take their walk together as had been agreed. On their return Ali Baba's son led Cogia Houssain through the street in which his father lived; and when they had reached the house he knocked at the door. 'This,' said he, 'is my father's house. He has desired me to procure him the honor of your acquaintance. I entreat you to add this favor to the many I have received from you.'

"Although Cogia Houssain had now reached the object of his desires by gaining admission into the house of Ali Baba, and to attempt his life without hazarding his own, yet he now endeavored to excuse himself; but, as the slave of Ali Baba opened the door at that moment, the son took him by the hand and forced him to enter the house.

ARABIAN NIGHTS

"Ali Baba received Cogia Houssain in a friendly manner, and gave him as hearty a welcome as he could desire.

"After a short conversation Cogia Houssain was going to take his leave, but Ali Baba stopped him. 'Where are you going?' said he. 'O my friend, I entreat you to do me the honor of staying to sup with me. The humble meal you will partake of is little worthy of the honor you will confer on it; but such as it is, I hope you will accept the offer as frankly as it is made.'

"'O my master,' replied Cogia Houssain, 'I am fully sensible of your kindness, and although I beg you to excuse me if I take leave without accepting your invitation, yet I entreat you to believe that I refuse you not from incivility or pride, but because I have a very strong reason, and one which I am sure you would approve were it known to you.'

"'What can this reason be?' resumed Ali Baba. 'Might I take the liberty of asking you?' 'I do not refuse to tell it,' said Cogia Houssain. 'It is this: I never eat of any dish that has salt in it. Judge, then, what a strange figure I should make at your table.' 'If this is your only reason,' replied Ali Baba, 'it need not deprive me of the honor of your company at supper. In the first place, the bread which is eaten at my house does not contain salt; and as for the meat and other dishes, I promise you there shall be none in those which are placed before you. I will now go to give orders to that effect. Therefore do me the favor to remain and I will be with you again in an instant.'

"Ali Baba went into the kitchen, and desired Morgiana not to put any salt to the meat she was going to serve for supper. He also told her to prepare, without any salt, two or three of those dishes he had ordered.

"Morgiana could not refrain from expressing some disapprobation at this new order. 'Who,' said she, 'is this fastidious man that cannot eat salt? Your supper will be entirely spoiled if I delay it any longer.' 'Do not be angry,' replied Ali Baba; 'he is a good man. Do as I desire you.'

"Morgiana obeyed, though much against her will. She felt some curiosity to see this man who did not eat salt. When

[422]

she had finished her preparations, and Abdalla had prepared the table, she assisted him in carrying in the dishes. On looking at Cogia Houssain, she instantly recognized him, notwithstanding his disguise, as the captain of the robbers, and she perceived that he had a dagger concealed under his dress. 'I am no longer surprised,' said she to herself, 'that this villain will not eat salt with my master. He is his bitterest enemy, and means to murder him; but I will yet prevent him from accomplishing his purpose.'

"When Morgiana had finished bringing up the dishes and assisting Abdalla, she availed herself of the time, while her masters and their guest were at supper, to make the necessary preparations for carrying out an enterprise of the boldest and most intrepid nature; and she had just completed them when Abdalla came to acquaint her that it was time to serve the fruit. She carried it in and placed it on the table. Then she put a small table near Ali Baba, with the wine and three cups, and left the room as if to leave Ali Baba, according to custom, at liberty to converse and enjoy himself with his guest while they drank their wine.

Cogia Houssain, or rather the captain of the forty thieves, now thought he had achieved a favorable opportunity for revenging himself on Ali Baba by taking his life. 'I will make them both drunk,' thought he, 'and then the son will be unable to prevent my plunging my dagger in the heart of his father, and I shall escape by way of the garden as I did before, while the cook and the slave are at their supper, or perhaps asleep in the kitchen.'

"But instead of going to supper, Morgiana, who had penetrated into the views of the pretended Cogia Houssain, did not allow him to put his wicked intentions in execution. She dressed herself like a dancing-girl, put on a head-dress suitable to the character she assumed, and wore round her waist a girdle of silver-gilt, to which she fastened a dagger made of the same metal. Her face was covered by a very handsome mask. When she had thus disguised herself, she said to Abdalla, 'Take your tabor, and let us go and entertain our master's guest and the friend of his son by the music and dance we sometimes practise together.'

"Abdalla took his tabor and began to play as he entered the room, walking before Morgiana. The wily slave followed him, making a low courtesy with a deliberate air to attract notice, as if to request permission to show her skill in dancing. 'Come in, Morgiana,' cried Ali Baba; 'Cogia Houssain will judge of your skill and tell us his opinion. Do not think, however, O my friend,' continued he, addressing Cogia Houssain, 'that I have been at any expense to procure you this entertainment. We have all this skill in the household, and it is only my slave and my cook whom you see. I hope you will find their efforts amusing.'

"Cogia Houssain, although he would gladly have dispensed with this addition to the entertainment, nevertheless pretended to be obliged to his host, and added 'that whatever gave Ali Baba pleasure could not fail of being agreeable to him.'

"When Abdalla perceived that Ali Baba and Cogia Houssain had ceased speaking, he again began to play on his tabor, singing to it an air to the tune of which Morgiana might dance. She, who was equal in skill to any professional dancer, performed her part so admirably that even a critical spectator must have been delighted. But of the company, perhaps Cogia Houssain was the least attentive to her excellence.

"After she had performed several dances with equal grace and agility, Morgiana at length drew out the dagger and, dancing with it in her hand, she surpassed all she had yet done, sometimes presenting the dagger as if ready to strike, and at others holding it to her own bosom, pretending to stab herself.

"At length, apparently out of breath, she took the tabor from Abdalla with her left hand, and, holding the dagger in her right, she presented the tabor with the hollow part upward to Ali Baba, in imitation of the professional dancers, who are accustomed to go round in this way appealing to the liberality of the spectators.

"Ali Baba threw a piece of gold into the tabor. Morgiana

MORGIANA DREW OUT THE DAGGER, DANCING WITH
IT IN HER HAND

then presented it to his son, who followed his father's example. Cogia Houssain, who saw that she was advancing toward him for the same purpose, had already taken his purse from his bosom to contribute his present, and was taking out a piece of money when Morgiana, with a courage and promptness equal to the resolution she had displayed, plunged the dagger in his heart.

"Ali Baba and his son, terrified at this action, uttered a loud cry. 'Wretch!' exclaimed Ali Baba, 'what hast thou done? Thou has ruined me and my family forever.'

"'What I have done,' replied Morgiana, 'is not for your ruin, but for your safety.' Then, opening Cogia Houssain's robe to show Ali Baba the poniard which was concealed under it, she continued: 'Behold the cruel enemy you had to deal with! Examine his countenance attentively and you will recognize the pretended oil merchant and the captain of the forty robbers. Do you not recollect that he refused to eat salt with you? Before I even saw him, from the moment you told me of this peculiarity in your guest, I suspected his design, and you are now convinced that my suspicions were not unfounded.'

"Ali Baba, who now understood the fresh obligation he owed to Morgiana for having thus preserved his life a second time, embraced her, and said: 'Morgiana, I gave you your liberty, and at the same time promised to show you stronger proofs of my gratitude at some future period. This period has now arrived. I present you to my son as his wife.' Then, addressing his son, he continued: 'I believe you to be too dutiful a son to take it amiss if I bestow Morgiana upon you without previously consulting your inclinations. Your obligation to her is not less than mine. You plainly see that Cogia Houssain only sought your acquaintance that he might gain an opportunity to carry out his diabolical treachery; and had he sacrificed me to his vengeance you cannot suppose that you would have been spared.'

"Far from showing any symptoms of discontent, Ali Baba's son replied that he willingly consented to the marriage, not only because he was desirous of proving his ready obedience to his father's wishes, but also because his own inclination strongly urged him to the union. They then resolved to inter the captain of the robbers by the side of his former companions; and this duty was performed with such secrecy that the circumstance was not known till many years had expired and no one was any longer interested to keep this memorable history concealed.

"A few days after, Ali Baba caused the nuptials of his son and Morgiana to be celebrated with great solemnity. He gave a sumptuous feast, accompanied by dances and other customary diversions; and he had the satisfaction of observing that the friends and neighbors whom he had invited, who did not know the true reason for the marriage, but were not unacquainted with the good qualities of Morgiana, admired his generosity and applauded his discrimination.

"Ali Baba, who had not revisited the cave since he had brought away the body of his brother Cassim, lest he should meet with any of the thieves and be slain by them, still refrained from going thither, even after the death of the thirty-seven robbers and their captain, as he was ignorant of the fate of the other two, and supposed them to be still alive.

"At the expiration of a year, however, finding that no attempt had been made to disturb his quiet, he had the curiosity to make a journey to the cave, taking all necessary precautions for his safety. He mounted his horse, and when he approached the cave, seeing no traces of either men or horses, he conceived this to be a favorable omen. He dismounted, and, fastening his horse, he went up to the door and repeated the words, 'Open, sesame,' which he had not forgotten. The door opened and he entered. The state in which everything appeared in the cave led him to judge that no one had been in it from the time when the pretended Cogia Houssain had opened his shop in the city, and therefore he concluded that the whole troop of robbers was totally dispersed or exterminated; that he himself was now the only person in the world who was acquainted with the secret of entering the cave, and that consequently the immense treasure it contained was entirely at his disposal. He had provided himself with a bag, and he filled it with as much gold as his horse could carry, with which he returned to the city.

"From that time Ali Baba and his son, whom he took to the cave and taught the secret of entering it, and after them their posterity, who were also intrusted with the important secret, lived in great splendor, enjoying their riches with moderation, and honored with the most dignified situations in the city."

The Sultan of the Indies could not but admire the astonishing memory of the sultana, his consort, whose stock of tales seemed inexhaustible, and who had thus continued to furnish fresh amusement every night for a long period.

A thousand and one nights had passed in this innocent amusement, and the lapse of time had very much tended to diminish the cruel prepossession and prejudice of the sultan against the fidelity of all wives. His mind had become softened, and he was convinced of the great merit and good sense of the Sultana Sheherazade. He well recollected the courage with which she voluntarily exposed herself to destruction in becoming his queen, without at all dreading the death to which she knew she was destined, like those who had preceded her.

These considerations, added to his experience of the excellent qualities which he found she possessed, at last urged him absolutely to pardon her. "I am well aware," he said, "O amiable Sheherazade, that it is impossible to exhaust your store of those pleasant and amusing tales with which you have so long entertained me. You have at length appeased my anger, and I freely revoke in your favor the cruel law I had promulgated. I receive you entirely into my favor, and wish you to be considered as the preserver of many ladies, who would, but for you, have been sacrificed to my just resentment."

The sultana threw herself at his feet, which she embraced most tenderly, and gave every sign of the most heartfelt and lively gratitude.

ARABIAN NIGHTS

The grand vizier heard the delightful intelligence from the sultan himself. It was immediately reported through the city and different provinces; and it brought down upon the heads of the Sultan Shahriar and his amiable Sultana Sheherazade the heartfelt praises and grateful blessings of all the people of the empire of the Indies.

THE END

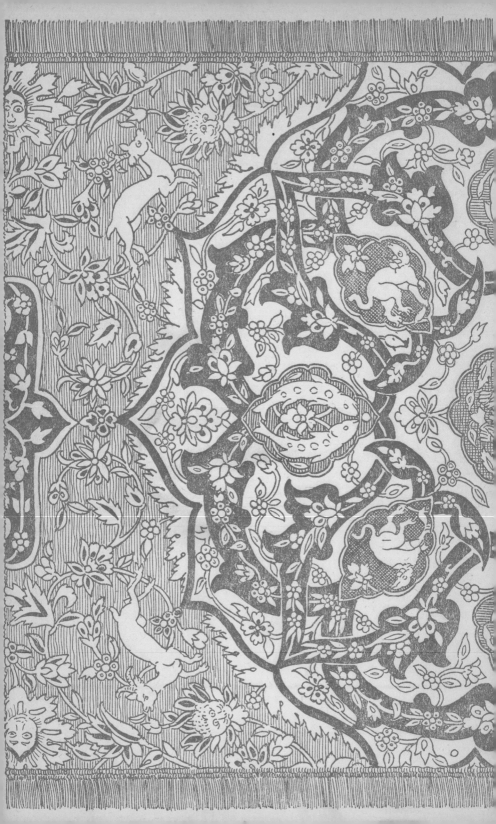